All on a Summer's Day

ALL ON A SUMMER'S DAY

by Judy Gardiner

St. Martin's Press
New York

Library of Congress Cataloging-in-Publication Data

Gardiner, Judy.
    All on a summer's day / Judy Gardiner.
      p.   cm.
    ISBN 0-312-07624-X
    1. World War, 1939–1945—Fiction. I. Title.
  PR6057.A627A74   1992
  823'.914—dc20   92-873
                                                     CIP

First published in Great Britain by Random Century Group.

First U.S. Edition: June 1992
10 9 8 7 6 5 4 3 2 1

For Zoë, Albert and Melanie

Acknowledgments

I would like to express my grateful thanks to Mrs Veronica Marchbanks from the Archives Department of the British Red Cross, and to Mr Terry Charman and his staff in the Imperial War Museum Reading Room for their help in supplying material for this book.

I also acknowledge with grateful thanks permission to quote from the lyrics of the song 'J'attendrai' (c. 1938 by Leonardi Piero Musikverlag, Italy) which has been granted by Francis Day & Hunter Limited, London WC2H 0EA.

It was barely light when the first sounds of chugging vehicles woke her.

Lying beside her husband she stared past the foot of the bed to the pearl-grey square of open window that looked across the front garden on to the Common. Casual picknickers sometimes parked on it, once a year the Boy Scouts camped over on the far side, and then in September there was always the Michaelmas Fair: a hardy, rowdy free-for-all with side-shows and glittering roundabouts which they both pretended to dread but in fact enjoyed. And after that the Common would settle down to thoughts of winter, with blackberry-pickers dwindling and the ferns turning fox-red, until the snow fell and the only signs of life to be read in it were the footprints of birds and other small creatures. And the footprints of the people who lived around the perimeter, like Miranda and her husband.

But this was the 15th of June, and she suddenly remembered that it was her birthday and that she was giving a small lunch party.

Quietly she got out of bed and walked over to the window, her movements a little stiff because of a twinge of arthritis in her knee. She could see the pale beam of headlights slicing the dawn; not many of them, but it was puzzling all the same. Tilting her head, she thought she heard the sound of voices, but couldn't be sure. She peered at the bedroom clock; four-thirty. Should she ring the police? No, stupid idea. The Common was precisely what its name suggested; common land, common to all. If a group of caravanners wanted to park there, so be it. It was a free country.

She went to the bathroom – another disadvantage to growing old was having to pee during the night – then she returned to bed. Her feet were chilly and she had no hesitation in warming them on her husband's outstretched legs. He grunted, made a little smacking sound with his lips and slept on.

She wanted to sleep too, but couldn't. Bored with wondering about the motor vehicles out on the Common she tried to recapture the dream that had been disturbed by their arrival. During these latter years Miranda enjoyed her dreams, and always tried to remember their content when she awoke so that she might have the satisfaction of going over them again later in the day. Nowadays, her dreams were invariably pleasant.

But this one remained elusive. However hard she tried to chase it, to catch it by the tail, it seemed to swerve out of reach. She dozed with one ear alert for any new sounds from the Common and her feet braced lightly against her husband's legs, and the dream began to float back to her like a story that had suffered interruption.

Childhood. Schooldays. And Florence. Dear, daft, infuriating old Florence, who was still keeping the brave little flag of her femininity flying in spite of bifocals, a hearing aid and white hair thinner than the down on a two-day chick.

And then, uninvited, the cavernous dark of Liverpool, and she knew what was going to happen next. This was the old dream back again after all these years; the blackness, the crushing weight of misery and guilt, and now, here it comes – the sound of screaming. The old high-pitched sound of a small creature facing death. She had heard it before, once in reality and then many many times in her dreams during the following years. And it had drawn a black line, black as Liverpool soot, across what should have been the golden days of youth.

She awoke, sweating. Outside on the Common she heard the sound of a man laughing. The time was 4.52 and the dream had brought the past rushing back.

ONE

She didn't know where to go or what to do. So she remained where she was, standing with her toes turned in, in the gateway of Queen Mary's College for Girls, which was in Liverpool. The date was the 4th of March 1936.

'It's a very famous college, and whatever happens no one will ever be able to take away the fact that you've been there,' her mother had said, and Miranda Whittaker had wondered briefly how one would go about removing facts from one place to another. It was typical that nothing was said about the benefit of a sound education for its own sake; so far as Miranda was concerned, it had merely been a matter of higher powers (on her father's side of the family) suddenly remembering her existence and deciding that something sensible ought to be done about her.

Nothing much had been done so far. Since the divorce when she was three Miranda had led an unsettled, picaresque existence, occasionally and very briefly with her mother, more often casually dumped on members of her mother's family, and from the age of five had attended a dizzying variety of schools, most of which had sought immediately to undo whatever she had learned at the last one. Philosophically she had endured, but now at the age of fourteen and in the early throes of adolescence, anxiety was creeping in.

Queen Mary's was a formidable, soot-encrusted Gothic building set behind a high wall with broken glass on top, and the girls strolling in the vicinity of the bicycle shelters looked equally formidable. Occasional whoops of laughter drifted across the asphalt quadrangle while Miranda continued to hover uncertainly, attaché case in hand and velour school hat smelling new and stuffy.

'Well, either go in or come out,' a voice said behind her. 'I can't stick people who dither.'

Miranda moved aside, mumbling an apology. The schoolgirl addressing her was of about her own height, with a chubby face and black curly hair tumbling from beneath a bashed-in hat. A worn leather satchel was slung on one shoulder. She strolled past, then a bell rang and everyone began moving towards a flight of stone steps leading down to the basement. Miranda followed like a stray dog.

There were two cloakrooms. Instinctively she chose the smaller one, but a large girl with short hair and a bust informed her that the Sixth Form cloakroom was out of bounds. So she mumbled another apology and went to the larger one where girls were divesting themselves of hats and coats and changing their shoes. Miranda began to do the same, and a girl wearing glasses said, 'Oi, that's my peg!' and dumped her belongings back in her arms. Then another bell rang and a tall woman dressed in grey appeared in the doorway, saw Miranda and said, 'You're the new girl, aren't you?'

'Yes.'

'Yes, Miss Wallace.'

'Yes, Miss Wallace.'

'And your name is?'

'Miranda Whittaker.'

'I think you're in Miss Wakeling's form. Don't stand with your toes turned in.'

Hastily adjusting her stance, Miranda saw the woman beckon imperiously. 'Natalie Ellenberg – Miranda Whittaker will be joining your form. Look after her until she knows her way about.'

And Miranda discovered Natalie Ellenberg to be the girl who had remonstrated with her for hovering.

Seen now in navy-blue skirt and winter jersey with striped school tie bunched under the collar, she had a less threatening look. Her curly hair clung round her face like thick tendrils of ivy and her eyes had an amused gleam.

'What did she say your name was?'

'Miranda.'

'My God.'

'No worse than Natalie,' Miranda said with a show of spirit.

Natalie grinned, then nodded through the crowd to the retreating form of Miss Wallace. 'Wally takes us for History. She's not too bad – most of them aren't too bad really – the one to watch out for is Nellie. Miss Nelson, the gym mistress.'

Miranda had never had a gym mistress before, but remembered the importance of gymnastics in all the best school stories. Being good at gym enabled the heroine to swarm down knotted sheets at dead of night, to climb trees, to swim rivers.

'One generally thinks of gym mistresses as jolly good sports,' Natalie continued as they headed out of the cloakroom with the rest of the crowd. 'But ours isn't. She ought to be in the Army.'

Miranda's polite sound, indicative of interest, was lost in the shuffle

4

of house shoes on stone floors. They passed into a gloomy corridor, then began to ascend an ornate mahogany staircase.

'Hands off the banisters!' cried a prefect stationed at the first bend. 'Feet off the stairs!'

'Fifty lines for you, Natalie Ellenberg. "I must not answer back." '

'OK,' Natalie said with resignation, then turned to Miranda. 'You'd better just follow the others now. It's Assembly, and I don't go in for the first part because it's prayers and I'm a Jew, although I'm not Orthodox.' She vanished, leaving Miranda a docile navy-blue sheep to follow the main flock.

Queen Mary's assembly hall was large and grim, its Victorian oak enlivened here and there by a brass plaque, most of which appeared to be dedicated to the memory of dead mistresses and diligent schoolgirls. One of them, Miranda saw, craning, had died for her country in Flanders.

There must have been close on two hundred girls standing in long rows, psalters in hand, facing the dais upon which stood a lectern and a highly ornamental grand piano. Behind the dais was a stained-glass window through which mournful Liverpool light filtered, while from behind the brick wall outside came the low keening of a tramcar.

Miss Lissett the headmistress appeared. She stood swinging her pince-nez in her hand, with the mistress known as Wally in close attendance. Miss Lissett said, 'Good morning, girls,' in equable tones and received a low murmur in reply.

They sang a hymn ('Jesus calls us o'er the tumult', which Miranda didn't know), and after the Lord's Prayer, led by Miss Lissett with her eyes closed and her head bowed, they launched into the long shuffling mumble of Psalm 23 which Miranda didn't know either. She was touched almost to tears when the girl next to her offered a share of her psalter.

Prayers were followed by announcements about hockey fixtures, netball practice, rehearsals for *Twelfth Night*, and about someone having thrown ink on the ceiling in Lower Vb. Failure to own up would be regarded with gravity.

Staring down at her new black-buttoned house shoes Miranda failed to see Natalie Ellenberg mount the dais and glide behind Miss Lissett and her companion to the grand piano. She merely heard the sudden cheerful rum-tum-tum of a march, and looking over the rows of heads in front saw her new friend, curls bobbing and plump decisive hands thumping out the chords. The sound filled Miranda with a strange and inexplicable joy as if she had just made a great discovery.

5

She watched the junior girls march out of the hall behind their form mistress, and when her own turn came she followed the girl in front, swinging her arms and stamping her feet and exulting in the bright conviction that everything was going to be all right.

Florence Whittaker stood up, buttoning her blouse and pulling down her skirt while the man on the bed lay watching her through a spiral of cigarette smoke.

'What about tonight? Your place or mine?'

She glanced at him over her shoulder, hair dishevelled and smile provocative. 'Haven't you had enough for one day?'

'Can't ever have too much of a good thing.'

She reached for her shoes, wobbling slightly as she thrust her bare feet into them. Then she stood hands on hips by the bed, looking down at him. 'Come on, Rob – you'll have to go. She'll be home any minute.'

'So when am I going to meet this daughter?' The cigarette in his mouth flipped up and down as he spoke.

'In a day or two, as we arranged. I mean, she hasn't even settled in properly yet.' She went over to the dressing table and ran a comb through her hair, then applied some lipstick and stood back, grimacing at her reflection. 'Do you think I'd look nice with my hair dyed red?'

'Red's a colour I'm not fond of.'

'Perhaps you're right.' She sighed, then returned to the subject of Miranda. 'In any case, she's my only child. I love her far more than anyone else on earth, and after – '

'Better than me?' He lay regarding her through half-closed eyes. A finger of cigarette ash fell on to his chest and he brushed it on to the bed.

'You're different.' She powdered her nose, then moistened both index fingers with her tongue and stroked them over her eyebrows. 'As I was about to say, after all the wickedness of her father's family – trying to keep me away from her and everything – I haven't finally got her just to share her with somebody else.'

'Get one thing straight. You've no need to worry about sharing her with me.'

'Although it would be nice if we could live like a proper little family, wouldn't it? I've been so starved of the kind of home life that other women take for granted.' She appeared to be retracting her previous words for fear of antagonising him. 'I never knew what it was like to have a proper home when I was a child.'

'Gettaway.' He smiled at her lazily, one eyebrow raised. Then he leaned over the side of the bed and stubbed out his cigarette in a saucer.

'You'll really have to go now. She'll be home any second and I must straighten the bed.'

'Come here.'

'No, I can't. There isn't time. . . .' But she went, sidling over to the bed in her high-heeled shoes. She stood looking down at him, and flinched pleasurably when he reached out to touch her. 'You're a bit of a tart, aren't you, standing there with your face all painted and no knickers on.'

He pinched her naked behind hard, and then abruptly swung his legs off the rumpled bed and stood up. He buttoned his trousers, then reached for the jacket that hung over the bedside chair.

'See you some time.'

'When, Rob?'

'When it's convenient.' He turned to look at her from the door, his jacket slung over one shoulder. 'Convenient for you and little Miss Whatsername, of course.'

'My daughter's name is Miranda,' Florence said. 'I love her best in all the world and you can go to hell.'

Sweeping the cigarette ash off the bed she tidied the covers, her lips tightening at the sound of the flat door slamming. Good riddance, she thought, and restrained herself from going to the window to watch his tall figure moving away down the street. Normally she admired his easy, swaggering walk, but now she felt tired and depressed and uncertain about the wisdom of having Miranda back to live with her after all this time. She loved her best in all the world, but there were difficulties.

The flat was small, she hadn't much money, and she cherished her freedom. And to Florence, freedom meant mobility. Unreasoning as a sparrow, she would flit from place to place, sometimes on her own and sometimes in company, driven always by an inexpressible need to escape from the present into the future. The future held a rosy promise that so far had not been properly fulfilled, but except in moments of deepest gloom she continued to believe in her own personal nirvana, the state of changeless peace to which she felt herself entitled.

She had tried marriage, and it had failed. She had fallen into other relationships as one would fall into a hole in the road; had clambered out of them and vowed to look where she was going in future. But caution had never been her strong point. It was too insipid, too monotonous, and her last relationship having reached an unsatisfactory conclusion, she had looked around in search of a new face, a new place.

The face belonged to Miranda, who had spent the last three years with Florence's long-suffering older sister and her husband in the East Riding of Yorkshire, and after that the place followed automatically. It must be a nice little flat with two bedrooms, a proper bathroom and a bit of garden where Miranda could play. (She imagined that girls of Miranda's age still played.) Her requirements were located without too much trouble on the third floor of a house not far from Prince's Park, and the quiet orderliness of the neighbourhood appealed to her freshly awakened sense of motherhood. A nice area for a nice girl to grow up in, she thought.

It had a living room, a kitchenette, a large, cold bathroom shared only with the occupant of the second-floor flat, two bedrooms (the second a small slip room containing the hot water tank), and, most gratifying of all, a thin slice of garden which Mrs Whittaker and her daughter were at liberty to use provided they knocked on the proprietor's door before going through his kitchen.

Negotiations concluded, she then looked round for a suitable school for Miranda, and became greatly taken with Queen Mary's because of its imposing portico. It must be a very good school, she thought reverently, and therefore very expensive, and upon approaching him via his solicitor, her ex-husband intimated that he would undertake the fees if she, Florence, would undertake not to remove Miranda before the age of sixteen. Florence promised, extracted a further sum of twenty pounds for school uniform, hockey stock, tennis racquet and first year's supply of books, and on her way home from meeting the headmistress bumped into Rob Allardyce, whom she hadn't seen for two years or more.

They walked down Prince's Avenue together, and when she told him that her daughter aged fourteen was coming to live with her, he became intrigued by a radiance, a sweet mature bloom about her that he had never noticed before. Women were made for motherhood, and motherhood had about it a strongly sensuous appeal that he saw no reason to reject. They had supper at a fish restaurant, and when later he said, 'Your place of mine?' she chose his, because she had vague feelings about the sanctity of motherhood.

'You mean you don't want to shit in your own nest?'

She recoiled, hurt, then thought, yes, that's what I am. A fluffy, loving mother bird guarding her one precious chick.

They saw a lot of one another during the couple of weeks that preceded Miranda's arrival, and she found herself falling in love with him. He was a good-looking man; tall, muscular, with brown eyes, strong teeth and dark hair brushed sleekly back from his forehead.

8

Often when they met he would greet her by clicking his heels together and bowing slightly – a mock deference that delighted her and made her giggle.

He seemed to have plenty of time on his hands, but his furnished rooms on the far side of Brownlow Hill betrayed no hint of either penury or affluence. There were books upon the windowsill, polished floorboards beneath the rugs, and over the gas fire a picture of King George V, which rather surprised her.

'Is he a friend of yours?' she asked jokingly.

'I am a friend of his,' he replied.

She waited for him to elaborate but he merely asked her to watch the toast while he made the tea. His kitchen was as neat and impersonal as the rest of the place, and curiosity about him increased, although she was by now aware that as an uncommunicative man he disliked being questioned. But she did ask him one day if he had a job and he replied that he was engaged in committee work. Again he refused to say more, and she was left to conclude that committee work was an occupation that combined easy hours with comfortable pay.

Casually she introduced him to Miranda. 'Chickabid, this is Mr Allardyce, an old family friend.'

'How do you do?' Miranda stood, toes turned in, in the doorway, in school hat and coat.

'Hullo.' He looked her over, smiling through a lazy twist of cigarette smoke. 'How's the world with you?'

Miranda replied constrainedly that it was all right, thank you, then vanished into her bedroom.

'Hasn't got much to say.'

'All little girls are shy at her age. I was terribly shy at fourteen.'

'I can imagine.'

'And don't forget, Rob,' she made an entreating little movement with her hands, 'I don't want her to know about us. It wouldn't be nice. . . .'

Miranda reappeared, divested of hat and coat and with smothed-down hair. Sitting on the stool by the fireside she tugged her skirt down over her knees.

'Isn't it a shame the way they have to wear black woolly stockings?' Florence said animatedly. She poured tea. 'Pass Mr Allardyce a scone, chickabid.'

'Rob,' he said, accepting one. 'Not Mr Allardyce, seeing that your mother and I are such good . . . friends.'

'I think we'd better make it Uncle Rob,' Florence said with a relieved little simper. 'Uncle Rob's been longing to meet you.'

Miranda, head bent, bit into a scone. She had never before had uncles who weren't proper uncles, and she was unsure how to proceed.

'Miranda and I are real pals,' Florence said, 'and now that we can be together again we're going to make up for lost time, aren't we?'

'Do you like your new school?' Uncle Rob asked. He had a watchful stare that disconcerted her.

'Yes, thank you.'

'Get a lot of homework?'

'Yes. But they call it prep.'

'Homework or prep – it's all calculated to keep young people out of trouble.'

'Yes.' She took another bite out of her scone.

'Do you belong to any clubs?'

'I'm sure you do, don't you, chickabid?' encouraged Florence.

'Well, I might join the Kingfishers, which is about nature study. They go up to Sefton Park once a week. But my friend's in the Debating Society and she also plays the piano for Assembly.'

'You must ask her home to tea,' Florence murmured.

'She's not just clever, she's very funny as well,' Miranda said, beginning to come out of her shell. 'I mean, she's got a lot of thick, black, curly hair and sometimes when no one's looking she puts an elastic band round her head and goes on working, and gradually all her hair starts rising up on end as the elastic band slides higher and higher up her head – ' Miranda choked abruptly, took a mouthful of tea and wiped her mouth on her handkerchief. 'She makes everyone die.'

White teeth gleaming in a smile, Uncle Rob asked the name of her new friend.

'Natalie Ellenberg, but we all call her Nat. Not the mistresses, I don't mean, but – '

'Natalie Ellenberg,' he repeated, laying heavy emphasis on the surname. 'She must be foreign.'

'Oh, no,' Miranda said warmly, 'she was born in a house in Rodney Street. They all think I'm a bit foreign because I don't belong here – '

'But you do now,' Florence chided, mindful of her promise that Miranda would stay at Queen Mary's until she was sixteen.

'Ellenberg,' Uncle Rob repeated. 'Is her father in the rag trade?'

'I don't know.' Miranda's animation shrivelled. 'Anyway, it's swanking to say what your father does.'

'Or perhaps he's a pawnbroker.' The words were lightly said, but she sensed hostility behind them.

'I don't know,' Miranda repeated. 'It's nothing to do with me.'

'Incidentally, I know one of your teachers.' He passed his cup and saucer to Florence for more tea. 'Her name's Miss Nelson.'

'Oh, golly.' Miranda looked aghast. 'She's the gym mistress and she's absolutely horrible. Everybody hates her.'

'I don't.' He spoke slowly, meditatively, and a sense of chill crept round the room. Outside in the street they could hear someone scraping away on a fiddle. Probably an unemployed ex-serviceman; there were plenty of them about.

Replacing her cup and saucer on the tea tray Miranda went to the door. 'I'd better get on with my prep.'

There was a lot of it. History (The Life and Times of Mary Tudor); Geometry (congruent and incongruent triangles) and then French and Latin revision. It was rather disheartening trying to revise something she had never done before – there had been no Latin or French at the village school she had gone to before Queen Mary's – so she dropped the books on the floor and sat staring out of her bedroom window. She wondered whether her mother had a pash on so-called Uncle Rob. She didn't like him much, and the fact that he knew Miss Nelson added to her general sense of unease.

Sighing, she picked up her history textbook and scanned through the part about Mary Tudor. She studied the picture of her; a woman with no eyebrows and a stare like two burnt holes in a blanket.

Mary Tudor was the daughter of King Henry the Eighth, she finally wrote, *and she married Philip of Spain but they didn't have any children. She was an ardant catholic and wanted everyone else to be the same. When they refused she had them tortured and set fire to at the stake which was wrong because peoples religeons are nobody elses business. What they feel about God is a private matter.*

She paused. She had not been asked for her opinion, merely for facts, but the martyrdom of Latimer and Ridley as described in the spare, dry tones of Miss Wallace had affected her deeply. *But Philip of Spain went back to his own country when she didn't have any children and she died all alone and ill and unloved. Which served her right.*

Defiantly blotting what she had written, she closed the exercise book and turned her attention to congruent and incongruent triangles.

Life in Liverpool was already proving very different from life in Beverley with Aunt Daisy and Uncle Frank. A childless couple, they had been married for year and years, kept rigidly to the same small circle of friends, and had little of interest to say to one another, probably because they had already said it all. The house was run with ruthless efficiency by Aunt Daisy – washing on Monday, ironing on Tuesday, bedrooms on Wednesday, and so on – the working week ending with a great baking session to see them through the rigours of the weekend. Roast on Sunday followed by the glory of late high tea and a game of whist before bed. It never varied, except on Christmas Day, and during Uncle Frank's annual week's holiday when they might take the odd day's excursion by train to Bridlington or even York.

It had all been very prosaic and predictable, something she felt that Liverpool could never be. To begin with, the city itself; huge, dark and cavernous after the country brightness of Beverley, it both appalled and fascinated her. She wanted to see more of it, but didn't like to venture far for fear of getting lost. When on a fine Saturday afternoon she asked Florence if they could go for a walk, Florence looked startled and said, 'Whatever for?' But after she had washed some stockings and painted her nails she repented and they took the tramcar down to Church Street where they had a pot of tea and two custard slices in one of the big stores.

Which was very nice, but not what she wanted. So she took to devising alternative routes home from school; little detours down parallel streets, walking slowly so that she could glimpse the life going on behind basement windows. Then home to Florence, who generally conjured up a bright smile and asked how school had been. And generally Miranda answered, 'Fine', and left it at that because she had already discovered that her mother's knowledge of the school world was limited and her genuine curiosity nil. Hence, presumably, its glamour for her.

One day Florence said, 'I think I'll change my name to Tania,' and this time it was Miranda's turn to look startled and say, 'Whatever for?'

'Florence is so working class,' Florence said. 'Some people even have the cheek to call me Flo.'

'Uncle Frank sometimes used to sing a song that went *Flo, Flo, why do you go, riding along in your motorcar. . . .* '

'I bet they always used to refer to me as Flo, didn't they?'

'I don't think they did.' Miranda frowned. 'They generally just said "your mother".'

'Well anyway, it's Tania from now on. If anyone calls me Florence I shan't answer. By the way, chickabid, I'm slipping out with Uncle Rob tonight, but I've made you a nice little supper and you needn't go to bed 'til half past nine.'

'OK.'

'You don't mind, do you? I don't very often go out these days, and you'll be quite safe and everything. If anything goes wrong, bang on the floor for Miss Lashley – I know she'd come up like a shot.'

'Yes, OK.'

Florence hesitated, then said, 'By the way, what was the name of your friend? The one you want to ask round to tea.'

'Natalie Ellenberg, and I didn't say I – '

'Well, ask her to come on Saturday. I'd love to meet her.'

Smiling briskly she tripped to the bathroom they shared with the downstairs tenant, and Miranda heard the subdued roar of the geyser as she ran a bath.

Dressed at last for departure, Florence seized Miranda's face between both her hands, kissed her, and said, 'I *do* love you, you know. Think I look all right?'

Releasing herself, Miranda stood back and surveyed her; black hat with veil tilted over one eye, silver fox fur slung across the shoulder of her black suit, and her feet in high-heeled patent-leather court shoes. 'Yes, you look jolly nice.'

Florence kissed her again, careful not to smudge her lipstick, then said, 'Why don't you part your hair in the middle, chickabid? It would widen your face.'

The flat doorbell rang and she scuttled away. Miranda heard the main door bang and watched from the window as she and Uncle Rob hurried arm-in-arm down the street. They were both wearing black – Florence said that black was very smart – but then she had never so far seen Uncle Rob in any other colour.

Halfway through doing her prep she ate the supper that Florence had prepared for her. Two tinned pilchards and some bread and butter, and an Eccles cake. She dropped a bit of fish on to her English composition and it left a greasy orange smear when she wiped it away. She continued writing doggedly, then someone banged on the door. Startled, she sat erect, and a blob of ink released itself from her pen and joined the greasy smear.

'Who is it?'

The banging was repeated. She went to the door and opened it, and saw to her relief that it was only Miss Lashley from downstairs. But her relief faded when she saw Miss Lashley's expression; it was one of unmitigated fury.

'I take it that either you or your mother used the bathroom recently,' she said without preamble, 'in which case *these* must be yours – ' and

13

she thrust a small soggy bundle at Miranda, who dazedly recognised a pair of silk stockings and a pink bath sponge. There were also some bits of cotton wool stained with red nail varnish.

'I'm very sorry,' Miranda said automatically.

'Sorry?' repeated Miss Lashley with heavy emphasis. 'Sorry? Well, I'll tell you something straight out. For the past three months I have been the sole user of that bathroom and it's been kept like a new pin. A new *pin*! But ever since you and your mother came it's been like a pigsty. Pools of water, steam everywhere – it would never occur to you to open a window, I don't suppose – the wash basin full of hairs, and now *this*!' She pointed a furious forefinger at the bundle in Miranda's helpless hands, water from which was already dripping on to the carpet. 'Wet stockings draped over the bath, a filthy sponge, and bits of cotton wool all red and *bloodstained*!'

Her rage appalled Miranda, who stood bowed before it like a sapling in a gale-force wind.

'When I think of the rent I pay – I pay far more than you do – and how hard I work, I feel that the least I'm entitled to is a clean bathroom without any *hairs* and without other people's personal belongings dripping revolting *water* – and if it happens once more – just *once* more – I shall write to the landlord suggesting that he gives you notice to *quit*!'

Without taking her terrible stare from Miranda she backed out of the door and slammed it violently. Transfixed, Miranda heard the noise of her footsteps pounding downstairs, accompanied by what sounded like sobbing.

Regaining the power of movement, Miranda spread the stockings over the kitchen draining board, squeezed out the sponge, then, after a moment's consideration, used it to mop the water from the carpet. She disposed of the bits of cotton wool in the bucket under the sink, then packed her books ready for the following day, and crept off to bed.

The incident, when she heard about it the next morning, roused Florence to a state of breathless indignation.

'How *dare* she speak to my child like that? Who the hell does she think she is?' Eyes flashing, nostrils flaring, she was as fearsome to behold as the outraged tenant from the floor below. Miranda wondered uneasily what would happen if they both chose to go to the lav at the same time.

'I'm going down there to have it out with her,' Florence declared. 'I'm putting my foot down once and for all. Nobody's going to speak to *my* child like that!'

I'm going down there directly she gets home; I'm going first thing tomorrow; I'm going when I've been shopping, had a rest . . . But she didn't. She seemed to find adequate satisfaction in telling Miranda how she proposed to deal with the Lashley woman's damn cheek, what she was going to say to her, et cetera, and Miranda was interested to note the way her mother addressed her as if she were a third party, and not Miranda at all. ('I'm trying to bring my child up decently and that's all the help I get – some sour-minded old maid bitching on at her the moment my back's turned . . .') In her furiously protective mood Florence was very impressive, at least to Miranda, but Rob Allardyce dismissed the display by saying that if Miranda left hairs where she shouldn't leave hairs, she must expect to be hauled over the coals.

But she didn't say they were my hairs, Miranda thought. Any more than they were my silk stockings or bits of cotton wool. She forbore to speak the words aloud however, because often when she proffered a remark in Rob's presence he would look at her but refrain from commenting, leaving her to conclude that she had said something stupid.

In fact the whole incident might have been forgotten but for Florence's innate love of drama and her great ability to turn most situations to her own advantage. She now saw that it would be undignified to skirmish with the Lashley hag and would be very upsetting for Miranda who was, after all, only a child – and as she couldn't bear living in an atmosphere they would have to move.

Blithely she set about flat-hunting again, and with a pocketful of estate agents' keys took Miranda round with her during the weekend to see what they could find.

'Just look, chickabid, doesn't it give you the *creeps!*' They would tiptoe in and out of damp and lonely rooms where mice scuttled and flies hung motionless in spiders' webs, and it was at times like these that Miranda loved Florence unrestrainedly because she was like a friend of her own age.

The flat in Morton Street was chosen because it had a sitting room and kitchenette on the ground floor, and two bedrooms and sole use of bathroom on the first. As Florence said, it made you feel you could breathe. There was also a cement-covered yard at the rear in which Miranda could play, despite the fact that she had never played in the previous garden.

They moved by horse and cart because it was so much cheaper than a van, and Miranda sat with her head under the standard lamp shade, its fringe slapping her nose. Rob and Florence walked the short distance together.

They were completely organised by late afternoon because Florence was expert at removing and good at providing a comfortable lived-in appearance at short notice. Edgar Wallace on the bookshelf, pictures on the wall and a vase of daisies on the strip of tasselled satin laid diagonally across the dining table. The floorboards surrounding the square of carpet had been stained with Brunswick black but were not quite dry so had to be stepped over for the time being. It was a pity that Rob had to be there too, but at least he was going away on business for a couple of weeks.

'So now's the time to invite your little friend to tea,' Florence said with a pleased sigh. 'What about sending her a little invite to your birthday – it's nice it's on a Saturday.'

'I don't need to send it, I could give it to her at school.'

'That's not the right way,' Florence said. 'You've got to learn the correct way of doing things.'

She also said that it would not be correct to ask her little friend the number of her house in Rodney Street, so they consulted the directory in a public phone booth.

'What's an FRCS, chickabid?'

'I don't know.'

'And to think of the money I'm spending on your education.'

So under Florence's direction Miranda wrote a careful, stilted note on pink scented paper bought especially for the occasion, and addressed it to Miss Natalie Ellenberg.

'That's one thing I will say for your father's family,' Florence said. 'They always knew how to do things properly, and because I was intelligent I picked things up from them very quickly. But it'll be different for you of course. You're going to a good school.'

'Yes.'

'But I do think they should have taught you what FRCS stands for.'

'Yes, I know. But listen, supposing she can't come?'

'Of course she'll come. No little girl could ever refuse such a dinky invite.'

And on the appointed afternoon at the appointed time Natalie duly presented herself, and Miranda, who had been restlessly keeping watch for her for the past two hours, greeted her offhandedly: 'Hullo, crow.'

'Crow yourself. Have I come at the right time?'

'No, you're three weeks late. Look, do you like our tree?' Carelessly

Miranda indicated the maple that dominated the tiny front garden. 'It makes patterns on my bedroom ceiling.'

'Is that your bedroom there?' Natalie squinted upwards. 'You could climb out on to that branch and shin down if you wanted to.'

Although tempted to lie and say that she had already done so, Miranda kept silent. 'Come in and meet my mother,' she said finally, then added, 'Thank you' when Natalie dumped a present in her hand. It felt like a book.

The flat looked very nice, flooded with summer sunshine, then Florence came in, smiling warmly and holding out both arms. She too looked very nice; her hair, now the colour of well-nurtured mahogany, was curled in a tight roll round her face, and her make-up had been generously applied. Her frock was bright-green artificial silk and her diamanté earrings danced animatedly. She drew Natalie into a loving embrace. 'How do you do, Natalie dear? I've heard *so* much about you!'

Natalie response was muffled, but once freed she smiled gallantly and said that she was very well, thank you.

'Do sit down, dear.'

She did so. She was wearing a pleated skirt, lisle stockings and a Fair Isle jersey with a small hole in one sleeve. The hole rather shocked Florence when she noticed it, and confirmed her opinion that being an FRCS couldn't be anything rich or important. But Natalie's black curls had been brushed into an orderly halo, and Miranda noticed for the first time what pale and powerful fingers she had. It seemed strange to see old Nat sitting on their settee. . . .

Florence was asking their guest about her family's plans for the summer holidays and Natalie replied that she didn't know – it depended when her father could be spared.

Spared, thought Florence, and decided that he was a bishop. Then remembering Natalie's surname, amended it to rabbi.

'We went to Derwentwater for three days at Whitsun,' Natalie said. 'My mother hoped to see a pair of Slavonian grebe, but she didn't.'

'Oh, what a shame!' cried Florence.

'It was really their courtship ceremony she was after.'

'Oh yes, I've heard it's wonderful! I've always adored animals.'

'Actually, grebes are birds – '

'Yes, dear, of course they are. Naturally.' Florence flashed a steely smile. 'Personally I've always loved Whitsun more than any other time of the year, what with everything so fresh and green and our dear Lord rising from the dead – ' She clapped her hand to her mouth. 'Oh my *dear*, I do hope I haven't said anything to offend you?'

17

'Oh, gosh no,' Natalie said composedly. 'We're not Orthodox.'

Somewhat nonplussed by this matter-of-fact admission to being Jewish (whether Orthodox or not), Florence turned to Miranda.

'Chickabid, show Natalie your nice little bedroom while I make the tea.'

Miranda led the way upstairs, depressed by the certain knowledge that no enjoyment would be gained from having Nat as a guest. Already it felt strange and difficult, as if an invisible and unsuspected chasm separated school from home. She now realised that she preferred the old familiar Nat in school uniform to the new one in pleated skirt and Fair Isle. She too had noticed the hole in the sleeve and for some reason it bothered her.

'It's absolutely sweet,' Nat simpered, looking round Miranda's bedroom, then her expression changed. 'God, do you still go to bed with a teddy?'

'No, of course I don't.' Mortified, Miranda plucked the shabby one-eyed bear from her pillow and tossed it on to the chair. 'It's just an ornament, that's all.'

'But it's wearing a doll's frock.' Nat's eyes gleamed with amusement.

'It's been like that since I was little. I can't be bothered to take it off.'

Nat's eyes continued to glint as she turned to the window. 'Yes, you could climb out of there as easy as anything. You just grab that branch there, then swing yourself on to that forked bit, and then – '

'Yes, I know, but I just don't want to!' Miranda's petulance was beginning to show. 'I don't like climbing.'

'I do, but I'm not much good at it because I'm too fat.'

The generosity of this admission had an instantly soothing effect. Miranda's scowl faded. 'You're not fat, Nat.'

Which sent them into giggles.

'Fat Nat sat on the mat – '

'Eating half a rotten rat – '

They collapsed, Nat pounding the foot of the bed with her fists, Miranda leaning drunkenly against the wall.

'Tea, darlings!' Florence's voice trilling sweet and ladylike from the foot of the stairs sent them into fresh paroxysms. Suddenly they were united, and if their sense of unity temporarily excluded Florence, then so be it. They had become ten-year-olds again.

'Come on, stinker!'

'OK, slimy slug!'

The table in the window had been laid with a lace cloth, and Florence

18

had made both cucumber and fish-paste sandwiches. Bought scones, buttered and jammed, were arranged on a doily-covered plate, and there were chocolate biscuits as well as the small birthday cake with fourteen candles wedged into its icing. Smiling gaily, Florence poured the tea.

'Aren't these cups and saucers pretty, Natalie? They belonged to my late husband's mother.'

On the point of saying *I thought late meant dead*, Miranda heard her mother add, 'My husband died in tragic circumstances two years ago. My poor little girl hasn't got a daddy.'

'Oh. Golly – ' Nat stopped chewing for a moment and looked at Miranda. 'I thought you said you were – '

'Shut up,' Miranda muttered, and kicked her under the table.

'I'm a widow lady,' Florence said, 'but Miranda is all I want. She fills my whole life.'

It was awful to laugh about anyone's daddy being dead (whether he really was or wasn't), and despite Miranda's obvious perplexity the giggles threatened to return. They rose in both girls like bubbles, and the more they strove to suppress them the more they floated bursting to the surface. Miranda choked on a sandwich and Nat thumped her on the back, which made it worse. Miranda took a hasty swig of tea and choked even more.

'Chickabid, what is the matter?' Conscious of the exclusion, Florence began to look annoyed. 'Where are your manners?'

'She left them at school . . . Take fifty lines – I must not titter when talked to – ' Nat stared fixedly at the birthday cake, striving to keep her voice steady.

'You sound just like old Lissett!'

'*Quairt*, garls!'

Relieved that they were not making fun of her, Florence began to laugh too.

'Nat, do Miss Hather!' cried Miranda. 'She's our chemistry mistress and she always puts an "ah" on the end of everything.'

Nat composed her features and drew in her lips. 'Miss Hathah put some watah in a beakah, added sulpha. . . .' She went on and on in a reedy Oxford accent, and Miranda wiped her eyes upon her paper serviette and said, 'Honestly, it's the dead spit of her!'

'How did you learn to be so good at imitations?' Florence asked finally.

'I think I've just got a good ear,' Nat said. 'Please can I have another scone?'

19

Miranda cut the birthday cake without making a mess of it, and tea passed off well, but afterwards the sense of constraint threatened to return. Brightly Florence suggested Ludo or I Spy, and after several other suggestions of an equally unsuitable nature, told them to go and play in the garden.

'Girls of our age don't play,' Miranda said, and Florence told her with a loving smile not to answer back.

'I wasn't.'

'You were, chickabid. And I don't expect it of girls going to a good school. When you think of the fees I pay. . . .'

Nat disassociated herself and silently appraised the picture that hung over the sideboard.

'You don't pay them. My father – '

'There you go, answering back again! Go and show Natalie the garden before it's time for her to go.'

Red-faced and mutinous, Miranda led the way across the hall and down the back steps. With its grey paving, and high walls propping up a series of derelict sheds, it could hardly be called a garden.

'Stinks of cats,' Nat said, sniffing. Suspecting further criticism, Miranda shot her a quick look.

'I love cats,' Nat added. 'We've got three at home.'

They walked round the yard and stopped by the gate at the far end. 'Does it open?'

'No.'

'Pity.'

'Sometimes,' Miranda said in a low voice, 'I hate my mother. She's always turning into somebody else.'

'You told me she was divorced but she said your father's dead.'

'She was telling lies. He sent me a Christmas card last year.'

'Did you get one for your birthday?'

'No.'

'Perhaps he's died since last December, then.'

Miranda shook her head. 'And she's trying to get everyone to call her Tania although her real name's Florence. Flo for short.'

'Never mind,' Nat said consolingly. 'Perhaps both your parents are dead and you're really a Grand Duchess or something.'

'I don't feel much like a Grand Duchess.'

'How do you know? You can't tell what it feels like until somebody proves to you that you really are one.'

'I wish I'd got a brother or a sister.'

'We always want what we haven't got.'

20

'You sound like my Aunt Daisy.'

Having circumnavigated the yard three times they made for the back door. 'I'll have to go now,' Nat said. 'My music lesson's in half an hour.'

'You don't need any more lessons,' Miranda said, feeling kindly again. 'You can play as well as anyone they've got on the radio.'

'I'm only Grade 6. I've got a long way to go yet.'

They found Florence sitting with her shoes off and her feet tucked under her. Laying aside her novel she smiled her loving-mother smile, the little unpleasantness with Miranda forgotten.

'Goodbye, Mrs Whittaker.' Nat advanced and held out her hand. 'Thank you for having me.'

Florence swung her feet down on to the floor and Nat took a rapid step back, fearing the onslaught of another embrace.

'Goodbye, Natalie dear. Tell your mummy from me that you're a very nice little girl.'

'She won't believe – ' Nat began to say, then halted. A man had appeared silently in the doorway. Wearing a black polo sweater and dark trousers supported by a thick leather belt, he stood staring at her intently.

Seeing Nat's expression Florence swung round, then cried, 'Rob – how nice!' She held out her hands invitingly but he continued to stare at Nat without speaking and without change of expression. The room felt suddenly cold.

It was Miranda who broke the silence. 'This is my friend Natalie Ellenberg.' She was unable to address him as Uncle Rob.

'Yes. I can see that.' He continued to stare at Nat for another long minute, then turned on his heel, and they heard the front door click quietly behind him.

'Who was he?' Nat asked Miranda as they walked together to the end of Morton Street.

'Uncle Rob. But he's not my real uncle.'

'You don't seem to have anybody who's a real anything, do you?'

'My Aunt Daisy and my Uncle Frank are real enough. I think I'll ask if I can go back and live with them. I'm not keen on it here.'

'Cheer up,' Nat said consolingly. 'As soon as you're grown up you can go and live wherever you like.'

'Where'll you go, Nat?'

'Germany. They make the best pianos over there.'

The warmth of summer increased. Liverpool's streets smelt of hot soot and melting tar, and the girls of Queen Mary's wore green-and-white check frocks, long black stockings and panama hats. Once a week they played tennis and rounders on a plot of ground reserved for the school in Sefton Park, and once a fortnight they marched in a crocodile with a prefect in charge down to the Cornwallis Street Baths where the gym mistress awaited them in the Ladies' Plunge.

Miss Nelson was a truculent woman with powerful legs and a crop of short blonde hair which was reputed to be dyed. The only girl in the school to have a pash on her was Fiona Addison, but as Fiona was forbidden both games and gymnastics because of her asthma, she was without personal experience of Miss Nelson's particular brand of nastiness. She bullied. And when she wasn't bullying, she sneered.

She was sneering now at a girl called Pamela, who couldn't bear getting her head wet. Standing up to her shoulders in cold green water she tried hard to obey the barked instructions 'One – two – three – *duck!*' but the instinct for self-preservation prevented her from submerging any lower than her top lip.

'Deeper, you ninny!' cried Miss Nelson from the water's edge, then drew a bunch of keys from her pocket and tossed them with a splash in front of Pamela. 'Now pick them up.'

The keys lay in a shuddering, luminous little heap on the bottom. Pamela tried to reach down for them while keeping her head erect but her fingers missed them by several inches.

'I'm still waiting, Pamela.'

Shivering wretchedly, Pamela drew a deep breath and tried again, but her head in its regulation rubber bathing cap remained as obstinately buoyant as a pingpong ball. 'It won't seem to go. . . .'

'You poor lily-livered thing.' Miss Nelson pranced derisively. 'Have you no grit at *all?*'

'I don't know. . . .' Pamela began to weep, and Miss Nelson was enjoying herself too much to notice the girl who appeared behind her until she had dived in and showered her with spray. She resurfaced with the keys, shaking the wet hair out of her eyes.

'You dropped these, Miss Nelson.'

'Thank you, Natalie, most kind. And in future when I want you to interfere I will ask you.'

'Yes, Miss Nelson.'

Witnessing the incident from a discreet distance, it occurred to Miranda that her friend was the stuff of which heroines were made. An avid reader of boarding-school yarns when she lived with Aunt Daisy, she had been greatly preoccupied with the idea of schoolgirl valour, and was readily prepared to admire anyone in real life who showed signs of exhibiting it. And now the tendency to idealise had revived. It had been more than brave to go to the rescue of Pamela, and to make Miss Nelson look ridiculous; there had been exactly the right flavour of careless chivalry to fill any onlooker with admiring esteem.

Yet in other ways Nat Ellenberg let herself down. For instance, the classic schoolgirl heroine getting dressed and undressed in the three-some cubicles of the Ladies' Plunge would manage to do so in a state of decent concealment. Everyone else faced a corner whenever either vestless or knickerless; Nat not only faced her companions in a state of brazen disregard, but on the afternoon of the keys incident she actually stretched her arms above her head in mock languor and said, 'I say, girls, just look at my beautiful bust. . . .'

There was self-mockery in the gesture as well as a prankish desire to shock, and Miranda's esteem was shaken. At the same time she was aware of a degree of fascination in Nat's creamy white skin, lustrous dark eyes and thick black hair dangling in little wet ringlets round her face. Blushing, she recalled reading the rude bits in the Song of Solomon: *Thy navel is like a round goblet which wanteth not liquor: thy belly is like an heap of wheat set about with lilies. Thy two breasts are like two young roes that are twins. . . .* There was something different about Nat, a faint sort of exoticism that Miranda couldn't place. It couldn't be because she was Jewish; you might as well say it was because she was in St Ursula's house and not in St Margaret's.

Reclothed now in regulation Queen Mary's uniform, the two girls rambled homewards, damp hair crowned by panamas, satchels slung on shoulders (Miranda having abandoned her attaché case after her first term upon discovering them to be considered unfashionable), and towels and costumes coiled in damp swiss roll shapes. They shared a Mars bar between them, and the warm streets were hushed with city lethargy. Passing the rear entrance to a police station they saw drawn up in the deserted yard a black van with a small barred window set high in one side.

'A Black Maria,' breathed Nat. 'For dangerous criminals.'

They stood contemplating its sombre bulk in silence.

'Come on,' Nat urged. 'Let's go and look at it.'

They tiptoed rapidly across the yard. There was no one about, but when Nat gently turned the handle of the van's back door, Miranda recoiled.

'Don't – we'll get arrested. . . .'

23

To their surprise the door opened. They peered inside, Miranda craning over Nat's shoulder, but there wasn't much to see. Two narrow wooden benches down either side and a few initials pencilled above them. The stream of sunlight they had admitted illuminated one of the scribblings. *M.W. 1930.*

'A murderer,' whispered Nat. They climbed in, and to Miranda's consternation Nat closed the door behind them. The sunlight died. Plunged in heavy shadow they stood close together.

'A murderer,' repeated Nat, eyes glittering. 'He drowned his children in the bath and stabbed his wife when she tried to interfere. They found her lying on the bed with her torn-out heart cupped in her motionless hands. . . .'

'Shut up,' Miranda giggled nervously.

'So they took him off to his trial, heavily manacled because he was a maniac, and the judge donned the black cap and condemned him to hang by the neck until he was dead, and on his way to Walton Gaol, in this very same Black Maria in which we are standing, he scribbled his initials. Then they took him to the execution shed and it took him a long while to die because the hangman had a fit of sneezing and didn't jerk the lever hard enough, so he went on dangling there . . . he dangled and dangled and he was still alive. . . .'

'He's got the same initials as me.' Unnerved, Miranda pushed past Nat and groped in the gloom for the door handle. There wasn't one. There was merely a small round hole through which a faint thread of light appeared.

'I can't open it – there's nothing to open it with – '

'He dangled . . . he dangled . . . he *dingle*-dangled. . . .'

'Shut up and help me open the door!'

Miranda's panic increased at the terrible vision of wives with their hearts in their hands while their children lay blanched and waterlogged in the bath. She banged on the door and then kicked it but it remained firmly closed. She couldn't breathe properly.

'His head was practically torn from his body when they finally cut him down. His eyes were sticking out and his tongue protruding like a slice of putrefying liver. . . .' Nat chanted in her ear.

Half-demented with horror, Miranda began to scream as she renewed her assault on the door. It opened abruptly, letting in a blaze of sunshine, and she fell into the arms of a startled policeman. Sobbing and incoherent, she clung to him.

'My poor friend,' Nat said, making a leisurely descent from the Black

Maria, 'is undergoing treatment at the Royal Hospital for Nervous Diseases. They have every hope that her condition will improve.'

The policeman held Miranda in a fatherly embrace, and demanded to know what they had been doing in there. Didn't they realise that they were trespassing? Then he added that trespassing in such a thing as a Black Maria was hardly the sort of thing for a girl alleged to be a bit weak in the upper storey.

'Don't worry, Officer, I will see her home.' Unruffled, Nat retrieved their satchels and swimming things, apologised for any trouble they had caused, then added that if any charges were to be preferred, her father was Mr Bruno Ellenberg.

They walked home slowly up Bold Street towards Mount Pleasant, Miranda red-eyed and still hiccuping occasionally. When they parted at the corner of Catherine Street she was sufficiently composed to remember Florence asking about FRCS.

'What's it stand for?'

'Fellow of the Royal College of Surgeons.'

'What's that mean exactly?'

'It means that he cuts people up,' Nat said with a satanic smile. 'Then sews them together again.'

'What was it like?'

'Very nice, thank you.'

'Yes, but what was it like?' Laying aside her nail file, Florence reached for a cigarette. 'Tell me about their house.'

Newly returned from her first visit to Nat's home, Miranda said that it was big. Then, seeing that Florence remained unsatisfied, she added that it had a lot of things in it. And that all of them were very nice.

'And were her parents nice to you?'

'Yes, thank you. Very nice.'

'What did her mother wear?'

'A sort of blue thing, I think.'

Florence smoked reflectively, then said, 'They're Jews, aren't they?'

'I don't know,' Miranda said gruffly.

Florence remained silent for a while. Then: 'Why were you so late back?'

'They asked me to stay for supper.'

'They might have known I'd be worried.'

'Yes, they told me to telephone you but I had to say I couldn't because we haven't got one.'

'We're not on the phone because it costs money, and your dear father, in case you haven't noticed, is very stingy.'

'Is he really dead or isn't he?'

'Don't speak to me like that –'

'Well, is he or isn't he?'

It was not like Miranda to insist, and Florence drew a quick, irritated breath. 'Yes. No – well, he might as well be for all the good he is.'

From the doorway Miranda said, 'I forgot to tell you, an FRCS is a Fellow of the Royal College of Surgeons.'

She went upstairs to her bedroom, and without switching on the light stood by the window watching the gleam of the street lamp illuminating the leaves of the maple tree. It occurred to her that a tree was the only thing she had got that Nat hadn't. But even the tree wasn't really hers; it was only rented.

The Ellenbergs lived in a big house on the corner of Rodney Street, that long and austere stretch of Georgian houses then occupied mainly by the medical profession. Mr Ellenberg had his consulting rooms on the ground floor, and following Nat towards the lift Miranda had muttered a confused hullo to the white-clad receptionist sitting behind a desk. Everything was pale grey and white and very silent, and Miranda had by now developed enough of Florence's sensitivity to atmosphere to sense that it would cost a lot of money to consult Mr Ellenberg FRCS.

But upstairs they stepped out of the lift into a new world. The long corridor had rugs strewn on top of the carpet, and the walls were liberally hung with pictures. Open doorways afforded glimpses into mysterious half-lit rooms, and the one into which Nat led Miranda seemed to be very large and filled with furniture. Sofas and easy chairs, many of them draped with colourful shawls and half-filled with cushions; tables and stools and lamps, and mountains of books, and standing between the two long windows was a large grand piano. There were more rugs, more pictures, and the whole rich and careless profusion astounded Miranda.

A woman was sitting by the fire, and on the rug at her feet a baby lay on its back making pleasant dreamy little sounds like a simmering kettle.

The woman stood up and came towards them, smiling rather gravely and holding out her hand to Miranda. She had large grey eyes and the same irrepressible black curls as Nat, which she wore in an old-fashioned style, caught back from her face and secured in a bunch at the back of her head.

'This is Miranda,' Nat said. 'And this is Ma.'

Mrs Ellenberg didn't gush a welcome, in fact she said hardly anything at all, but her smile was kind and her handshake firm.

'And this little bit of nonsense,' Nat said, scooping up the baby, 'is my sister Rachel.'

Miranda was totally unprepared for the sight of her best friend holding a baby against her rumpled school uniform. Thunderstruck, she watched it grab at Nat's tie, then bend its head close to examine the stripes. A bead of saliva escaped from its intently pursed lips.

'I didn't know you'd got a sister.'

'Yes, you did.'

'No, I didn't. You only said you'd got three cats.' It sounded like an accusation, a cry of complaint.

'Well, OK, this is Rachel, aged ten months, and I've got a brother called Sammy but he's older.'

'I think we ought to make some tea, don't you?' Nat's mother said, but instead of leading the way to a dining room and a primly laid table, she conducted them into the kitchen, which gave a first impression of being large, warm and untidy. Freshly amazed by this casual approach, Miranda hovered by the door while Nat and Mrs Ellenberg began to produce tea in a rather disorganised kind of way, and the baby crawled round the floor. A grey striped cat jumped down from a chair and examined Rachel's face with interest, as she chortled and made grabbing motions which the cat deftly avoided.

Talking busily, mother and daughter produced a loaf of poppyseed bread, a tin of fruit cake and a glass jar full of florentines.

'Here,' Nat proffered a knife to Miranda, 'you butter while I cut.'

Miranda did so, aware that beneath the table the baby had grabbed her ankle in her busy little hands. She wanted to giggle, but didn't quite like to.

'I told Miss Fleming that I didn't want to play that stuffy A major thing any more because it's full of repetition and it hasn't got one decent tune to its name,' Nat was saying, 'but she said if I didn't play it I'd be back on Czerny and I said, OK Miss Fleming, I'll go back on Czerny if I have to because he does at least teach me something – '

'Miss Fleming must find you rather a trial,' said a deep voice, and Miranda saw a large man with unruly grey hair standing by the open door.

'She'll miss me when I leave,' Nat said. 'How many slices for you, Pa?'

'Bruno,' Mrs Ellenberg said, busily making the tea, 'this is Miranda, Nat's friend.'

'How do you do?' Miranda said.

'Delighted to make your acquaintance, Miranda.'

'Yes, this is my pa,' Nat said, flinging herself on him in a paroxysm of affection. Still holding the bread knife she began to saw the blunt side of it against his neck. 'This unfortunate man is in urgent need of a double tricotomy – '

'What's a dooble tricotomee?' he asked in a Liverpool singsong, and seized her hand. 'Careful with that thing or you'll have my head off.'

'Miranda, would you mind capturing Rachel for me? She's eating coal,' said Mrs Ellenberg.

Relieved to have something more to do, Miranda dropped to her knees and nervously removed the baby from the vicinity of the stove, deeply impressed by the small wriggling warmth of her. Mercifully she didn't scream, neither did she bite or scratch, so Miranda was able to sit down on a chair while she gently prised the fragments of coal from Rachel's clenched hands. Knowing nothing about babies, she was further impressed to see that her tiny fingernails had half moons.

'So, how's young Mozart?' Mr Ellenberg sat down at the table and ruffled Nat's hair. Then he turned to Miranda. 'Do you play, my dear?'

'No.' Miranda was thrown off balance. 'Well, just a bit of tennis.'

Some people, she realised later, might have laughed, but the Ellenbergs didn't. They merely regarded her with a frank and serene kindness, as if they had no suspicion of any shyness or constraint on her part.

They ate tea in the kitchen, Mr Ellenberg, in shirtsleeves and a blue-and-white spotted bow tie, scraping jam out of the pot with his knife, and Mrs Ellenberg talking about a lecture at the Rushworth Room by Harold Craxton. Miranda had heard neither of the Rushworth Room nor of Harold Craxton, and felt a stab of envy when Nat said that she would like to go. The baby, on her mother's knee, swooped suddenly upon the florentine on the plate in front of her and crammed it into her mouth.

'Piglet,' said Nat, then asked Miranda if she had done her Biology.

Miranda said that she had, and Nat asked her what she had put for the answer to the question about how did bladderwort and bird's nest orchis obtain their supply of nitrogen.

'From rain,' Miranda said, 'but I don't suppose it's right.'

'Righter than Wendy Hicks, who said it came from God.'

'She's a twit.'

Mr and Mrs Ellenberg smiled, then asked Miranda if her parents both came from Liverpool. She told them that they didn't, and that, well, it was all a bit complicated.

'She's got this funny background,' Nat said helpfully, 'full of uncles who aren't really uncles, and sometimes her father's dead and some-times he isn't – I think she's really the spurious offspring of an illicit union. I mean, suppose she's the rightful heir to the throne of France of something, but can't claim it through being out of wedlock?'

'Apart from the fact that the French show little sign of hankering for a Restoration,' Mr Ellenberg said mildly.

'No, but it'd be very interesting to have a friend like that, wouldn't it? My own poor life is so very, very dull. . . .'

Dull? thought Miranda, as the baby made a sudden lunge towards her from her mother's arms. The florentine had now been disposed of, mainly around her mouth and nose and down the front of her clothes. It lunged again, and pink-faced with gratification, Miranda opened her arms wide.

'I wish I had a little sister,' she whispered.

'You can have the Piglet any time between four and five pm,' Nat said.

Gripping Miranda's shoulders in a tight little pinch the baby stood facing her and began to spring up and down on her lap as if she were a trampoline.

'Why's she doing that?' Miranda was entranced.

'Instinct is telling her to strengthen her leg muscles in preparation for learning to walk.'

'Golly. Fancy something so little having an instinct!'

'All living creatures have them from the moment they're born. Instincts have to take the place of reasoning power.'

'You've probably seen fledglings flapping their wings in preparation for take-off from the nest,' Mrs Ellenberg said.

'We had a lot of birds where I lived in Yorkshire with my auntie and uncle – I liked it up there very much. . . .'

As if released from a spell, Miranda suddenly found herself able to talk to them. There was none of the tension she remembered from the afternoon Nat had come to tea at Morton Street, which was strange, because her mother (unlike the Ellenbergs) had tried so hard. Had made everything so nice. Perhaps that was the trouble.

Carefully carrying Rachel, she followed the Ellenbergs back to the big colourful room where the firelight was now making dim patterns on the lofty ceiling, and Nat sat down at the piano and began to play by the dying light that came through the two big windows looking down on to Rodney Street. The music she played was nothing like the rackety rum-te-tum that signalled the end of Assembly at Queen Mary's. It was very slow, and not so much sad as thoughtful; a wistful kind of thoughtfulness that somehow transported Miranda back to the clean-swept countryside outside Beverley, and suddenly she could see it all. The big skies and lonely trees and coarse tussocky grass growing among rocky boulders. The clean smell of it, and only grazing sheep for company. It had never been so close to her since she had left Aunt Daisy and Uncle Frank on Beverley railway station, and she wanted to cry, but in a curiously fulfilled sort of way she was too happy for the tears to form. She didn't notice when halfway through the music Mrs Ellenberg quietly took little Rachel away for bath and bed, but when Nat finished playing she saw the last gleam of light catching Mr Ellenberg's strong profile as he sat listening.

'Quite good,' he said when the last notes had died away.

'Play some more,' Miranda begged.

'Too dark to see.' Nat drooped over the keyboard, then suddenly tinkled out a little waltz. 'But I can play this without looking. I learned it for my Grade 4.'

Afterwards they sat on one of the brightly coloured rugs and Nat taught Miranda to play backgammon – 'It's only like an extra spiteful Ludo' – then they tiptoed into Rachel's room to say goodnight, but she was already asleep. Leaning over the bars of her cot Miranda gazed down at the unblemished face and closed eyes, and the golden glow of the nightlight made everything look so safe and warm.

'Not a bad old Piglet,' Nat said as they finally withdrew.

She showed Miranda her own bedroom which was large and carelessly opulent like the rest of the place, and Miranda admired the gilt-framed painting of a snow scene that hung over the bed.

'It belonged to my great-grandmother. Some of us came from Russia.'

The casual statement gave Miranda a sharp stab of envy. 'I thought you said you were dull!'

'So I am. I've never lived anywhere but in this house.'

If it was me I wouldn't ever want to live anywhere else, Miranda thought. I'd just want to go on living here until I died.

It was at that point that Mrs Ellenberg asked her to stay for supper, and she immediately accepted.

Back in her own bedroom in Morton Street she switched on the light and drew the curtains, looking round at the ordinariness; the square of thin carpet surrounded by floorboards stained with Brunswick black, the folkweave bedspread, the cheap varnished dressing table. No pictures except for a calendar with a dog on it and a snap of Aunt Daisy in a deckchair doing her knitting. No colour, no warmth, no life; the only thing she had for company was a one-eyed teddy bear in a doll's frock.

She went to bed without saying goodnight to her mother.

Miranda had left for school and the flat was very quiet when Florence went to the bathroom and swallowed the small white pill with a sip of water. Then, while the bath was running, she undressed, covered her hair with a frilly waterproof cap and stroked some nourishing skin cream into the pores of her apprehensive face.

She stepped into the bath, wincing at the sting of hot water, then slowly lay down. The ceiling was barely visible through the rising steam. She closed her eyes and thought, soon be over. Nothing to it.

She wished she had remembered to prop the door open and to leave the radio on. It would have been company. Not that she really needed company of course, particularly at a time like this. This was one of those times that a girl had to go through on her own; a bit nasty for a couple of hours perhaps, but after that bobbing back bright as a robin and full of beans. It was the first time she had ever had to do this, and she was only doing it now because of Miranda. And because of Rob, who was in London for a week.

Rob didn't know. She hadn't told him. Hadn't told anyone, because, of course, no one would want to broadcast such a thing round the neighbourhood. These things had to be managed quietly and discreetly. After all, girls had to preserve their mystique and their glamour.

Sweat began to break through the oily mask of skin food. She mopped her face with the sponge, then turned the hot tap on again with her toe. Fresh steam arose and she wondered what Rob would have said, supposing she had told him. Left her flat, most likely. As it was, he was in London helping to put the world to rights in his grim and manly way. She loved his grimness, loved melting it with soft arms and warm mouth, and of course she admired what he was doing; helping to make the world a better place for people like her and Miranda to live in. She didn't quite follow all the things he said, but she knew they were right, and after all if a girl goes by her intuition it seldom lets her down. Soon she would be all right again and Rob would be back and everything would be fine.

She dozed. Awoke, and turned the hot water on again. But this time it was only lukewarm. Damn, she must have drained the tank.

She dried herself, sprinkled her body with some highly scented talc and then, because nothing seemed to be happening yet, manicured her toenails and painted them red. She took off her bathcap and fluffed out her hair, and she didn't look too bad, considering. Considering she was half scared to death.

The pain started as she was sipping the second gin. Good. Soon be over now. And tomorrow she was going to buy a new frock.

It was midday before the thing got out of control. Sobbing and shuddering drunkenly, she lay on the bed, curled in a ball with her arms folded tight round her stomach. She crawled back to the bathroom and was sick. Soon be over . . . soon be over . . . . The last thing she remembered to do was to leave the front door on the latch for Miranda, then she lost consciousness.

Miranda, bathing her forehead with cold water, brought her back to life. Through clouds of griping pain she tried to smile and say hullo, chickabid.

'What's happened? I think you've got your period. . . .' Wide eyes in a white face; schoolgirl hairslide and striped school tie.

'Yes. I get it badly . . . sometimes. . . .'

Then another face looking at her. One she didn't recognise, but she heard the word *doctor*. Then the pain screaming as they lifted her on to the stretcher and carried her out into Morton Street, where a small knot of interested spectators had gathered. She managed a broken little smile at Miranda before the ambulance doors closed and she was driven away.

Miranda spent the evening in a state of shock, passing from one room to another, picking things up and then putting them down, looking at things and not seeing them. She tried to clean the mess off the bed, then, shuddering with cold, made herself a pot of tea. She carried it up to her bedroom, and then started convulsively when someone knocked on their front door. It was the tenant from the top floor, the elderly gentleman who had suggested sending for the doctor. His name was Mr Brewster and he kept himself to himself.

He asked if Miranda was all right. Miranda said yes. So Mr Brewster said that if she wanted anything she had only to knock at his flat door. Any time after six-fifteen, which was when he got home. She thanked him, and almost took him at his word after she had gone to bed but couldn't sleep because of all the fears and horrors, and because of not knowing what she was supposed to do next. What she was supposed to do if her mother died. But she didn't see Mr Brewster again until he passed the front-room window on his way to the tram stop next morning.

She went to school because it seemed the obvious thing to do, but at mid-morning recess she asked her form mistress if she could visit her mother in hospital. Her pallid face and stammered words allayed any suspicion of ulterior motive, and permission was given. She left without seeing Nat.

The Women's Hospital was not far from Morton Street, and they looked at her curiously when she asked to see Mrs Florence Whittaker. They asked which ward she was in and Miranda said she didn't know, so they consulted a register and then said that they had only a Mrs Tania Whittaker. When Miranda said yes, that's her, they looked at her more curiously than ever.

She found her way up to the ward, where a sister in a billowing headdress barred her way. 'Visiting hours are from two until three only.'

But Florence had already seen her, and was waving to her. Overcome with sudden love, Miranda ducked past the sister and ran down the ward.

Florence looked much better. Pale and drawn and with her mahogany curls congealed with sweat, her smile nevertheless had something of its old indomitable gaiety.

'I'm so *sorry*, chickabid – are you all right? Did you find some supper and everything?'

Forgetful of the fact that she was frequently left to find her own supper anyway, Miranda marvelled at Florence's tender unselfishness.

'Are you better now?' she asked in a low voice.

'Almost.' Florence pressed her hand. 'But I think I've got to have an op.'

'An operation?'

'Only a tiny one. They think it would be advisable. The doctor's such a nice man with blue eyes – '

'How long will it take?'

'Oh, only a day or two. But in the meanwhile I think you'll have to pop up to Daisy and Frank – you can't stay in the flat on your own.'

'Yes I can.'

'Of course you can't – ' The first sign of peevishness showed. 'Rob won't be back for five more days and I've got enough on my mind without. . . .' She put her hands over her face and already they looked pale and thin, the hands of a sick woman.

'OK,' Miranda said resignedly.

'You'll find some money in the leather purse under the tablecloths in the sideboard drawer. Take three pounds. And you'd better send a wire to Daisy and Frank to let them know you're coming. Do you know

33

where to turn the gas off? And before you go could you bring me my hairbrush and make-up and I'd better have my curlers, chickabid. I do wish they'd let us wear our own nighties instead of these God-awful things. . . .'

Miranda nodded dumbly. Having weathered the parting from her aunt and uncle, she didn't want to go back. It wouldn't be the same any more. So she allowed the sister to bustle her out of the ward, and because she had no intention of going to Yorkshire until the following day, retraced her steps towards Queen Mary's. Outside the high sooty wall she remembered that the afternoon held the promise of a double period of Latin. She walked on.

Back in the Morton Street flat she made herself a marmalade sandwich and a cup of tea. The place seemed dank and spiritless, so she switched on the light and tried to get on with *Sohrab and Rustum* which they were doing for English, then chucked it aside and had a go at one of Florence's Edgar Wallace novels. That was no better, so she went up to her bedroom, flung herself on the bed and went to sleep.

It was late teatime when she awoke. Hungry, and uncertain of what to do next, she washed her hands and face, combed her hair and went out for a walk. She walked down towards the new, half-built cathedral, turned right, and found herself as if by chance in Rodney Street. It felt very quiet and orderly; very solemn. There was no one much about. Without really considering what she was doing she mounted the steps of the Ellenbergs' house and rang the bell.

They took her in, of course. No fuss, no more questions than were strictly necessary, but when she asked Mr Ellenberg if he would be doing her mother's operation he smiled regretfully and said, 'Afraid not, my dear. It sounds more like a gynaecologist's job.'

She slept in a small room across the corridor from Nat, and when she lay down in bed she was enchanted to see that the ceiling was decorated with a dark blue paper speckled with stars. She had never seen anything like it before. She went back to the hospital on the following day and was shocked at the change in her mother. Her face was yellow and her little thin hands clutched and plucked at the sheets as if they were trying to find a way out of the pain. A nurse told Miranda that she hadn't come round properly yet.

Helplessly Miranda went on sitting there, watching her and trying not to smell the fumes of ether that still clung about her, and the woman in the next bed said, 'Don't fret, love, she'll be as right as rain tomorrow.'

So Miranda slipped away, and when she got back to Rodney Street she found that Nat's brother was there.

She had imagined him to be younger than Nat, even though Nat had said he was older; the picture of a small chubby boy in short grey trousers had somehow presented itself, but in reality he was slightly taller than Mr Ellenberg and had a faint shadow of down across his top lip. He smiled at Miranda without knowing who she was or why she was there, then went on with the book he was reading.

There were other people at the Ellenbergs' house as well. Elderly aunts and uncles who called in for perhaps an hour or two, others who stayed for a few days. Some of them had foreign accents, but they were all very nice to Miranda and accepted her presence with the same incurious courtesy as that shown by Nat's parents. One aunt whom she particularly liked giggled like a schoolgirl and also played the violin while Nat accompanied her on the piano. Her husband was a bent, bald old man who wore a little embroidered skullcap on the back of his head (to protect it from draughts, Miranda concluded). They were all faintly exotic and she decided that foreigners were jolly nice, no matter what other people said.

'It's rather nice having two schoolgirl daughters,' was one of Mrs Ellenberg's few comments concerning Miranda's presence.

'Rachel will be going to school one day,' Miranda said, holding the baby in her arms and kissing the top of her head. She loved Rachel with the same strange deep love she had felt for a border collie pup which she had been given by Uncle Frank, and which she had had to leave behind when she came to Liverpool. The parting had been too painful for her ever to want to see it again.

'Wouldn't it be funny if she ended up head girl?'

'Supposing Queen Mary's is still there,' Nat said from over by the piano.

'Why shouldn't it be?'

Nat shrugged. 'You mustn't rely too much on anything.'

Strange words from a cheerful extrovert like Nat, and for some reason they sent a shiver of disquiet through Miranda, although no one else in the room appeared to notice.

She had been staying with the Ellenbergs for four days before she went back to the Morton Street flat. Quietly she let herself in through the front door, and dumped her school satchel on the hall chair before going through into the living room. It was warm and airless. Flies buzzed in the window, and sitting motionless on a dining chair, his arms folded, was Uncle Rob. The sight of him made Miranda jump convulsively.

'Where is she?' He remained seated.

'In hospital. She's had an operation.'

'What for?'

'I don't know exactly,' Miranda said rather nervously. 'Something to do with her stomach.'

'Appendicitis?' He stood up, as Miranda didn't answer. 'Which hospital?'

She told him, then added, 'I've just been to see her and she's much better. Well, she must be because she's angry that they won't let her use make-up in there. She says that none of them seem like women, although it's a women's hospital.'

He walked towards the door and automatically Miranda stepped aside, suddenly filled with a premonition that he was about to give her a comforting hug. But he passed her, and asked from the hall whether she was all right, living on her own.

'I'm not living here, I'm staying with friends.'

'Oh. Good.' He looked back at her with the faint trace of a smile. It made his face look much nicer, and prompted Miranda to add, 'With the parents of my best friend Natalie Ellenberg.'

'Oh. Really.' The faint smile was instantly obliterated.

Annoyed by her own impulsiveness, Miranda asked how he had got into the flat. 'I have a key,' he said. 'Didn't you know?'

On the following afternoon Florence broke the news that when she left hospital next Monday she was going for a week's convalescence in Blackpool. Wasn't she lucky?

Miranda agreed. 'Did Uncle Rob arrange it?'

'Uncle Rob? Good God no, chickabid. He may have popped in to see me last evening, but that was all.' Florence buffed her fingernails on the sheet. 'It's a home for nice convalescent ladies, facing the sea, but in the mean time you'll really have to go up to Yorkshire because – '

'I can't,' Miranda cried, panic-stricken. 'We haven't finished exams – '

'Well, you'll just have to miss them. Exams aren't everything.'

'They are! If I don't pass I won't go up next year.'

Florence gave a cluck of impatience. 'Well, the minute the exams are over you'll have to go up to Beverley. I expect your friends will be going on holiday and they won't want to take you with them. In any case,' her voice took on a wheedling tone, 'it's time you had a change, chickabid. I sometimes think that Liverpool doesn't agree with you like the country. In fact I'm wondering – '

'I want to stay here – I want to stay in one place!' Miranda's voice rose, then dropped to an agitated whisper as she saw neighbouring patients looking at her. 'I've grown to like Liverpool and being with you. I like Queen Mary's and I like my friends and I don't want to start all over again!'

Florence looked nonplussed for a moment, then smiled her loving-mother smile. 'Yes, of course, and I'd feel just the same – supposing I'd had the chance of a good school and everything.'

So they said no more, but Miranda spent the following Saturday morning at the Morton Street flat, sweeping and dusting and tidying, and then carrying the sheets and towels round to the laundry. Although she was alert for the sound of his key in the lock, Uncle Rob didn't appear, so she took two shillings out of the leather purse in the sideboard drawer and bought a bar of chocolate for Nat and a bunch of flowers for Mrs Ellenberg.

She stayed with them during Florence's seven-day convalescence in Blackpool. The last of the exams were over and so now was the summer term, and she and Nat spent their first two days of freedom lounging on their beds reading and then taking Rachel for walks in her pram. They took turns pushing her to Prince's Park and round the squares of Georgian houses that were sunk deep in August torpor, while they gossiped and giggled and sometimes remained companionably silent. And Rachel, sitting plumply upright, peered about her from beneath the fringed sun-canopy and chewed the feet of her woolly rabbit.

On the Saturday afternoon before Florence returned, the Ellenbergs took Miranda with them to the Adelphi for afternoon tea. It was very large and magnificent, but even waiters and crystal chandeliers failed to subdue the characteristic family atmosphere. Eight in number, they settled themselves like a flock of vivacious birds, and Sammy, who had shown no more than a polite interest in Miranda, leaned close to her and asked which she would prefer – a bear in front or a bear behind?

Miranda turned bright pink and dropped a blob of strawberry jam in her lap, and Nat indicated the elderly lady playing sweet nothings on the grand piano and said, 'If I couldn't play better than that I'd drown myself.'

'The quality I most admire in my daughter is her modesty,' observed Mr Ellenberg.

'What is the point in hiding one's light under a bush?' demanded one of the aunts. She was very old, and one of those with a foreign accent.

'Bushel,' said Sammy.

'Bushel – what bushel?'

'It's what I'm supposed to hide my light under,' Nat said. 'Can I have another cake?'

'You've had three already,' Mrs Ellenberg said mildly. 'Pass one to Miranda.'

'What is a bushel, please?' pursued the old lady.

'A dry measure of eight gallons,' someone told her.

The waiter poured more tea and replenished the empty hot water jug. The lady pianist strayed into one of the slower pieces from Schumann's *Carnival*.

'Jesus, just listen to that,' breathed Nat.

'Don't blaspheme.'

'It's not blasphemy if I'm not a Christian.'

'Your own beliefs, or lack of them, are beside the point. One does not challenge other people's gods in public.'

The teacups tinkled and the conversation became increasingly animated. Sammy and Nat and their father became engrossed in the question of whether or not Jesus Christ was a god. He was if one took the word in a general sense – Mars was a god because he was the son of Jupiter – 'What's that got to do with it?' 'The same as princes are royal because their fathers are kings.' 'We're not talking about kings, we're talking about gods – '

'Gods or God?'

'I can envisage hiding one's light under a bush, particularly if it is large, but how can it be hid under eight gallons of something or other?' went on the old aunt, dusting crumbs from her bosom.

'It's an old English expression, darling,' someone told her. 'Lost in the mists of antiquity.'

'Like Jesus,' muttered Nat with her mouth full.

'Are you being deliberately provocative?' demanded Sammy.

The pianist left Schumann in favour of a tasteful ballad, and Miranda sat back in her chair and watched waiters with silver trays held aloft as they passed smoothly between the tables. Pale smoke from scented cigarettes tinted the air and she became aware of other people watching the Ellenberg family with interest.

She hoped that she would be taken for one of them. Although she wasn't joining in the conversation much she felt totally at ease in their company, perhaps because no matter what their ages they seemed to

38

enjoy everything so much. There was a freshness, an unselfconscious charm about them which called up a deep response in her that she had never experienced with anyone before, and she wondered whether it had anything to do with some of them having come from Russia before the Revolution. Yet beneath the charm was something wise and profoundly sophisticated which gave her the sure knowledge that they would never let her down. Would never change in their attitude of relaxed geniality towards someone who, she now saw, had had the luck to be admitted to their charmed family circle. She felt privileged and very happy.

Then there was Sammy, whom she now liked in a different kind of way. Nervous constraint in the company of an adolescent schoolboy had faded on the day he said he was very sorry to hear that her mother was ill – was it something serious? And the rather clinical concern bred by a medical background melted into a guffaw when Miranda said she didn't know, except that it was something to do with her innards. And when the guffaw suddenly cracked on a disastrously high note and he laughed more than ever, she became aware for the first time that the male gender could also suffer pubescent embarrassment. It recalled the afternoon in the Ladies' Plunge when Nat had said, 'Just look at my beautiful bust!' and Miranda now knew for sure that it had been the Ellenberg delight in self-mockery, and not swank, that had prompted the exhibition.

They lingered over tea that afternoon in the Adelphi until Mr Ellenberg glanced at his watch and said that he must call in at the clinic to have a look at one of his patients. He signalled for the bill, and someone asked Sammy if he was going to study medicine when the time came.

'I expect so, if nothing else crops up.'

A curious little silence fell, as if they were listening for the first sounds of the future, then Nat said, 'I know exactly what I'm going to do. I'm going to make it my life's work to rescue music from people like *her*.'

As if in answer, the lady pianist rippled a last arpeggio up the keyboard, then closed the piano lid, gathered up her music and her little gold handbag and departed with a gracious inclination of the head to left and right. A polite patter of applause followed her.

No one noticed Nat glide over to the piano until she began to play. Mr Ellenberg smiled interrogatively at the waiter, who gave his assent by a slight tightening of the cheek muscles. The rest of the family left their preparations for departure half completed.

She began to play Mendelssohn's 'Rondo Capriccioso', and the music came out slow and weighty and melted into grandeur. It had a beautiful tune that Miranda had heard several times on the Rodney Street piano, and watching the decisive movements of Nat's small plump hands she thought, if this were a film everyone would fall silent, their expressions would go soppy and the man over there would turn out to be a Hollywood producer or something. . . . But no one seemed to be taking much notice. The tea-sippers and scone-nibblers continued with what they were doing and the Ellenbergs went on talking.

Then Nat left the Mendelssohn and plunged abruptly into a slow, ringing jazz tune, crashing down on the heavy bass chords and letting the treble cry out its irresistible lament. Teacups paused then, and conversation was still, but only for a moment. Someone tittered, and Miranda saw a woman with a small dog on her lap nudge her companion and indicate the pianist with her cigarette holder.

But that was all. And when Nat rose from the piano stool only the waiter who had served them clapped his hands noiselessly and discreetly together.

'What on earth was that?' Mrs Ellenberg asked.

' "Aunt Hagar's Blues". I found the music in a box outside a junk shop.'

'Not quite the thing for the Adelphi, my dear,' Sammy remonstrated.

'It's real music though. And that's what I'm going to play, and I'm going to play it the way the composer meant. I'm never going to play anything like that awful woman there – '

'She's a professional,' someone pointed out.

'I'm going to be one too, but a different sort.'

'I take it you mean better?'

'No. The best.'

Mr Ellenberg leaned forward and ruffled her hair. 'Your arrogance is sufferable only because of your age.'

'Didn't you want to be the best surgeon?'

'Of course. But as my father used to say, there comes a time in every man's life when he realises that he's not going to be prime minister.'

'That's stupid. Somebody's got to be, haven't they?'

'I think Nat's a jolly good pianist,' Miranda said, 'although I can't understand anyone wanting to take up politics.'

They left the Adelphi, and outside the vast splendour of St George's Hall a man on a stepladder was haranguing a crowd. They were too far away to hear what he was saying, but they saw his head jerking and his fist beating the air while his audience appeared to be listening with rapt concentration.

'Our next prime minister,' Sammy murmured to Miranda, and her cheeks burned with pleasure when he took her arm as they crossed the street.

When they reached Rodney Street the daily woman who had been minding Rachel said that a telegram had come for Miss Whittaker. It was from Florence saying that she had been advised to extend her convalescence for another three days.

'May I go on staying here?' she asked.

Smiling at her worried expression they said, 'Yes, of course you can.'

Florence was to return on the following Thursday, and the day before, while Nat was having a music lesson, Miranda went round to Morton Street and once again swept and tidied the flat. But it was an effort to get going; Domestic Science was not her favourite subject, although this time she was made less dispirited by the difference between the careless and romantic abandon of Rodney Street and her own home. At least this *was* her own, and she crouched on her knees polishing the black-stained floorboards and thinking how much she loved Florence. Florence, Tania – what did names matter? – had been very ill, and someone who was so bright and brave in spite of having had a rotten husband (Miranda still wasn't sure whether he was really dead or not) was worthy of a loving, understanding daughter. She would be nicer in future. Kinder, gentler; more like the Ellenbergs.

She made Florence's bed with clean sheets and turned the corner down invitingly, and with the last shilling piece from the purse in the sideboard drawer bought a bunch of antirrhinums which she arranged in a vase and placed next to Edgar Wallace on the bookshelf. Welcome Home, the place said.

She was about to leave when there was a knock on the door. It was Mr Brewster from the top floor.

'I haven't seen you for some days, Miss er. How is your mother?'

'She's fine now,' Miranda said, beaming. 'And coming home tomorrow.'

'You will be very glad to have her back.' He was a wistful, elderly man who always wore a trilby that looked too large. 'I take it,' he added, lingering, 'that she is a widow?'

'Well, I'm not quite sure,' Miranda admitted. Then, seeing Mr Brewster's expression, added hastily, 'Yes, I think she is.'

'A personal tragedy, no doubt.'

'Yes, it'll be lovely to have her home again.' Miranda decided to change the subject. 'I've been staying with some nice friends in the meanwhile, but I've just spent all morning here putting things to rights and polishing and sorting things out, and I've left a note for the milk-man – '

'What a good girl you are,' Mr Brewster said, then added after a thoughtful pause, 'and your mother is a very sweet woman.'

'Yes, I know. And my friends – the ones I've been staying with – have asked her to lunch as soon as she's well enough.'

'Perhaps one evening you and your mother would care to come up and have coffee with me?' Mr Brewster suggested diffidently.

'Oh yes, we'd like to very much!' Miranda said heartily.

'Splendid, splendid. . . .' Mr Brewster smiled, disclosing crooked front teeth, then touched his trilby and departed towards Upper Parliament Street.

The Ellenbergs were packing up to go on holiday when Miranda left on the following day. The old aunt who played the violin looked vaguely surprised to learn that she was not going with them. 'Perhaps next year.' Mrs Ellenberg detached Rachel's sticky fingers from Miranda's hair. 'In the meanwhile she's going to look after her mother.'

'Can you come back when she's better?' Nat asked from the piano.

'I don't know – it's your turn to come to us.' Miranda felt suddenly awkward, as if the parting had already taken place, the thread of intimacy already broken.

She said goodbye and thank you to them all, with the exception of Sammy who wasn't there, and went down in the lift for the last time. Mr Ellenberg's consulting rooms were empty, the telephone on the reception desk silent. She let herself out into Rodney Street where the pavements radiated a dusty August heat, and began to hurry towards Morton Street, intent upon reaching home before her mother.

But Florence had already arrived and was standing in the sitting-room window as Miranda reached the house. Her face brightened and she opened the front door before Miranda could use the key.

'Chickabid!' Same radiant smile, same silly pet-name, and Miranda noticed with instant contrition that she winced when she hugged her.

'Sorry, was that your stitches?'

'No, they took them out before I left hospital.'

'Did you like the flowers? And did you see I'd polished everything?'

They walked through the hall with their arms around one another, Florence rather bent in the middle, and Miranda's smile vanished when she saw Rob Allardyce standing in the sitting-room doorway.

'Oh – hullo.'

'Hullo, Miranda. How are you?'

He had never asked before how she was; she didn't think that he had ever addressed her by name, but there was a new affability in his smile. He looked tanned and fit, and somehow taller than she remembered from their last encounter.

'Very well, thank you,' Miranda said. Then, releasing Florence, she asked if he was staying to lunch. 'I've only bought enough for two, but – '

'Darling,' Florence said, 'we've got something to tell you. Rob and I were married very quietly last week.'

'What – in the convalescent home?' Miranda blurted incredulously.

'Well, it wasn't exactly a convalescent home.' Florence's smile took on something of the old sweetly wheedling character. 'It was more like a small private hotel, and we just slipped away to the registry office round the corner when we realised that we love each other so very much – '

'So my father really is dead?'

'Yes, chickabid. He died very peacefully and there was no pain so you mustn't grieve, but in any case we were already divorced.'

'Oh.' There was nothing she could add. She couldn't think of any more questions, yet neither could she move away. So she just went on standing there, white-faced and with her toes turned in.

'She obviously doesn't feel like congratulating us,' Rob said. 'Never mind.'

He went over to the table and uncorked a bottle of sherry, Florence and Miranda watching motionless as he poured three small glasses full.

'I don't really – ' Miranda said in a stifled voice as he handed one to her.

'Just a wee sip to drink our health,' Florence said, and raised her own glass with a flirtatious little gesture. 'Here's to us – the three of us – and we're going to be wonderfully happy, aren't we?'

Miranda sipped, trying not to grimace. 'I hope you'll be very happy,' she managed to say, 'and I think I'd better go and unpack now.'

Conscious that they were watching her she walked out of the room and up the stairs, carrying her small suitcase. Her mother's bedroom door was ajar and her cheeks burned suddenly crimson when she saw the carefully turned-down sheet. She certainly hadn't meant to turn it down for *him* . . . .

She went into her own room, sat down on the edge of the bed and thought, Oh gosh, isn't it ghastly. Nothing's ever been quite as ghastly as what's happened now.

So far as Florence was concerned, the worst part – breaking the news to Miranda – was over, and everything was going to be fine. She was in love with Rob, definitely in love, and if one or two slight adjustments in the truth had had to be made it was only out of consideration for Miranda. For she loved Miranda too; she loved her very much indeed because she was her child, her sole chick. And as it's love that makes the world go round, there was no reason why the three of them shouldn't all be wonderfully happy together.

They ate lunch (cold ham and salad) at the table in the window and Miranda silently discarded one topic of conversation after another. School seemed remote during the second half of the summer hols, she didn't read newspapers, and instinct told her to avoid mentioning the Ellenbergs. Finally she said that she had been to the pictures and seen a film about Queen Cleopatra, but didn't say that she had been with Nat at the time.

Sensing her shyness, Florence attempted to enliven the proceedings with a light-hearted description of hospital routine – all bums and bed-pans and nurses with moustaches – and Rob asked Miranda if she would pass the mayonnaise. She did so, and didn't like it when their fingers touched.

After lunch she washed up while Florence had a nap on the settee, and Rob put his head round the kitchen door and said that he was going back to the office.

'Is that where you work, in an office?' She realised then how little she knew about him.

'I have to wade through a certain amount of paperwork, yes.'

'What are you?' she asked bluntly.

'I'm an area organiser.'

Miranda considered, staring down at the tea towel. 'It sounds very important.'

'It will be, one day,' he said, then gave her a terse smile and departed.

And so the days began to form a new pattern which consisted to a large extent of politely avoiding the company of Florence and Rob. It wasn't difficult, and they seemed easily satisfied with the answers she gave to their occasional enquiries. I was out for a walk, upstairs reading, writing a letter, going out to post it. . . . And she wasn't all that unhappy because an unstable home life had formed in her the ability to ignore the unacceptable and to concentrate on the agreeable. Like most only children she found pleasure in solitude.

And now she had the Ellenbergs to think about. She spent hours dawdling around Prince's Park and remembering how it had been when she stayed with them. They had made everything so easy, so uncomplicated, and she pondered their ability to indicate love without words, without grabbing each other in sudden fervent embraces. Their style of laconic, amused affection had impressed her even more than their colourful, casual home above the consulting rooms; even more than the music that she was beginning to enjoy more and more.

There seemed nearly always to be music. If Nat wasn't playing the piano, then it would be pouring from the gramophone; Bach, Beethoven, Schubert, Brahms, Russian ballet music, and Maggie Teyte singing Fauré and Debussy. She had learned to hum some of the tunes so gorgeously embellished by symphonic writing, and no one had minded when she asked if she could hear them again. She vowed to herself that a gramophone was the first thing she would buy when she had a home of her own. If she couldn't live with the Ellenbergs, then to live on her own was the next best thing.

But when Nat sent her a picture postcard from Snowdonia, giving it to Florence to read sparked off an ominous little row between the two of them.

'Yes,' Florence said, having glanced at it briefly, 'very nice.'

'They're coming home on Saturday, so I'll be able to see them on Sunday.'

'Don't forget school starts on Wednesday.'

'Yes, I know. But I want to see them before then – anyway, they want you to go to tea or supper or something at their house.'

Florence said nothing, and Miranda remembered that the invitation had been issued in the days before Rob had become a permanent fixture in their lives. 'I daresay they wouldn't mind him going too,' she added half-heartedly.

Florence looked at her in silence for a moment, then said in a low voice, 'We don't like you being friends with the Ellenbergs.'

'Why?'

'Because – well, because they're Jews.'

Miranda made no reply, but the colour drained from her face.

'They're not being a good influence on you,' Florence went on, 'and besides, it's very awkward now because of Rob's work and everything. He's got a great future career which I can't tell you about just yet, but everything's going to be different very soon and then you'll be glad you listened to my advice.'

'I don't understand what you're saying,' Miranda said. 'What's his work got to do with my having friends – '

'I've just told you, they're Jews.'

45

'But they're nice – '

'They're still Jews.'

'But doesn't being nice come first? It's stupid to put being Jews first.'

'Don't argue!' Florence stamped her foot, then said bitterly, 'You've changed a lot since you went to stay with them. I knew you would, that's why I wanted you to go back to Yorkshire where you'd be safe. They're influencing you – that's what Jews do to people – and you're young and silly and easily impressed.'

'I'm impressed by how kind and nice – '

'Shut up!' Florence cried, and burst into tears. She stood bowed, holding on to the edge of the table. 'Stop arguing and listen to me. I'm trying to explain that I've got two people to consider now, not just you, and it's not easy trying to make the happy little home I'd planned. Why can't you be nice to Rob?'

'He's not all that nice to me.'

'You don't give him a chance! Rob is kind and good and trying to help us both, and one day soon he's going to be very important. And when you're older you'll see exactly what we mean about the Jews and everything.'

'He makes me feel like David Copperfield with Mr Murdstone.'

'Who was – ? Oh, it doesn't matter. For God's sake lend me your hanky. . . .'

Miranda did so, and Florence sniffed and wiped her eyes, leaving little streaks of mascara. 'Please, chickabid, do be nice. I've been so ill and everything, and all I want is for us to be happy.'

Incapable of saying that she was sorry, Miranda offered to make Florence a cup of tea but Florence patted her curls back into position and said that they must wait for Rob. He would be back from his meeting any time now, and it would be fun to have it all together, wouldn't it?

The awkward age, Florence told herself consolingly after Miranda had slouched from the room. Sulky, moody, spotty, greasy, grumpy . . . I don't think that school's doing her any good either. She doesn't seem any more educated than I am and she's making friends with all the wrong people. Rob's quite right, you never see a Jew digging a hole in the road, do you? They never get down to an honest day's work like we do. They're parasites. . . . But one day everything's going to be different and we'll all be happy. Really happy. . . .

And although Miranda said nothing about having been discouraged from visiting the Ellenbergs, and the reason why, she very much enjoyed breaking the news to them of her mother's remarriage. Nat looked

gratifyingly impressed while her parents listened gravely and sympathetically, and only showed signs of remonstrating when Miranda's self-pity
began to overflow.

'Step-parent must be a difficult role to play,' Mrs Ellenberg said,
'and an equally difficult one to accept until a relationship can be
established.'

'Pity you can't divorce him,' Nat said. 'I don't see why you've got to
be married to someone before you can get shot of them legally.'

'The Nazis appear to be getting shot of a great many people, and I
believe they would describe it as legal.' Mr Ellenberg scooped little
Rachel off the floor and held her aloft. 'There's nothing to prevent
people from changing the law once they're in power.'

'What's that got to do with it?'

'Wait and see, my child.'

They turned to other subjects. Rachel made a grab at her father's
bow tie and squawked with joy when she pulled it undone. They told
Miranda about the cottage in Snowdonia, and Mrs Ellenberg said that
the hen harrier was at last becoming established in Wales.

'A bird,' Nat said laconically, noting Miranda's expression.

'I know it's a bird,' Miranda said, slightly miffed. 'And I know your
mother's going to write a book about them.'

Sammy came in as Miranda was leaving but they didn't say much to
one another. He seemed to have grown much taller during the holidays
and there were pimples on his chin. But from the way he smiled as he
held the lift gates open for her, she had a strange and uncomfortable
feeling that he was aware of Florence and Rob's attitude towards his
family.

Then school started, and as autumn set in there was less constraint
in the Morton Street flat because Rob was away more and more.
'Another meeting in London,' Florence would sigh. 'But you have to
hand it to chaps like Rob, they're so dedicated.'

Depends what to, Miranda thought, but didn't say the words aloud
because she now had no desire to know anything more about Rob than
was strictly necessary. She didn't want him impinging on her own
private world of dreams which still involved living either with the
Ellenbergs or on her own in a nice little flat somewhere with a gramophone.

But he was back with them on the Friday in November when the
Ellenbergs asked Miranda to spend the weekend with them. Solomon

the pianist was giving a recital at the Philharmonic Hall on Saturday evening and they already had a ticket for her.

'So can I go?'

Florence looked undecided, even harassed, then hurriedly gave her permission. 'Don't tell Rob where you are,' she whispered. 'Say you're with some other friends . . . . He's got a terribly important meeting on tomorrow so he'll be busy.'

'Thank you.' She gave her mother a quick hug. 'I've never been to a recital before.'

'Neither have I, but I'm determined that you're going to have all the advantages that I never had,' Florence replied with exquisite logic.

So on Friday afternoon Miranda went to Rodney Street with Nat after school, and on Saturday morning they reverted to the old practice of taking Rachel out for a walk. As usual they took turns to push the pram (You go up to the pillar box then I'll go up to the end of the street . . . .) and they dawdled and chattered while Rachel, in a rabbit-wool bonnet knitted by one of the aunts, rocked to and fro and made a simmering, bubbling noise that she had recently invented. She could also walk a few steps unaided now.

It was a very still grey day and Liverpool's great soot-encrusted buildings wore a strangely ominous look. There were few people about. The two girls walked down Rodney Street and crossed Mount Pleasant towards Brownlow Hill giggling about the new Latin mistress who sprayed saliva when she talked. They looked in a few second-hand shop windows and shuddered at sounds coming from the abattoir in St Andrews Street.

'God has forbidden Jews to eat pork,' Nat said. 'But we're OK because we're not Orthodox.'

As they rambled through the small back streets that lay behind Lime Street Station, the city was still oddly quiet, almost as if it were waiting for something to happen. Coming to the steep slope of Lord Nelson Street, Miranda was pushing the pram when they saw the sweetshop, and it was all that a sweetshop should be: small and intimate, with jars of fruit sherberts, bullseyes, dolly mixtures and wine gums glittering like jewels in the gaslight. On the cluttered marble counter lay a slab of palm toffee and a little brass hammer with which to break it.

The shopkeeper was a very old woman, peering through wire-framed pince-nez. Patiently she laid her hand on one glass jar after another as her customers' attention was diverted yet again by something that promised deeper delight and more of it for the money, for Nat was as congenitally short of pocket money as Miranda.

'I'm sorry we're taking so long,' Miranda said apologetically, 'but we'll be too old for sweets and things before long.'

'We'll prefer cocktails and cigarettes,' Nat explained, and added liquorice bootlaces to her purchases.

Outside, Rachel had stopped rocking and bubbling. Bored with trying to look through the shop window she leaned forward, straining against the harness that secured her, but was unable to reach her feet. She had recently discovered how to remove her shoes and socks and wanted to do it again. Frustrated, she threw herself back on the pillow and began to pick at the braid lining the pram's hood. It remained firmly attached. She sat up again and began to rock, but stopped bubbling when she heard the sudden commotion coming from the street opposite. A lot of men were running towards her, pursued by three mounted police. The men were shouting, but the noise was drowned by the clatter of hooves as the horses came nearer. One of the policemen was swinging a stick above his head which made Rachel laugh.

Excited, she rocked harder, making the pram bounce as she held one hand out towards the horses. As they pranced closer, the pram broke loose and began to move. The men were now running down Lord Nelson Street just ahead of her, pelting headlong down the steep slope that led towards the St George's Plateau.

Then one of them turned abruptly and stood braced in the path of the pursuing police horses. He was waving a red flag at them. The pram gathered speed towards the men, and Rachel's delight changed abruptly to the primitive terror of a defenceless creature facing death. Her cries were lost in the harsh stamping and trampling. Tightly reined, the second horse reared at the man and his flag. The man jumped aside and covered his head with his arms. The flag fell unheeded and the pram sped crazily towards the kerb, tilted, and then fell beneath the flailing hooves and foam-flecked jaws.

She was lying discarded, limp as a little rag doll when they released her, and the trembling policeman who held her so tenderly looked up at the two ashen-faced schoolgirls and said, 'If I had my way you'd both go to prison for life.'

Ahead of them the British Union of Fascists grimly ignored the boos and catcalls and marched eight abreast towards Church Street with banners aloft. Standing in the crowd Florence clutched her fox fur tightly round her neck and thought how attractive Blackshirts were, Rob in particular. She waved to him and cried, 'Coo-eee!' but he stamped by without seeing, his eyes fixed on some distant glory in which she had no place. Two rows behind him marched a woman with cropped blonde hair whose name was Miss Nelson.

Florence's first reaction upon hearing the news was to burst into tears. Sobbing convulsively, she held Miranda tightly to her breast.

'How awful – how awful – oh, that poor little baby! And her poor mother – ' Abruptly her sobs ceased and she held Miranda at arm's length. 'And what about you? What's going to happen to you and your friend?'

'I don't know.' Miranda wept too, great silent tears that rolled unchecked. 'A policeman said we'll go to prison for life, but Mr Ellenberg came to the hospital and said it was an accident – an *accident* – although he was crying too . . . But I don't know what's going to happen now because I loved little Rachel so much and now Nat won't speak to me. . . .' She broke down and sobbed.

'It's not fair of her to blame you.' Florence blew her nose. 'If you were there together it was her fault as much as yours.'

'Yes, but – '

'But what?' The loving-mother demeanour vanished behind sudden suspicion.

'Nothing.' Miranda dried her eyes.

'It's not fair of your friend to be cross with you,' Florence went on. 'What's happened is absolutely dreadful – how I feel for the poor mother – but what's done can't be undone and least said soonest mended. I daresay that's why she's not speaking.'

'Yes,' Miranda said, and tried to blot out the memory of Nat's face when she'd said, 'It's your fault. You were pushing the pram and you forgot to put the brake on.'

'So we'll send some nice flowers to the funeral,' Florence said with the air of someone who has found the practical solution to a problem, 'and I'll perhaps pop round to see your friend's mother in a day or two when she's had time to get over it, poor soul.'

For some time now Florence had made a point of referring to Nat as 'your friend', and Miranda had a sense of her steady withdrawal from any association with the Ellenbergs. Not that there had been very much to start with, but she had made no further suggestions about inviting Nat to tea again; even if she had done so, Miranda would no longer have felt sufficiently confident to pass them on. She had been made aware of her mother's newly found distaste for Jews, and the possible presence of Rob, silent and accusing, deterred her completely. The Ellenbergs now had to occupy a completely separate part of her

50

life, and the sense that she herself was being divided into two halves was confusing and difficult to deal with. It would have been a tremendous relief to have told Florence about the brake, but it was no longer possible.

Unexpectedly, however, Rob also attempted to offer comfort in her initially harassed state. He sat with her in front of the fire one evening.

'Sooner or later we all have to come to terms with reality,' he said. 'Some people can avoid it longer than others, while idiots and halfwits remain in perpetual ignorance so long as we have a system that believes in the strong protecting the weak. And just now, Miranda, the system is in the process of change, and like the rest of us you're in on the dawn of a great new age. When you're old you'll be proud to be able to say, yes, I remember the early days of struggle. I saw it and I took part in it.' He leaned closer. 'Wouldn't you like to take part in the struggle for a better world, Miranda?'

'I don't know. . . .' Striving to control her tears, she was barely listening.

'But in any struggle towards an ideal there is bound to be a stage of what may seem like senseless destruction, so think of it this way. Think of a beautiful room which is full of fine furniture, valuable pictures and windows giving on to a superlative view. It's all there. But the room hasn't been cleaned for ten years. No one has entered it. No one has bothered. They've just left it to look after itself, and so, when you and I finally open the door and step inside, what do we find? We find dust and dirt; spiders, Miranda, weaving grey webs over all the bright colours and reducing them to a dull monochrome. And hordes of mice are nibbling the fine carpets, making nests in the silk cushions, leaving their filthy droppings everywhere. And rats in the wainscot are chewing the panelling and squabbling and devouring each other, leaving bloodstains on the brocaded chairs. There are dead flies littering the place, rooks have fallen down the chimney and their carcasses are putrefying. . . . It's all dirty and brutal and without any sense of order. So what are we going to do, Miranda?'

She was listening now. She could see the Ellenbergs' big room in all its silent, tarnished splendour, and although the spiders would make her shiver, she would still want to go back to it.

'So what we've got to do, Miranda,' he continued without waiting for her to answer, 'is to take brooms and brushes and dusters in there and clean it out. Open the windows, clean away the dirt in our big metaphorical room so that we can see the fine view through the windows. Then we must set mousetraps and rat-traps and get rid of all

51

the vermin, and then sweep and polish and make it a room fit for decent people – people like you and me – to live in. Don't you agree?'

She nodded. Then said in a small voice, 'I quite like mice.'

'I know,' he smiled. 'So do I, until I remember that they spread disease. Mice are vermin, Miranda, and so are rats. It was rats that were responsible for the Great Plague which you must have learned about at school. Bubonic plague which killed thousands but only after they had suffered days, even weeks of agony. Flies, wasps, spiders – all these things we can do without because they live outside our scheme of things, and it's the same with the march last Saturday. I was marching with the British Union of Fascists, Miranda, because I believe in the creed of Britain for the British. I don't believe in sharing our countrymen with vermin who contribute nothing except dirt and disease.'

He paused, as if waiting for Miranda to comment, but she remained silent.

'In any struggle towards an ideal there is bound to be an initial stage of what may seem like wanton destruction, and inevitably some of the weak and supposedly innocent will be crushed underfoot.' Miranda winced. 'Like your friend's baby. All very sad, but at this stage of development we have to be sternly practical. And the practicalities of this incident are that a baby in a runaway pram – and don't forget that the pram ran away because of someone's negligence – collided with the mounted police who were merely trying to keep order against a gang of ruffians – '

'Someone said they were Communists,' Miranda said.

'A gang of ruffians who like to challenge us and then lay the blame for any resulting violence at our door. It is their policy, their strategy.'

'But Rachel was a person, not a fly or a – '

'I know, I know, but – ' Rob looked as if he were about to say more, then changed his mind.

'Did you see – ?' Miranda began to weep again.

'No.'

'She was so little. . . .'

'Yes, all very sad, and this is one of the reasons why we must never allow Communism to gain a foothold in this country. Don't you agree?'

His handsome features emphasised by the dancing flames of the fire bothered her almost as much as his words. Distractedly she remembered the sounds that often came from the bedroom he shared with her mother – strange rustlings and creakings and little cries – and switched her mind hurriedly to the things he was saying about the evils of Communism. But none of it seemed to have anything to do with

Rachel's death. Except that perhaps he was just saying all that to ease the pain of her responsibility. Timidly hopeful, she steeled herself to look at him again, but at that moment her mother came in.

'Ah, you're having a chinwag,' she said. 'Don't let me interrupt.'

'You're not.' Rob stood up, legs braced, thumbs stuck in his belt. 'I was just explaining some of the facts of life to Miranda – some of the other facts, I mean.'

The phrase made Miranda blush deeply and uncontrollably.

'And I'm reasonably sure that within a year or so she'll be joining us, won't you, Miranda? After all, one of Queen Mary's teaching staff is already an active member of our branch. June Nelson, you know her, don't you?'

'Miss Nelson's our gym mistress,' Miranda managed to remind him, before bolting from the room.

She fled upstairs and flung herself on her bed, then after a moment or two pulled the eiderdown over her and lay huddled beneath it. But she would never be able to shut out the powerful presence of Rob, or the things that he had been saying. Neither would she ever for the remainder of her life shut out the vision of Rachel in the policeman's arms and Nat saying, 'It was all your fault. You forgot to put the brake on.'

She lay there for a long while, trying to get rid of the searing impressions of the last few terrible days so that she might think what to do; where to go for comfort for all the pain and misery of guilt.

She couldn't face school, and on Monday and Tuesday had played truant. But neither could she face the old haunts of Prince's Park and the Georgian squares, so she'd wandered down to the big shops of Church Street where she moved listlessly through the various departments. She'd bought herself a film magazine and a fourpenny book of Schoolgirls' Stories and read them sitting in an armchair in the Ladies' Restroom in John Lewis's. But she was too old now for schoolgirl yarns, and not yet sufficiently knowledgeable about the cinema to care greatly about the marital goings-on of film stars.

They were two long days, and she had nothing to do but remember bursting out of the sweetshop with Nat – both of them running and screaming – too late to halt the pram in its crazy progress down Lord Nelson Street. Gazing in shop windows she saw only Rachel's little arms raised high above her head in an attitude of frozen terror, then the man jumping aside from the police horse and the pram tilting and falling, the great threshing hooves crushing in its side. She remembered the wheels still spinning after the policeman had leapt down from the saddle and run to release Rachel. She remembered how red and clumsy his hands had looked, and she remembered their infinite tenderness as he'd held Rachel close to him, and had slowly reached for the pram blanket with which to cover her. And she remembered the look in his eyes when he had said, 'If I had my way you'd both go to prison for life.'

It brought back the memory of that summer afternoon when she and Nat had climbed into the back of the Black Maria on the way home from swimming, Nat grinning in the stuffy gloom and maliciously fanning Miranda's apprehension into a state of niddering panic. She realised now that it had been an omen; Rachel had died because she had forgotten to put the brake on the pram, so now she would be taken in a Black Maria to a reformatory until she was old enough to be hanged.

She played truant again on Wednesday, but this time walked down Upper Parliament Street and turned in the direction of Rodney Street. It surprised her that it should look much the same as usual; quiet, sedate, unruffled. Her hand hovered over the Ellenbergs' house bell, touched the one beneath it that served the consulting rooms, and then withdrew. She walked away; she looked round the new Anglican cathedral, slowly rising on its hillock above the old houses, the wide splendour of the city proper, the docks, and then finally at the steel-grey River Mersey.

It was a dark day and there were lights in the houses she passed and in the trams that sang their sad iron songs as they coasted down towards the Pier Head. She couldn't afford to go to a milk bar for lunch so she bought herself a doughnut and ate it out of the paper bag. The first few mouthfuls were all right but she couldn't finish it. She hadn't felt hungry since Saturday morning – *the* Saturday morning. She was passing a quiet alleyway when a man in overalls stepped out of the shadows, fumbled with his fly and asked her if she would like to see something. Miranda declined in a small prim voice, and walked on, trying not to quicken her pace.

And the incident recalled the Saturday afternoon she and Nat had spent among the classical statues in the Walker Art Gallery, examining the various examples of male equipment and deciding that on the whole they were unimpressed. It was Nat who had told her the facts of life as they walked along Lime Street.

'How long does it take to get the seed in?'

'Oh, it can be hours and hours, depending on how long it stays upright.'

54

'Suppose it gets stuck and they have to go about like Siamese twins for the rest of their lives?'

The helpless tittering and cruel schoolgirl sniggers had helped Miranda to deal with the embarrassment of her mother getting married to Rob Allardyce. In an odd kind of way it had made her feel cleansed, and she and Nat had since kept off the subject.

But everywhere she wandered was full of Nat. Nat slouching along beside her with her dusty black curls bouncing under her old bashed-in school hat, her satchel slung on her shoulder. Nat's voice, low and rather husky, arguing, laughing, teasing, joking, imitating other people. The intense glow of her dark eyes and the smile, half-affectionate and half-sardonic, that disclosed small, even teeth and dimples in her cheeks. She wasn't pretty, and Miranda had realised some time ago that when they were old enough, she would make little attempt to fall in line with lipstick and high-heeled shoes. She laughed at long, thin women in *Vogue* and at the débutantes in the *Tatler & Bystander*, copies of which were available in her father's waiting room, and said that when the time came she would probably marry a piano-tuner.

Music seemed to be the only thing she took seriously. 'Do you realise how many different ways there are of playing one single note?' she once asked Miranda. 'How many ways you can just press down one key? There's hundreds and hundreds and they all sound different. Sad, happy, frightening – anything you're feeling at that particular moment. It's only a slice of ivory attached to a bit of wire but it can mean anything you want it to. The pedal helps of course; it produces what they call resonance. But there's more power of persuasion in one note of music than any old politician's got. Beethoven knew that, which is why he sounds so livid sometimes, and Chopin too, but in a different kind of way. He had a long pash on a writer called George Sand – '

'Fancy having a pash on another man.'

'George Sand was a woman, dope. That was just her *nom de plume*.'

'Oh.'

Sometimes it seemed to Miranda that she was gaining as much education from Nat as she was from Queen Mary's.

But presumably that was all over now. She had lost Nat and all the other Ellenbergs because she had forgotten to put the brake on the pram and Rachel, with her rocking movements, had dislodged the front wheel from resting against the sweetshop wall. It was Rachel's fault too. But Rachel was only a baby, and Rachel had paid with her life. Rachel was presumably one of the poor little mice innocently nibbling the carpets in Rob's hypothetical room. What a stupid idea.

Yet she had to examine it. She began taking notice of people in the streets, looking into their faces and wondering whether they were Communists or Fascists, vermin or humans. At home in the evenings, when Rob and Florence were out, she read the newspapers; Rob's *Action* described the Jews as a river of grey slime, while the *Liverpool Echo* quoted Lady Baden-Powell's statement that ill-health was caused by the motor car, the wireless and higher education. Which seemed neither here nor there.

Listening one evening to a talk on the wireless about current affairs, she learned that Germany had been rearming at a breathless pace for the past two years and that under the guidance of Herr Hitler they had reoccupied the Rhineland. She already knew that Abyssinia had fallen to Mussolini and the Italians, and that they, like Hitler (and Rob), were Fascists. All of which needn't concern her greatly except that the Fascists for some reason hated the Jews, and that was what her best friends were. Jews. But not Orthodox.

She went to the Picton Library to look up the word Orthodox, hoping against hope that its negative form would somehow exempt the Ellenbergs from racial hatred, but she had just reached the word orthodontia (rectification of abnormalities in the teeth) when she saw Helen Pritchard, the head girl of Queen Mary's, consulting another large volume close by. Miranda closed her dictionary and glided swiftly away.

That was on Thursday, and when Miranda arrived home at the duly appointed hour on the following day, Florence said without preamble, 'It's no use kidding me you've been to school, because you haven't. A mistress called Miss Lacey or something came here looking for you and asking why they hadn't received a doctor's certificate if you were ill.'

Still in her school hat and coat Miranda sank down on to a chair.

'So where have you been? Today's Friday and you haven't been there all week.'

'I know.'

'Well, why haven't you?'

Florence stood with her hands on her hips and Miranda thought dully, if you can't guess why not, there's no point in me trying to explain.

'So, why?'

'I was fed up.'

'Fed up? What sort of an excuse is that? Don't we all get fed up sometimes? God knows I do, what with one thing and another – trying to look after you, and help Rob with his work, and cook and clean and everything – ' Then abruptly her mood changed. Her eyes softened, grew tender, and she held out her arms. 'Oh, poor little chickabid, tell me about it. Is it the baby?'

Miranda nodded, incapable of speech. She sat with her hand shielding her eyes.

'I've been so worried about you – mothers do know about these things, you know. And I've been saying to myself, Oh my poor chickabid, she looks so pale and doesn't talk much, how can I help, what can I do . . . ?'

The temptation after five long days of aimless wandering up and down the streets of Liverpool was too much. Miranda succumbed. 'I feel so guilty because it was all my fault. She was such a lovely little baby – a bit like Nat must have been – and now she's dead and it was my fault because I forgot to put the brake on. And they're all so kind and lovely, all the Ellenbergs, they love music and art and they're wise and gentle and they love all the family and being together – ' Her voice broke. She got up from the chair and like a lost child groped her way towards Florence's arms.

Although Miranda was now two inches taller than her mother, Florence held her tightly, then after a moment or two gently removed her school hat and smoothed her hot forehead and tangled hair while Miranda cried without restraint for the first time since Rachel's death.

'Darling . . . darling . . . poor little chickabid. . . .' The words soothed and healed even as the pain and guilt poured out, until at last Miranda scrubbed at her swollen eyes, sniffed raucously and then withdrew from Florence's arms.

'Sorry.'

'Don't be. If mothers can't understand these things, who can?' Then she made a tenderly conspiratorial face and whispered, 'Isn't your period due about now, chickabid?'

'I don't know. I suppose so.'

'That's what it's all about. I expect you remember me telling you that us girls always feel a bit down in the dumps just before it starts – what nasty old things we have to put up with! I don't see why men shouldn't have some of them as well. . . .'

In no mood for jokes, Miranda nodded dourly and retreated towards the door.

'By the way, darling, Rob and I are popping out tonight so I've left you a nice little supper in the kitchen. Cold ham and tomato and bread and butter and there's some chutney if you fancy it and a piece of apple pie I bought. . . .'

She left soon after for Rob's office, dressed in her new black coat and a little felt hat tilted over one eye. Her fox fur lay abandoned on the arm of the settee and Miranda picked it up, stroked it and gazed into its mournful little eyes.

'Poor old Fido, I suppose you're one of the vermin too,' she said. 'But at least they like you after you're dead.'

She went back to school on the following Monday, and didn't know whether she was sorry or relieved when she discovered that Nat wasn't there.

But everyone knew about it. She could tell from their faces that they had all read the papers, had all talked about it, as she tried to slide inconspicuously back into the rhythm of school life.

Rather to her surprise no one said anything; no mention was made by either staff or girls of her week's absence and neither did anyone speak of Natalie Ellenberg. Miranda didn't – couldn't – say anything either. It seemed as if the burst of weeping in her mother's arms had effectively sealed the flow of emotion, leaving her in a state of frozen inertia. She went through the days like an automaton, only dreading and yet longing for the return of her best friend. Nothing else mattered much.

Because they were minors, neither she nor Nat had been called to the inquest, where a verdict of death by misadventure was recorded, and Florence had also vetoed any idea that she and Miranda should attend the funeral.

'For one thing we don't know when it is. They've probably had it by now anyway – and, after all, they haven't bothered to let us know, have they? In any case it'll be some sort of ceremony we don't understand, chickabid. It'll be in a synagogue with a lot of old men with long beards all wailing, and we won't know what to do. . . .'

She then went on with greatly increased animation to speak of Mrs Simpson.

'She doesn't love our King, she just wants to be Queen of England. You can see it written all over her face – oh, yes, she's very chic and who wouldn't be, dressed by Worth and Molyneux and all those people, but she's calculating, chickabid. She's as cold as charity. . . . No, no, she's got it all worked out that she's going to be our Queen, and she damn well isn't!'

Miranda was beginning to recognise that Florence hated all other

58

women, whether personally known to her or not, in the same way that Rob hated Jews and Communists. Fumbling about on the edge of the adult world she pondered the human capacity for impartial hatred while she tried to get back to the Confederacy of Delos becoming an Athenian Empire, and did her best to endure being bawled at on the hockey field by the strutting and peroxided Miss Nelson.

On the Saturday afternoon, when she could bear it no longer, she walked round to Rodney Street, mounted the steps of the Ellenbergs' house and rang their private bell. There was no answer. They had gone away. Upped and gone somewhere else to escape from the memories of Rachel, and of Miranda Whittaker, murderess. She rang again, then peered through the big brass letterbox. Blackness, and silence. She rang once more, then sank down on the top step with her hands between her knees, her head drooping, so filled with despair she could have died of it.

'Miranda?' Mr Ellenberg had opened the door noiselessly. He was standing there in a baggy old suit and slippers but the spotted bow tie was still poised in place. She rose to her feet and stood confronting him uncertainly.

'I'm sorry.' She didn't know whether she meant sorry for intruding or sorry about her part in Rachel's death.

'Come in, child,' he said, and gently took her arm. He continued to hold it without speaking as they went upstairs in the lift, Miranda's heart now thumping heavily.

Mrs Ellenberg and the small gathering of aunts and uncles greeted her calmly and quietly and without surprise. Seeing her glance hastily round the room they told her that Nat was in bed with tonsillitis, and – in order to give her a little more time to compose herself – added that she had been to London to take a music exam.

'Can I see her? I mean, will she want . . . ?' These was so much that needed to be said that she could only stand there with her toes turned in while she repeated the old instinctive words of a child out of its emotional depth: 'I'm sorry.'

'It was an accident,' Mrs Ellenberg said, taking her hand. 'We are all holding tight to that fact, and you must do the same.' She looked pale and very tired, but quiescent.

The big room was lit by a bright fire, and a tea table was drawn up in front of it. The cats were asleep on cushions, the piano stood open between the long Georgian windows, and the rugs and shawls were scattered with their usual careless profusion. But there was no Rachel.

They gave her a cup of tea and told her that Nat was asleep but would be glad to see her when she awoke, and Miranda sat next to an old aunt who smiled and nodded her head as if in time to secret music.

They asked her about school and she told them that she had joined the Playreading Club, but without mentioning that it was merely an excuse for coming home later on Wednesdays, which were the afternoons Rob invariably spent at home.

Mr Ellenberg said that he had once played Malvolio in a school production, then they fell silent. It wasn't an uncomfortable silence – the family circle still appeared to be open to her – but things weren't the same. Miranda sensed that it was an effort to make conversation, to drag themselves from the sad shadowland of their thoughts.

It was the old uncle with the little round cap to keep off the draughts who finally suggested that she should look in on Nat.

The door was ajar, the bedside lamp switched on, but Nat made no move as Miranda tiptoed fearfully in. She was still asleep, lying on her back with her thick tangle of curls tossed on the pillow and one hand still supporting a pocket edition of Holmes' *Life of Mozart*. She breathed with a slight buzzing sound.

As if becoming aware of another presence she slowly opened her eyes.

'Hullo, wombat.'

'Gosh, you sound awful.'

'Hurts to talk.'

'Don't then.'

Nat continued to stare up at Miranda, her eyes darkly bright, and Miranda tried hard to decipher their expression.

'Sorry you're ill.'

'Me too.'

'Your mother said you'd been to London. Did you catch tonsillitis there?'

'Probably.'

It was difficult to tell whether the weary monosyllabic replies were really because of a sore throat or because of what had happened to Rachel. She desperately wanted to know, but couldn't ask.

'Myra Patterson's nose bled in French yesterday.'

'She always was a clever clogs.'

'No, I didn't mean – '

'Oh, dry up,' Nat whispered. 'Go and ask if I can have some more orange juice.'

Miranda did so, and returned with a glass tumbler standing in a basin.

'They've fobbed you off with gargle.'

'I know. They said it was time.'

Nat sat up, chucking the *Life of Mozart* to the foot of the bed. She gargled with head thrown back and eyes shut, then spat vigorously, and handed the tumbler and basin back to Miranda.

'If you were any sort of friend you'd finish it for me.'

'Am I still your friend?' The anxious, yearning words were out before she could prevent them.

'Dunno about friend. More a sort of habit.'

'Nat – I. . . .'

'Save it,' Nat said brusquely. 'Save it.'

Miranda left soon after, and tipping the remains of the gargle into the basin took it back to the kitchen. She said goodbye to the Ellenbergs and walked back to Morton Street telling them in her mind about Rob's involvement with the British Union of Fascists; that he had been among those marching along Lime Street that day, and that her mother now shared his beliefs. They sympathised, and were gratified when she told them that she herself would never join the Party because she knew that Jews were very nice; a jolly sight nicer than Hitler.

Refreshed by the imaginary conversation she entered the flat with a light step and found Florence sobbing over a bowl of washing-up because she had had a row with Rob.

'He called me all sorts of horrible names and told me I was too stupid to understand the Union's aims – but I do understand, I do!' Moaning, she dried her eyes on the tea towel. 'I understand that we're aiming for a peaceful revolution and that if some people have to be sterilised it's only because we want Britain for the British and not clogged up with a lot of foreigners taking our jobs and buying up all our property and things. . . . I do understand and I agree with every word. . . . Put the kettle on, chickabid, and let's have a cup of tea. . . .'

'Do you think you'll get a divorce?' Miranda asked hopefully, and lit the gas with a plop.

'Perhaps. Maybe. I don't know.' Florence hung the tea towel back on its nail. 'And if that Simpson bitch had a single shred of decency she'd go straight back to America and stay there. Who the hell does she think she is, anyway?'

'You said she thinks she's going to be our Queen.'

'Well, she's bloody well not!' Florence returned to the bowl of tepid washing-up and sloshed the mop round a couple of cups. 'Queen Mary won't stand for it, for one thing. Neither will Baldwin and neither will people like us. We'd all see her in hell first.'

61

Miranda made the tea but poured only one cup.

'Where's yours, chickabid?'

'I've just had some.'

'Oh – where?' She paused. 'I take it you've been round to see those friends of yours again. Why can't you take my advice and leave them alone?'

Walking out of the kitchenette, Miranda said from the door, 'You never used to hate so many people before you married *him*.'

But any hopes Miranda had that Florence and Rob might divorce were unfulfilled, and the year 1936 dragged to its weary conclusion. In London the Crystal Palace burned down and in Germany the school-leaving age was lowered to meet the needs of military education. Mrs Simpson married the King but didn't achieve her alleged goal of being made Queen, and the British government grew weary of the proliferating street battles between left- and right-wing elements and introduced measures to ban the wearing of uniforms by political associations.

But all this was of scant importance compared with the news that Nat, at the age of fifteen, had won a scholarship to the Royal Academy of Music and would be leaving for London on the 7th of January.

TWO

'I don't think it'll look bad,' Florence said. 'A bit like those quaint old windows you see in costume films.'

'You mean mullions?'

'Yes, that's what I said.' She detached another strip of brown paper, wiped one side of it on the damp sponge and then applied it to the window. She smoothed it with her fist. 'It also makes you feel very patriotic, doesn't it?'

'Not so much patriotic as apprehensive,' Miranda said. Sitting cross-legged on the floor she was sewing brass rings on to blackout curtains.

'I still don't think there'll be a war. He wouldn't dare.'

'I'm not much of a judge. Politics baffle me.'

'But why should he want Poland, chickabid? It sounds such a mouldy little country – anyway he's got quite enough already.'

Florence and Miranda were now living in a rented top-floor flat in Maida Vale, the move from Liverpool having been decided and accomplished with Florence's accustomed ebullience. She had parted from Rob – thrown him out and metaphorically dusted her hands of him, according to her own version – Miranda had left school, and so now the time was obviously ripe for a change. And Florence was at her best when on the move; lively, excited, busy, with sparkling eyes and laughter never far away. She taught Miranda to rumba, and they rumba'd up and down the long narrow passageway where once again the floorboards had been stained with Brunswick black bought in an oilcan from the ironmonger's on the corner. Wherever Florence went she was accompanied by Brunswick-black floorboards, and Miranda had now learned to disassociate them from the sinister black of Fascism. Black floorboards made a more striking background to whatever thin and impoverished carpets they had.

'There won't be a war,' Florence repeated when the last strip of paper had been stuck in place, the last ring sewn on the blackout curtains. 'But if there is, then by Christ, chickabid, we're ready.' With advancing age she swore more than she used to.

As for Miranda, now rising eighteen, life was pleasanter than it had been for some years. For the first time in her life she felt that she had some semblance of control over her own destiny; she had discovered that Florence, in spite of her forthright character, was really quite easy to manipulate. A new idea, a new suggestion, might well call forth expostulation and a flash of temper, but a few reasoned words would generally cause her to subside into acceptance. 'Well, if you really think so, chickabid . . . After all, you've had the benefit of a first-class education. . . .'

Which wasn't so, if interpreted to mean much of it had been absorbed and not how much had been offered. Frequently bored, frequently miserable, she had played truant increasingly, and growing bolder had sometimes filched small amounts of money from the fancy ashtray into which Rob emptied his black trouser pockets each night before retiring. With the proceeds she went further afield; on the ferry to New Brighton, on the train from Central Station to Hoylake and West Kirby, and no one ever questioned the schoolgirl in Queen Mary's uniform who wandered along deserted beaches and up and down the little streets filled with 'Sea Views' and 'Sunnyside's. No one seemed to notice her at all, for which fact Miranda was duly grateful.

She rather liked the idea of being invisible. It was enabling her to grow up in peace.

When Florence and Rob finally parted – 'Get out of my life and take the photo of the bloody Führer with you!' – there was every indication that a change of scene was now due. Impatiently Florence asked how much longer they had to wait before Miranda did her exam-thing, and when Miranda told her not for three months, said, 'Can't we persuade them to let you do it sooner? I mean, we could always tell them a little white lie about simply having to move because of urgent family business. . . .'

Increasingly aware that due to lack of application there was little prospect of getting School Cert. anyway, Miranda, with a tinge of Florence's own manipulative skill, offered to sacrifice her chance of further education by leaving school before the exams were due – 'After all, you sent me to that school in the middle of a term, so I suppose I might as well leave in the same way.'

She didn't want to stay in Liverpool any more than Florence did. She still called on the Ellenbergs, she still loved them with the same uncritical romanticism of a child, but Nat, it seemed, had gone for ever. After two years at the Academy she had now gone to Paris to study with Nadia Boulanger. They wrote to one another occasionally; not dutiful letters, but long rambling epistles when the mood took them, which Miranda took as a hopeful sign. They never mentioned Rachel. No one ever mentioned her, and Miranda endured, without telling anyone, the recurring nightmares in which her death was re-enacted in all its obscene violence. She had never walked down Lord Nelson Street since, and always looked the other way whenever she was within sight of it.

'What about your divorce?' she suddenly thought to ask Florence when they were packing up the Morton Street flat. 'Won't you have to go to it?'

'Oh, we could probably arrange to have the hearing in London,' Florence said airily. 'It's not the song and dance it used to be.'

'I could come with you.'

'How sweet of you.' Florence seized another sheet of newspaper and wrapped the clock in it. Carefully she tucked it in the packing case among the dinner plates and kitchen utensils. Then she straightened up and said, 'I suppose I'd better tell you, chickabid. Rob and I weren't married.'

Miranda too straightened up. 'You mean you were living in sin?'

'You could call it that.'

'But why?'

'People talk,' Florence said. 'So I called myself Mrs Allardyce because I had you to think of. You were going to a good school and having a good education, and it was up to me as your mother to sacrifice myself.'

'But if you had married him you wouldn't have had to sacrifice yourself, would you?'

'Don't nag, chickabid!' Florence cried sharply. 'I can't stand being nagged.'

They continued the packing without speaking, then Miranda finally broke the silence. 'Is my father really dead?'

'Of course he's dead,' Florence retorted. 'I sent arum lilies.'

'So in that case, why didn't you and Rob – ?'

'Don't mention his name in this house. Go and make a cup of tea.'

'I can't. I've just packed the teapot.'

'Sometimes,' Florence said, sighing, 'I think I'd have been better off barren.'

Shortly after, Miranda went round to Rodney Street to say goodbye to the Ellenbergs. Mrs Ellenberg was alone, sitting at a table classifying snapshots of birds. Two of the old uncles and one aunt had now died, but during recent years other members of the family had arrived, birds of passage blown off course by the gathering Nazi storm in Europe. They stayed for weeks, sometimes for months, before attempting the hazardous business of living independently in a strange country. Miranda felt sorry for them all.

Sammy was now up at Oxford, and all that remained of Nat was the big piano standing between the two windows.

'Bruno's still at the clinic,' Mrs Ellenberg said, then indicated the albums of photographs. 'He's promised to buy me a movie camera, but it all sounds rather technical.'

'You'd soon learn,' Miranda said encouragingly. 'Then you could go to Hollywood and film Garbo.'

'I'd sooner film the great crested grebe.'

'That's spectacular.' Miranda peered over her shoulder. 'What is it?'

Mrs Ellenberg said that it was a hoopoe. Together they studied the dramatic plumage and raised crest. 'A rare visitor from the Continent. It never gets as far as Lancashire.'

'You ought to move to a nice place down in the south. The only birds in Liverpool are seagulls and sparrows.'

'Bruno says he would like to when he retires, but we seem to have so many family commitments here now.'

'Rare visitors from the Continent. Take them all with you.'

'It would be safer, if there's a war.'

'Rob Allardyce said that Great Britain would surrender to Hitler in a bloodless coup, but he was barmy.'

'I don't believe it would be bloodless. And I'm quite sure that, whatever happened, the old and the sick and the Jews would bear the brunt of it.'

It was the first time Miranda had heard the word Jew mentioned by an Ellenberg with the exception of Nat saying carelessly on the day they first met, 'I'm a Jew, although I'm not Orthodox.'

'I wish I was a Jew,' Miranda said suddenly. 'Been born one, I mean.'

'Good heavens, why?' Mrs Ellenberg looked amused.

'I don't know exactly, but you all love beautiful things and you all seem so happy. So sort of enclosed.'

'Enclosed . . . . How very perceptive. Perhaps we give that impression because we're the product of six hundred years in the ghettos of Europe.'

'Did they lock you up because they were afraid of you?'

'On the contrary, we were considered inferior.'

'I saw the photos in *Picture Post* taken inside the Warsaw ghetto. The little children looked so beautiful and so frightened. And they were innocent because they weren't even allowed time to be anything else.'

'Beauty, innocence and fear count for very little, I'm afraid. And

Hitler will invade Poland before very long.' Mrs Ellenberg began to tidy up the photographs and to stack the albums in a pile. 'But we must try to be philosophical. Bruno and I share a wonderful life, and if we all strike you as happy it's because we really are.' She turned to Miranda, and the smile in her large eyes seemed to have limitless depths. 'You will come back to see us, won't you?'

'Do you really want me to?'

'We love you.'

The simplicity of the words came like a shock to Miranda. Her face turned red and her voice shook.

'It was all my fault. I forgot to put the brake on.'

'Have you been trying to say this to us ever since it happened?'

'Yes.'

'Nearly three years ago.'

'Two years, seven months and four days.'

'Oh, Miranda.' Mrs Ellenberg turned away. 'It wasn't your fault, it was mine. I forgot to have the brake mended.'

Miranda, who had considered herself past the emotional turbulence of adolescence, began to weep. She stood with her toes turned in, hiding her eyes with the back of her hand.

'Whatever you say, I'll never forgive myself, never. I'll never forget what happened. I loved Rachel and not because she was a Jewess or anything but because she was a dear little *person*, and I forgot to put the brake on when I was in charge of it – I was doing the pushing, I mean – and it was my fault in another way, too, because my stepfather or whatever he was was in the march – and so was Miss Nelson, our gym mistress – and my mother was there in the crowd *admiring* it all – but she's different now . . . And when I think it was Nat's little sister and how much I loved you all and wanted to be especially kind and nice and everything . . . and I keep getting these nightmares about it and hearing it happening all over again and I sometimes think I'll go mad. . . .'

'Come to me,' Mrs Ellenberg said, and Miranda blundered closer, crying with a convulsive hooting sound. She buried her hot wet face in Mrs Ellenberg's neck.

'If there has to be a fault,' Mrs Ellenberg said, 'it was mine. But apportioning or accepting blame really means very little, except additional anguish. It was a set of circumstances that took Rachel away from us, not any one person. And we have borne the sadness, we have comforted each other, we have all drawn closer. . . .'

Six hundred years in the ghetto makes you talk like this, Miranda thought with her nose pressed against Mrs Ellenberg's collarbone. It makes you resigned and stoical, which isn't good. It can't be.

Gently the older woman detached herself, lent Miranda a handkerchief and then said, 'As this is the last time we'll see you for a while I think we ought to drink to your future in London, don't you?'

Miranda assented, and after blowing her nose and stroking her hair back behind her ears, accepted a glass of sherry.

'Thought I heard the clink of glasses.' Mr Ellenberg came into the room, forcing a bright smile on to his obviously fatigued face. 'Ah Miranda, how nice.'

He kissed his wife, then poured a whisky and soda. 'I've been performing an emergency op on a poor old girl of seventy-four today. She was hurrying to catch a tram and slipped. It meant amputation above the knee.'

Here lies the body of Martha Black, a tramcar hit her slap in the back, Miranda silently recalled. In the Lower Fifth she and Nat had been seized by a brief compulsion to invent epitaphs; that had been one of Nat's less ghoulish efforts.

'Miranda called round to say cheerio,' Mrs Ellenberg said. 'She and her mother are off to London tomorrow.'

'Hope you'll come back to us.'

'No, I won't be coming back here, you're all coming to live with me in the country one day. We've got it all planned.'

'Sounds idyllic.' Mr Ellenberg shook her hand with great warmth, then suddenly hugged her close to him. 'Keep in touch – particularly with Nat.'

'How much longer has she got with this Mademoiselle Boulanger?'

'About six months. It's now a question of getting a good repertoire together – no concert manager will take you on without.'

When she had finished her sherry they walked with her to the lift. Mr Ellenberg pushed the button and the old expanding metal gates clattered open.

'Come and live in the south when you retire,' Miranda said, embracing them both again. 'Don't forget it's what we've planned, and I'll come and watch hoopoes with you.'

She slid down past their eyes as Mr Ellenberg put his arm round his wife, and walked back to Morton Street conscious that an almost intolerable weight had at last been lifted from her shoulders. She had been able to broach what had always seemed an unmentionable subject and had confessed to being responsible for Rachel's death. And the confession had been unnecessary because the brake on the pram had been faulty anyway.

Yet the dream came back worse than ever that night, and when she finally broke free of its evil tendrils she knew with a feeling of desolation that Mrs Ellenberg had lied to her, had taken the blame on her own shoulders because she was that kind of person.

'What's happening? Where am I?' Dazed and dry-mouthed she gazed through the shifting, flickering blackness pierced every now and then by a harsh dazzle of light. The jolting sensation made her feel sick.

'We're on the night coach to London, of course,' said Florence, who was sitting beside her. The whites of her eyes gleamed eerily in the dark. 'You must have been dreaming.'

Miranda lay back in her seat, trying to stretch her cramped legs. From behind them came the sound of snores.

'I'm far too excited to sleep,' Florence rattled on. 'We're due in at Victoria coach station at seven-thirty, and the first thing we'll do is have a wash and brush-up and then go and find some breakfast. And once we get settled in a nice little flat somewhere I think you ought to start powdering your nose. Women are so much more chic in the south, chickabid.'

'Then you'll be able to drop the "k".'

'Pardon?'

'You'll be able to call me *chic*-abid. Sorry, just a weak joke.'

'Oh yes, I see,' said Florence, who didn't. She yawned, and switched her thoughts back to the coming delights of flat-hunting. She visualised a nice little street somewhere in the vicinity of Buckingham Palace.

But in the end Maida Vale, with its wide, quiet roads lined with blocks of florid Edwardian mansion flats, suited her very well. There was no lift, only five flights of stairs, but the brown lino with which they were covered and the wide strips of brass that protected the edges were polished twice a week, and the porter who sent scuttles of coal up on the wooden hand-pulley outside the kitchen window always called her madam.

It would be a nuisance if war broke out, but her annoyance was soothed by the knowledge that Rob Allardyce had already been interned under Section 18B along with all the other filthy Fascists, Mosley included. She hoped that he was having to sew mailbags, or better still, make bombs which would be used to blow up Hitler.

In the meanwhile a very nice man had called at the flat one evening to see about issuing their identity cards. Elderly, but not too old to be interesting, he had sat, pen in hand, taking note of their names and marital status, and Florence, after a swift calculation, had admitted to Florence Amy Whittaker (Mrs), but had defiantly clipped five years off the date of her birth.

He had promised to call again when the identity cards had been prepared, and she thought how nice it would be if he came during the afternoon when Miranda was at work. The days sometimes passed rather slowly without her little chickabid.

Dear Miranda,

Just a quick line to say I'm OK. Everyone's in a bit of a state about the war but received opinion has it that the Jerries won't invade France. They've got enough on their plate anyway, and this time the French are well prepared. Everyone puts great faith in the Maginot Line. It was fun seeing you in July and I'm glad you enjoyed the concert. I was fair piddling with nerves but they say everyone's like that just before it starts. Once I got going I felt fine and just forgot all about You Out There.

Mlle Nadia is marvellous, and meticulous as ever. Everyone wants to strangle her at one stage or another apparently, and I'm no exception, but she's a wonderful teacher. She's got integrity. I'm still living in the same room – one bed, one piano, meals in the café opposite, but Paris isn't as lonely as it was. I've made friends with quite a few other students and we all go out together sometimes – and my *dear*, one of them has actually propositioned me! But I honestly can't – his front teeth slope backwards and his ears move up and down when he talks. Must rush off now – take care of your dear old self. When I've finished with Nadia I expect I'll be based in London like you, which will be fun. Ma and Pa are asking me to go back to England now but I'm determined to finish here first. When we do finally meet up again properly we'll really go on the razzle.

Much love,
Nat.

Miranda reread the letter while she waited for the iron to get hot. The casual good humour and the careless, rapid handwriting brought old Nat very close, and pressing the creases out of the blackout curtains her mind went back to the concert, which had been Nat's official début. She had received two complimentary tickets from the Ellenberg parents and had persuaded Florence to go with her. They had found their way to the hall in Hammersmith, and although it was a warm summer evening Florence had fussed about feeling chilly.

'Put your coat on, then.'

'I don't want to, it's too old. I can't make an entrance in it.'

'Nobody'll notice.' Miranda urged her onwards.

'You do say the most hurtful things,' Florence panted, trying to keep up. 'I'm only trying to be a credit to you – anyway, I hate music.'

'Perhaps this'll make you change your mind.'

As previously arranged they met Mr and Mrs Ellenberg and Sammy in the foyer, which was already buzzing with conversation. Sammy and his father were wearing dinner jackets and Mrs Ellenberg a brightly coloured skirt and black velvet coatee. Pink-faced and nervous, Miranda introduced Florence, who switched on a great show of animation, shook hands and said, 'I can't imagine why we've never met before!' Her bare arms were goosepimpled but her frock looked very nice.

'May I?' Sammy stepped forward and relieved Miranda of her coat, and watching his tall, self-confident young figure moving through the crowds towards the cloakrooms she thought, how he's grown! And I wonder if he's thinking the same thing about me?

'I can't believe we're going to hear Nat,' she confided to Mrs Ellenberg. 'I feel dreadfully nervous.'

'So do I.'

'Has she arrived yet?'

'Yes. She'll be in the green room, probably having a last run-through.'

'Sipping a gin and tonic more likely,' Mr Ellenberg said heartily, and led the way into the auditorium.

They were in the front row of the balcony and as the orchestra filed in, Florence tweaked at a stray curl and thought, just look at all those lovely men. She glanced at Miranda, who was sitting between her and Sammy, but Miranda was gazing reverently at her programme. It contained a photograph of Nat looking uncharacteristically remote.

'I meant to buy us a box of chocs,' Florence whispered.

First public performance given by a young English soloist who last year won the Broadwood Prize and who is now studying in Paris with Nadia Boulanger, Miranda read for the third time.

The applause made her look up to see the conductor take his place. They began with an overture, which was followed by some quiet Delius, during which Florence fidgeted, then a man came on and raised the great lid of the piano, struck a few desultory notes, and departed. They waited, and the applause began again when the audience spied the conductor leading Nat by the hand down through the brass and woodwind and past the violins. She was wearing a long emerald-green frock that left her arms bare, and the bright lights picked up the shimmering lustre of the skirt as she sat down.

'Taffeta,' murmured Florence.

'Rather ambitious, kicking off with Liszt,' someone whispered from the row behind. 'Hope she doesn't come a cropper.'

That's Nat down there, Miranda thought incredulously. Old *Nat.* . . .

Then silence. Tension. Nat sitting crouched like a watchful cat, her dark curls piled on top of her head. The conductor turned to her, arms raised, and the soft sound of strings and woodwind was interrupted by a great crash from the keyboard. Up the whole length of it and then down while the orchestra listened in silence. Nat's hands flew faster, scurrying with a speed that dazzled, and Miranda heard Sammy draw a deep breath.

The orchestra joined in. Nat seemed to be speaking to it and it began to reply, weaving little strands in here and there, and then Nat calm and quiet, not hurrying, as she played a tune Miranda thought she had heard before back in the Rodney Street days. The tune dissolved in ripples beneath a sudden blare of orchestral wrath, and the piano answered with gathering fury, the conductor shaking like a man trying to maintain his balance in the teeth of a gale. A great tumult of sound filled the hall, and while Nat's flying fingers stormed down the keyboard Miranda jumped violently as Sammy took her hand and held it gently imprisoned. Glancing down she saw that most of her programme lay shredded in her lap. He smiled without taking his eyes from the platform where muscular power was giving way to a sweet delicacy that brought back the memory of Nat saying, 'Do you realise how many different ways there are of playing one single note?' No, she hadn't realised. Not until now.

The mood shifted again, becoming irritable and turbulent and full of disquiet, as if Nat were trying to say something. Was Liszt a Jew? Why do I keep thinking about Jews? Miranda wondered. What's really so special about them that so many people make such a fuss about them? How many people in the hall are Jews? How many of the men in the orchestra? What does it really *mean*, being a Jew? It must be far more than not believing Jesus was the son of God, otherwise Hitler wouldn't be so paranoid about them.

She listened to Nat playing a long, long high trill – so steady, so calm, like a canary chirruping on its perch – before tripping away into a musical game of hide-and-seek with a man at the back of the orchestra tinging a triangle. Then another blaze of brass. And Nat fighting back, curls bouncing – one had escaped from her topknot and was swinging delightedly in time to the march as she skittered along the top of the violins. Flash bang crash – it couldn't really be old Nat in charge of all this marvellous musical din, the hugely dramatic conclusion, strong, slow chords. And then silence.

Slowly, as if coming out of a dream, Miranda and Sammy loosened hands and joined in the applause. Glancing across Florence she saw Mr Ellenberg standing and clapping his hands above his head, his cheeks glistening with tears, then she turned back to Nat on the brightly lit platform.

Slumped over the keyboard, she straightened up slowly and stumbled awkwardly to her feet. She managed to execute an indeterminate little movement, something between a bow and a curtsey, then the conductor seized her hand and shook it warmly and all the orchestra rose to their feet and applauded her. A little girl in a party frock proffered a large bouquet of flowers, and some more of Nat's curls burst from their unaccustomed confinement. Typical, thought Miranda, weeping.

They called her back again and again, and still clutching her flowers she bobbed hasty and confused little acknowledgments.

'She's quite plump, isn't she?' Florence mouthed as they went on clapping. 'But I daresay she'll fine down.'

Miranda had only a hazy recollection of what happened afterwards. Hurrying with the Ellenbergs and Florence along cold stone corridors to a room where Nat, in a little crowd of people, was drinking glass after glass of water and saying, 'But I'm not sure the *Allegro Animato* really came off. . . .' She looked very hot, but depositing her glass in someone's hand rushed forward to embrace her family and Miranda. She shook hands very affably with Florence, who murmured, 'Lovely, dear.'

They had dinner in an expensive restaurant where the head waiter offered to put Nat's bouquet in water, and other diners stared respectfully as he carried it high above his head like a trophy. Which of course it was. And Miranda, still dazed by the thunderous grandeur of Liszt's first piano concerto, and by her first glass of champagne, remembered the way Sammy had taken her hand and held it warmly and protectively. By the time his father had seen her and her mother into a taxi bound for Maida Vale, she had fallen in love with him. Too wonderfully in love to remonstrate when Florence stopped the taxi round the corner and they finished the journey by Underground.

'They must think we're made of money!'

'They only ever think nice things about people.'

'Most Jews only think nice things about other Jews.'

They went to bed, Miranda too engrossed in thoughts of Sammy to notice that Florence was sulking.

That had been last May. Now it was Saturday, September the 2nd, and Britain and France were on the brink of declaring war upon Germany.

'He'll win, of course,' said Florence, whose spirits swung between highest optimism and deepest foreboding. 'I mean, what good is one old man in a bowler hat?'

'I don't think Chamberlain's going to do the actual fighting any more than Hitler is. They always get the young men to do their dirty work.' Young men like Sammy, Miranda added silently. She hoped very much that he would be going back to Oxford next term.

She finished ironing the curtains while Florence cooked lunch, and during the afternoon they took a bus down to Selfridges and bought two siren suits because Florence had read that they were what the smart woman would be wearing in the air-raid shelter.

'They're like combinations,' Miranda objected. 'I had to wear them at Aunt Daisy and Uncle Frank's.'

'Piffle.' Florence preened this way and that, and smoothed the heavy material over her backside. 'They're not merely practical, they're also extremely seductive. Don't you want to be seductive, chickabid?'

They also bought two torches, each one fitted with a mask of dark paper in case the beam attracted enemy bombers. And when they reached home they discovered that the porter had placed a large red bucket full of sand outside their front door.

'What's that for?' Florence asked suspiciously.

'For dumping incendiary bombs in. If you'd read the ARP leaflet instead of fussing about being seductive you'd know.'

'Well at any rate, we're all ready now.' Florence's mood was once again on the upswing. 'We know exactly where the air-raid shelter is, we've got a lot of nice food in the cupboard, and I've just ordered some more coal. So what with the blackout done and a bucket of sand and our torches and everything we should be OK.'

'Don't forget our gas masks,' Miranda said dourly. 'If we have to wear them all the time you won't need to put on any make-up.'

'Oh, don't be such a grump, chickabid!'

But next morning the reality broke through. They sat at their open sitting-room window looking down on to the quiet Sunday street while they listened to Chamberlain's slow, sad voice.

'We are now in a state of war with Germany,' Florence repeated, and began to sob.

'So is France,' added Miranda, thinking of Nat who was still in Paris. Hopefully she would be coming home today.

She watched as the door of the block of flats opposite burst open and a man hurriedly snatched a basking ginger cat from the low wall and carried it protectively indoors. She glanced up at the strip of blue sky between the rooftops just as the curdled wail of the air-raid siren split the silence.

'Oh Christ, they're here!' Florence halted in mid-sob, and, dragging Miranda by the arm, ran with her to the bedroom. Flinging off her housecoat she began to plunge into her siren suit while urging Miranda to do the same.

'I thought they were to keep us warm at night – '

'They're for the air-raid shelter whenever there's a raid – oh, bugger the bloody zip!'

Designed as trousers and jacket combined, they were not easy garments to put on, and for Florence, ingress was further hampered by having been tempted to buy a size too small.

'It's stopped blowing – the siren – '

'Oh God, this is it!'

'Come *on* then – where's your gas mask? No, that's mine – '

'I want my torch.'

'In broad daylight?'

'It is now, but we might be in there for days – '

They met other residents of the flats as they all hurried down to the underground garage that had been converted into a shelter. The air, warm and heavy and still smelling faintly of petrol, made Miranda feel sick. She and Florence sat close together and a helmeted ARP warden bossily forbade people to smoke.

'I've got a funny feeling,' Florence said, 'that I'm going to turn Catholic.'

'What on earth for?'

'Because I need something to hold on to.'

All I want to hold on to is Sammy Ellenberg, thought Miranda sentimentally.

The all-clear sounded, and an old lady indicated Florence and Miranda with a disparaging sniff, saying, 'Look at those two women dressed up as workmen.'

'What do you expect when there's a war on?' Florence enquired. 'Crinolines?'

Swinging her hips at the ARP warden she took Miranda by the arm and marched with her back to the flat.

After a couple of brief false starts – once as a clerk and once in a hat shop where the chief saleslady referred to the owner as His Yidship, Miranda was now working in an antique shop in the St John's Wood Road. The pay was modest, the hours reasonable, and the work not unduly arduous. Swann's Antiques was owned by Emrys Arundel, a pale-faced man with a wide countenance and a froggy smile, who wore his hair a little longer than was usual. He had an easy casual charm and a way of expressing himself that was either sophisticated or rather childlike, Miranda was unable to decide which. He wore a lemon-coloured cravat tucked inside a brown silk shirt, but his corduroy trousers bagged at the knees and his suede shoes were slightly down at heel.

'I've never actually had an assistant before,' he said. 'I do hope we'll get on.'

'Well, I'm here to do as I'm told.'

'Oh my dear, how subservient! I might tell you to do the most dreadful things.'

'Such as?'

'Scrub the floor. Make my bed.'

'I'd sooner sell antiques.'

'And so you shall. . . .' He put his arm round her shoulder and gave her a quick hug. She caught a faint whiff of lavender water. 'Come along, I'll show you the ropes.'

She quickly learned to respect his expertise and to enjoy his company. In a way it seemed less like work than helping a friend, and on the day she made her first unaided sale (a pair of Staffordshire figures to a clergyman), he said that they must celebrate with a Harry Sippers, and poured two gin and tonics. He seemed to like Miranda, and it was not difficult to like him in return.

The shop was not a large one but the window was enticingly arranged and the interior was an agreeable accumulation of gleaming wood, glowing silver and sparkling glass. In a way, it reminded her of the Ellenbergs' profusion of beautiful objects. He lived above the shop, an area she had not been invited to enter, and sometimes she speculated idly about the kind of life he lived when the shop was closed. She saw no evidence of either family or friends. Florence said that he must be a pansy.

Considering that he had so far managed without an assistant, it seemed strange that he should decide to acquire one when the outbreak of war had brought a slump in trade, and it was not long before Miranda discovered the reason why. He was a sick man.

'Kidneys, dear,' he said on the first morning she found him still in pyjamas and dressing gown. 'One doesn't function and the other one's irresolute. The pain's devastating.'

She offered to make him a hot drink but he said that he would go back to bed for an hour and try to sleep it off.

'Shall I send for your doctor?'

'No, dear. I already have tablets and there's nothing more he can do.'

She felt very sorry for him, and because trade was slack she swept the floor and dusted the stock, and when it was time for her lunch break at one o'clock she brought him back a hot steak-and-mushroom pie from the Spinning Wheel Café.

He was up and dressed, but looked paler than ever and walked with a slow dragging step. 'What a dear girl you are. I'll try to eat it for supper,' he said, then added inconsequentially, 'I'd adore to go off and fight the Jerries but the medics say no.'

'Someone's got to keep the antique trade running.'

'So I suppose it might as well be crocks like me. Do you think they'll invade us, dear?'

'Oh, I shouldn't think so,' Miranda said with the airiness of youth. 'My mother says Hitler wouldn't dare.'

'And your mother's invariably proved right?'

'Not exactly. I've just got into the habit of believing the cheerful things she says.'

'Tell me some of the uncheerful things.'

'She wants to become an RC.'

'Is that so awful?'

'Knowing her, she'll try and make me one too. And Catholics are even more anti the Jews than C of Es are.'

'You're pro-Jewish, then?' He looked at her curiously.

'My best friends are Jews.' There was pride in her voice. 'One of them, the girl I was at school with, is a concert pianist. She's studying in Paris with a woman called Boulanger, and I went to a concert she gave over here in the summer. She was marvellous.'

'I take it she's left France now.'

'Well, no. She says she won't until she's finished the course or whatever it is. But I know her parents are dead worried, and so am I because none of us have heard from her recently. She's got a lot of aunts and uncles, and I realise now that some of them are refugees from Nazi persecution. She's also got a very nice brother and he's a friend of mine too.' Reference to Sammy slipped out of its own volition.

'And you really like him?'

'Oh, yes. But not – well, not especially, if you see what I mean.' Her cheeks flamed.

Mr Arundel smiled sympathetically, then heaved a deep sigh. 'Think I'll go and lie down again, dear. I really do feel rather dished.'

As autumn hardened into a long cold winter of blackout and the first signs of food rationing, Miranda discovered that Mr Arundel was forced to spend as much time in bed as out of it. His kidney trouble subsided a week before he developed shingles. 'If they meet round my waist, dear, I'm a dead man.'

'Let me get the doctor.'

'There's no cure for shingles. It's all caused by nerves, and whose nerves aren't at snapping point with this ghastly war?'

'He's a pansy all right,' Florence commented when Miranda recounted the latest news. 'At least you're safe with him, chickabid.'

In the meanwhile it was time to think about Christmas. Florence bought Miranda a powder compact with butterflies on it, and Miranda bought Florence a pair of fluffy bedroom slippers. And Florence broke the news that Captain Cordelier was coming to share their roast chicken and plum pudding. 'He's that nice man who did our identity cards. Terribly upper-class and was out in India with his lady wife who is dead now, poor soul.'

'Does it mean I've got to buy him a present?'

'Not necessarily. Well, just a nice cigar, perhaps.'

'I thought of asking Mr Arundel as he's ill and all alone,' Miranda said tentatively.

'Oh, I wouldn't do that, chickabid. Being what he is he'll probably embarrass Captain Cordelier.'

There were several notable gaps in Miranda's worldly knowledge, one of them concerning homosexuality, which wasn't so surprising since Queen Mary's had remained mute on the subject of sex, apart from providing rather perfunctory instruction on the reproductive cycle of the rabbit. Florence, who was very strong on advice about mantrapping by means of slinky dresses and cunningly applied make-up, was also decidedly coy about the cruder facts, although she did warn Miranda of the dangers of sitting on the seats of public lavatories. Apart from the memories of giggling with Nat and reading the doleful back page of Florence's weekly women's mag where sex was called Intimacy and the more alarming queries were turned sharply away – *I cannot possibly answer your letter in this column, but if you send me a stamped addressed envelope I will do my best to advise you* – the only way to find out seemed to be through personal experiment, but being romantically in love with Sammy Ellenberg prevented it. In any case, she didn't know how to begin; there was only Mr Arundel, and according to Florence he was a pansy, whatever that was. All she knew was that she was supposed to be safe with him.

So she dismissed the subject for the time being and concentrated on learning about the hallmarks of silver and how to tell Sheraton from Hepplewhite.

Christmas Day passed off quite well; Captain Cordelier was small, white-haired and gallant, and kissed Florence under the sprig of mistletoe she had thoughtfully suspended from the centre light in the sitting room. Then after a slight hesitation he kissed Miranda as well, scratching her cheek with his moustache. He had brought a bottle of claret, and after lunch they sat listening to the British Expeditionary Forces singing 'Roll out the Barrel' and 'Run, Adolph, Run' on the wireless, while Captain Cordelier smoked the cigar that Miranda had given him. He referred to Florence and Miranda as 'you two dear young ladies'.

'Old twerp,' Florence said after he had left. 'Who does he think he is?'

The winter was a long while departing; like the war, it seemed to hang, a perpetually cold and motionless presence, above their heads, and on the day Mr Arundel heard Miranda sneeze he beseeched her to go home.

'Flu, dear. I can always tell a flu sneeze from a dust sneeze. You look hot and your eyes are too bright. Go home, dear; if I catch it in my weakened state it'll be curtains.'

So she went home, and developed no more than a mild head cold, and on the second evening of toasting herself over the fire Florence said, 'For God's sake let's go out, chickabid. I mean, what are we doing cooped up in here when there's so much going on outside?'

So they took a bus down to Piccadilly and went into the lounge of the Regent Palace, where people were sitting in Lloyd Loom chairs, sipping coffee and ogling one another in an agreeable kind of way. Florence, wearing Old Fido, and with her hat tilted provocatively over one eye, ogled back.

'That officer over there's staring at you, chickabid.'

'So what?' Miranda was listening to the small string ensemble playing selections from *The Desert Song*, and thinking nostalgically of Nat and Sammy.

'I think he's a major, but I can't see for sure.'

'Uh-huh.'

'Your father was a major, you know.'

'No. I didn't.'

'He looked marvellous in uniform. I suppose that's why I married him.'

'Bit frivolous, wasn't it?' Funny, thought Miranda, how old and weary she makes me feel.

'He gave me you, chickabid.'

'What was it like?' Miranda asked tonelessly, and Florence gave a seductive little chirrup and stroked Old Fido. 'You'll find out on your wedding night – although of course you've had the benefit of a good education, haven't you? They'll have taught you all about everything at Queen Mary's, whereas I just had to – had to find out for myself.'

'I'll bet you learn more down dark alleyways than you ever do at a classy girls' school.'

'Miranda!' Florence looked deeply shocked. 'I've never been down a dark alleyway in my life! And if that's how you're going to talk to me we might as well go home. I suggested we came here for a treat, and God knows there aren't many of them to be had during this stupid, bloody war.'

'Sorry.' Miranda watched the elderly pianist accompanying the ensemble with little careful mincing movements, so unlike Nat's great passionate sweeps. 'I miss my friends.'

'The Jews, you mean?'

Filled with sudden rage, Miranda gripped the edge of the glass-topped table and said in a low, shaking voice, 'Their name is Ellenberg. Their daughter was my best friend at school. The Ellenbergs were very kind to me when you were ill; I enjoyed staying with them, I enjoyed their sort of life – the way they talked and the way they did things. They invited us both to go and hear Nat play at the concert, in case you've forgotten, and they took us out to dinner. They let us share in it all. They're big and generous and wise and they wouldn't refer to anybody as *the* Protestants or *the* Catholics or *the* Seventh Day Adventists or *the* – *the* Pansies – they'd just call them by their proper names because they're gentle and civilised which is more than you can say for the people who've been slanging the Jews and persecuting them for a couple of thousand years – '

80

Florence leaned closer, and stared piercingly at Miranda with one eye. 'They've been getting at you!'

'No, they haven't! They never mentioned politics or religion.'

'Maybe not directly, but they've influenced you. Oh yes, I've seen it all along but I haven't said anything because I hoped that it was just a silly schoolgirl pash – '

'I've never had pashes – '

'Shut up when I'm talking. A schoolgirl pash on them just because they're different from us, but take my work they won't be happy until they've converted you.'

'You're pretty busy getting converted to Roman Catholicism.'

'That's different, it's all Christian. We all believe that Jesus was the son of God.'

'How do you know he was? I mean, what proof have you actually got?'

'A little more coffee, madam?' A cruising waiter flourished the silver pot. Without glancing at him Florence shoved her cup in his direction.

'There you are, you see. They've already sown doubts in your mind about him, haven't they? Well, take it from me, Jesus was the son of God and God sent him – '

'Miss . . . ?' The waiter suspended the coffee pot above Miranda's cup. She nodded tersely.

' – God sent him down via the Virgin Mary to save us from our sins – '

'What had she got to do with it?'

'She *had* him, stupid. And Catholics get the Virgin Mary to intercede for them because they love women, particularly mothers, because they know what a hell of a lot we all have to go through – '

The waiter slapped the folded bill down on the table and went off in search of more appreciative prey.

'I don't say that I hold with what Hitler's doing to the Jews,' Florence resumed a little more calmly, 'but a lot of their troubles they bring on themselves. All the top jobs are pinched by Jews – '

'Because they're better at doing them, not because they pinch – '

'And all they think about is money. Making money out of other people's hard work. . . .'

Mr Ellenberg doesn't. But she didn't say the words aloud. Filled with a sense of weary futility she leaned back and tried to concentrate on the string ensemble, who were now striving to instil a little syncopation in a Glenn Miller tune.

'They couldn't swing on the end of a rope,' Florence commented.

81

'You're right.'

It was comforting to think that they could agree about some things, and when the man who had been staring at Miranda followed them through the foyer and said, 'Pardon me, I think we've met – ' they swept contemptuously past, arm-in-arm and with old Fido's tail flicking the stranger's cheek.

It was a mild moonlit night and they walked part of the way home. The streets were deserted.

'I can't help feeling that the Holy Mother and I have got a certain amount in common.' Florence gazed dreamily at a wandering search-light.

'I don't think you're as meek and mild as she's cracked up to be.'

'Perhaps not, but I'm trying hard.'

'When are you due to be admitted?'

'Received, chickabid. Father Donovan thinks some time after Easter. He's taking such pains with me, bless him. . . .'

Spring brought a shimmer of green and yellow to the London parks, and it also brought the war to life.

After a winter of inactivity Hitler's troops occupied Denmark and Norway, then Belgium, the Netherlands and Luxembourg. In May they invaded France, and the Ellenbergs received a postcard from Nat to say that she was coming home and would telephone as soon as she reached England.

She didn't tell them that she was hoping against hope to play for Darius Milhaud. She admired the composer's music, and the recital to which he had accepted the guest-of-honour invitation from Nadia Boulanger was to take place during the evening of Friday, June the 14th. She was going to play Poulenc, Ibert and Satie, and end with one of Milhaud's own compositions.

In the meanwhile there was the protection of the Maginot Line, that impregnable fortification stretching from Switzerland to Belgium; there was also Maréchal Pétain in charge, a man whose military glory had been won on the battlefields of the First World War, and who, at the age of eighty-three, was considered to be at the height of his powers. Far more experienced people than Nat imagined that there was no need to worry, even after the Germans had crossed the Meuse, the last obstacle on the road to Paris.

The only person to sound a warning had been her landlady, Madame Triboulet, and when Nat tapped on her door with the news that she would be returning home the day after the recital there had been fear in her eyes.

'*Allez maintenant, Mademoiselle! N'attendez-pas – vous devez partir avant que les Allemands arrivent!*'

'But why? It's only a few days now.'

'*Pourquoi? Parce que vous êtes Anglaise! Et aussi parce que je pense que –* '

She turned her head away.

'*Quoi?*'

'*Vous êtes aussi juive.*'

Nat smiled, but said nothing. She went back to her room and sat down at the piano. Milhaud's bright contemporary music danced from under her fingers, and out in the street the life of Paris flowed on as usual.

But the break-up had already begun. Accelerated by the bombing of Paris's airports and the news that Italy had declared war on France, government departments were hastily preparing to evacuate to the safety of Bordeaux. Museum treasures were carted away and the doors locked behind them, theatres and restaurants were closed and, infected by *la grande peur*, the ordinary Parisians began to take flight. On the morning of the 11th, Nat learned that the recital had been cancelled and that Darius Milhaud had unobtrusively departed for America.

'But where's the British Army?' she asked the caretaker of the shuttered and silent Conservatoire.

'Your army?' He shook his head pityingly. 'Your army is no more. The fragments that remained were picked up on the beach of Dunkerque more dead than alive.'

'So it's time for me to go, too?'

'I think it best, Mademoiselle.' He shook her hand, then impulsively leaned forward and kissed her on both cheeks. '*Bonne route, ma petite.*'

She returned to her room and packed her bag, leaving Milhaud's score on top of the piano and the following week's rent on the table. She left without seeing Madame Triboulet, who worked in a baker's shop during the mornings, and found that all trains in and out of Paris had already been cancelled and that the trickle of citizens leaving Paris had become a flood.

She saw cars with luggage piled to the roof, bicycles with suitcases lashed on the back and string bags swinging from the handlebars; handcarts, horse-and-carts, and a long snaking column of people on foot pushing prams, lugging bags and boxes, urging old people and children on at a faster pace. They streamed along the Boulevard Haussmann where the windows were already shuttered, and an agitated little dog darting underfoot jumped fleetingly at Nat and licked her hand. Absently she patted its head and it fell in behind her, trotting on thin nimble legs and holding its tail briskly aloft.

Changing her suitcase from one hand to the other she listened to the babble of voices and smelt the sharp smell of fear as she tried to feel at one with the people who jostled and shoved in an agony of frustration. And they had crossed the Seine and were heading for Montparnasse before it occurred to her that she was travelling in the wrong direction. She needed to head north-east to reach the Channel and they were all going roughly south-west.

It took a certain willpower to extract herself from the crowd and begin walking in the opposite direction. One or two people glanced at her and a man with a beard shouted something that she couldn't quite hear. She shook her head and smiled, then a stream of cars loaded to the roof with bedding and boxes hid him from view. The dust and the noise was making her head ache and she turned off the main road, hoping to thread her way through the back streets. She wondered how many days it would take to walk to Calais.

The babel had died. And the quietness that followed it was extraordinary. The small shops and houses were shuttered and locked, and no sign of life seeped out of them. No burble of radios, no whiffs of cooking, no cries of children. It was as if a giant door had suddenly slammed shut, leaving her alone outside. But when she dropped her suitcase and stood rubbing her arm she saw that she was not quite alone after all. The little dog had followed her. It sat down on the empty pavement and looked up at her with humble brown eyes.

'Someone's forgotten you in the rush,' she said. 'So you'd better come back to England with me.'

It was quite nice to have someone to talk to, and the little dog listened as if it were hungry for a few kind words. They walked back to Montmartre through streets so deathly silent that she could hear the soft padding of her companion's paws. The dog was walking at her side now, and no longer at her heels in a subservient manner.

'You'll have to learn English, of course,' she told it, 'and I hope you like music.' By the time they reached Pigalle she had christened it Maurice, after Ravel.

The heat of the day was dying and Paris appeared emptier than ever, although now it seemed to Nat as if the silence was a listening silence. Trudging onwards she imagined the deserted houses to be full of shadowy people standing motionless with their ears pressed close against the locked doors and shuttered windows, hardly daring to breathe as they listened for the first sound of German troops. The roar of tanks, the rhythmic slam-slam of marching boots. Paris had been declared an open city, which presumably meant they wouldn't bomb it, but Madame Triboulet's radio had spoken of atrocities committed by the invading army against the people of Brussels and Amsterdam.

She should have been afraid, but she was walking in a strange dreamlike state that somehow excluded fear. Her mind was still dealing with the disappointment of the cancelled recital and with the shock of Milhaud's precipitate flight.

'He scarpered,' she told Maurice bitterly. 'Your namesake wouldn't have done that. He drove an ambulance in the last war and survived to go on composing.'

When her mind switched from music it ran ahead to Liverpool and to the welcome she would receive when she eventually arrived home. Her mother soft-eyed and striving to maintain her shy dignity; her father vociferous, weeping, probably, and not giving a damn who saw. The family would rally to welcome her – with a bit of luck Sammy would be there – and the welcome would extend to her new friend Maurice because their family circle, however close, seemed capable of limitless expansion. She thought about Miranda, and began to plan how she would appear at her door unannounced. . . .

In the meanwhile she was becoming increasingly convinced that the houses she passed were full of people watching and listening; it was ridiculous to think that the whole population of Paris had taken to the roads in a panic-stricken attempt to escape, and in order to prove it she dropped her suitcase and rapped on the door of a *charcuterie*. No reply, but she leaned her head close against the woodwork in an attempt to catch the telltale sound of breathing on the other side. Maurice sat down and watched, ears pricked expectantly. No reply. No sound.

She walked on, conscious now of nagging tiredness and rumbling hunger. She had been a fool not to ask Madame Triboulet for some sandwiches for the journey. More as a means of breaking the monotony than with any kind of hope that she would receive a reply, she knocked at several doors and rang several bells, but the sounds echoed dismally, emptily, and it became an increasing effort not to imagine that she was tampering with the dead.

'We're not going much further tonight,' she told Maurice. 'Surely to God there's someone open somewhere who'll give us a bite to eat, even if we have to spend the night in a graveyard.'

She had never realised that Paris was so big, so sprawling, with suburbs far more spreading than those of Liverpool or even London.

They came to a small park with seats and dusty evergreens and a row of children's swings; it was a poor little place surrounded by tall gaunt houses. Sinking down on to one of the benches, Nat slipped off her sandals and spread her toes with a sigh of relief. Maurice, after a moment's hesitation, jumped up beside her.

But evening brought no relief from the sense of silent waiting, of listening and watching. On the contrary, the impression intensified as the midsummer shadows crept through the bushes. There was no sound of birds preparing to roost – perhaps they had all gone south-west with the people fleeing the city.

Then she felt Maurice's hair stiffen beneath her caressing hand. His ears were pricked with such intensity that they stood on end. Motionless, she heard the slight dragging sound before she was able to distinguish the figure walking slowly along the path towards her. A man, limping. She watched his approach with her hand on Maurice's neck, and the man halted a short distance away, saying softly in French, 'Will he bite?'

'I don't know. We haven't been acquainted all that long.'

'I wouldn't wish to be bitten in addition to suffering a German invasion.'

It was a young voice, and Nat leaned forward trying to penetrate the gloom. 'You're not the only one suffering it.'

'Ah, you a foreigner, I think. American?'

'Certainly not.' Nat spoke with dignity. 'I'm English and I'm on my way home.'

He came closer and she could see that his eyes were gleaming and his hair was cut *en brosse*.

'I speak English,' he said. 'And if you will pardon me I think it is advanceder than your French, Mademoiselle.'

'Which isn't claiming a lot. And in England we say *more* advanced.'

'Ah.' He sat down beside her and Maurice gave a little growl, then thought better of it and wagged his tail.

'You've got a bad leg,' Nat said.

'Foot.'

'What's wrong with it?'

'Why do you ask?'

'Sorry. I was brought up in a medical family.'

'I have a *pied-bot*. What it is in English I don't know.' He stretched out his legs, feet together, and Nat craned forward to scrutinise them.

'Oh – a club foot.'

'Club foot,' he repeated, '*pied-bot*, which one you prefer. Both names mean cripple.'

'I'm sorry,' Nat said, and suddenly thought, what am I doing here waiting for the Germans to arrive and discussing deformities with a stranger? 'I must go,' she added.

'Where to?'

'I'm making for Calais.'

'Too late. All the Channel ports are sealed off.' He peered closely at her when she made no reply. 'So what you do – swim?'

'I might at that, except I wouldn't be keen on the mines.' She sat silently stroking Maurice's neck and inadvertently her hand touched that of her companion.

'So what you do?'

'I'm not sure.'

'You are student?'

'Piano.' Then bitterness welled. 'I was going to give a recital of modern French music and Milhaud was going to attend, but he's run away.'

'There has been much running away, but only by people inferior.'

'Aren't you running away, then?'

'No, I live here. What is your name?'

'Natalie Ellenberg.'

He turned to her, striving to distinguish her features in the gathering dark. 'Ellenberg. Are you a Jew?'

'Yes, if it's any business of yours.'

'The Germans will make it their business soon enough,' he said. 'They don't like Jews and they don't like cripples. They will get rid of us both very soon, I think.'

'Your optimism does you credit. Well, I must be going now. . . .'

'Where do you sleep tonight?'

'Don't know exactly,' she shrugged. 'Behind a bush, probably.'

'And supper? Have you ate?'

'Eaten. No. . . . Perhaps you could tell me where I could find something?' For the first time her nonchalance wavered and she sensed that the reality of what was happening might at last overwhelm her. She didn't want that to happen; she didn't want to be like the panic-stricken crowds streaming out of Paris. 'I'm so hungry – we're both so–' She stopped abruptly.

'I have food, and two fine beds – one big and one little.'

'Just some food will do, thank you.'

'Come then.' He stood up. 'Is the dog coming too?'

'If you don't mind.'

'Typical English. Always dogs. . . . We laugh at you.'

'Well, don't,' Nat said shortly. 'Remember that it's a French dog.'

Despite his dragging limp he was able to walk quite fast and Nat made no more than a token protest when he insisted upon carrying her suitcase. Maurice trotted silently between them, and after a while they turned under a deep archway off the rue du Cherche Midi where it was so dark that Nat stumbled. They crossed a stone courtyard, and from the bleary light that came from the one lamp in the middle she gained the impression of tall stone apartment houses surrounding them. There was a smell of drains and damp plaster, but the same deathly silence prevailed.

Taking her arm her companion led her through heavy double doors and past the concierge's vacant cubbyhole. They began to climb a circular stone staircase lit by flickering gas jets. On the fourth floor he set down the suitcase and took a key from his pocket.

'We are home,' he said, and switched on the light.

It was a large attic, so large that the far corners remained in shadow and Maurice pressed close against her leg for reassurance. There was a round table beneath the shuttered window, a few chairs dotted about, some cupboards and a small cooking stove and, taking pride of place on the big wall opposite the window, a large and extremely ornamental brass bed.

'Tante Honorine,' he said, indicating it with a flourish. 'She offers great comfort.'

'It's – ' she began, then turned to him and stopped abruptly.

'What is wrong?'

'Nothing.'

'Then why you stare?'

'I'm sorry.' Then aware that the apology might not be considered sufficient, added with a sudden painful honesty, 'I'm sorry, but you're the most astounding-looking bloke I've ever seen.'

'Tell me more!' He stood in front of her, hands on hips and laughing, and once the shock had passed she was able to laugh too.

She had met a good many young men, mostly students, since coming to Paris, and had become familiar with continental charm. Easy good looks coupled with French vivacity and the heady scent of Gauloises had pleased her without in any way rocking the foundations of her true love, which was music. She had been out with them in noisy groups in cafés, and sometimes in a twosome, and, apart from a little good-humoured kissing and fondling, had remained uninvolved. Brought up in a naturally gregarious household she had adapted with ease while keeping her head and heart unaffected.

And she was still unaffected at this moment, although the man into whose attic room she had been invited had casually turned upon her a face of classic male beauty; features of a remarkable purity enhanced by warm, living colouring. Thick chestnut-brown hair, a skin already lightly tanned by early summer sun, and large and amused eyes of a deep cerulean blue. He was dressed in a torn open-necked shirt and a pair of old dark red trousers held up by a striped necktie in place of a belt.

'So now we prepare ourselves for eating,' he said, rolling up his sleeves.

He limped over to the cupboard by the cooking stove, and it was so wicked that a man with a god's face should have to drag one foot in an ungainly surgical boot.

'Can I help?'

'No, I do well by myself. You stroke the dog.'

So she sat on the edge of the big brass bed while he warmed some soup and cut thick chunks of *baguette*. Whistling, he produced some slices of ham, and she watched, almost faint with hunger, as he mixed dressing for the lettuce. Taking two glass tumblers from the shelf he uncorked a bottle of white wine then turned to face her. 'Come, Mademoiselle. We are prepared.'

'Please call me Natalie,' she murmured, suddenly constrained. Then politeness impelled her to add, 'I'm sorry, I don't know your name.'

'Raoul Lefevre, age twenty-one, unmarried man.' He sat down opposite her. 'What is English for unmarried man?'

'Bachelor – and unmarried women are spinsters. I'm one. Can I have a piece of bread?'

He passed it to her on the end of the knife. 'Eat while you can, English spinster.'

'They really are going to occupy Paris?'

'They are on their way.'

'So I'm going to be stuck here until it's over.' She spoke soberly, yet even now the full reality of the situation evaded her. Nothing was real at the moment but the taste of bread and soup; it took precedence over everything, including the company in which she found herself.

They ate in silence, then he said, 'Tell me, what is a bloke?'

'A bloke?' Nat pushed her empty soup bowl aside. 'It's a . . . well, you're one.'

'I am a bloke? It is something good?' He looked suspicious.

'You could get called far worse things.'

'So I shall call you a bloke too,' he said, and poured the wine. 'Help yourself to ham, my dear bloke.'

She did so, then sat back and watched as he diced some pieces for Maurice, mixed them with little bits of bread and put the bowl on the floor. Maurice approached warily, sniffed, then ate without pause until every morsel was gone. Staggering slightly he retired under Nat's chair and composed himself for sleep.

'It's still so quiet outside, we might be the last three creatures left on earth.'

'Perhaps we are. In that case we had better marry and have children.'

'No one to perform the ceremony.'

'So, we will abandon ourselves to the life immoral and have children without marriage.'

'Sorry, I'm planning to be a pianist.'

'But for whom will you play, my dear bloke?'

'Oh, they'll all come back again. In the meanwhile I've got to keep practising – I suppose you haven't got a piano?' She glanced round.

'No, but I have music.' Pushing back his chair he limped to the far side of the room, and after a moment or two she heard the hiss of a gramophone needle followed by the wistful slow foxtrot that everyone in the streets had been whistling during the past weeks.

> *J'attendrai . . .*
> *Le jour et la nuit*
> *J'attendrai toujours*
> *Ton retour . . . .*

Sung in the high, rather disembodied voice of Tino Rossi in that big shadowy attic where they sat waiting for the Germans to arrive, the tune had a new sadness, a poignancy that neither would ever forget.

He played a lot of records – Jean Sablon, Charles Trenet, Django Reinhardt – while they drank the last of the wine and Nat tried to make up her mind to walk back to her old room at Madame Triboulet's house. It would be fairly easy to say goodbye and walk out, but very difficult to find her way across Paris in the dark. Montparnasse was a long way from her own rented room, and even if Madame Triboulet hadn't scarpered like all the others she would never allow a dog in her house. She hated dogs, and Nat had no intention of abandoning Maurice now.

Her host seemed to be following her thoughts. 'You can sleep here if you want.'

'Well. . . .'

'It is not wise outside, I think.'

'I know, but . . .' She put her hand down by the side of her chair, feeling for Maurice's rough coat. She touched him and he shivered in his sleep.

'You can have Tante Honorine and I the little bed.'

'I haven't even seen the little bed yet.'

'He is a good little bed. Look, I show you.'

She contemplated the small divan piled with books and papers; on the floor by the side of it stood the portable gramophone and the pile of records.

'I could sleep on it,' she said finally. 'I don't want to deprive you of your own bed.'

'I have another alternative. We could both sleep in the Tante Honorine.'

'No, thanks.' She looked up to meet his dark blue eyes and he gave a shrug of smiling resignation.

'You do not care for me?'

'I think you're very nice,' she said, turning away. 'Very kind and very nice.'

'Is it the foot?'

She turned back, startled. 'The – ? Good God, no. I hadn't really noticed it.'

'All the nice blokes say that. I think you are a very nice bloke.'

'Thank you,' she said formally. 'But talking of bed, is there much point in going, anyway?'

'It is a pity to spend the last hours of freedom in sleep,' he agreed, 'but people go to bed for other reasons too.'

'I know. But no.'

'She is very comfortable, the Aunt.'

'I daresay. But honestly, I haven't got the urge.'

'English blokes prefer to go to bed with their dogs and cats. I forgot.'

Nat grinned. 'Don't forget the odd horse – '

'Listen – ' He inclined his head sharply. 'Was that a shot?'

She listened too, but the only sound was Maurice snoring and the sudden thumping of her own heart. 'Shall we go out and see what's happening?'

'I think not. We will learn soon enough.'

She helped him to clear the table, to wash the dishes at the little sink in the corner with its one cold tap. 'Are you a student, Raoul?'

'No, I am a working bloke. I sell books on the Left Bank, but I expect all that is finished now.'

There was nothing wise or comforting she could say, so she remained silent. Tiredness had crept into her bones and the long bewildering day had sapped her emotions. She felt dull and inert, incapable of conversation, and for the second time he seemed to sense her mood.

'I think that after all we sleep. It is no good to sit waiting for Hitler like two children waiting for Santa Claus. We will sleep now, and tomorrow we see what happen and we make our plans.'

She took her nightgown out of her suitcase and undressed, indifferent to his presence, while he swept the books and papers from the divan and peeled back the old travelling rug. They bade one another goodnight, then he switched off the light and quietly opened the shutters. Chill night air refreshed the room but their straining ears caught no sound. Turning her face into the pillow she was sleepily conscious of breathing in the scent of its rightful occupant, and fell asleep thinking that tomorrow should have been the day of the recital.

The distant throb of motorised transport woke them when it was barely light.

'They're here,' she whispered, and padded barefoot to the window. Maurice awoke and went to join her, nuzzling her hand and whining. 'Don't worry, old boy, they won't hurt you.'

'He is saying he wants to *pipi*,' Raoul said.

'Hell, I never thought of that. I'd better take him down now.'

'No, I do it.' He had already pulled on trousers and shirt and was now rapidly lacing the heavy boot. He whistled briefly and the dog followed him, a little uncertainly.

I must get him a collar and lead, Nat thought, and went on to wonder whether such ordinary, innocent tasks would still be possible under German occupation. She decided that it would be wise to postpone for the moment any new plans for going home.

The light was beginning to strengthen, and from the window the courtyard looked as if it might be in the same state of picturesque dilapidation as so many other courtyards in Paris; wrought iron, peeling plaster, cobblestones, and the smell of Gauloises and drains. A string of washing hung like ghostly bunting from one of the balconies opposite, but most of the shutters were still closed. Craning, she watched Maurice and Raoul walk slowly across the cobblestones to the ornate lamp standard in the centre, against which Maurice cocked his leg.

Leaving the window she began to dress, hurrying into her crumpled clothes and thrusting her feet into her sandals. The sound of vehicles had increased quite rapidly and she was thankful to see that the court-yard was empty. Raoul and Maurice would be on their way upstairs.

She ran to the door to meet them, peering over the stone balustrade. The staircase was empty. She called their names and her voice echoed back to her. Breathlessly she scuttled down the first flight, peered again, then scuttled back and into the attic. From the window she could see that the courtyard was still empty.

'Where are you?' The useless words were lost in the heavy whine of engines. Downstairs, the first pale finger of sunlight was probing the shuttered windows. She ran under the arch towards the street, where she was in time to see the last of the motorbikes and sidecars and the first of the tanks. They filled the street with their massive alien presence, each man staring ahead from beneath his low-fitting steel helmet, but there was no sign in either direction of Raoul and Maurice.

Bewildered and very frightened she went slowly back through the double doors of Raoul's apartment block. The dusty curtain was still drawn across the concierge's window and there was no one about. She stood in the middle of the attic, looking round her. The Tante Honorine with rumpled sheets and the other small divan surrounded by a careless heap of books, the portable gramophone and the pile of records. *J'attendrais . . . le jour et la nuit j'attendrais toujours . . . .*

During the past twelve hours the place had been home to a cripple, a stray dog and a Jew, and she sat down at the table where they had eaten supper, feeling as if she had lost the only two people left to her.

Emrys Arundel celebrated the passing of shingles and the return to fitness by taking Miranda out to lunch. They went to The Volunteer at the top of Baker Street and had poached salmon and a bottle of hock. Afterwards they strolled in Regent's Park where weeping willows overhung the lake and ornamental waterfowl gave occasional nasal cries.

'So like my Aunt Freddie, dear.' Mr Arundel indicated a bird with a prominent red beak. 'Dear old girl, Frederica; master of foxhounds and a pillar of the church. By the way, how's your mother coming on?'

'She's officially RC now, but I don't think it's going to last. Father Donovan's been replaced by Father Phipps who's got halitosis and no hair.'

'Oh, the poor dear.'

Uncertain whether he was referring to Florence or to Father Phipps, Miranda contented herself with watching the sun sparkle on the silver barrage balloon moored over by the Zoo. It was a wonderful summer, war or no war, and even the blackout was no more than a mild nuisance

93

at this time of the year. Apart from a few strollers in Service uniform, the park was deserted. Mr Arundel indicated two vacant deckchairs.

Miranda hesitated. 'What about the shop?'

'Trade is dead for the duration, dear, so we might as well wring whatever advantage we can from the situation. I noticed yesterday that nearly all the little shops in St Christopher's Place are shut.'

'You're not going to need me much longer, are you?'

'Ah. I was just coming to that.' Cautiously he lowered himself on to the striped canvas. 'Listen, dear, I'm thinking of moving. Packing up the business here and perhaps opening a little business in the country. Everyone with money has gone to the country – London's *dead* – and if we should get bombed and I lost all my stock I should be distinctly cross. So I think it only sensible to fold my tent and depart.'

'Oh, what a pity!'

He looked pleased. 'But I've also been thinking of asking you to come with me.'

'To the country?'

'Yes.'

'Whereabouts?'

'I don't know yet. We've got to find somewhere.'

'We?'

Mr Arundel gazed steadily at two swans and their infant progeny paddling towards the island in the lake. 'In a roundabout way, dear, I'm asking you to marry me.'

'Oh, my God – '

'God has nothing to do with it, it's all my own idea. Quite honestly I never really regarded myself as the marrying sort – I loathe babies, for instance – but there's no denying that I find you most restful to be with. You're pretty and charming and reasonably intelligent and you know when to shut up – '

'Thanks, I'm overwhelmed.'

'Oh dear, now you're cross. Perhaps I put it a little too bluntly, so let me rephrase it. You have a sensitive nature, Miranda dear, which, added to all your other qualities, makes you pretty well irresistible. So there.'

It's the wine, Miranda thought. The wine and the hot sun on top of his having been ill. Dazedly she stared down at her lap.

'So what do you say?' Gently he took her hand, compelling her to look at him. His pale face, wispy hair and froggy smile were not without a certain curious attraction and she liked him very much because he made her laugh. She was also sorry for him because of his delicate health.

'I'd miss you very much indeed,' she said slowly. 'But I don't know about. . . .'

'Think it over. Discuss it with your mother if it would help.'

She agreed to do so, and after a little while they walked slowly back to Baker Street and said goodbye at the tube station. He kissed the tips of his fingers to her and disappeared behind a passing bus.

She didn't discuss it with Florence. Instinct told her that this was something she needed to think about in solitude, and at leisure. Mr Arundel didn't say any more either when she went back to work on the following day, except to tell her to stop calling him Mr Arundel. His name was Emrys. So she called him Emrys, and the only time he tried to kiss her was when she trapped her finger in a drawer. Even then it misfired slightly and he kissed her ear instead of her mouth.

But if sales were poor it was an excellent time for buying as so many people were leaving London homes, and Emrys bought cheaply and with discrimination. Miranda helped him to carry longcase clocks, davenports, chests and credenzas upstairs to his flat, and tried to imagine herself living there with him as Miranda Arundel. Sometimes she could, but mostly not. It made her feel rather mean and ungrateful, but the trouble was that she was already in love with someone else; had been for over a year now.

Yet however much importance she attached to the dream of being in love with the person she married, she found herself unable to reopen the subject by means of a blunt rejection. She didn't want to lose him as a friend, or come to that, as an employer, but neither did she particularly want to go to bed with him, and although she was still very inexperienced this struck her as an ominous sign.

So the summer weeks drifted by, enlivened for Londoners by the daily scores notched up by RAF Spitfires and Hurricanes against marauding German planes seeking to destroy the main airfields in the south-east of England.

'Never before have so many owed so much to so few,' misquoted Florence, gazing entranced at a news photograph of Squadron Leader Douglas Bader with dark wavy hair and spotted silk cravat tucked with careless bravado inside the neck of his flying suit. 'My God, I could go for him.'

'More than Father whatsisname?'

'Father Phipps is a priest, and priests are not men.'

'You once told me that priests have to battle like mad with their animal instincts – '

'You're still a child, you know nothing about it.'

I'm old enough to have been proposed to, so *there*, Miranda thought, and it was the only source of comfort she had against the increased jarring of her mother's personality.

The odd flashes of laughter, of insouciant happiness were still there, but Miranda was becoming steadily more aware of the gradual erosion of whatever bond had been between them. For some time now Florence had had the uncanny effect of making her feel old and jaded and rather spinsterish, while Miranda had been longing to breathe a deeper, fresher air that was not compounded of men and clothes and how to attract the former by means of the latter. Camiknicks and Chanel Number 5; high heels and smart little hats; powder compacts, silver cigarette cases with matching lighters that always lit first time . . . . Miranda had tried, and failed. She couldn't afford Chanel Number 5, and camiknickers were uncomfortable. High heels were a nuisance and so were hats tilted provocatively over one eye, and she had obediently tried cigarettes and given them up. Far from helping her to look sophisticated the smoke had invariably gone down the wrong way, and she had finally come to the conclusion that she couldn't be bothered to fiddle about with all these little bits and pieces any longer. On the day she accidentally trod on her powder compact and broke the mirror she chucked the whole lot away and decided that rightly or wrongly she would be plain Miranda Whittaker as nature had seen fit to fashion her, and damn the rest of them.

So Florence made occasional remarks about Girl Guide captains scrubbed in Lifebuoy soap, and Miranda retaliated with pseudo-naïve questions about the Virgin Mary: 'How did God pick her out – with a pin?' Then events suddenly stopped marking time and plunged them into a new situation.

It began on the Saturday afternoon when Miranda was crossing Piccadilly Circus in order to meet Emrys, who was taking her to a matinée at the Criterion. Quite by accident her eyes met those of a young man in Air Force uniform who hesitated, walked on a pace, came back again and said, 'My God, if it isn't old Miranda!'

'Sammy. . . .'

He grabbed her arm, hauling her from the path of an oncoming bus. 'We haven't met up since I can't remember when!'

'Since Nat's concert.'

They reached the other side of Shaftesbury Avenue and she tried to

96

stop the sudden burning of her cheeks, the sudden impulse to cry. Still holding her arm he led her past the Empire Theatre, shouldering a path through the afternoon crowds looking for pleasure, for relief from wartime tedium. He led her into the Coventry Street Corner House with all its marble and gilt, and cakes only a little less ostentatious than they had been a year ago. Downstairs a gypsy orchestra was playing and the waitresses had crisp uniforms and bows in their hair. He found an empty table and pulled out a chair for her, then seated himself opposite.

'Well now,' he said, beaming at her, 'what are you doing with yourself these days?'

'Nothing very exciting.' She tried to look away from him, but couldn't. Same black hair as Nat but not so curly, and same brown eyes gleaming with amusement, but his features were better defined. He looked tidier, more neatly put together than his sister; perhaps it was the Air Force uniform. Perhaps it was because she loved him.

'What are you, exactly?' She nodded towards the braid on his sleeve.

'Flight Lieutenant, you ignorant woman.'

Her eyes travelled to the emblem above his top left pocket. 'And a pilot.'

He hailed a cruising waitress and ordered tea, toasted teacakes and pastries. Then he sat back gleefully rubbing his hands.

'Tea's always been my favourite meal,' he told her, 'and there hasn't been too much of it just lately. This is my first forty-eight for over three months and I've got a lot of ground to cover.'

'Are you going up to Liverpool?'

'Doubt if I'll have time.' His face shadowed a little, making him look suddenly older and more like his father. 'We keep in touch by phone and they seem to be surviving pretty well. The old man keeps talking about retiring but that's as far as it gets.'

'And Nat?'

'Still nothing.'

The waitress arrived with the loaded tray. In silence they watched her deftly set out the cups and saucers, the teapot, milk jug and hot water. The toasted teacakes glistened and so did Sammy's eyes.

'I still can't understand why she didn't come home as soon as war was declared,' Miranda said when the waitress had departed.

'The last thing they had was a postcard saying she'd be home shortly and would phone as soon as she reached England. Pa's been in touch with the Foreign Office but they weren't much help.'

'She *must* be all right,' Miranda said in a low voice.

'Just two snags. She's English and a Jew.'

'Of course they'll know she's English, but how can they prove she's – '

'Oi yoi yoi.' He slapped his hand to his cheek and wagged his head from side to side. 'The Nazis claim to be the world's leading experts on racial classification. No Jew, no gypsy, no person of non-Aryan breed is likely to escape their amazing expertise. Himmler claims to be able to smell a Jew three miles off and one can only marvel at the skill involved.'

He spoke lightly, but she was deeply conscious of his sense of being excluded; someone from an ancient tribe who had learned to accept the stigma of inferiority with an amused and rueful pride. It sent her back into the old confusion of the Liverpool days; of the young Nat saying with elderly gravity, 'We're Jews, but not Orthodox', and she remembered clinging to the fact that the Ellenbergs weren't Orthodox as if it were some sort of alibi; as if the word itself would automatically deflect the strange hatred of Florence and Rob and the gym mistress and all the others who had been part of the march through the city on that terrible Saturday.

She didn't know much more now, and hadn't progressed any further in the understanding of impersonal hatred since she was a troubled fifteen-year-old. Still unclear about Jewish traditionalism it did nevertheless become very obvious to her, sitting in the Corner House that afternoon, that it shouldn't matter whether any living creature was so-called Orthodox or not so long as it was kind and nice and loving and gifted and funny. In other words like the Ellenbergs, and Sammy Ellenberg in particular.

Brimming with love, she watched the greedy schoolboy manner in which he munched through his teacake and then chose a chocolate-coated choux bun, stabbing it with his pastry fork so that the interior oozed cream. She poured more tea, feeling wifely, motherly, and the world outside had no existence. Even the people at the next table had no more substance than ghosts.

Under her prompting he told her that he had been stationed at Coltishall in Norfolk but was now at Duxford and that he was currently flying Hurricanes. Then he leaned across the table towards her and said quietly, 'Get out of London.'

'Oh . . . ?' His closeness dazzled her.

'It's going to be bad.'

'You mean air raids?'

He nodded, then suddenly grinned in the direction of the gypsy band that was currently murdering a Hungarian czardas. 'If Himmler heard that, he'd nab the lot.'

'Nat would be pretty scathing too.'

'Dear old Nat. . . .'

'And dear little Rachel.' She had had no intention of saying that, but having done so, added, 'My mother's boyfriend was on that march. So what with that and the fact that I'd been pushing the pram when we stopped outside that sweetshop – '

He reached for her hand across the table. 'Rachel was a baby,' he said. 'I only remember a little pink creeping thing whose life had barely started – '

'You're just saying that to make me feel better.'

'Like my parents did? Oh no, there's no comfort without truth. Be peaceful, Miranda, be happy.'

'I am now,' she said huskily, and gazed at their entwined hands. She was still gazing as his fingers slid gently away towards his tunic pocket.

'Look,' he said, 'I've got something very exciting to show you.'

He drew out a jeweller's box, opened the lid and displayed a platinum ring with a small diamond at its centre. She felt the colour flare back into her cheeks.

'Oh, it's lovely. . . .'

'Her name's Rose. I do hope you'll like her.'

Her world disintegrated. She nodded, without trusting herself to speak.

'You're the very first person to know,' Sammy said, tilting the box this way and that so that the diamond caught the light. 'They don't even know anything about it back home yet.'

'Congratulations. I hope you'll. . . .'

'I know we will.' Reluctantly he put the little box back in his pocket. 'She's an absolutely wizard girl and I'm on my way down there now. They're expecting me to dinner, but of course her parents have no idea either.'

'No,' said Miranda. 'I see.'

'But it seems as if it's very important to get things right in her sort of family. Do everything in the proper order – produce the ring after an interview with her old man and so on.'

'They'll love you,' Miranda said. 'Love you. But I really must go now – I've just remembered that I'm meeting someone. In fact I'm about an hour late.'

'Is he nice?' He regarded her with the bright and perky look of someone who wants everyone to be happy.

'Yes, he's marvellous.' She gathered up her handbag while he hurriedly beckoned the waitress for the bill. 'No, don't worry, I'll just slip out by myself – ' and she dabbed at his hand with a quick and inconclusive little movement and threaded her way rapidly between the tables towards the exit.

It was far too late to meet Emrys now and she walked part of the way home, up Regent Street, along Oxford Street, stopping at Marble Arch to buy a pound of plums from a street barrow. Then she caught a bus up the Edgware Road and when she reached home Florence was sitting in her kimono with her hair in a turban and her face concealed behind the rough-textured ramparts of a mud-pack. Only her nostrils, her lips and her two slitted eyes were visible.

'Enjoy the show?' She spoke carefully, in case the over-use of facial muscles cracked the mask.

'Yes, fine.' Miranda flung her handbag on to a chair and peeled off her coat. 'In fact he's asked me to marry him.'

'Who – your old antique dealer? Oh my God, chickabid, what did you say?'

'I said yes.'

Florence gave a high whinny, leaped to her feet and then swore as chunks of dried mud thudded to the floor. 'Oh *chickabid*, are you happy and excited? He must be very well-off, all antique dealers are – oh, just hang on a minute while I get rid of this bloody stuff!'

She darted to the bathroom and Miranda heard the sound of frantic splashing and gasping until she returned, still dabbing at her pink and startled face with a towel. 'Go on, go on – what exactly did he say?'

'Well, not very much really – '

'And to think I thought he was a pansy – '

'Incidentally, it's high time you explained to me what pansies actually do.'

'They poke other men, chickabid. Now, where's your ring?'

'I haven't got one,' Miranda said. 'But look, I've bought us a pound of plums.'

Deflated, Florence collapsed into a chair. 'I'll never understand you. Never, never. All I can say is you're going to be an old maid like your Aunt Daisy.'

'Aunt Daisy's married to Uncle Frank.'

'That doesn't stop her being an old maid. Being an old maid's a state of mind. But never mind her – when am I going to meet him?'

Puzzled and frustrated by Miranda's evasiveness, Florence nevertheless put on her new blouse and her beads and poured them both a gin and orange while she made two Welsh rarebits for supper. The gin made her weep a little ('A pound of *plums* . . .'), then she put her arms round Miranda's neck and said, 'Honest to God, you'll never know how much I adore you.'

'I adore you too,' Miranda said, moved by the old affection, and when Florence dropped one of the rarebits sticky side down on the floor and then tried to scoop it up with the bread knife they both laughed helplessly and uncontrollably.

The ring that Sammy had bought for the girl he was to marry was of modern design; the one that Emrys Arundel slid on to Miranda's finger was antique, with seed pearls surrounding a small sapphire.

'What thin little fingers you have, dear. I've never looked at them closely before.'

'Would you prefer fatter ones?'

'No, no, they're very pretty.' He kissed her lovingly, and with dreams of Sammy Ellenberg now put firmly away, she was able to respond with surprising ardour.

'Careful, dear, or I shall explode.'

'Will it matter?' She refused to open her eyes.

'I'm not sure whether semen dry-cleans and I'm particularly fond of these trousers.'

So they left it at that, and went off arm-in-arm to meet Florence for lunch. Emrys had booked a table in a small French restaurant noted for its impeccable cuisine and in spite of anticipatory qualms Miranda admitted privately that Florence's appearance was a credit to both of them.

She was wearing the new navy-blue spotted dress and jacket that Miranda liked, and her hair, now dyed black, was curled beneath her pink felt hat in little flat snails. Her skin glowed and her eyes shone with the old unquenchable zest, and she seized Emrys' hand and said 'My dear *boy*!' in deep motherly tones that were both affecting and impressive. The only slight feeling of discomfort came when Miranda realised that Florence was closer to Emrys' age than she was. She wanted them to get on well together, but not too well.

They were still sipping aperitifs when it became obvious that Florence had also tumbled to the fact. With both elbows on the table she tilted her chin provocatively and said, 'I do hope you'll take care of my little chickabid. She's still rather a baby, you know.'

'You must have been very young when she was born,' Emrys responded gallantly.

101

'I was a child bride,' Florence said with downcast eyes. 'In fact you could almost say that I was sold to the highest bidder. My parents were poor, although they came from a very long line, but my husband's family were nobility.'

'Really?' Emrys looked intrigued. Miranda's heart sank.

'His father was a Sir. Very aristocratic, but also a bit *nouveau riche*, if you get me. He always smoked cigars with the band on, which I was brought up to believe was very common. But then you can't have everything in this life, can you?' She sighed gustily and nibbled a toasted almond. 'It was worth everything just to have darling chickabid.'

'You are a widow?' Emrys glanced at his fiancée. 'Miranda has told me very little, so far.'

'Yes, unfortunately. He was killed in a typhoon on the way to Zanzibar. He always flew his own plane however much I pleaded with him not to. Take the *Queen Mary*, I said, it may be a little slower but it's so much safer. . . .' She shook her head. 'The dear silly man.'

'Can we eat now? I'm starving,' Miranda said.

The food was marvellous, despite the moment of embarrassment when Florence, having tried to slice her globe artichoke with a knife and fork, complained that it was too tough. The waiter removed it without change of expression.

Undeterred, Florence balanced her chin upon her linked fingers and asked whether the happy date had been fixed yet, and where would the ceremony take place. And had Miranda mentioned that she was a Roman Catholic?

'I'm not one,' Miranda said, 'and if I'm allowed to have any say in it at all I'd like to be married in a registry office. Quietly, and without any fuss.'

'I second that,' Emrys said, greatly to her relief. 'Formality brings me out in a rash. But before we proceed any further with the wedding plans I must confess that I have just put in an offer for a little place up in Suffolk. Very rural I believe, but so far I've only seen photographs of it.'

'How lovely!' cried Florence. 'London can become such a bore.'

'Miranda and I have already discussed the possibility of moving the stock out of town, at least for the duration, and as soon as our plans are made we will let you know, Mrs Whittaker.'

'Please call me Maria,' said Florence. 'I'm sure we're going to be great friends.'

'I'm equally sure,' he said, and the lunch ended on a graceful note.

'He's really rather delicious,' Florence commented as they both strolled homeward. 'Not good-looking, with that rather squat little face, and a bit old for you, chickabid – I always imagined you falling for a glamorous Spitfire pilot or something – still, older men can be very attractive.'

'Yes. Hands off.'

'I hope that was a joke. I'm your mother, in case you've forgotten.'

'But I daresay you've already got your hands full with Father Phipps.'

'Father Phipps,' Florence said as they paused to look in the window of a shoeshop, 'may be a good parish priest but he has his limitations. He's got no sense of humour.'

'I don't think any of that lot have. Certainly not God or Jesus.'

'Jesus did turn water into wine, chickabid. Look at those slingbacks – I wonder if they've got them in my size?'

'Yes, I know, but there's no record of him falling about with laughter at the party.'

'I don't think there was a party. He was just proving a point.'

'What a wasted opportunity.'

'It must be Emrys and all his antiques that's making you so cynical. It's dreadful in a young bride-to-be.'

They went into the shoeshop and Florence tried on a pair of open-toed sandals, decided that she couldn't afford them and they resumed their leisurely stroll.

'I sometimes get a bit impatient with the Holy Mother,' Florence confessed as they cut through Portman Square. 'All that meek and mild business. I mean, you can be a mother and still have fun, can't you?'

Miranda grunted, then said, 'My grandfather wasn't really a Sir, was he?'

Florence sighed. 'Well, no. I was just trying to keep our end up.'

'And my father never flew a plane to Zanzibar, did he?'

'Well, not exactly. As I say, I was just – '

'Next time, I think you'd better check the *Queen Mary*'s route. I've got an idea it only goes between Southampton and New York.'

'You can't expect me to know everything,' Florence retorted crossly. 'I was just giving a general impression, that's all.'

They were side by side in their twin beds that night and the bedside lamp was out when Florence said, 'By the way, chickabid, where exactly is Zanzibar?'

But Miranda was already asleep. Turning on her side Florence bunched her pillow comfortably beneath her curlers and closed her eyes. She sank into oblivion and slept peacefully until breakfast time.

On the following night the London blitz began.

Although the area in which Emrys lived came unscathed through the first night of terror, he was badly shaken, and greeted Miranda on the following morning with a pale face and trembling hands.

'It was terrible, dear, terrible. All the Meissen was rocking on its shelf – '

'We didn't hear much in Maida Vale but we had to go down to the shelter. We didn't sleep much and Florence got hiccups – '

'Who's Florence?' He sounded testy.

'My mother. Maria.'

'So why does she – ? Oh, never mind. Listen, dear, I still haven't heard any more about the place in Suffolk. Apparently the owner's died, which doesn't exactly help, does it?'

Miranda made a pot of tea and he calmed down. 'I wouldn't mind so much being bombed if I didn't have kidney trouble as well. I wonder if they'll come back again tonight?'

'Oh, I shouldn't think so. It must cost thousands to come over here, let alone the cost of bombs.'

'What a divine comfort you are to me,' he said, and gloomily stirred his tea.

They did come back, the night after that and the night after that. Flares lit London with a ghastly light, then the Dorniers and Heinkels came throbbing in over the Thames and the bombs whistled down over the city, bursting open its buildings and obliterating its streets with smoking rubble. The bells of ambulances and fire engines were the only sounds to break the dazed silence which followed the dawn all-clear, and the night that Paddington recreation ground received a direct hit, Florence and Miranda clung together in the stifling dark of the air-raid shelter as it rocked and swayed around them.

'Chickabid, I think you ought to get married straight away.'

'Fancy thinking about that now.'

'This is just the very time we should. We don't want to lose him, do we?'

'We?' Another bomb fell closer, possibly in Shirland Road.

'You, then.' Florence wiped her forehead on the sleeve of her siren suit. Over in the corner someone groaned in terror.

'All right, duck,' the warden on duty said. 'It hasn't got your number on it. Not tonight.'

'I mean, you are his fiancée, aren't you? But not his wife. And if anything happened to him – God forbid and hail Mary full of grace I hope it doesn't because he's a darling and so right for you – but if anything happened you wouldn't come in for a penny. And he's obvi-

104

ously made of money. . . . That suit he wore when we had lunch was what they call bespoke tailoring, chickabid. I know good clothes when I see them, and if anyone really appreciates them, I do – '

Her voice ceased during the next explosion, then resumed its murmured monotone of logic in Miranda's ear.

We, she thought. When do girls logically get rid of their mothers? I always hoped it was when they got married.

She was looking forward to marrying Emrys. She loved him because he was kind and knowledgeable and made her laugh, and because the tentative fondlings had made her want to go to bed with him. She also felt pleasantly proprietorial about his poor state of health, and told herself that it would improve when he had someone sensible to look after him.

'Take my tip and hurry things forward, chickabid.'

'You make me feel as if I'm pregnant.'

'*Are* you?' Florence peered closely in the gloom.

'No.'

'Oh, thank God. Just as a matter of interest, have you – ?'

'No. I haven't.'

'All right, I was only joking, chickabid. No need to sound so gruff.'

On the late September morning when they emerged from the shelter clutching their torches, gas masks and woolly blankets to find that their windows had been blown out and that there was no electricity, Miranda drank a glass of yesterday's milk and ate a marmalade sandwich, then dressed herself and set off for the antique shop in St John's Wood Road. Stepping over fire hoses and chunks of smouldering brickwork, she rehearsed what she was going to say to Emrys, not because of Florence's advice but because she wanted him to replace her mother as the premier influence in her life.

There was no need. With a white towel wrapped round one arm and a cut over one eye he greeted her groggily, confusedly, and then said, 'Never mind, dear – fear no more the heat of the sun. The estate agent received instructions from the dear departed's lawyer to say that the house is ours, and that taking into account the exceptional times in which we live, we may move in as soon as we like.'

They hadn't even seen it, and after Miranda had attended to the cut above his eye and stuck plaster on the two small scratches on his arm, Emrys went round to the garage where he kept his old two-seater.

'I've been drawing my petrol ration since last September,' he said, 'but I fear this will be our last little jaunt until peacetime.'

They set off, and the nearer they drew to the East End of London the more devastating were the signs of bombing. Time and again they made forced detours around roped-off areas, but when they reached Havering-atte-Bower Emrys stopped the car and put the hood down.

'Look, dear,' he said. 'We're in the country.'

The sudden effect on her of trees and grass and a quiet meandering road was one of unmitigated pleasure. She got out of her seat and ran across to the bulging overgrown hedge crying, 'I can see some spindleberry!' The colours glowed sealing-wax pink in her hand as she dashed back to the car and gave him the little bunch of twigs. There were cows grazing in the meadow on the opposite side of the road and a blackbird eyed her beadily as it scuffled among dry leaves in the ditch.

'I remember gathering spindleberry in Yorkshire with my Aunt Daisy,' she said apologetically. 'It sort of takes you back.'

They drove on, following the road to the top of a long rise, and away to the left stretched London. Here and there plumes of smoke still rose in the quiet air, but seen from this distance the sweet passivity of the countryside seemed to have calmed the violence of war.

At midday they found a pub which served them with bread and cheese and brown ale, and on the outskirts of Chelmsford Emrys woke Miranda by digging her in the ribs and asking her to locate Sudbury on the map.

The countryside had grown deeper, more mysterious and more untouched by hand when they finally found themselves on Clatterfoot Common. A few young bullocks were grazing nearby and stared impersonally for a moment or two before losing interest, and the sun was casting long shadows from the timbered house that still bore the estate agent's sale notice.

It faced the Common, and there were apple trees in the garden and a well outside the kitchen door. It had two gables, a thatched roof and small-paned windows, and Emrys unfastened the front door with the big old-fashioned key, saying, 'Welcome home, dear.'

She embraced him wildly and exuberantly, then ran from room to room while she called out to him to look at this and that. She was tousled and excited as a child, and he followed her slowly, panting from the exertion.

'What an appalling colour they've painted this room.'

'Let's do it white. I love painting.'

'I can smell mice in here – '

'I love mice too.'

'Calm down, dear. You're becoming hysterical.'

106

'I wish we could get married now,' she said. 'And never go back to London.'

He took her hand and gently kissed her fingers. 'Is it me – or the house?'

'Both. But mainly you.'

She wandered upstairs again, touching the crooked walls and contemplating a patch of late sunlight lying like a faded rug on a dusty oak floor, and only one thought filled her mind. I've come home. This is mine and Emrys' home and I'll never ever leave it.

This sudden sense of intrinsic and deep-rooted belonging to a place was something she had never experienced in all the past years of restless and disordered change; perhaps the nearest approach to it had been during the Ellenberg era, but even then it had been an involvement with people rather than place. Her love for their rambling and colourful flat had merely been an extension of her love for them.

This is my home. *My* home. And I will always love it and cherish it, and it will shelter me from hardship and fear. . . . Then, suddenly sickened by a vision of herself as Florence's type of sensibly acquisitive female, she rushed downstairs and cast herself into Emrys' arms.

'I love you, I love you – I honestly do!'

'And I love you too, dear.' He rumpled her hair, and his wide, froggy smile, hidden by her clinging arms, was that of a man sunnily content with his lot.

They drove back to London as the sirens were moaning and the anti-aircraft guns beginning to limber up, and they were married a week later by special licence.

When Raoul returned to the big attic room with the dog Maurice on a length of pale blue silky cord, Nat said with her back turned, 'I thought you were both dead.'

'We are not only living, we have found a beautiful *laisse* – no shops open for such things but this we discover in a bundle of things outside a house.'

'Somebody's dressing-gown cord.' She turned to look at Maurice's adornment. 'I suppose we'll have to take the tassels off.'

'Ah no, they are very *à la mode*.' He removed the improvised collar and Maurice bounded across to Nat and licked her hands. 'You stupid old dog,' she said, and hid her face in his rough coat.

That was a week ago, and now the Germans had completed their occupation of Paris. Swastika banners hung from all ministry buildings, from the Chambre des Députés and all the requisitioned hotels; road

107

signs written in German had been set up at all the main points in the city, and the monocled General von Studnitz had been declared temporary military governor. Very early on, the morning after the armistice had been signed, Hitler made his one and only lightning tour of the city, the convoy of cars sweeping rapidly past the famous sites on every tourist's itinerary before depositing him at Le Bourget airport.

The occupation had been effected with a smooth efficiency that even now was difficult to credit. No shots had been fired although there were several discreet suicides, and the Parisians who remained opened their shutters and their doors and accustomed themselves fatalistically to the sight of German soldiers in green uniforms. Before long they had been nicknamed *les haricots verts*.

For Nat, life in the big shadowy attic with Raoul was a strange and dreamlike interlude, a not unpleasant pause between the life that was past and the life that was to come. It never seriously occurred to her that there might not be a life to come, but Raoul was insistent that precautions must be taken. He introduced her to the concierge as his sister, shouting the word into her deaf ear while the old girl nodded and smiled, and had forbidden her to go into shops or to speak with strangers because of her English accent. On one occasion he suggested that she might consider dyeing her hair.

'Which colour would you prefer – blue or green?' But the flippancy of her words hid her sudden feeling of sickened disgust at the idea of trying to disguise herself.

'You are not wise to laugh if you wish to live.'

'I tell you one thing,' she retorted, 'I live my life on my own terms and on no one else's. *Je suis moi* – and I propose to stay that way.'

'All very strong and brave, but not worth to die for.'

'Why are you so obsessed with death?'

'Wait and see,' he said, and hobbled over to the stove to make coffee.

Several times she considered moving out, but there were difficulties, and money was one of them. Her last allowance from home had dwindled almost to nothing, and in spite of rejecting Raoul's careful circumspection she was hesitant about putting her trust in strangers. Her first sight of a French girl walking arm-in-arm with a German soldier had shocked her, and a paragraph in the German-controlled press stating that Nadia Boulanger had made her home in America had left her with a sense of youthful outrage. First Milhaud, then Mademoiselle; two people whom she had respected and revered had behaved like the proverbial rats leaving the sinking ship.

A further reason for not going was Raoul himself; in spite of occasional disagreements she liked him very much, and, all things considered, the life they had both embarked upon suited her very well. She still occupied the Tante Honorine every night and invariably awoke in the morning to the voice of Tino Rossi or Jean Sablon coming from the gramophone on the floor by the side of the other bed. He would be lying with his hands clasped behind his head and a Gauloise between his lips.

'It's a disgusting habit, smoking in bed.'

'Denied the other pleasures I can think of, it is the only one left to me, my dear bloke.'

'Beds are for sleeping in.'

'So they told me when I was a child. But I learned they were telling untruth.'

After the first week had passed and life appeared to have assumed a pseudo-normality, he returned to selling secondhand books, pitching his barrow in a variety of small street markets rather than trundling to the better-known sites. And while he was gone Nat and Maurice would go for long rambling walks through the city where the leaves of the chestnut trees were already hanging listless and dull, and where the quiet was occasionally broken by the thud of jackboots as the guard was ceremoniously changed outside some big requisitioned building. Through listening but not speaking, she learned that the Conservatoire had already reopened, but she didn't feel like going back there now. In any case they probably wouldn't accept her again because she was English. And despite Raoul's rather clumsy suggestion about disguising her curly black hair, she felt far more conscious of being English than of being Jewish, although suddenly coming upon a chalked sign on a wall saying *Mort aux juifs* had given her a momentary jolt.

I know about being English but I don't know much about being a Jew, she thought. Still, I suppose ignorance is my protection.

One afternoon she and Maurice turned in to a narrow thoroughfare where, on the pavement outside a secondhand shop, stood an old upright piano. She stood looking at it for a moment or two, her fingers drumming against her cotton skirt. She hadn't touched a piano since leaving Madame Triboulet's house, and the hunger was muscular as well as emotional. She walked up to it, and Maurice sat down by her side as if he were waiting for her to begin.

It had a better tone than she would have imagined, but was very out of tune. Gently she struck a bass chord, then ran her fingers lightly up the scale. Unaware of faces looking out from the dim interior of the shop she tried a few more chords, an arpeggio or two, and then, still

109

standing, launched into the first piece of music that came to mind: Mozart's 'Rondo à la Turque'. The bright patter of sound brought the proprietor of the shop to his doorway and he stood there, hands on hips. Unaware of him she continued playing, still standing up and conscious only of the hunger for making music. She went on playing, anything which came into her head, stretching out one foot to reach the sustaining pedal as Mozart changed to Liszt and Liszt to Bach.

It was like coming out of a dream when someone tapped her on the shoulder and said close to her ear, '*Bien joué, Mademoiselle! Mais maintenant la musique Française. . . .*'

Her fingers hesitated, slipped from the keys as she remembered the Milhaud she had been going to play at the recital before he scarpered. He was to have been guest of honour, but now she would never play Milhaud again. Then her hands returned to the keyboard and as if of their own volition began to crash out the 'Marseillaise'. The sound of it seemed to bounce defiance off the houses opposite and then come ringing back. Some of it escaped and fled up into the sky and when she had played it through twice she stood back, easing her stooped shoulders as the echoes died.

Turning, she saw for the first time that a small group of people had gathered behind her; several children, two women with shopping bags, a man in a beret holding a bicycle and then, a little apart, a German soldier in a forage cap pointing a camera towards her.

She stood motionless, staring at him with her hands at her sides, then very slowly reached down for the length of cord that secured Maurice, and walked away.

She didn't tell Raoul about it because she knew that he would upbraid her for taking unnecessary risks, although as far as she was concerned the incident of the German had already become an irrelevance compared with the shock of suddenly being able to make music again. She could remember only the piano outside the shop, and her immediate response. Merely touching its yellow keys with her fingertips had released the powerful hunger to play, to hear the sounds flowing from beneath her hands and to fill the whole world with them.

And the hunger, once awoken, would not be stilled. Casually she asked Raoul whether any of his friends had a piano – was there anyone in the other apartments surrounding the courtyard who had one? But he shook his head.

'I regret not. Most people these days play the gramophone.'

So her fingers drummed on the table top and on the arm of her chair with all the furious frustration of mice in a revolving cage. Every now and then he would capture them with his own, his expression a mixture of sympathy and exasperation. 'You suffer a crisis of the nerves. Be calm, my dear bloke, be calm.'

'I am calm, for God's sake! I'm just trying to endure a sense of bereavement.'

And so she would go for another walk; another silent trail round the warm Paris streets with Maurice on his blue dressing-gown cord, and the music would go with her, filling her ears and her brain and blotting out the occasional sound of armoured cars or stamping jackboots as the German army went about its business.

In other respects life in the city seemed to have returned to normal; theatres had reopened, the big shops were busy and the pavement cafés filled with customers idly sipping aperitifs and reading *La Gerbe*, the new daily paper launched by collaborationists and approved by the Nazi hierarchy. She looked away from the sight of Frenchwomen fraternising with German officers, and once when a Luftwaffe pilot tried to stroke Maurice she jerked him sharply away from the outstretched hand. Her brother was a pilot too; on the opposite side.

'Isn't there anything we can do?' she demanded that evening. 'Isn't there anyone prepared to tell them where they get off?'

'Only those who welcome a bullet between the eyes.'

'Your timidity sickens me!'

'I do not force you to endure it.'

'Oh Raoul, can't you *see*?'

'Only too well, my poor bloke.'

'And you're prepared to endure it for the rest of your life? For ever?'

Receiving no answer she would sit at the table as the evening shadows lengthened across the attic floor and play scales and arpeggios with fingers that sometimes seemed almost mad for action. Again she thought about moving out but did nothing, and what seemed as if it would prove to be the end of the interlude came one afternoon in late autumn.

Nat had developed the habit of going down to the courtyard to help Raoul carry books upstairs when he arrived home, and now they were sitting on the edge of the barrow enjoying the damp stillness that precedes the cold of winter. Maurice was with them, and they watched while he examined the variety of animal scents clinging to the base of the solitary lamp. Cooking smells drifted down, and from one open window they heard the sound of a woman singing. This is the heart of Paris, thought Nat. Beautiful, picturesque, casual, romantic and hostile. No one had bothered to make her acquaintance during all the weeks she had been sharing Raoul's attic, although other tenants eyed her curiously if they passed on the stairs. Even the old concierge gave her no more than a curt nod. Perhaps they think I'm a whore, she told herself. Well, so what?

The peace was disturbed by the sound of a motorised convoy turning into the street outside, and by the sudden appearance of a large black dog. It stood in the archway, busy tail curved over its back in a querying attitude. A red tongue lolled from its open mouth. When it caught sight of Maurice, who was in the act of raising his leg, it closed its jaws and charged.

Taken unawares Maurice yelped and sped towards Nat and Raoul, who immediately rose to their feet. Then with sudden loss of logic he turned, the black dog in pursuit, and ran under the archway and out into the street.

The last of the armoured cars had just passed as Nat and Raoul arrived panting on the pavement, but they were in time to see the marching column that followed. Three marched over the body, then the fourth, with a grimace of disgust barely visible beneath the deep helmet, kicked it into the gutter.

Nat screamed and hurled herself forward, evading Raoul's grasp. She grabbed at the soldier who had kicked Maurice, missed him, and hooked strong savage fingers on to the tunic buttons of the man behind. He shoved her hard with his elbow and she almost fell. Regaining her balance she freed one hand and slammed her clenched fist into his jaw. The column of marching men lost its rhythm for an instant then regained it as the soldier stamped hard on Nat's foot and shoved her with both hands. She fell close to where Maurice lay, and although her eyes were closed, one hand slowly reached out as if to comfort him in death. The convoy disappeared, and with it the black dog.

There was only Raoul to help her. No one else had seen anything, heard anything, except from behind the safety of their shutters. He put his arms round her but she shrugged him off. 'Bring Maurice – don't leave him.'

Her face was bruised and her foot hurt where it had been stamped on. She limped upstairs and Raoul laid Maurice down outside the door on the landing, then boiled water and poured it into a bowl to bathe her face.

'Thanks. I'm OK now. . . .'

'Oh, my poor old bloke. . . .' But this time he didn't remonstrate; didn't scold her for her reckless stupidity. He took off her sandal and gently propped her foot on his lap while he cleaned dirt and blood from the broken skin. Nat watched him, stony-eyed, and when it was done she insisted upon carrying Maurice downstairs, wrapped now in an old shirt of Raoul's, and then waited while he dug a small grave behind the bushes that grew against the opposite wall. The old concierge watched without comment from her cubbyhole.

They had no appetite for supper, and that evening the gramophone remained silent. It was only after she had crept into the sanctuary of the Tante Honorine that her tears began to flow. She tried to cry quietly but he must have heard because she sensed the bedsprings move beneath his weight. Without speaking she drew the covers back and he came in beside her. Her tears soaked his hair and trickled down his neck and he held her and kissed back the hot tumbled curls from her forehead.

'He didn't deserve it, that brutality . . . he was small and innocent and trusting like my baby sister all over again . . . the same sort of mindless marching people killed her and she didn't deserve it either. The only thing she did wrong was to get in the way . . . be in the wrong place at the wrong time and even then it wasn't her fault because she was too young even to walk properly, but she suffered the same terror and the same brutality – why does it have to be like this always?'

He didn't know. He had no answer. He just held her closely and stroked her hair and gently kissed the swelling bruise on her cheek. She stopped crying and they lay side by side staring at the darkened outline of the big unshuttered window.

'They'll come here, won't they? After what I did.'

'I think perhaps not. A dog is not too serious, to them.'

'I wanted to kill him, to kill them all, but I'd nothing to do it with.'

'Fortunately.'

But they'll come here, I know they will. She turned to him, put her arms round his neck, and they made love for the first time, and Nat thought fragmentarily, I see it all now; the rhythm of music is the rhythm of life itself.

They slept, her head on his shoulder and a strand of her hair rising and falling each time he breathed. Church clocks struck their way through the small hours and she kissed his nose in the darkness and said, '*Je t'aime.*'

'I love you too, my dear old bloke. You are the bloke *la plus adorable.*'

'Shall we get married?'

'Sure. First thing tomorrow.'

'I think it's tomorrow now.'

'So, we just do this one time more and then we rise from the bed and get married.'

'I've always felt so at home in Auntie. . . .'

The sound of a shot awoke them, or perhaps it was only a German car backfiring. The French had no cars now, and in any case there was a curfew.

'Tell me about your little sister. What happened to her?'

She told him, and he sighed and said, 'I too had a little sister. Her name was Hélène but she died of the *diphtérie*. I did not know her well for we were parted as children.'

'Wish I could believe in a heaven, then I could picture Rachel and Hélène playing hopscotch together.'

'You do not believe?' He raised his head to look at her in the murky November dawn. 'You are a bad bloke.'

'How can I believe? How can anyone, with all this going on? All this wickedness and pain.'

'To believe in something helps the pain.'

'Are you a Catholic?'

'Yes. But not strong, you understand.'

'I'm a Jew, and I'm not strong either.'

'Perhaps that's where the world is gone wrong. If we had believed in God hard enough the anti-Christ would not have come to power.'

'Is that why he persecutes religious people? Because he hasn't got a religion himself?'

'How can one tell with a madman?'

'I suppose he is his own religion,' Nat said. 'He's got a Narcissus complex, or something.'

'Whatever his complex, it goes badly for millions of people.' They fell silent for a while, dozing and at peace.

Then Raoul said, 'But everything is changed now. You are changed because I love you and you will be my wife, and the Germans will change very soon because they are finished with their first months of politeness here and will be cruel and *épouvantable* like they are in Poland and Czechoslovakia.'

'So what do we do?'

'It's what we do not do. And you, my dear bloke, because you are a Jew, must stay in here safe and not go out any more – '

'But I can't!' Aghast, she bounced round to face him and then yelped with pain when she banged her cheek.

'You can, and you must. Not only have you not papers to pretend you are French, but your accent, if I may say so, is scarcely *comme il on plaira*, and I have also heard that all Jews are to wear a yellow star so that they may be – may be – '

114

'Identified?'

'Exactly.'

'Identified for what?'

'We do not know. We can only guess.'

'I see.' She tried to sound dignified and formal on behalf of the race to which she belonged by birth but not conviction. My parents are not Orthodox Jews and neither am I, but she didn't speak the words aloud because the new, heightened sense of menace turned them into the craven and paltry excuses of a coward. And when one is in love, perhaps the hardest defect to admit to is any form of cowardice.

He left her reluctantly, and made coffee and cut up the stale remnants of last evening's *baguette*, then brought them back to bed. They sat close together, dipping the bread in their bowls of hot coffee, and Nat flinched when she caught sight of Maurice's bowl and the wooden box he had used as a bed.

'Do you really think they'll come for me, Raoul?'

'Let us be cheerful and say not.'

'Hitting German soldiers isn't really a good thing to do, is it?'

'Scarcely, my dear bloke. We must just ask providence to provide them with many distractions so maybe they will be too busy to remember.'

'It's going to be very boring shut up here all day without you and – and him.'

'Jews are used to incarceration. It is part of their history.'

'For Pete's sake!' she exploded. Then halted abruptly, silenced by mingled recollections of Old Testament illustrations and contemporary press photos of Jews herded inside the Warsaw ghetto.

'You really believe that Jews are somehow different from other people, don't you?' she asked finally.

'I am not saying that.' He swallowed the last coffee-soaked crust on his teaspoon, then laid the bowl aside. 'I am only saying, be prudent and remain in hiding.'

Thinking of Maurice she began to weep again.

'We are looked after,' he said, putting his arm round her and holding her close. 'Someone is in charge. And soon all *les haricots verts* will be gone and we will be married and have our children and you will play the piano on the radio and on the gramophone and I will listen and be proud.'

'It really will be like that, won't it?'

'But naturally, my dear bloke. What else can you imagine?'

115

So she stayed in hiding. During the following days her foot became less painful where the *haricot vert* had stamped on it, and the bruise on her cheek turned from black to purple, from blue to pink. Her eye closed to a slit then opened again as the swelling subsided, and with the improvement in her appearance so did their dread of the knock upon the door begin to fade. Perhaps it had been officially viewed for what it was: the rash and unpremeditated action of a hysterical female.

Christmas came, and they celebrated with two horsemeat steaks and a rather grey-looking *tarte aux pommes* washed down with half a litre of Burgundy which one of Raoul's regular customers had given him.

Food ration cards had been issued as far back as last September, and as Nat had been unable to apply for one they had to manage on Raoul's alone. Like a provident housewife he scoured the street markets for such imperishables as rice and noodles, and by the time they were rationed in December he had amassed a nice little store which he hid in the clothes cupboard. Nat learned to make vegetable soup, but bread was rationed to only 300 grams a day and every evening Raoul came limping home with news of further shortages. All the shops were emptying; clothes, shoes, household goods – *ils nous prennent tout*, everyone was lamenting; the Germans are swiping everything, and that included the little tin boxes of gramophone needles. They had to ration themselves even to Tino Rossi and Jean Sablon now.

Snow fell, and the iron grasp of winter became relentless. There was no more heating oil, and coal was hard to find, and in mid-January Raoul gave up trying to sell secondhand books to people whose main preoccupation was the search for food, and got himself a job as a café waiter. At least he was working indoors, and after a day spent limping rapidly between tables, bearing trays of Nazi beer or small cups of acorn coffee, he was sometimes able to bring home a couple of slices of bread or maybe an egg.

He waited on Germans and Parisians with equal passivity, and if, during the odd respite, he thought of anything at all, it was of Nat. Everything else was in abeyance, including plans to study law when he had saved enough money. He had never told her of this, and was grateful and astonished that she should accept with such equanimity his present status as secondhand bookseller turned waiter. She seemed to exist by a set of values different from those of most girls, and although he occasionally dreamed of being presented to her father, Monsieur le Docteur, native prudence told him that it was unlikely to happen. As soon as the war was over life would return to normal and dreams would end.

116

In the meanwhile, all he could do was try to take care of her; to be wise and cautious and diligent in everything that concerned her, because for a man who had been abandoned to an *orphelinat* because of a club foot it was the most stupendous thing in the world to have someone who loved and relied upon him for their safety.

For Nat, the winter months passed in a strange and dreamlike trance of love, hunger and loneliness. Love made her sweep and tidy the attic for when Raoul returned, while hunger and loneliness drew her to other small activities to induce a state of mind over matter.

Slowly she read through the stock of unsold books stacked against the wall, and her French improved. She devised a series of exercises to keep herself pianistically in trim. Not merely the fingers but also the network of muscles in hands, wrists, arms and shoulders upon which their agility depended. Music seemed to have deserted her temporarily, but she knew that it would come back and that she must be ready. She found an old exercise book in a drawer and began to keep a diary, until it petered out for lack of anything to record. And when the long, steel-cold hours threatened to overwhelm her she went to bed – it was the only place in which to keep warm – and fully clad she would prop herself up in the Tante Honorine and stare through the window at the lifeless apartments opposite, longing for the time when Raoul would be home.

Thoughts and memories of England she rationed severely, preferring to regard them as a rather dangerous indulgence, and it was the same with making plans for the future. To discuss marriage and children was at this stage a semi-joke, a pleasant fantasising that did neither of them any harm provided they didn't believe it too literally. To do that would be tempting fate. The time for serious planning would be after the war, and in the meanwhile they were as good as married, living this strange, shadowy, secretive life in the big attic high above occupied Paris.

She was trying to keep warm in the Tante Honorine on the afternoon when there came a soft tapping on the door. She remained motionless for a moment, then slid from the bed, straightened her skirt and went to investigate.

A middle-aged woman, vaguely familiar, was smiling and proffering a small paper bag. 'A little coffee for Madame and Monsieur,' she said. 'My daughter has sent me a parcel from the Midi.'

Surprised and touched, Nat mumbled her gratitude.

'We are living in bad times,' the woman said. 'It is important to share what we have.'

Nat repeated her thanks, then after a slight pause asked the woman to come in. She did so, glancing swiftly to left and right before shaking hands and saying that she was Madame Boudot from the second floor. She asked after Monsieur, and when Nat replied that he was very well and working hard, Madame Boudot sighed and said that times were hard for them all.

'And what do you do with yourself all day, Madame? You must find the days long.'

'I have plenty to occupy me,' Nat said. Then added, 'I am Mademoiselle, not Madame.'

'A thousand pardons.' Madame Boudot smiled understandingly. 'And I think from her accent that Mademoiselle is not French?'

'Madame thinks correctly,' Nat replied, and forbore to elaborate.

They stood smiling at one another politely and a little uncertainly. Madame Boudot had a long nose and dusty black hair and was wearing a man's cardigan over a flowered overall. Nat remembered having watched her shaking mats down in the courtyard, and on sunny days last summer hanging her canary's cage on a hook outside her window. She seemed a pleasant, friendly woman.

'I must go now,' Madame Boudot said finally. 'I have work to do. *Au revoir, Mademoiselle*, and enjoy the coffee.'

When Raoul arrived back from the café he unloaded a demi-sel cheese and two slices of salami from his pocket.

'So tonight we dine in state!' Nat began to lay knives and forks and plates on the table. 'And Madame Boudot from downstairs brought us two spoonfuls of real coffee – '

'Why?' He stood motionless.

'Why? Well, I suppose because she's a neighbour and because, as she told me, she's just received a parcel from her daughter in the Midi.'

'Did she call here with it? And did you invite her in?' His beautiful classical features took on a look of sharp suspicion that both alarmed and irritated her.

'Well yes, but she only came in for a minute.'

'What did she say? What did she ask – and what did you tell her?'

'I didn't tell her anything. For God's sake calm down – '

'But don't you see that times are not normal and that we must regard everyone as unreliable and insincere? I work among people – I listen and I know about collaboration with the Germans. . . . That woman Madame whatsername has never called here before, has never spoken a word to me since first I came, and now suddenly – '

'All right, all *right*! I take your point and I won't speak to her ever again! If she knocks on the door with a kilo of beefsteak I won't answer in case Hitler sent it. I won't answer the door to anyone – I won't speak to anyone – I'll live like a blasted deaf mute if that's what you want – '

'Don't shout, you stupid bloke!'

'I don't shout during the daytime,' Nat said, quivering with rage. 'I don't talk during the daytime, I don't even whisper during the daytime. I stay shut up in here like a white mouse in a cage and when you come home in the evening I beg leave to talk. To talk and laugh and sing and dance – to shout my head off if I've a mind!'

'You are *mad*!'

'I will be if I stay shut up on my own much longer.'

'Go then. Go!'

'OK, I will.'

They both paused, and the little silence that ensued was tense with foreboding. They were both on the verge of shattering their fragile relationship like two wanton children throwing stones at a window.

'I'm sorry,' Nat muttered finally, and without looking at him put out her hand. He took it, stroking the fine contours of it with his thumb. Her hand closed over his and he marvelled at the soft strength of it; it seemed to have a boneless power quite out of keeping with the rest of her. Gradually she increased the pressure. He winced, and was about to protest when he caught the gleam of laughter in her eyes.

'Are you sorry too?'

'Yes – yes. . . .'

'Promise not to boss me any more?'

'Yes. What is boss?'

'Dunno – be *autoritaire*.'

'OK, I will not be *autoritaire*.'

'Or be jealous of Madame Boudot?'

'Jealous of her? You are crazy, my poor bloke – '

She released his hand, they embraced, and because of the cheese, salami and coffee they played some of the old gramophone records for the first time since Christmas.

But the quarrel had been a warning. All lovers had quarrels, but, as Raoul frequently pointed out, they were living in a new reign of terror, where one small and unpremeditated action could plunge them into the dark abyss of death.

'In other words, I'm a Jew,' she said later.

'You are both English and a Jew,' he replied, kissing the wild curls back from her forehead. 'You are also the woman I love, and that is why I care so much.'

119

The sound of screaming. The high, wild, animal sound of it piercing her skull like arrows of glass. She struggled to get away, to hide from its demented terror, but hands pinned her shoulders and prevented her from moving.

'What on earth's the matter?' Miranda awoke to find Emrys leaning over her, spikes of thin, ruffled hair silhouetted in the dawn light.

'I don't know – I'm. . . .' Real life came flooding back. 'Sorry, just a bad dream. . . .'

'But my dear, you frightened me to death!'

'Sorry,' she repeated as the wild pounding of her heart subsided. 'I'm afraid it's a sort of nightmare that comes back every now and then. Sorry. . . .'

Why do I feel the need to apologise, she wondered. *Sorry . . . I'm afraid that . . .* I'm always apologising for everything; I suppose it's because Aunt Daisy used to say that the test of good manners is not to cause unnecessary annoyance or inconvenience to others. I daresay she was right, but . . .

'Sorry,' she said for the third time, then relaxed against the pillows and smiled at him. 'But I think we'll have to take it as part of the for better, for worse clause.'

'I'll have to go, dear,' he said. 'Being woken so brutally has made me feel sick.'

He padded away and Miranda dozed disjointedly until he returned in due course with a pot of Lapsang and two antique cups and saucers on a lacquer tray. They sipped, side by side and comfortably at peace. 'I've just breached our last packet of China tea, dear,' he said. 'No more now until after the end of the war.'

It was typical of Emrys that he didn't ask what her nightmare had been about, and perhaps typical of Miranda that she couldn't tell him without some form of encouragement. Obviously very fond of her, he nevertheless evinced not the least curiosity about her as an individual, and she was aware that her thoughts, her reactions, her past life, seemed to hold no interest for him whatsoever. So far as he indicated, her life had begun on the day she applied for the job of assistant in his antiques business, and from that moment onwards he was all charming, if faintly amused, attention. He was equally evasive about his own family and past, and she could only glean that his father had been a West Country bishop, that he had been educated at Haileybury and had always preferred things of beauty to people with high ideals.

He had taken her maidenhead briskly and efficiently on their wedding night, which seemed to dispose of Florence's theory that he was a pansy, but had shown little inclination to pursue their sexual relationship since then, explaining that the act of love, performed in whatever position, gave him backache.

She became familiar with the aches and pains of his ever-recurring kidney trouble, and was once awoken at 3.30 am by Emrys switching on the bedside lamp and looming over her in his bathrobe.

'Look, dear, at what I've just passed.'

Squinting painfully she saw what appeared to be an extremely small and not very spectacular diamond cradled in his moist pink palm.

'Heavens, is that a kidney stone?'

'My dear, I thought I was in labour.' He looked round for a suitable receptacle for it, then placed it carefully beneath his pillow. 'Never mind, perhaps it'll have turned into a bag of gold by morning.'

'You're getting mixed up with milk teeth,' Miranda said sleepily. 'Come back to bed before you get cold.'

'Honestly.' He subsided gratefully beside her. 'It was every bit as awful as giving birth.'

'If there's to be any giving birth, kindly leave it to me.'

'Miranda – ' His head shot up in alarm. 'You're not . . . are you?'

'Not that I know of.'

He collapsed again, tucking the covers into the small of his back and then clasping his hands under his chin. 'I love you dearly, Miranda, but I doubt if I'll ever be able to put you in pod. I think perhaps we'd better look out for a nice little kitten somewhere.'

But life at Trellis House was proving very agreeable. There had been one or two preliminary ups and downs of course; rumblings of discord over which colour to repaint the drawing room – Emrys insisted upon ivory while Miranda took a sudden fancy to eau-de-Nil – and then a short sharp altercation about the removal of Virginia creeper from over the hall porch.

'Virginia creeper is so common, dear – '

'Rubbish, rubbish – it's beautiful! And soon it'll turn bright red. . . .'

Emrys shuddered, but the creeper remained and the drawing room was painted ivory.

A local builder was employed to trace the damp in the scullery, to patch some of the plaster, and to make habitable for Florence the small outbuilding that had once been a wash house.

The realisation that Florence had taken it for granted that she would be joining them at Clatterfoot Common had been a shock. Miranda had been quick to point out how much she had always hated the country. 'You couldn't get away from Yorkshire soon enough – '

'I've matured, chickabid. I've formed new values, and towns hold nothing for me, these days.'

'You'll be bored stiff – '

'I won't, I won't! Not with you and Emrys.'

'But we want to be on our own!' Miranda blurted, red-faced. 'We've just got married and we want to live our own life – '

'Of course you do, chickabid. No one understands that more than I do, and believe me I wouldn't dream of intruding in any way. You won't even *see* me.'

'Yes, I will, every time I go in the garden I'll see your curtains hanging up – '

Tears misted Florence's eyes. 'I never thought you'd begrudge me even an old wash house to live in.'

'I don't begrudge you – I think it would be lovely for you to come and stay for holidays, but not to – '

'I don't think I can stand the bombing any more.' Florence broke down. 'All that crouching in the dark waiting to be killed. And the thought of dying all alone without you and Emrys – '

'You'd feel much happier if we died with you?'

'Oh, stop being so bloody *clever*, chickabid!' Florence dashed away her tears and snorted furiously into her handkerchief. 'All right, we'll say no more. I'll go back to London and I'll spend another winter without any windows. Bits of plywood stuck in will do fine. And just in case you're interested, I don't think I'll bother to go down to the shelter any more – after all, what's the point? With no one to live for, no one to care whether I'm alive or dead – '

'Oh, shut *up!*' bawled Miranda, shaking with remorseful fury and standing with her toes turned in. 'Go and live in the blasted wash house and much good may it do you!' She stumped off to break the news to Emrys.

'Look here, I'm awfully sorry but I'm afraid she's coming to live with us.'

'Who – the Mother Mild?'

'Yes. We shouldn't have mentioned the wash house even as a joke.'

'But my dear, she can't possibly live in a wash house.'

'You don't know my mother. She'd live in a piss pot if it meant being somewhere different.'

'Miranda dear, how coarse.'

'Yes, I know. Sorry. . . .'

There it was again, that word *sorry*. Damn Aunt Daisy and her outmoded good manners.

So the wash house was divested of spiders' webs, the walls replastered and a small modern wash basin installed to replace the old brownstone sink.

'But you mean there's no actual tap?' Florence's paean of praise faltered. 'So what do I do for – ?'

'Draw it from the well, same as us.'

'And what about – ?'

'There's a little wooden hut down the garden which it's time you were introduced to.'

'You don't mean it's back to one of those old – ?'

'Yes, I do,' Miranda said brutally. 'It's a bucket and chuck it.'

But even the prospect of an earth lavatory failed to daunt Florence for long, and she moved up from Maida Vale with her furniture crammed into the back of an odd-job man's Morris van.

'I've sold your bed, chickabid, and I've got rid of the wardrobe. This is Bert, who lives in Kilburn.'

Bert stayed the night, sleeping on a pile of spare blankets in the dining room of Trellis House, and next morning helped to unroll the carpet and to arrange Florence's furniture. He seemed in no hurry to return to London, and commiserated with Florence as they hung the blackout curtains.

'Expectin' a lady like you to live in a bloomin' outhouse and them with all them rooms to theirselves. . . . They're no better than Adolf Hitler the way they're treatin' you, madam.'

'I am a mother and a Christian,' Florence said, 'and I have learned to be grateful for small mercies.'

She had, however, already forsaken the Church of Rome, having found Father Phipps too unresponsive and the bowed meekness expected of her too much of a bore. She was able to acknowledge that flirtation with Fascism, via the sexiness of Rob Allardyce, had been a mistake, and that any attempt to embrace Roman Catholicism had been yet another slight error. She sometimes wondered whether she was too intelligent to embrace any of the faiths, creeds or beliefs that appeared to keep other people happy, but concluded that this could not be so. She had the native wit that had prompted her to leave home at an early age and to shift, however precariously, for herself, but when it came to the difficult and lasting choices she knew that she was fatally handicapped by the lack of knowing the right things.

Miranda knew them all of course because she had been to a good school. She had come home night after night with a satchel stuffed full of books that had explained to her everything she needed to know in order to become an educated woman. Florence had watched her sitting at the table in Morton Street while she pored over them all, had watched while all the wonderful facts and truths had been sucked up from the page by her darling eyes and stored away in her brain like a bee storing honey in a hive. Once or twice when Miranda was absent from the room Florence had glanced through some of her textbooks – Euclid, Froude, Lord Macaulay, Shakespeare – and had hurriedly retreated in the direction of Edgar Wallace. Obviously that type of book meant nothing unless taken in conjunction with a good school.

So at the moment of becoming installed in the wash house she was at an emotional loose end, and although partially aware that for her it was more important to be *seen* as a certain kind of person without necessarily bothering to *be* it, without an assumed role to play she felt vulnerable as a creature in a state of metamorphosis. Bert the handyman had unwittingly offered her the role of downtrodden mother-in-law, but she rejected it, sensing that it was one she would be unable to sustain for long without losing her temper.

Over tea and Spam sandwiches consumed in the privacy of the wash house she learned that Bert was a Labour man, and strong on working-class rights.

'If I was you, I'd get in there.' He indicated Trellis House with a jerk of the head. 'Take all your pots and pans and dump 'em down in their bloomin' hall. I'll help you stake your claim to what's right.'

'But I think I'm going to like it here,' Florence ventured, looking round. 'It's beginning to look rather sweet.'

'Whether you like it or not's got nothing to do with it, madam,' Bert explained patiently. 'It's what's right. What's fair.'

'But we can't expect life to be fair. We must be prepared to accept what we're given – '

'Bollocks! Beg pardon I'm sure, madam.' Hastily he clapped his Spam sandwich against his lips. 'I mean, that sort of attitude'll get you nowhere. In this world we have to fight for what's due to us – we have to band together.'

'Yes, I'm sure,' Florence said vaguely, and poured some more tea. 'I think I've got a little bit more sugar somewhere. . . .'

'I wouldn't take your sugar ration, madam, any more than I'd take your – ' Bert stopped, overcome, then shoved the sandwich into his mouth and chewed vigorously. 'Trouble is, I'll never get nowhere with you because you're a perishin' saint.'

'I had a go at being one once,' Florence said, 'but it didn't really work. I think I'm too impatient or something.'

'I wouldn't mind living here.' He gazed out of the window at the tangled garden. 'London's no place to be.'

'There's a row of dinky little cottages over on the Common. I think some of them are empty, but I haven't had time to explore much.'

'I wouldn't mind at all.'

'So that you could stir up all the farm labourers?'

'Oh no, madam – I'd be a sort of guest, wouldn't I?' Bert looked hurt. 'But if ever they wanted putting right about certain things . . .'

When the tea and sandwiches were finished he returned to painting the bookshelves he had made, and Florence trailed out to the well with the white enamel jug Miranda had bought for her in Sudbury. ('This,' Miranda had said, 'is for filling at the well with your *drinking* water, which you must boil, and this,' she indicated a sort of galvanised bowl with a handle on one side, 'is your pannikin. It's for dipping in the water butts for *washing* water.')

Bloody Miranda, thought Florence, panting with the effort of winding the bucket up from the well. She knows it bloody all, doesn't she, just because I sent her to a good school.

The sprinkling of ancient houses around Clatterfoot Common had all in their youth been connected with the great woollen cloth trade which had made that part of East Anglia rich during the fourteenth century. Soaring and grandiose churches still paid tribute to the wealth of pious wool merchants but the money had run out long ago, although in nearby villages the timbered houses, heavily carved and pargeted, still remained to tell the tale of past glory.

The Common itself had earned its name from the clatter of wooden looms coming from the weavers' cottages that stood in a row on the far side from Trellis House. A little to their right, and half-hidden in a belt of trees, stood the Overseer's House, gabled and jettied and with tall barleysugar chimneystacks. It had been empty for years and then at the outbreak of war pressed into service to shelter London evacuees.

The operation had not been a success; hurriedly swept and filled with a variety of furniture that was part government issue and part local jumble sale, the mothers of babies and small children who had been wrenched from the familiar back-to-backs of Stepney and Bethnal Green had been resentful tenants. It was cold and unfriendly, there was nowhere to go, nothing to do, and the deep silence of the country-side filled them with far greater fear than the Luftwaffe was able to impose. The weaker ones cried, and those of greater resource walked

125

the two and a half miles to the Bird in Hand and got resolutely drunk on brown ale.

They went back to London; some blatantly and furiously, while others stole quietly away, trundling prams filled with babies and suitcases the long lonely march back to the railway station.

By the summer of 1941 the Overseer's House was empty again, and exploring its sad shadows and bird-haunted garden Miranda suddenly said to Emrys, 'I'm going to persuade my friends the Ellenbergs to come and live here.'

'The parents of your friend the pianist?'

'Yes. They're the best friends I've ever had, with the exception of you.'

'Sorry I'm not much of the other, dear. Husband, I mean.'

'I've no complaints.' Fondly she touched his cheek, and then her thoughts went back to Nat. For Miranda, worry about her safety alternated with bouts of exasperation that she hadn't bothered to come home until it was too late. But the worst times were when the nightmare came back and the screaming face of Nat was superimposed upon that of little Rachel.

Like everyone else, she had read about the Nazi attitude towards the Jews and had seen the grainy black-and-white photographs of atrocities in *Picture Post*, but for her their impact was sharpened and made infinitely more terrible by the memory of Florence's boyfriend. As a schoolgirl she had been unwittingly exposed to the face of impersonal hatred, to the sense of watching an orderly and inexorable march towards violence and the death of everything precious. More than most people around her she was aware of the sense of remorselessness behind the German behaviour because she had seen it at first hand in the eyes of Rob Allardyce. It hadn't needed words or photographs.

Yet hope plus a slight sense of the ridiculous continued to prevail. In Suffolk the war against Hitler was still embodied in the Home Guard and the Women's Institute – home-made jam without sugar, knocking off airborne Jerries with grandad's sporting rifle; the sheer optimism of such crackpot notions was marvellously reaffirming. She tried hard to bury herself in the slow, good-natured busyness of rural England at war while Emrys made himself infusions of tea from strange-looking weeds dug up in the garden before trundling back to bed with a hot water bottle. Any hope that his numerous aches and pains would be cured by life in the country had long since faded although he still refused to bother with doctors. They decided not to attempt to open another antique shop until after the war.

126

Initially tempted to return to London like the evacuees, Florence had thought better of it and joined the ARP because the local branch happened to be an all-male affair. Twice a week she fire-watched on the church tower in company with the local butcher and Bert the odd-job man from Kilburn who now rented one of the weavers' cottages for ten shillings a week. She also learned to ride Miranda's bicycle, and one evening borrowed it and cycled all the way to the cinema in Sudbury with Bert – he being the only man available and his company endurable provided he didn't go on about politics.

The film had been about Ziegfeld Girls, a subject which would normally have absorbed all her attention, but she returned to the wash house thinking, in spite of herself, about Socialism, and buttonholed Miranda about it on the following day.

'Yes, I know it's dreadful they've been invaded, but it's the same for all the other countries in Europe.'

'No, chickabid, it isn't. All the capitalist countries were rotten to the core – that's why they gave in – but Russia's got so much to fight for. They all believe in something.'

'So do we.'

'What, for instance?'

'Well, Mr Churchill.'

'Churchill is a warmonger.'

'Good job somebody is, apart from the Jerries. I wonder how Rob Allardyce is, by the way.'

'You know perfectly well he's been interned under 18B, chickabid. Don't try to rile me.'

Miranda's letter to the Ellenbergs telling them about the Overseer's House included an invitation to stay for a few days at Trellis House, and they arrived at the little branch line that served Clatterfoot Common one sweet summer evening. The setting sun was flaring its last crimson rays over pastureland that had been hastily ploughed and set with corn at the instigation of the Ministry of Agriculture, and when the train had puffed away the air was full of late birdsong.

The two Ellenbergs were the only people to alight and they stood looking about them rather bemusedly.

'I've managed to get the local taxi,' Miranda said, gleefully embracing them. 'It's really wonderful to see you.'

Yet being with them again after a long absence made her feel curiously shy and robbed her of small talk; it was too soon to mention Nat, and they jogged across the Common in smiling silence.

Emrys greeted them cordially, hands outstretched and smiling broadly, and glancing round it suddenly occurred to Miranda that between them they had succeeded in making Trellis House very beautiful. The old cut-glass oil lamps made pools of soft light on choice pieces of furniture, and pale smoke drifted lazily from an applewood fire on the drawing-room hearth.

And she saw the Ellenbergs responding with gratitude. Seen outside their own particular setting they looked smaller, older and rather tired. Sympathetically she blamed the long wartime journey and the effects of the Liverpool blitz, in addition to worry about Nat and Sammy.

They were drinking sherry when Emrys suddenly put down his glass and hurried from the room, then returned a few minutes later with something held carefully in his cupped hands.

'I almost forgot – here's a present for you,' he said to Miranda, and the black kitten opened its small pink mouth in a silent miaow. She took it from him and held it rapturously against her cheek. The two Ellenbergs came close, Nat's father stroking the top of its head with his forefinger, and Miranda grinned across at Emrys as she remembered his remark about giving her a kitten instead of a baby. From his rueful smile she saw that he remembered too, and loved him for it.

They dined well that night on off-the-ration roast chicken and garden vegetables, and the kitten disposed of a morsel of chicken breast mashed up in gravy and then went to sleep on Emrys' lap. Drinking coffee round the dying fire Miranda heard herself say, 'I wish Nat was here.'

A small silence followed her words. She sensed rather than saw Mrs Ellenberg nodding her head as she gazed down at her folded hands.

'We believe that she will be here one day,' Mr Ellenberg said, and the constraint imposed by nervous sensitivity was broken. They talked about her openly and freely, laughing at old jokes, old incidents which they recounted to Emrys who smiled his wide froggy smile as if he too had known and loved Nat, and Miranda, between laughter and tears, thought fragmentarily that love of Nat was forging a new and unbreakable bond between them, and that the bond itself must surely in some way be helping Nat, wherever she was.

'She'll be back,' she said. 'She's got more zest for life than anyone else I know.'

There came a tap on the drawing-room door and Florence appeared, clad dramatically in trousers and tunic and steel helmet.

'Just popped in to say I'm off on duty.' She smiled round at the four of them. 'So sleep well, all of you.'

Emrys and the Ellenbergs rose politely to their feet.

'You remember my mother,' Miranda said. 'You met her at the concert.'

Greetings were exchanged, and Miranda was swift to recognise the role that Florence was playing. 'What's that thing stuck in your belt?'

'That? It's my hatchet.'

'What on earth do you want a hatchet for?'

'In case there's a fire, chickabid. All the seniors have been issued with them to break down doors and things.' Florence turned to the Ellenbergs. 'I live in the wash house, you know. It took a bit of getting used to, but I adore it now, and quite honestly I don't really care where I live so long as I'm near to my chickabid – and her darling husband.'

'You'd better hurry or you'll get a black mark for being late,' Miranda said, then thought, here I go again; why do I always sound like an elderly parent trying to deal with an irrepressible child?

'Yes, miss,' replied Florence, saluting, then winked at the two Ellenbergs. 'She's not bossy, she's just got my welfare at heart. I find it so touching, bless her.'

She departed, and Emrys kicked the last smouldering log into place and said, 'Ah well, we can all rest confident in the knowledge that my mother-in-law is keeping the enemy at bay from the church tower.' But there was affection in his voice; Emrys, thought Miranda, seems totally devoid of malice. I bet he'd ask Hitler in for a cup of tea, supposing he appeared.

Seen by daylight on the following morning the Ellenbergs' appearance endorsed Miranda's first impression. They were ageing; six years seemed, in her eyes, to have served them more like twenty-six. A little more hesitant in their movements, their old warmth and assurance had been tinged by a touch of nervousness, an apprehensiveness that she had never seen before. It filled her with rage.

But they were obviously enjoying themselves at Trellis House; the peace of the countryside was doing its healing work, and after they had explored the Overseer's House Mrs Ellenberg clasped her hands and said, 'Oh Bruno – please let's live here!'

Mr Ellenberg made no reply, but walked round again on his own. They heard his footsteps, slow and deliberate, pacing across the bare floors upstairs, then hesitating by a window, and glancing upwards from the hall Miranda saw him run his hand over the ancient newel post on the landing.

'He likes it,' Mrs Ellenberg whispered. 'He's just saying goodbye to the old way of life.'

'He's really retired now?'

'The clinic was bombed and I sometimes think he'll never recover from the shock of it. He still does a little consultancy work, but somehow. . . .'

'I know.'

'And we've still got some friends in Liverpool but the family's nearly all gone now. Most of the aunts and uncles have died – poor Aunt Gretel went in the big raid, you know – and with Nat away and Sammy married. . . .'

So Sammy was married. Presumably to the girl whose engagement ring he had shown her that day in the Coventry Street Corner House. She thought of him with affection, but nothing more. At least . . . . Resolutely she switched her mind to other things.

'Please come and live here,' she said. 'And be near us.'

They talked about it later, sitting in the garden at Trellis House while the kitten rushed through the long grass, hiding and pouncing with its tail fluffed up and its eyes wide with astonishment.

'It's idyllic,' Mr Ellenberg admitted, 'but there's a lot to think about, my dears. Perhaps I should get used to retirement in the place that I know, or on the other hand perhaps I should sever all connection with the old life with one quick – '

'Stroke of the scalpel?' Emrys captured the kitten and held it aloft.

'There is another reason for staying in Rodney Street. It's the first place that Nat will go to when she arrives.'

They fell silent. Emrys replaced the kitten on the grass at his feet, and, observing the spasm of pain that passed over his face, Miranda was unable to tell whether it was of a physical or an emotional nature. Nat was becoming a real person to him, too.

Lulled by the drowsy beauty of rural Suffolk the Ellenbergs extended their stay and the days passed serenely. They strolled on the Common where blackberries were beginning to form and families of rabbits played in the twilight, and Mrs Ellenberg saw a pair of wrynecks perched together in a tall tree. Impressed more by her excitement than its cause they offered their congratulations and she told them that the wryneck, a cousin of the woodpecker, was becoming increasingly rare.

'Like Jews,' Mr Ellenberg murmured.

But the war was far away, its voice only heard on the six o'clock news as the summer shadows lengthened and Miranda and Mrs Ellenberg prepared the evening meal. Even Florence's activities in the ARP seemed to be losing their sense of urgency and she often joined them in a mood of pleasant unassertiveness. Miranda concluded that she was between roles. Resting, as the theatrical profession called it.

But it had to end. And it did so, dramatically and disastrously on the evening Miranda came in from the garden with the news that the kitten had climbed the walnut tree and couldn't get down.

They all went outside and Miranda fetched the stepladder.

'No, let me – ' Emrys propped it securely and began to climb.

'Emrys, you can't – come down!' Miranda pulled at the back of his shirt.

He took no notice but continued to mount one step at a time towards the kitten, who was peering down at him and mewing distractedly. Mr Ellenberg steadied the ladder with both hands, laughing and chirruping encouragement.

'Emrys, *please* be careful. . . .'

He was on the last step from the top. Stretching up, he clasped the main branch above which the kitten was crouching and endeavoured to brace his knee against the top of the tree trunk. He hung there for a moment like an unwieldy sack while summoning the strength to reach the main fork which would give him a safe perch.

'Emrys. . . .'

'Kitty, come here – ' With a sudden violent effort he lunged upwards, and with a crack the branch that was supporting him gave way. Miranda and Mrs Ellenberg screamed, and Mr Ellenberg kicked away the ladder and held out his arms as Emrys plummeted heavily against him and crashed to the ground.

'Oh God, my back. . . .' He lay with his eyes closed.

Miranda flung herself on her knees beside him, distractedly smoothing his hair, then stopped as the hands of Mr Ellenberg took over. Speechlessly she watched them ripping Emrys' tie undone and pulling open his shirt, careless of buttons. He felt Emrys' heart, then laid his leonine grey head against the white skin.

'He's OK. Find something flat to carry him on.'

Instinctively Miranda and Mrs Ellenberg rose to their feet. Miranda began to run towards the house then veered abruptly towards the old barn that housed Emrys' laid-up car. Propped against the back wall was a door that had been taken from Florence's wash house. Panting, she and Mrs Ellenberg carried it back and the three of them lifted Emrys on to it. His eyes were still closed and he appeared to be unconscious.

It seemed a very long while before Mr Ellenberg rolled down his sleeves and said, 'Shock, bruises and strained muscles, but I hope that's all. Definitely no bones broken.'

'Then why's he still unconscious?'

131

'I did mention shock, and he's not a particularly fit man, is he?'

Emrys was put to bed, a procedure to which he acquiesced with grace, and Miranda relaxed sufficiently to take note of the change in Mr Ellenberg's demeanour. Previously she had only known him as the personification of jovial family man but now he had become transformed into doctor and expert. She felt calmed by his presence, and when the kitten – to whom they had given no further thought – strolled into the kitchen and demanded his supper she snatched him up in a surge of love and thankfulness. But later, when she took him up to the bedroom, Emrys merely opened tired eyes and then closed them again as if the little creature were of no importance.

That night she slept on the folding bed under the bedroom window, and when she took Emrys a cup of early morning tea he was awake and smiling at her.

'Was I a *total* nit, dear?'

'No, of course not.'

'My motives were of the purest, but alas. . . .'

'Are you feeling OK now? Think you can get up for breakfast?'

His expression changed, became hesitant and irresolute. 'Don't rush me. I think I'll stay here for a mite longer.'

Same old Emrys, she thought with a touch of impatience. Funny and sweet but fatally undermined by self-indulgence. 'OK,' she said. 'I'm going down to the village to collect the newspaper.'

She cycled off across the Common and when she returned he had fallen asleep again. She made him an omelette for lunch, and eating downstairs failed to stifle a remark about hypochondria.

'Who is your doctor?' Mr Ellenberg asked her.

'Well.' Miranda looked nonplussed. 'We haven't needed one since we've been here and I know Emrys isn't too keen on seeing them anyway, but I believe there's one down in the village. Do you think I should send for him?'

'Not at the moment,' he replied.

But by evening it appeared even to Miranda's untutored eye that Emrys was very ill. During the few hours since his fall from the tree he seemed to have dwindled physically. He lay immobile, except for the occasional restless tossing of his head on the pillow.

After spending half an hour alone with him, Mr Ellenberg came slowly downstairs and said, 'I think we must get him to hospital.'

'Is it some internal injury?' Miranda tried to keep the fear from her voice.

'Could be – I don't know.'

The ambulance arrived from Sudbury Hospital an hour later and Miranda and Mr Ellenberg travelled with him. Emrys seemed unaware of what was happening and Miranda held his hand and occasionally wiped his forehead with her handkerchief. Once or twice she glanced across at Mr Ellenberg, seeking the reassurance of a smile, but he was staring at the floor.

Emrys was put to bed in a small private room while Miranda sat outside in the corridor. The hospital was quiet except for the distant wail of a child, and she sat, arms folded, staring at a row of red fire-buckets filled with sand. He must have twisted something inside, she told herself. Perhaps they'll have to operate. . . . Perhaps Mr Ellenberg'll do it. She realised, not for the first time, that Emrys was very precious to her.

They allowed her to see him and he smiled at her drowsily. Mr Ellenberg and another man were standing by the bedside while a sister in a frilly cap stood nearby.

'He's going to be all right, isn't he?' She badly needed the reassurance.

Mr Ellenberg smiled and introduced her to the doctor, and the doctor said, 'Yes, yes of course, Mrs um Arundel.'

Nervous of hospital discipline and sensing that they wanted her to go, Miranda bent to kiss Emrys' forehead. He opened his eyes and smiled at her. 'Dear, what are we having for supper?'

'I've got four lovely fillets of plaice and I'll do them the way you like.'

'How wizard.' The youthful Air Force slang sounded quaint on his lips. 'Do save a nice little bit for the kitten, won't you?'

The hospital had arranged for a taxi to take them home. They left after Emrys had fallen asleep, and Miranda gazed across the darkened countryside to where a lone searchlight roamed the sky.

'But he really will be all right, won't he?' She was praying for reassurance.

'It might take a bit of time, but try not to worry.' He reached for her hand and pressed it and she suddenly thought of Nat; this was the hand that she must have held on so many occasions when she was a child.

'You mean a lot to me, Mr Ellenberg.'

'Try calling me Bruno.'

'Thank you. But I still tend to see you as a sort of – '

'Father-figure?' He chuckled. 'Don't worry, Nat used to address me as Bruno – but generally when she was cross with me.' Releasing her hand he groped in his pocket for change as the taxi bumped across the Common to Trellis House.

They didn't operate upon Emrys. They didn't seem to do anything, and once or twice a combination of fear and frustration caused Miranda to cry out that he would be better off at home.

But home was different now. Sinister with shadows and heavy with unexpressed fears, the long hours dragged. The Ellenbergs remained, for which she was numbly grateful, and even Florence was at her best. She was charming to the two guests and sent a saucy postcard and a bunch of flowers to Emrys, but on the morning that he died she had gone with Bert the ex-odd-job man to a talk on Advanced Fire Fighting.

Strangely enough it was the Ellenbergs who wept, and Miranda who remained stony-faced with shock. In the matron's room at the hospital Mr Ellenberg – Bruno as she tried to remember to call him – clasped her in his arms and rocked with her to and fro crying, 'Daughter – oh my daughter, daughter . . .' and through her own blankness she sensed the deeply buried anguish of an elderly man who had lost both his own girls; one at the beginning of her life and the other at the beginning of her career. She sensed too, in the wailing and rocking, a strange and foreign unashamedness in grief, an uninhibited display of natural feeling quite extraordinary in a man of his professional eminence, and blunderingly she tried to comfort him. The attempt made her own eyes mist, but nothing more.

Emrys was dead. Because of falling from the walnut tree. The fact was like a towering monument dwarfing her with its presence, and the more she tried to assimilate it, the greater the sense that the whole thing was some kind of crazy hoax. Trellis House was still as filled with his presence as it was with his fine furniture and charming bibelots. Sunlight falling across an inlaid table, violet evening shadows dusting a yellow velvet chair, the ting of a French clock . . . all these things spoke of his charm, his gentleness, his funny froggy smile.

The day she finally broke down and wept uncontrollably was the day when she suddenly seized the kitten by the scruff of its neck and said that it was to be put down. It had been the cause of Emrys' death and therefore had no right to live.

'Spare it,' Bruno said. 'He was merely hastening the inevitable.'

'Meaning?' She held the twisting kitten fiercely aloft, glad when it scratched her.

'Emrys was suffering from inoperable cancer. He had only a very short time to live.'

Miranda closed her eyes, then steadied the kitten's gyrations with her other hand. 'Did he know?'

'I think so.'

'I thought he just had trouble with his kidneys.'

'That as well.'

There was nothing more to ask; nothing more to say. She wept, and moved through the following four days with red eyes and quivering chin. Esme Ellenberg took over the cooking and the running of the house, and the small village funeral was only bearable because Miranda was able to concentrate on her feeling of irritation with Florence.

Despite the warmth of the weather and the country simplicity of the interment Florence had put on her black suit, black hat with the eyeveil, and had even resurrected Old Fido, the silver fox. Teetering into the church on her high heels she sobbed loudly and convulsively into a handkerchief hastily concocted from a square of blackout material, and Miranda heard awestruck whispers from casual observers standing by the lych gate.

'That must be 'is widow, pore soul.'

'Reckon so. Lonnon folk from up the Common.'

Florence continued to sob throughout the service and Miranda nudged her fiercely to shut up.

'I *loved* him, chickabid. . . .'

'Sshhh. So did I.'

'How he must have suffered. . . .'

'For God's *sake!*'

'The days of our age are threescore years and ten,' intoned the clergyman. 'Yet is their strength then but labour and sorrow; so soon it passeth away, and we are gone. . . .'

'No need to rub it in.' Florence dabbed at her eyes. 'How old *was* Emrys, by the way?'

'Forty-eight. Now shut up.'

After seeing the coffin lowered into the grave and the first ceremonial handfuls of earth sprinkled upon it they returned to Trellis House and made a pot of tea, which no one drank. Florence departed for the wash house saying that Miranda wasn't the only one to feel bereaved, but half an hour later she was back with a bottle of Odds On Cocktail tucked under her arm.

The taste was awful; sweet and sticky and with a slight hint of floor polish; yet strangely enough it proved far more efficacious than tea. All four of them downed the first one quickly, and made no objections

135

when Florence refilled their glasses. She had not yet divested herself of Old Fido, whose tail swung busily as she moved.

'It grows on you,' Miranda admitted, sipping. 'Where on earth did you get it from?'

'Aha.' Florence winked through her veiling. 'Let's just say that the ARP runs on it.'

'Then God help us all.'

'Don't blaspheme, chickabid, particularly today.' She turned to the Ellenbergs, one hand on her hip and the bottle held aloft. 'Isn't she naughty?'

'Depends on your yardstick,' Bruno said.

'I don't think I've got one,' she simpered roguishly.

But the clouds of sadness were dissolving. Perhaps they were all four willing the bottle of ready-mixed cocktail to perform its task of allevi-ation, of painting over the loss of Emrys with its temporary balm, and when Florence asked Esme whether Jews buried their dead, Esme smiled at her and said, 'No. We store them in the Frigidaire.'

The kitten came in and Florence whisked it up and held it close, and roared with laughter when it spat violently into the face of Old Fido.

'There was a time,' Miranda recalled sentimentally, 'when that thing was like a brother to me. I used to look into its little eyes and imagine I could see the flickering of a kindred spirit. I was a very lonely child.'

'Nonsense, chickabid. You had me.'

'Some of the time.'

'All the best children are brought up by nannies,' Florence declared, launching into fantasy. 'Look at our two little princesses.'

'I was brought up mainly by Aunt Daisy and – '

'Aunt Daisy was a nanny before she married. She was with the de Bone family.'

'The de Bones?' Bruno repeated. 'I knew old Judge de Bone quite well at one time.'

Florence proffered a little more Odds On. 'My husband was at Oxford with one of the sons. Afterwards they both went into the Guards – the Blues, you know.'

'My father . . .' began Miranda, then fell silent. Nothing felt real any more. Tomorrow I will grieve, she thought – the truth about Emrys will become unbearable – but for the rest of today I'll take refuge in Florence's fibs. It can't do any harm.

'. . . and I pray for your daughter's return. I'm a lapsed Catholic, by the way,' she heard her mother say, 'but I dream about her every night

136

and a little voice tells me that she's being taken care of – ' Then she gave a sudden yelp and sprang to her feet. 'Jesus, I'm supposed to be on duty.'

Silence fell as she scuttled from the room. They heard the kitchen door bang and then the patter of her feet as she hurried back to the wash house.

Suddenly aware that it was a long while since they had eaten, Miranda went out to the kitchen and made some lettuce-and-tomato sandwiches, lacing the tasteless margarine with home-made chutney. She found a bottle of Emrys' favourite Puligny-Montrachet and took it back to the drawing room with three glasses and a corkscrew.

'He'd want us to drink it tonight,' she said. Then added, 'I wish I believed in heaven.'

'Nothing to stop us trying.' Bruno pulled the cork and held it to his nose for a moment.

Quietly and lovingly, they drank a toast to Emrys, the two Ellenbergs sitting in easy chairs and Miranda on a low stool between them. And as daylight drained from the room and mulberry-dark shadows stole into the corners it became suddenly easy, after the day's events, to speak of matters previously prohibited by constrained good manners. The past became the present.

'When I told you that what happened to Rachel was my fault because I'd been pushing the pram and forgot to put the brake on outside the sweetshop, you tried to help me by taking the blame. You told me that you'd forgotten to have the brake mended, and although I pretended to believe you, I didn't really because I knew that there was nothing wrong with it.'

Esme began to speak, but Miranda hurried on. 'The only thing I'll ever believe in is your kindness, your sort of unthinking goodness that I'd never known anywhere except in your house. But it *was* my fault, Rachel dying, and sometimes I feel that if you'd both blame me as I deserve – be really bitter and awful about it, I mean – it'd stop the nightmares I still have. I keep hearing and seeing it all over again, and I wake up thinking if there's nothing I can do to bring her back I'd better die too. It'd just be sort of tidier and more satisfactory somehow. It was much better when I had Emrys – I used to frighten the life out of him sometimes, but he was so patient and understanding once I'd told him about what happened. He used to get up and make a cup of tea and talk to me until I could go to sleep again. But now I've got the added awfulness of knowing that I've let him down, too.'

'In what way?' Bruno's face was in shadow.

'I didn't know he was dying.'

'Only because he didn't tell you.'

'But *why* didn't he? It must have been because he decided that I wasn't capable of dealing with it. Like you felt I wasn't about Rachel.'

'You were a child,' Esme said.

'So you do admit now that – '

'I admit nothing, dear Miranda.' She leaned forward and touched Miranda's hair.

Silence fell. Miranda took a sip of wine and swallowed it slowly, willing its fragrance to overcome the heavy fumes of Odds On.

'But ever since I've known him he's never even seen a doctor!' Her thoughts returned to Emrys. 'Only ever taken aspirins and gone off to bed with a hot water bottle, and there was me as good as telling him that he was a hypochondriac.' Sniffing, she helped herself to a sandwich.

'People need to make their own decisions,' Bruno said. 'Once Emrys had learned the truth he decided to ignore it, that's all.'

'I don't know how I'm going to fill in the days now.'

'One thing you could do is to help us with the removal.'

Both women looked at him sharply and Esme clasped her hands. 'We're not by any chance moving to the Overseer's House?'

'It mightn't be a bad idea.'

'But what about Nat?' Miranda stifled a surge of joy.

'We'll leave a note on the door in Rodney Street.' And his words, spoken so lightly, were a first salutary lesson in the art of dealing with grief.

THREE

America had joined the war on the day after the Japanese bombing of Pearl Harbor, and Hitler had invaded Russia. In the Middle East the British Eighth Army was fighting both Italians and Germans while the Japanese overran Singapore and Burma. During the first half of 1942 any hope of an Allied victory seemed remote, and while huge armies struggled to gain ascendancy the people of occupied Europe were left with two main priorities: how to stay out of trouble and how to keep starvation at bay.

In the Paris attic Raoul and Nat were doing the same as everyone else; he still worked long hours in the café, and because of the increasing scarcity of food was finally forced to allow Nat to queue for unrationed vegetables in the street markets. It felt marvellous to be outside again; the fresh air was intoxicating and she clenched her hands and breathed deeply.

But there was a difference. Even during the first year of occupation there had still been something of the old Parisian *élan*, but the faces in the streets were different now. No one looked at anyone else any more, clothes were shabby and eyes haunted. She became aware of a new and sinister element, and despite the sudden surge of high spirits she was always relieved to regain the sanctuary of the attic.

Which is stupid, she told herself afterwards, but I suppose it's natural after being shut up indoors for so long.

Raoul agreed that that must be the reason, and bestowed extravagant praise upon the six potatoes and the handful of carrots she had managed to buy. There seemed no point in telling her of his unsuccessful attempts to provide her with a forged identity card through a contact given him by one of the other waiters. He had met the man, had gone to him with the money in his pocket, but at the last minute had mumbled an excuse and hurried away. Perhaps he had been a coward not to trust him, but he found it impossible not to be a coward on behalf of Nat. He loved her too much, and there was too much at stake. All he could do was to reintroduce his rule forbidding her to leave the attic, which she appeared to accept with docility.

If only they could be married she would become a French national, but it was impossible to marry without first producing her French identity card. He tried to reopen negotiations with the forger and discovered with a shiver of apprehension that he had been arrested by the Gestapo.

The sense of an invisible net slowly closing round them was heightened by the increased café gossip about the deportation of Jews. Synagogues had already been burned down, and during the previous autumn an anti-Jewish exhibition which had been opened in the Palais Berlitz was said to have attracted almost a million visitors. Jews and Communists were becoming increasingly linked in the public mind as the twin perpetrators of all evil, and the German SS had already been briefed by Heydrich on plans for the Final Solution.

Deeply worried and trying not to show it, Raoul again suggested that Nat should consider dyeing her hair. Again she refused, and two evenings later greeted his arrival home by indicating a small, brown-paper-wrapped package lying on the table.

'I've had a present.'

He opened it and drew out a six-pointed yellow star with the word *Juif* in the centre of it.

'Where did this come from?'

'Someone knocked on the door but when I opened it they'd gone. I just heard the sound of feet running downstairs and found it on the doormat.' She looked very pale but her voice was steady.

'The concierge will know.'

'I tried to ask her. She pretended not to understand.'

'What about that *rosse* downstairs – Madame Boudot?'

'She's not a *rosse*, she's a friend. And God knows I don't see much of her.'

'God also knows that you can't trust anyone these days. My dear, stupid bloke, this is not your kind and gentle Liverpool.'

'Liverpool's hardly kind and gentle – '

'Liverpool is not under occupation!'

Stifling a childish urge to reply that Liverpudlians would never allow anyone to occupy them, she picked up the yellow star – the Star of David – and held it against her breast. 'So where is it supposed to go, exactly? Which side?'

'I don't know. I don't suppose it matters.'

'Ah, but it does. With their mania for accuracy I bet the krauts have passed a decree saying that it must be worn so many millimetres above or below the left or right atrium. The most important thing in this life is exactitude. I learned it in music and I'm learning it all over again under the Third Reich. Kill a Jew a day – it doesn't matter whether it's a good Jew or a bad Jew or whether it's never entered a synagogue in its life – ' She burst noisily into tears. 'The only thing I keep trying to make clear to anyone who'll listen is that I'm not a Jew except in some kind of old biblical or racial sense. I don't support any of the dogma, I don't even know what it is because my parents aren't interested either. They're happy enough just to be *people* – '

'I worry because I love you so.' He put his arms round her, trying to stifle her wild sobs.

'Perhaps you'd better stop. Perhaps being a Jew, however reluctant, is infectious. . . .'

'I love you, my dear crazy own bloke. I love you. . . .'

'I love you too.' She grew calmer, then raised her head and looked at him. 'Do you think we'll still argue and get cross in peacetime?'

'We'll try it and see, won't we?'

She made no reply.

'*Won't we?*'

'Yes, of course we will.'

She made no attempt to sew the yellow star on to her coat, but neither did she put it away out of sight. Instead she left it in the middle of the table like a doyly, and occasionally stood the coffee pot on it.

Although the months of summer precluded any need to go to bed to keep warm, she spent an increasing number of hours each day lounging listlessly, dreamily, on the Tante Honorine. She watched the pigeons strutting on the roofs opposite; watched the opening and closing of shutters and the twitch of net curtains while her fingers drummed endless scales and arpeggios on the rumpled quilt.

Madame Boudot called to see her occasionally, and it was impossible to tell whether her swift darting glances round the attic were caused by shy constraint or by something of a more sinister nature. Possessed of the gregarious Ellenberg character Nat always felt a lift of the heart whenever she appeared, but the stilted conversation born of nervous mistrust soon bored her and she longed for solitude again.

The 7th of July was Raoul's birthday, his twenty-third, and she spent days trying to devise a means of celebrating it. Every way she thought of involved firstly going out, and secondly spending money. She now had two francs of her own money left, which was not a great deal but if spent wisely might be capable of bringing him a little fleeting pleasure. In terms of worldly goods he was not exactly over-indulged.

Clothes were out of the question; in any case he appeared to care for them as little as she did. Gramophone records, like gramophone needles, were scarcer than hens' teeth, and extra food and wine were equally elusive. In any case, she wanted to give him something in which she would take no share.

It was Madame Boudot who solved the problem.

'Does Monsieur smoke cigarettes?'

'He did, until they disappeared like everything else.'

'Go to the Place Maubert – I will explain how to get there – for that is the place for black-market cigarettes. They are not always first-class tobacco, you understand, but they are better than nothing. A poor young man who works so hard deserves to have a little smoke every now and then.'

It seemed a good idea, and on the morning of the 6th she suppressed all qualms and set off directly Raoul had left for the café.

She found the locality without difficulty, and having expected to queue long and patiently for packets of Gauloises was appalled to discover that trading was mainly in discarded cigarette butts. She couldn't bring herself to touch them, and was about to turn away when an old man in a greasy jacket and a beret tapped the side of his nose with his forefinger and whispered, '*Attendez, Mademoiselle.*'

He disappeared behind a group of gesticulating men, and waiting for him to return she became aware of a heightened sense of unease. Turning, she saw two gendarmes watching her. Trying to remain calm and unconcerned she began to move away, then a voice said, '*Pardonnez-moi, Mademoiselle, puis-je voir votre carte d'identité?*'

'*Je m'excuse, mais c'est chez moi,*' she stammered.

'*Alors, je dois vous demander votre adresse.*' He spoke politely, but his expression was obdurate.

She told him her name, and after toying fleetingly with an imaginary address, gave him the correct one. They both continued to stare at her, then slowly walked away. Automatically Nat began to hurry off in the opposite direction and jumped violently when the old man in the beret touched her shoulder. He handed her four cigarettes, wrinkled and hand-rolled, but at least they were complete, and she dropped the two francs into his hand without any idea whether the sum was too large or too small.

It was a beautiful morning of serene gold but she was in no mood to enjoy it. She hurried home without glancing at anyone, oblivious even of fellow Jews wearing the prescribed yellow star on their coats.

And the attic was safety, was home, was sanctuary. She closed the door behind her and leaned against it, trying to brush away the apprehension and fear. Perhaps it would be all right. Perhaps most ordinary people when challenged would find that they had left their identity card at home, and perhaps most police were too preoccupied with other things to pursue the matter further. Anyway, there was nothing she could do now but hope for the best. The one thing she had no intention of doing was telling Raoul; with his capacity for worrying she would never hear the end of it.

But his birthday supper was a feast. He had filched two slices of cold pork from the café and had managed to buy a lettuce and some tomatoes on the way home. They still had a scraping of butter left for the bread roll they shared between them, and when Raoul leaned back in his chair and lit a cigarette which crackled like an autumn bonfire, it was the peaceful contentment that can sometimes exist between an old married pair.

They played a couple of Django Reinhardt's lazy jazz records and then the old favourite 'J'attendrai', listening as the words fell softly and sadly in the big attic where summer shadows were gathering.

He was tempted to break the now unspoken taboo; to talk about plans for the future because the future suddenly seemed very near. The first twenty-two years of his life had passed so fleetingly, with one day, one year, melting smoothly into the next, that he knew the war was bound to end very soon. It would end as suddenly as it had begun and then there would be no more danger and no more fear.

'The cigarettes are magnificent,' he told her, instead. 'But please, my bloke, don't go out into the streets again.'

'OK.'

'The risk is too great and there is only a little time to wait in patience now.'

'You really think so?' She wanted to believe him, but found it difficult.

'Of course, of *course*.' He smoked the cigarette down to a thin little rim of charred paper then deposited the final remains in the ashtray. He looked speculatively at the remaining three, then carefully replaced them in their wrapper. 'One for the next three days. After that, who knows?'

They played the Tino Rossi record once more, ignoring the blunt needle hiss, and she fell asleep with her cheek against his bare shoulder, thinking, they won't bother to check up on one solitary identity card, will they? They must have far more important things to do.

But they came three days later. Gendarmes again, but a different pair, and the younger one who had a narrow black moustache asked if she were Mademoiselle Natalie Ellenberg.

143

She said yes she was, standing by the table where a pot of red berberis twigs from the courtyard was standing on the yellow star.

Holding his hand out he asked to see her identity card, while his companion, older and shorter, stood by the door as if on guard.

She had tried to plan for this moment, had visualised it and cast about for a plausible explanation, but still had nothing to offer. She could think of no lies or excuses that would stand a chance.

'I'm sorry, I haven't got one.'

'May I ask what happened to it, Mademoiselle?'

'Nothing happened to it because I never had one.'

The gendarme by the door shifted from one foot to the other and his boots creaked.

'I think perhaps that Mademoiselle is not a French citizen?' pursued the younger one, his manner polite and his face expressionless.

'I'm English.' There was no point in saying otherwise.

'Perhaps you are unaware that you should have registered as an enemy alien at the time of the Occupation?'

'I may be an enemy of the Germans but I didn't realise that the same thing applied to the French. I'd always thought we were on the same side.'

'Times change, Mademoiselle,' he said dryly. 'So I must ask that you accompany us to the Mairie for further questioning.'

'OK.' She tried to speak lightly. 'Shall I need a coat?'

'It would be advisable to pack a valise, Mademoiselle. We will wait while you do so.'

J'attendrai ... le jour et la nuit j'attendrai toujours .... The words of the song floated in her mind as she got out the suitcase with which she had arrived. Her old student scores of Beethoven and Mozart sonatas still lay in the bottom and she packed her clothes carefully on top. They were very shabby now and her shoes were down at heel. She took her nightgown from beneath the pillow, reassembled the contents of her sponge bag and removed the clean underwear hanging to air over the stove. Finally she latched the case.

They watched without speaking while she took down her coat and then said, 'May I leave a note?'

'With whom do you share the apartment, Mademoiselle?'

'With no one,' she said quickly. 'I was just thinking of the cleaning woman, but it doesn't matter.'

She stood by the door, suitcase in hand and with the coat over her shoulder while she looked round the attic for the last time. She knew that it was for the last time; and so did they, because they didn't hurry her.

She drove off to the Mairie comforted by the fact that Raoul had one last cigarette for when he came home and found her gone.

Upon arrival she was conducted to a waiting room and left there for two hours on her own. It was a small room with a bare wooden floor and grubby walls, and a window that refused to open. She sat on a hard chair opposite the door, trying not to speculate about the future and listening to the quarter-hours struck by a nearby church clock. She walked up and down; from the window to the opposite wall was fourteen paces, twenty-four if she placed one foot directly in front of the other. . . . She sat down again and did finger exercises on her knee, then placed the chair in a corner and sat leaning against the wall. She dozed, trying not to think of Raoul.

At last they came to fetch her. Another gendarme led her up a flight of stairs and she followed, the suitcase banging against her leg. She was shown into an office where a German officer sat at a desk, writing. He continued to do so for several minutes while Nat remained standing. Then he glanced up at her, pen poised, and asked her name. He spoke French with a heavy accent.

'Natalie Ellenberg.'

'You are not French?'

'No. English.'

'Were you not aware that all aliens had to register immediately France came under the protection of the Third German Reich?'

'No, not really.' The indifference in her voice was at odds with the heavy pounding of her heart.

'Who was sheltering you?'

'No one.'

'You were living with someone.'

'No. I lived alone.' A useless lie, when all they had to do was return to the attic to find Raoul, even if the two gendarmes had ignored signs of his occupation in the first place. But the lie made her feel better.

'How did you eat, without a ration card?'

'I have a very small appetite, and live mainly on vegetables.'

He put down his pen and folded his arms on the desk. He had little grey eyes and very short hair, and despite the warmth of the room his tunic was buttoned to the neck.

'Why were you living in France?'

'Because I was a music student. And I stayed on after war was

145

declared because I was due to give a recital that would have been important to my career.'

'And our arrival spoilt it for you.' He gave her a small sarcastic smile. 'Please accept my apologies.'

'I don't need them. I discovered that the two guests of honour had already run away.'

He sat looking at her in silence, the smile extinguished. He took up a pen. 'What is your religion?'

'I have none.'

'I feel sure you were born of a certain – persuasion?'

'In that sense, yes. I'm a Jew.'

Perhaps because she was tired and hungry she couldn't be bothered to lie; or perhaps in spite of Raoul's warnings to the contrary she still believed that only self-confessed Orthodox Jews were the subject of Nazi persecution. The third possibility was the normal human response of, this may happen to others but it will never happen to me.

She realised that he was speaking again. '. . . to an internment camp for the time being while your case is being considered. . . .' He stood up, indicating that the interrogation was at an end, then suddenly asked, 'Were you training to be a singer or an instrumentalist?'

'I was studying piano.'

'Pity.' The small sarcastic smile flashed again briefly. 'Personally, I prefer the harp.'

'I see no point in studying for an afterlife in which I don't believe.'

'You must believe in something.' For a split second he looked nonplussed. 'Everyone does.'

'I believe in myself,' Nat said, and picking up her suitcase followed the gendarme from the room.

She was driven in the same small Citroën van to the Paris suburb of Saint-Denis, and peering through the window caught her first glimpse of a barbed-wire fence. Dry-mouthed and suddenly longing for Raoul's protection she endured the arrival procedure of further questioning, of being searched for hidden offensive weapons and of having her head perfunctorily checked for lice. The ritual was carried out by large and bellicose women wearing some kind of uniform.

She was then led away and eventually shown into what at first sight seemed to be a large hospital ward filled with narrow iron beds down either side and a long wooden table and matching chairs in the centre. A second dazed glance showed that the room was occupied by women of varying ages, some lounging on their beds, some sitting at the table; one or two of them were busily knitting.

146

'Good evening,' said a cultured voice. 'I take it that you are English?'

After the long strain of the preceding days it was difficult to suppress a sudden rush of tears. She managed to do so by looking round again, and with a touch of the old derisive humour thinking, so there really is some corner of a foreign field that is forever England. . . .

Saint-Denis was the internment camp set up during the early days of the Occupation for British subjects who, like herself, had left the return to their own country too late. There was a young woman with two small children, a couple of girls who had been dancers at the Moulin de la Galette, three Irish nuns, and a bevy of elderly ladies dressed mostly in hand-knitted grey who had been either nannies or governesses. Looking at some of the more elderly, Nat wondered whether they, like poor Maurice, had been callously left behind in the initial stampede.

The woman who introduced herself was Mrs Gaston-Haigh, the wife of a British Embassy official, who some two years ago had hurried back from Deauville to Paris intent upon retrieving some of her country's silver and porcelain rather than let it fall into enemy hands. She had been too late; she was now incarcerated in Saint-Denis, and the British Embassy had become a furniture depository to be plundered at the invaders' leisure.

Still remaining the courteous hostess in a world temporarily deprived of its sanity, she showed Nat to the one vacant bed and asked whether she had her own supply of toilet things. ('I'm afraid that soap is in rather short supply now. . . .') then gave her a briefing on the general routine.

'Reveille at six I'm afraid, bread and margarine and weak so-called coffee in a *mug* of all things, then tidy our bedspaces and wash our smalls as best we can – we take turns with the washing line and of course there's no iron – in other words we try to keep ourselves sensibly occupied between breakfast and luncheon, luncheon and supper. We're a mixed bunch, but we get along very well considering. . . . Then lights out at nine. The people in charge of us are German women of the servant class called *fridolines*, which apparently is German for auxiliaries. They can be surly and somewhat spiteful, but seem to respond best if you stand no nonsense. Use simple words and enunciate clearly, is my motto. Presumably we shall all be shut up here for the duration – two years almost gone by, and how many more to go, I ask myself – but it's up to each one of us to show tolerance and good humour and *esprit de corps*. We have two packs of playing cards, one jigsaw puzzle and a variety of books, some of a religious nature' – she glanced significantly in the direction of the three nuns – 'and now and again we are issued with a Red Cross parcel.'

Providentially Nat was in time for the supper which was slapped down in silence by one of the uniformed *fridolines*, and she gulped her portion of thin vegetable soup without bothering to savour the taste. Her piece of bread was hard and dry, and when the thin little lady sitting next to her covertly offered her own untouched slice, she refused.

'You need more food at your age, my dear.'

'Thanks, but I've had more than enough.' She was still ravenous.

She slept badly. The bed was hard and chill after the sensuous comfort of Tante Honorine and she tried to banish the memory of Raoul's lovemaking; the scent of his hair, the flicker of his eyelashes against her cheek, the whispered words as their arms tightened about one another. . . . But perhaps the war would be over sooner than anyone realised; perhaps against all hope someone would assassinate Hitler, and the German race would come to its senses. They couldn't all be permanently insane.

Snores, and the little cries of women frightened by their dreams, constantly jerked her back to consciousness, but she was sound asleep and curled in a tight defensive shape when someone shook her and said, 'Come along, dear, you must wake up – it's roll call.'

My first day in captivity as a wholehearted Englishwoman and a reluctant Jew, she thought as she stumbled into her clothes. But in terms of a straightforward category, what am I? I'm a musician, and I must hold on to that.

Almost before he opened the door Raoul sensed that she was no longer there. The big attic was more than silent and shadowy; it held a sense of loss.

He stood on the threshold listening intently because once in the early days of their love she had hidden in the clothes cupboard, one knee balanced on the tin of hoarded rice and noodles, and then jumped out, wild black curls bouncing and face alight with a child's glee. But he knew without going to look that she was not hiding in the cupboard now. There was no sense of expectancy, no suppressed snort of laughter. Only a heavy evening silence that told of her absence.

Limping across to the bed he saw that her nightgown had gone. So had her clean underwear that he remembered seeing airing above the stove. Her coat had gone, so had her shoes, and the suitcase with which she had arrived.

'Bloke!' he called sharply. 'Where are you, my bloke?' His voice seemed to shatter the silence and his panic rose. In an agony of fear he hauled the covers from the Tante Honorine, snatched at the pillows and threw them on the floor. With a child's lack of proportion he looked in drawers and behind the door and under the table.

He called her again, then wrenched open the door and hobbled downstairs. Madame Boudot had been sewing buttons on a blouse, and she opened the door to him still wearing her thimble. She cried out when he seized her arm. 'Where is she? What happened?'

'To Mademoiselle? *Ai-eee*!' She gave a cry of pain and tried to wrench herself free. 'I don't know, is she not with you upstairs?'

'You know perfectly well she is not because you watched them take her away. You denounced her.' He grabbed her other arm and shook her violently. Her thimble fell off and rolled under the chair.

'I have done no such thing! I beg you, Monsieur, she is my friend so why should I do that?'

'I don't know – because you are jealous or because you are paid money by the Germans to denounce people – '

'Lies! Wicked lies!' Her spectacles glittered and shivered as he held her roughly, and when abruptly he let go of her she almost fell.

'Where is she? What have they done with her?'

'I don't *know*!' she screamed back at him, now equally distraught. 'I haven't seen her for four days and this afternoon I was out visiting a friend – '

He left her, knocking over her workbox and banging the door behind him. He went down to the ground floor only to discover that the old concierge had seen nothing either. In these days of uncertainty and terror, the less one saw the better. Limping hurriedly through the archway he went out into the street. It was already curfew and the only living creature out was a striped cat prowling the gutter in search of food.

He returned, looked up at the silent shuttered windows of the other apartments, and was furiously aware that many pairs of eyes, other than those of the concierge, must have watched discreetly as she was taken away. He drew a deep breath in preparation for bellowing insults or pleas for help, whichever fell out of him first, then turned away without uttering a sound.

He turned on the light in the attic. The place was cold and cavernous without her presence. He began to search calmly and painstakingly for a scribbled note, for anything, however small, that could be construed as a message. The only thing that remained of her was the six-pointed star lying like a nice little mat on the table beneath the pot of berberis leaves. How like the bloke to put the emblem of terror to such airy and inconsequent use.

He removed it from beneath the pot and sat with it on his knee. It was approximately the same size as the palm of his hand. Tracing the word *Juif* in the centre he became increasingly certain that whoever had left it outside the door had denounced her. It was one and the same person. His rage rekindled and he rose from the chair, intent upon returning to Madame Boudot's apartment and confronting her with it. Or beating her stupid face with it – or cramming it into her stupid mouth and forcing her to eat it.

The rage left him. He went to the stove and made a jug of coffee, and the bitter ersatz taste matched the bitterness in his soul. But perhaps the moment of greatest desolation came with the sudden thought that perhaps she had not been arrested, but had merely left him of her own accord.

For what had he been able to offer her? A life of poverty and near imprisonment; long hours of solitude, and constant nagging about the risk of going out, of making friends. He had even condemned the pathetic little friendship with the poor old *rosse* downstairs. What had he done to her? In his jealous efforts to provide and protect he had diminished the life of a lovely, lively and highly intelligent woman to that of a bird in a cage. With closed eyes he remembered the restless drumming of her fingers – those small, strong, pale fingers, each one of which seemed to have an independent life of its own. With her hand lightly cupped on the table she could raise each finger high in turn and drum it with woodpecker speed. (He had once tried to do the same and had found it all but impossible to raise his fourth and fifth fingers on their own, and she had laughed gleefully, delightedly. . . .)

He also remembered her reaction to his club foot. In the time of sleeping in the little bed beside the gramophone he had always been careful to remove the surgical boot last of all, and to put it on again first thing in the morning. But on their first night together she had deliberately sought his foot, capturing it between her own small, warm feet and rubbing it in a breezy, friendly way as if to say, it doesn't matter, it's of no importance. And in the morning she had insisted upon seeing it and he had finally allowed her to because her father was a doctor and because she had said that she loved him.

He had never been loved before, and neither had he loved. As a child, no adult, as an adult no man, woman or child. He had even to begin with regarded the poor lost bastard of a dog Maurice with antipathy.

Sitting with the yellow Star of David on his knee he endeavoured to trace the memory of his feelings on the night he invited her to shelter with him; the night the Germans arrived. Pity? No. Not even sympathy. Curiosity maybe, boredom certainly, but the main purpose had undoubtedly been that of seduction. After all, everyone had to start some time and he had already left it later than most. He had thought her a reasonably attractive proposition (apart from the dog), and had imagined that once in the sanctuary of the attic the rest would follow naturally.

It hadn't, because he had been unprepared for what had happened, or rather, for what had not happened. Perhaps he should have seduced her immediately and provided her with supper afterwards. As it was, he had given himself time to consider her as a person, a character in her own right, and not merely as the physical means of transforming his status from that of boy into man. He had made the mistake of liking her, and then the further mistake of not noticing as liking turned into love. And now he was bound to her indissolubly – this Englishwoman, this Jew, whom he had tried so hard to shield from the escalating barbarity outside.

So far as he knew she had heard no whisper of the coming *Grande Rafle*, the mass round-up and deportation of Jews to Eastern Europe. He himself had learned of it in *Au Pilori*, the French version of the savagely anti-Semitic German paper *Der Sturmer*, which was read openly and eagerly in the café in which he worked. He had seen the photograph of the man who was to be in charge of the operation – SS Hauptsturmführer Theo Dannecker, the dashing young protégé of Heydrich and Himmler – and had kept his worries to himself.

Perhaps he should have been more forthright; should have brought home copies of *Au Pilori* for her to read, and stood over her while she did so. Then maybe she would have stifled her boredom with him and his attic and realised her good fortune. . . .

He drank the last of the coffee then replaced the tumbled bedclothes on the Tante Honorine and smoothed them into some semblance of order. He replaced the yellow star under the pot of twigs where she had left it, and went to bed without bothering to undress. Lying in the silvery summer dark the bloke seemed very near to him and he knew that she had not left him of her own accord. She had been arrested, but her magic was such that she would find her way back to him.

He made no attempt to go to work on the following day, or on the day after that; he went only to the local *boulangerie* for his ration of bread and then continued to sit in silence on a chair by the attic window, waiting for her to return.

151

On the fourth day Madame Boudot knocked timidly at the door and asked if Mademoiselle had come back. No, he said, not yet. She hesitated by the door, then, emboldened by his mildness of manner, asked if she could do anything to help. He sat looking at her in silence for a long while, his eyes of deep cerulean blue filled with thoughts she was unable to read, then finally asked if she would lend him a needle and some thread.

'But certainly, Monsieur,' she said gladly. 'May one ask what colour?'

'It doesn't matter.'

She hurried back with a generous-sized needle stuck in a reel of dark cotton. He thanked her politely but made no effort to detain her.

Down in the courtyard a woman was standing with a baby in her arms while she gossiped with a friend, and outside Madame Boudot's window her canary sang sweetly in its cage. He continued to sit there for another half-hour, watching and waiting, then took his jacket down from behind the door, carefully threaded the needle, and began with fumbling fingers to stitch the yellow star on to the top pocket. It took a long while, and when it was done he flexed his cramped fingers a little before putting on the jacket and buttoning it up.

Then he locked the door behind him and went slowly downstairs and out into the street. If she was unable to come to him, then he would take the quickest route available and go to her.

For Miranda, the sense of loss incurred by Emrys' death was increasing rather than diminishing. Picturesque but somewhat unassertive in life, absence appeared to be strengthening and sharpening the personality she had always found amusing and attractive.

So much of his character was in the collection of beautiful furniture and charming bibelots rather than in memories of things he had said and done, although she recalled with tenderness his air of helpless indignation at the antics of Hitler: 'The man's completely beyond the pale, dear. The worst kind of schizoid and a first-class shit!'

Everyone had loved him; the Ellenbergs because they had sensed an inner quality of grace, and Florence because he had obviously come from a good background and had treated her with the kind of gentle gallantry she had read about but seldom experienced. Even the kitten, now grown into a lithe hunter of creatures smaller than itself, appeared to have withdrawn from the human race, as if Emrys had been the only acceptable member of it.

Miranda had helped the Ellenbergs to move into the Overseer's House; she had engaged the same firm of country builders who had made Trellis House habitable and had ordered them on the Ellenbergs' behalf to replaster, redecorate and refurbish. She had then gone up to Liverpool by train, crouching uncomfortably in the corridor among the kitbags of Lancashire Fusiliers going home on leave, and had helped the Ellenbergs to pack up the Rodney Street house. She had been unprepared for the poignancy of the experience; each chair, table, picture, spoke of her adolescence at Queen Mary's, of the initial shyness and confusion she had felt in their company. For she had been aware even then that she was gauche and irresolute, a confused mixture of Aunt Daisy's stern working housewife and Florence's attempts at sophistication which she had sensed even then to be hollow as a tin can.

But most of all the place reminded her overwhelmingly of Nat. Nat of the wild curls and bashed-in school hat. Nat with her gleaming eyes and sardonic smile. The piano that stood between the two long windows was moved out in careful stages, its legs taken off and its vast body, wrapped in removers' sacking, inched into the old lift that creaked and sighed beneath its weight.

Without its colourful furnishings the big rambling flat looked shabby and dusty, the life already drained from it. And Liverpool itself looked much the same; stricken by the bombing and stripped temporarily of its old cheerful toughness it seemed to Miranda to be suffering from apathy laced with malevolence. Tired shop assistants snapped at disgruntled customers and someone tried to steal her handbag on Lime Street Station.

On the afternoon before she left she strolled towards Upper Parliament Street and Queen Mary's College, but it had been evacuated. The windows were boarded up and weeds sprouted on the majestic front steps. She wondered what had become of Miss Nelson, whether she had been interned under Section 18B like Rob Allardyce. . . . But most of all she wondered about Nat.

They had rambled round all these streets together, teasing, joking, giggling. The bombing had made the streets look different but they were still redolent of Nat intoning without punctuation, 'Caesar entered on his head his helmet on his feet . . .' Under Miss Daly's direction they had always pronounced Caesar *Kaiser*, and had stared in lofty incomprehension at the advertisements on the backs of trams that said *Caesar cup of hot Oxo*.

She remembered having a crush on Nat's brother Sammy. For a crush it had gone on for quite a long time, but only because she had not met many other young males. And now Sammy was married to

Rose, whose silver-framed photograph she had helped to pack with all the others. Rose was now up in Scotland in the WAAF and Sammy was serving in North Africa. She hadn't seen him since the chance encounter at Piccadilly Circus, since when she had been married and widowed. Dear old Sammy, she would always be fond of him because he was an Ellenberg.

Upon impulse she called in at the local police station and asked if they knew of any organisation that could help to trace a British subject who had been in Paris at the time of the German invasion.

'Left it a bit late, haven't you?' Nothing like Liverpool bluntness. Then the desk sergeant added, 'No, chook.'

She thanked him and turned away.

'Tried the Red Cross, have you?'

'Can you give me their address?'

He did so, and gave her the sudden amiable grin which is typical of Liverpool, but when she reached the Red Cross office it was closed, and the following morning she left for home so that she would be ready to welcome the Ellenbergs when they came to live at Clatterfoot Common.

Bruno and Esme had now been settled there for six months. Bert the handyman had made himself increasingly at home in his weaver's cottage, and Florence was the ever more reluctant tenant of the wash house.

'Are you sure you want me to go on living in there, chickabid? I don't mind for myself, I'm used to having to make do, but other people seem to think it's a bit funny.'

'What's it got to do with them?'

'Nothing, of course. But gossip can be very unpleasant.'

'I always imagined you were impervious to it, Mother dear.'

'It's not me I'm thinking about,' Florence said. 'To be quite honest, you're the one who's coming in for it, chickabid.'

'Come over to supper and we'll talk about it,' Miranda said. 'We can have pilchards on toast.'

Florence went, taking with her half a bottle of British sherry that tasted like cough mixture but had a more enlivening effect. They ate in the kitchen because it was warmer, and the sherry made them talk fondly of Emrys – 'Did you ever notice his dinky little ears, chickabid?' – and from there they roamed back to the old days in Liverpool, finding that the passage of time had already dimmed the unpleasant realities and substituted a kind of prolonged knockabout farce.

'Do you remember that evening we dressed up as Clapham and

Dwyer – where did we get bowler hats from? – and we pranced up and down the hall singing "Sandy You're Bandy" . . . ?'

'That wasn't Clapham and Dwyer – '

'No, but we started off as them. Then we did Noël Coward – a roooom with a vieuuuuuu. . . .'

'Rob Allardyce never smiled once.'

'That's the main trouble with people who like politics, chickabid. Bert's just the same, they never know when to have fun. I've always adored Noël Coward, he's got such *style*. . . .'

'So had Emrys.'

'Yes. And so have you, chickabid.' Florence poured some more sherry. It went surprisingly well with pilchards.

'Have I really?' Miranda dropped the perpetual guard she maintained between herself and Florence and gazed at her hungrily. 'I don't see myself as having anything at all – neither style nor non-style, if you see what I mean. I'm just a sort of nothing.'

'No daughter of mine could be a nothing.' Then Florence took her hand, gazing at her mistily. 'In fact you've got everything I haven't. Poise, charm, sex appeal, and of course you've had the benefit of a good education.'

'It was only a good standard secondary education.'

'Oh no, chickabid. You went to a college where they had mistresses not teachers and you played hockey and lacrosse, didn't you? I mean, all that *matters*.'

'All right then, it was a High School education – '

'No it wasn't,' Florence said, getting cross. 'It was a College education and it cost me every penny I had!'

'Cost *you*?'

Storm cones were being hoisted. They both recognised them, and Miranda got up to clear away the dirty plates. She returned with two coconut-covered madeleines on a Famille Rose plate of the Ch'ien Lung period.

'Ooh, they've got glacé cherries on top! I thought they'd gone for ever!'

'The village baker's a marvel – '

'And you know he's bedding the woman from the Three Swans, don't you? I think it's dreadful while her husband's away.'

'Would it be better if he was there?'

'Now you're being silly and challenging again, chickabid. I merely said that it's in rather questionable taste to do that kind of thing when a man's away fighting for his country and all that he holds dear.'

155

'We're living in funny times,' Miranda said, dreamily reading the label on the sherry bottle.

'Exactly. And I can't help thinking that we'd be far better off together, chickabid, than this silly idea about you all on your own and me all on my own . . . in the wash house.'

'OK,' Miranda said. 'You win.'

'It's not a question of anyone winning,' Florence said with a tinge of asperity. 'I'm merely trying to protect you.'

'What from?'

'Gossip. As I said.'

Miranda munched her madeleine in silence, then wetted her finger and captured the last errant grains of coconut. 'I'm resigned to your coming here,' she said finally, 'but I'm damned if I'll resign myself to the idea that *you're* doing *me* a favour, and not the other way around. So you can have the spare room as your own domain to do whatever you like in, but the rest of the house is mine; my drawing room, my dining room, my kitchen, in which you will be a guest. You may be my mother, but let's not confuse the issue – I'm not married to you as well.'

'In which case I'll stay where I am.' Florence jammed the cork back in the sherry bottle which she then seized by the neck. 'So goodnight and thank you for the pilchards.'

They parted, both spent the night fuming and awake, and Florence moved in to Trellis House three days later.

The result was much as Miranda had drearily foreseen: the house was no longer hers. Florence changed the furniture round in the drawing room, draped wet stockings over the kitchen stove and chattered endlessly, sometimes amusingly and sometimes not. The funny, gentle ghost of Emrys was retreating, driven into the walls by the scent of ersatz nail varnish (in natural shade only, its real function being the gluing together of various aircraft components), and although it was nice having the Ellenbergs near, Florence was not averse to making jealous scenes while displaying an outward demeanour of cloying sweetness.

Food rationing was tightened, and the monthly allowance of jam or marmalade replaced without warning by black treacle the consistency of cart grease. There were no cigarettes, clothes were rationed, and the bus service into Sudbury was severely curtailed. Then Florence met a sergeant from the American airbase near Lavenham; they met in a pub and she was instantly charmed by his soft blond features and by the tight little male rump made so provocative by well-fitting USAF pants.

156

Our boys didn't have pants; they had the hairy and strictly noncommittal British version called trousers.

They conversed easily, and she was touched by the respectful way he addressed her as 'ma'am'. She told him that her name was Victoria and he said, 'My, that's real pretty.'

'After the Queen,' Florence said, and accepted her first Lucky Strike cigarette.

'Would you be a relative, ma'am?'

His respect increased, and Florence exhaled a long and luxuriant plume of smoke from her nostrils and said well no, not exactly. But there was mystery in her smile.

He told her that his own name was Clark, and Florence said, how nice. It made her think of Clark Gable, whom she greatly admired. 'I don't suppose you've ever met him, have you?'

'He grew up in my home town, just a freckle-faced kid like the rest of us.'

They sat at the bar for a long time, drinking flat wartime beer and busily impressing one another, Clark's patriotic claims involving the magnitude of everything in the States while Florence countered with the antiquity of everything in Britain.

'You're not old, Victoria!'

'I'm what you might call a woman of a certain age, Clark. In fact I've got a beautiful daughter old enough to have been married and widowed.'

'That's real tough.'

'She's getting over it.' Florence sighed and twiddled her glass. 'Our family is used to tragedy.'

'How come?'

'My husband left me for another woman. He sold our home and she spent every penny he had, and when she had finished she abandoned him with only a poor old broken chair in a one-room flat over a tobacconist's, and then went out to India and married a maharajah. I don't know what happened to her after that, but of course if her husband dies before her she will be expected to commit suttee.'

His blue eyes opened wide and questioning.

'Burn herself to death on his funeral pyre, which some might say would serve her right.'

'And your husband, did he come back?'

Florence bent her head low, but not before he had seen a little tear slide down her cheek. 'He took the last shilling out of his pocket and put it in the meter and then turned the gas tap on. They didn't find him until weeks later, the poor lonely man.'

'*Two* widows. Gee, that's terrible. . . .'

They parted fondly at closing time, and Florence gave him her address and invited him to visit her when he next had time off and nothing better to do with it. 'You boys must be so lonely, so far away from home. . . .'

He promised to do so, and gave her a jaunty American salute, his blue eyes beaming gratitude.

Florence returned home feeling emotionally replete, but for some reason didn't tell Miranda about the encounter. Which was a mistake.

On Christmas Eve they were startled by the sound of hooting outside Trellis House, followed by voices. Miranda opened the front door and five American airmen cried, 'Merry Christmas!' from the shadows, their arms full of parcels.

'Pardon me, ma'am,' added one, 'would this be Victoria's place?'

Bewildered and slightly apprehensive Miranda began to say no it wasn't, then Florence appeared from behind her and said with a little gasp, 'Oh chickabid, this is Clark!'

'And you're the beautiful daughter!' Clark appraised Miranda with unashamed admiration. 'Thought we'd just drop by to bring you a little festive cheer, girls!'

Even Florence seemed nonplussed that he should have brought four companions, then, noting the parcels, came swiftly to the conclusion that he couldn't have carried them all by himself.

So they trooped inside, and the parcels contained bottles of bourbon and bottles of scent, packets of amazingly ultra-fine stockings called nylons, yet to be seen in England, boxes of candy and cigarettes, and lastly a lump of butter, hastily hewn and the size of a brick.

Poise now recovered, Florence indicated with a graceful wave of the hand the softly lit drawing room, and one of the airmen standing next to Miranda said, 'Gee, your mom's sure got a nice place here.'

'It's not Mom's place, it's mine,' Miranda said, smiling. 'So do sit down.'

They all did so, and for a while the conversation remained politely banal: 'How do you like our country?' 'Just great. And all that history your mom was telling us.' 'My mother has always been good at history.' (Not to mention composition.) 'Ever bin to the States, ma'am?' 'Not so far. But of course I should like to, one day.'

Gradually they began to make themselves at home with laughter, wisecracks and easier conversation, yet there was still something of the clean and politely polished little boy about them all; despite the glug-glug of bourbon into glasses and the thickening clouds of cigar and cigarette smoke, they were oddly like children who had been instructed to watch their pleases and thank-yous when they went out to tea next door.

But it was Christmas Eve, and, three thousand miles from home and taking part in a war that didn't seem to have much to do with them personally, made it particularly poignant. Clark and the one called Larry seemed disposed to reminisce about their folks while they sat and sipped together on the sofa, but the big freckled one they called Chuck asked if Victoria had a record-machine and then maybe they could dance a little.

'*Victoria* dear,' drawled Miranda, 'have we a gramophone?'

In place of one they tuned in to Geraldo's dance music being played on the Forces' programme, and Chuck's friend Louis tried to teach Miranda to jive. She was unwilling, particularly when she caught sight of Florence wriggling away as if she had been doing it all her life, then in an effort to shake off the old self-accusation of spinsterly spoilsport, tried hard to follow his instructions.

She began to get the hang of it, and for a brief space of time felt at ease with these smiling, finger-snapping men-children who were trying to banish loneliness and fear of the dark. But when Chuck's other friend Sim tried to kiss her she shook him off in disgust.

Laughing and tousled, Florence sped to the kitchen and made sand-wiches spread with bloater paste, which was off the ration. The brick of butter had already been concealed at the back of the larder in case they should suddenly demand it back.

Then Clark and Larry recovered from their bout of retrospection and suddenly demanded to know where the party was. They had been drinking steadily if not all that heavily, and Clark broke off singing 'I'm Dreaming of a White Christmas' to grab Miranda and draw her protectively close. 'No kidding, honey – you really a widow?'

She stiffened in his grasp. 'Yes. As a matter of fact.'

Larry, grinning, mimicked her accent: 'Yers . . . s'metterafect . . . boy, I just love the way you Limeys talk.'

'Thank you.' She wanted to add, *most gratifying*, because she still didn't quite know how to cope with this unexpected invasion and because she was furious with Florence; obviously, it was all her doing. But she didn't say any more. Instead, she tried very hard to loosen the constriction caused by shyness, lack of experience and genuine apprehension on behalf of Emrys' beloved antiques. She still thought

159

of them as his, as if he might come through the door at any moment, smiling his wide froggy smile and saying, 'But my *dear*, what on *earth's* going on?' The realisation that this was Christmas Eve and that he wasn't here to enjoy it made her eyes fill with tears.

'Have another bloater sandwich,' she said. Hours seemed to have passed since their arrival. It was two and a half, in fact.

In the meanwhile Chuck and Louis had now succumbed to alcohol-induced evocations of home. They produced snapshots from between the pages of their pay books.

'That's my kid sister – she wore her hair in braids until she was going on sixteen.'

'That's my ma in the backyard. She's number one in the church choir.'

'The most wonderful relationship in the world is the one between mother and child,' Florence said, perching a little unsteadily on the arm of a chair. Her eyes were very bright and her breath smelt of bourbon. 'Don't stand with your toes turned in, chickabid.'

Tired, irritated and bored, Miranda leaned smilingly towards her and said in a whisper heavy with menace, 'I will stand with my toes turned in if I want to. I will stand with my toes turned out, one lot facing north and the other lot facing south. I will stand with my toes pointing bloody backwards if it pleases me personally, and if anyone happens not to like it they can go back and live in the bloody wash house, can't they?'

'Bitch,' Florence replied, smiling back. 'Hard-faced, hard-arsed bitch.'

'Put it down to my college education.'

Geraldo was now playing 'In the Mood', and the volume was turned up to its highest level. Chuck was weeping gently over a letter from home, Louis was lying full-length on the floor, and two of the others were snapping their fingers and singing, *'Mister whatchercallit, whatya doin' tonight? Hope you're in the mood because I'm feelin' jus' right. . . .'* While Clark, who had undertaken the role of host, was pouring more drinks, a kitchen towel tied round his waist. It was miraculous that anyone should hear the sound of the front-door knocker.

'Oh Christ, not more of them,' Miranda said wearily.

It was the Ellenbergs. They came in a little uncertainly, Bruno looming over his wife's dark head and both of them blinking at the loud music. Someone had the courtesy to turn it down.

'We just walked over with these,' Esme said, holding out a locally made osier basket covered with a white cloth. 'Bruno's been up to town to see an old colleague who used to be at the London Hospital.' She gave the basket to Miranda.

'Fresh from the Whitechapel Road!' Bruno added.

Beneath the white cloth nestled a dozen bagels and a dark brown packet that smelt of freshly ground coffee. Louis hauled himself up from the floor and straightened his tie.

'Please don't let's spoil the party,' Bruno began, but Miranda patted his arm. 'Come and meet Victoria's new friends.'

They all shook hands, the Americans once again polite little boys, and it was strange how attention seemed to become focused on the Ellenbergs in spite of their obvious reluctance.

Miranda, having offered them a drink, went to the kitchen to make coffee. The kettle simmered perpetually on the big iron range, and the rich scent coming from the earthenware jug brought back the memory of Emrys, who had always made exquisite coffee, though with a lot of puffing and blowing and an inordinate fluttering of fingers.

Esme came in and stood hesitantly in the shadow of the hanging lamp.

'I'm so sorry if – '

'Don't apologise for the best thing that's happened all evening,' Miranda said. 'God knows where that lot turned up from, but you can guess who's to blame.'

'They're lonely. A bit like us.'

'I know.' Miranda softened. No Nat, no Sammy.

'We wondered if Rose would be able to get leave, but if she does I expect she'll want to spend it with her own family.'

'You're my family,' Miranda said abruptly. 'And when Nat gets home you'll have the two of us to cope with.'

'You do really think she'll come home, don't you?' She moved closer, her hands clasped in the old familiar way. The light fell on her face and Miranda noted with a pang of sorrow how lined it had become.

'If faith has anything to do with it, she will.'

Together they placed the cups and saucers on a tray and heaped the bagels on a plate.

'They should really be buttered, but they're probably fresh enough without,' Esme said. 'Just think, in the old days we used to have them with smoked salmon.'

'Fear not,' cried Miranda, suddenly joyous, 'we're OK for butter!'

She produced the large, rough-hewn brick from the larder, and saw Esme's large dark eyes open wider still. 'Nothing like having friends in high places. . . .'

161

They buttered the rolls swiftly, then Miranda hacked off half of the remaining butter, shoved it in a paper bag and thrust it at Esme, who backed off in alarm.

'No, no, I can't!'

'Yes, you can – don't be daft!'

'No, Miranda – put it back.'

'I'm giving you this bit of butter,' Miranda said through gritted teeth, 'because I want to. I want to share it, and what's more I'm going to share it. Hell, we're all in the same war, aren't we?'

'Well, just an ounce, then – '

'Ounce be damned, you're having half!'

Defeated, Esme clutched the bag in both hands, and then said, 'Do you know, you're becoming just a shade dictatorial, my dear Miranda?'

'That's what Florence says, but she puts it a bit more forcibly.'

Miranda picked up the tray of coffee and led the way back to the drawing room. Outside the door she paused. 'When I said that faith would bring Nat back, I didn't mean religious faith. I just meant the ordinary common or garden sort.'

'That's the only sort I know,' Esme Ellenberg replied.

And they were talking about faith in the drawing room, Bruno sitting in an easy chair with the young Americans grouped close. Someone had prodded the fire into a fresh blaze and Florence, temporarily deserted, sat on a low stool, yawning and buffing her nails on the front of her sweater.

'I have my faith and it helps me stay outta trouble,' someone was saying. 'I'm over here and mixed up in things I don't understand too much, but I know Uncle Sam'll see me through.'

'I'll bet the Nazi boys are saying the same about Hitler.'

'But I *know* I'm right. I *know* it's wrong to take over the little guy.'

'Not if you think what you think is right.' While bringing profundity, the mists of bourbon were also obscuring the issue.

'Sure. For instance, I don't think it's the right thing to come over here and fornicate with other men's wives – beg pardon, ma'am,' Sim shot an apologetic glance in the direction of Florence, 'because that's just doing the dirty – '

'Shitting in the Allies' nest – '

'Pipe down, Larry.'

'Sex isn't necessarily dirty.'

'Do unto others as you would have them do unto you – '

'So OK, which would you sooner be, a Nazi general or a GI Joe?'

'It's a matter of what you believe.'

162

'That's my point. A matter of faith.'

'I believe in God,' someone said.

'We all do. Everyone's got to believe in God.'

'Or *a* God. You can stick a cabbage on a pole and call it God.'

'I'm talking about God the Creator – back home we go to church and stuff – '

'It doesn't matter what God you have,' someone observed, 'so long as it's on the side of what's right. What's kind and humane and considerate to other folk.'

'We're not getting anywheres,' someone else objected. 'We're just going around in circles.'

'What do you believe in, sir?' They turned their clean, trusting young faces towards Bruno, who smiled upon them; the archetype father-figure with comfortable bow tie and copious grey hair.

'If I believe in anything at all, which I sometimes doubt,' he said slowly, 'I believe in the family group. In taking care of the pence and the pounds will take care of themselves, in other words. Yes ... I believe in the ties which bind protectively in childhood, which loosen in adolescence and which fall away in adulthood. I believe in the sheltering of all young growing things, in the giving of love, in the sharing of such poor wisdom as we have managed to acquire, and I believe that in the end those who have been in our care owe us nothing.'

Someone began to protest, and Bruno raised his hand. 'I believe in esteem; love, if you like, but not that terrible cold commodity which is called a sense of duty.'

Esme and Miranda passed round the coffee, and it was Louis who suddenly cried, 'Egad – onion bagels!' with his mouth full. He chewed convulsively. 'Back home the bagel man used to call all along our street when the kids were let out of school. . . .'

'Bagels?' said Florence, sulkily accepting one. 'Oh, I thought they might have been mince pies.'

'Pardon me, sir, for asking, but are you also a Jew?' Louis directed his gaze at Bruno.

'I'm a husband and a father – you mean I have to be something else as well?'

'Not necessarily, sir, but – '

'I'm a lapsed Catholic,' Florence said, suddenly tired of being left out. 'I tried very hard at the time but it just didn't take, any more than any of the other things did. And now I think I only believe in human beings.'

'And oh boy, that's some faith,' Sim murmured.

163

'Whatever our creeds and beliefs, it's Christmas,' someone said, 'and I guess you don't have to believe in Jesus to enjoy it.'

'I believe in Jesus,' Louis said, 'but I don't dig the idea of him being the son of God, that's all.'

'Does it matter who he was?' enquired Bruno, 'apart from sounding a nice young chap who suffered a particularly unpleasant death uncomplainingly.'

'Sure it matters. He did it for *us*.'

'So OK, who'll I be doing it for if I get crucified by the Jerries or the Japs? Boy, I'm in no hurry to be crucified.'

'You'll be doing it for Uncle Sam and the free world, knucklehead.'

'Aw come on, kid, I'll hold your hand.'

'Hell you will. I'll be up too high to reach. . . .'

The deeper perplexities which could only surface with the aid of alcohol dissolved into levity. Bruno the father-figure regarded them fondly, as if in memory of times past, then Clark glanced at his watch and shot to his feet. 'Holy cow – it's just on midnight!'

'Which means two things,' Bruno said. 'The arrival of a Christian festival and the departure of visiting servicemen likely to be declared absent without leave and dealt with accordingly.'

Coffee cups were drained, the last bagel crammed into the last young mouth, and handshakes and kisses were exchanged. But now the kisses were warmly fond rather than hungrily sensual.

'So long, Victoria!'

'So long, Miranda!'

'Be seeing you, sir – and you too, ma'am. . . .'

Cries of 'Merry Christmas' mingled with the roar of the jeep as they sped hurriedly away across the Common. The Ellenbergs left after helping to wash the coffee cups, and Miranda hid the last of Florence's bloater sandwiches which had been abruptly forsaken in favour of the Whitechapel bagels.

Christmas is no time for jealousy, Miranda thought, no matter who or what you believe in.

The internment camp at Saint-Denis was a very large place where men greatly outnumbered women. One of the two showgirls told Nat that there were reputed to be between sixteen and eighteen hundred internees within its perimeter, and added that it was wrong to segregate the sexes; God knows, there wasn't much else to do, was there?

'Tell your beads?' suggested Nat, nodding in the direction of a nun praying rapturously by her bedside.

164

It had taken a week or two merely to become accustomed to the idea of being confined before she could face the fact of confinement itself. The secluded life spent in the attic had irked her now and then, but ultimately she had always accepted the reason for it. There, she had been loved; here, she was an enemy alien.

Lost and disorientated, she studied the other women in her room in an effort to discover how they dealt with the problem of captivity, for most of them had been in Saint-Denis since the summer of 1940. Mrs Gaston-Haigh and her ilk behaved with a patrician indifference threaded with insolence, while others, particularly the grey hand-knitteds, tended to react with the nervous promptitude bred by a lifetime of scurrying to answer bells and receive commands. The nuns remained piously docile while the two showgirls had perfected to the level of high art an aptitude for releasing strings of English epithets from behind smiles of guileless charm. She came to the conclusion that it mostly depended upon that station in life to which you had previously been called.

She also discovered that for purposes of self-protection it was extremely unwise to dwell upon past life, past happiness. Two of the room's inmates spent their days in a state of either brooding silence or red-eyed apathy, and it was obvious that Mrs Gaston-Haigh, the self-appointed head girl, had lost patience with them long ago. Serve them right, thought Nat, and every time a chance word or gesture triggered a youthful memory or a sudden vision of life with Raoul she became increasingly adept at suppressing it, at swerving her thoughts aside into other, calmer channels. It was an accomplishment that would serve her well until the very end.

Determined to survive, she forced herself to take an interest in the small twitterings of the grey hand-knitteds, who complained in quiet and ladylike voices about the food, the *fridolines*, the airless heat and the lack of basic amenities.

'Miss Nettlefold hung her wet washing all over my vest and knickers. She could *see* they were dry. . . .'

'Miss Simmons asked me for another of my corn plasters but I had to say no. I've only got two left, dear, I said, and they've got to *last* me. . . .'

'I do wish people wouldn't snore so. . . .'

'I was forced to have a little word with Mrs Gaston-Haigh this morning about the nuns. We all know how sweet they are, but wearing those heavy, unhygienic garments in this hot weather. . . .'

The war was seldom mentioned, and and then only with the head-shaking disparagement one would normally use towards the antics of small and unruly boys.

There were few rows and no slanging matches; disagreement or displeasure was invariably shown by a brisk sigh and a tightening of the lips, followed by a temporary refusal to engage in conversation. A case of serious umbrage could result in silence between two ladies lasting for several weeks, during which time other occupants of the room were inevitably (and enjoyably) drawn in to take sides, but only covertly. Mrs Gaston-Haigh alone appeared immune to any form of petty intrigue and Nat concluded that it must have been because of her husband's job in the Diplomatic Corps.

The heat of August gave way to the chill nights of September. In November they all caught colds, and one of the showgirls, whose name was Dawn, went down with chickenpox. She lay in bed sobbing about the scars it would leave on her face ('Nonsense, dear,' said Mrs Gaston-Haigh, 'you're thinking of smallpox.'), and when the two small children caught the infection they kept everyone awake at night with their grizzling and their mother refused to speak to Dawn, who called her a silly fat *vache*.

With all of which, Nat dutifully sympathised. The past was past for the time being, and already there were times when she thought she could no longer remember the smaller details of Raoul's appearance. Because she wanted to survive whatever lay ahead, it was like a small victory.

Christmas came. Apart from the steadily increasing cold, boredom was the worst feature of Saint-Denis, and the celebration of *Noël* seemed to offer a temporary reason for increasing the struggle against listlessness.

In Nat's room, small gifts were exchanged: a newly scrubbed pocket comb, a blurred snap of Queen Mary taken at Badminton House, a pair of number 10 knitting needles . . . . The old girl in the bed next to Nat gave her a necklace of glass beads, and Miss Nettlefold said without rancour, 'I gave those to Mrs Kingston last year. . . .'

Nannies and governesses kissed one another with dry, polite lips, and everyone made a fuss of the two small children. Someone even attempted to cut paper chains out of filched copies of the magazine *Signal*, but although they tried hard to achieve a festive atmosphere, the accent lay on bravery rather than on jollity.

At the suggestion of Mrs Gaston-Haigh they ended the day with the Lord's Prayer and a few carols, while the three nuns made the sign of the cross and outside they heard the stamp of boots as the guard was changed. When lights out finally released them from the compulsion to appear undaunted, Mrs Salmon and Miss Yates were not the only ones to weep themselves quietly to sleep.

But if Nat was succeeding in her resolution to turn her mind away from the past, an even greater torment began to fill the empty space. Perhaps it had been prompted by the sound of carol-singing, or perhaps it was bound to happen anyway. The torment was music.

It was now assuming an almost diabolical aspect, seeping stealthily into her mind and filling her with a fury of frustration. It no longer brought her the pleasure as in the old days when a Scarlatti or Beethoven sonata would run vivid as a bright ribbon through her mind as she travelled between the Conservatoire at Fontainebleau and her room at Madame Triboulet's. For one thing, it no longer ran smoothly; like a badly scratched gramophone record it would repeat one bar over and over again, and although the years of learning how to learn had developed the painstaking ability to perfect her technique bar by bar, phrase by phrase, this was different. It was an insistent and essentially meaningless reiteration over which she had no control. It drove her mad.

She tried to placate it with the finger exercises that she had practised so assiduously in the attic, running up and down scales and arpeggios on her knee under the table as they waited for the *fridolines* to bring their scanty meals, lifting each hammer finger in turn and tapping it with machine-gun rapidity, and then spreading the palms of her hands to their utmost width so that they might still be able to stretch an octave when the war was over. Her chief problem had always been the smallness of her hands.

She performed the exercises unobtrusively because she needed neither commendation nor condemnation from outsiders. There was only one person qualified to comment and she had bunked off to America with all the others.

But despite her efforts, music now seemed to have broken loose from its boundaries. Like a great tide bursting through a sea wall it was engulfing her in a roar of cacophonous fury, and her companions would occasionally nod in her direction and exchange significant glances as she sat, head drooping, on her bed. They had no idea that she was slowly starving to death.

Then, early on the morning of the 2nd of February, she was awoken by one of the *fridolines* thumping the bed with her fist and shouting in guttural French, 'Get up! You are being moved, so pack your things!'

She did as she was told, dry-mouthed and with a rapidly beating heart. No one else in the room had been given similar orders, but most of them were awake. They watched quietly in the cold, dim light, and when Nat was ready to leave, Mrs Gaston-Haigh slid from her bed and accompanied her to the door.

'We'll all be thinking of you, my dear,' she said. 'And when you get back to England do tell everyone that we're coping splendidly, won't you?'

Nat promised. They shook hands and touched cheeks, and as the *fridoline* pushed her roughly on her way the chorus of brave good wishes made her eyes sting with tears. Strange, how kindness was harder to bear than cruelty.

The camp at Drancy, near Le Bourget airport and conveniently close to Drancy-le-Bourget railway station, was a large and shambling affair fashioned in haste from a half-completed council estate. In full view of the outside world the inmates gathered in aimless groups by the electrified fence, hands stuffed into the sleeves of their jackets, feet stamping against the iron cold. They were mostly Jews, many of them refugees from countries already overrun by the Nazis, and occasionally a sympathetic outsider would aim cigarettes or a small parcel of food at them, like people feeding bears at the zoo.

Despite the hard frost and flurries of snow, outside was better than in, for, accustomed to the relative refinements of Saint-Denis, Nat was unprepared for the conditions in the women's block. Herded fifty or more to a room, they slept on the floor; there were six cold-water taps to eighty-six inmates for washing and drinking, and no one was allowed to visit the lavatory more than once in every sixteen hours. Children, and many of the older women, gave up the hopeless struggle with nature, and the resulting stench was all-pervasive.

A diet consisting solely of watery cabbage soup did nothing to help; dysentery and infectious skin diseases were rife and the old straw palliasses were crawling with lice. Perhaps it was not surprising that no one bothered to welcome Natalie Ellenberg, to smile, extend a hand and say, *Bonjour, Mademoiselle. Je m'appelle Madame* whatsername, *et comment vous appelez-vous?. . . .* No one took any notice of her at all because they were too engrossed in their own business; the business of how to keep warm, how to assuage the constantly nagging hunger, how to keep the children quiet, how to stay sane, how to stay alive.

For the first time she saw life without the ordinary constraints to which she was still accustomed. She saw two women brawling over a slice of bread; an old woman in a headscarf rocking to and fro in an agony of mental confusion; a young dark-eyed girl with blood running down her legs because no sanitary towels were available.

She watched it all, silent and aghast, and a little Jewish boy ran up to her with a gap-toothed smile and said in a strong Austrian accent, 'We're all going to Pitchipoi where it's warm and happy with lots of food and beautiful toys to play with!'

She managed to smile back. 'And where's Pitchipoi?'

'Oh, it's a long way from here,' he gestured in the direction of the railway station, 'but we'll be going in a big train. I've never been in a train before, have you?'

'A couple of times.'

'They say it travels very fast. Much faster than a bus, and that you can have meals while you go along.'

'Yes,' she said, 'I believe that's true.'

Pitchipoi . . . Pitchipoi . . . . It had a charming, childish, rhythmical sound, not unlike the chuffing of a steam engine. She tried hard to believe that Pitchipoi, wherever it was, would be an improvement upon the domestic horrors of Drancy.

These domestic horrors were her first impression; it took a day or two longer to realise that for the first time in her life she was living in close proximity to hundreds of people of her own race. In the male compound she saw old men wearing long grey ringlets and prayer shawls and reciting the *Sh'ma Yisrael*, 'Hear, O Israel, the Lord our God is one. . . .' She saw bearded men in black suits and hats walking solemnly together, and in her own room she listened to the voices of her own sex talking in rapid, emotional Yiddish. They were all sorts and types and ages, and they had all been herded together because Hitler had chosen them to represent evil in a demonstrably human form, and she was one of them. And in the Europe of 1943 few non-Jews had the courage to challenge his choice.

Finding little in common with her fellow room-mates Nat spent as much time as possible with the children. The camp was swarming with them, and they soon learned to gather round her because she told them stories in French with a funny accent. By which they meant an accent funnier even than their own. And as spring reluctantly returned they tried to stifle endless hunger and endless ailments by talking about Pitchipoi.

'It won't be long now. Soon we'll be there – and did you know that Pitchipoi is by the sea? Oh yes, there's a beautiful, warm blue sea to swim in, and if you're lucky you can even make friends with a mermaid or ride on a hump-backed whale . . . and there's lots of beautiful yellow sand where you can make the biggest sandcastles in the world. . . .'

'And there's lots to eat?'

'You can eat all the time, if you want to. Cakes and chocolates and puddings and roast chicken . . .'

'I hope the chicken has been killed by a *shochet*,' added a grave-faced little girl with long tangled hair.

'Of course it has,' Nat said heartily. 'Anything you say.'

'And *chollah* and bagels – ' put in someone else.

'And lumps of Palm toffee that stick your jaws together – '

'What please is Palm toffee?'

'I'll tell you tomorrow,' Nat said.

The children were helping her as perhaps she was helping them.

La Grande Rafle, the Big Round-up, had begun the previous July, and the herding and transporting of Jews had by now become a slickly organised routine, the brainchild of Hauptsturmführer Dannecker with the approval of Himmler and Eichmann. Everyone in Drancy knew that one day their name would be called, and almost everyone clung tightly to the rumour that the next place would be better. To stop hoping is to die.

Music was no longer plaguing Nat with its insistence. It seemed to have fallen away quite voluntarily, like all the memories of her old life, leaving her in a state of quiescence. She moved through the days in a trancelike state from which only the children could rouse her.

I am not hungry. I am not thirsty. I am not me, I am not a person. I am an inanimate object; indifferent, unfeeling, uninvolved. Nothing can touch me or harm me because I'm inorganic; non-animal; non-vegetable. . . .

She caught ringworm from the children, and the old woman on the louse-ridden straw mattress next to her own died quietly, her eyes closed and her gaunt beak of a nose pointing at the cracked ceiling. Another woman, with a deeply lined face, crossed the old woman's hands on her breast and then recited *kaddish* on behalf of whatever sons she may have had.

The little boy with the gap-toothed smile disappeared, and so did the little girl with long tangled hair. The children who came to her for stories were changing all the time; old inmates introduced new ones.

'Edek has gone to Pitchipoi with his three sisters – isn't he lucky?'

'He said he was going to have hot milk to drink and a bed all to himself.'

'I do wish I was Edek – '

'Don't worry, we're all going next week. The man told me – '

'Listen, do you want to hear the story of The Cat that Walked by Himself . . . ?'

For I'm the woman who walks by herself. I'm talking to you because it passes the time and I forget about hunger and fear. . . . Music has left me because it's too fastidious to be associated with a place like this and I'm glad, glad, glad. . . .

The name Natalie Ellenberg was down for the convoy which left for Pitchipoi on the 24th of October. At six o'clock in the morning it was still dark, and the deportees, heavily laden, crowded into the tarpaulin-covered trucks waiting for them. They had been urged to take all their possessions, particularly anything of value, and the assumption that they would be needing them in the next place was reassuring.

'It's when they tell you to leave everything behind that you know you're in trouble,' someone joked.

The optimism faded a little when they reached the marshalling yard and saw the train waiting for them. It was old, rusty in parts, and in place of the normal compartments were cattle trucks.

'*Mais que voulez-vous? C'est la guerre,*' said the gendarme helping with the proceedings. Carefully he handed a small baby up to its mother.

They settled in as best they could, the strongest and most able scrambling for places against the sides of the trucks while the old and infirm made do with the space in the middle. At least the straw was clean and there were two buckets in each truck; one filled with clean water for drinking and the other provided for sanitary purposes. Not ideal, but, as the gendarme had pointed out, there was a war on.

When the engine jerked into life and the trucks clanked together everyone raised a cheer. They were off to Pitchipoi at last.

'My husband's a Jew, as a matter of fact,' Rose Ellenberg said.

'Really? Pity.' The Brigadier caressed her foot beneath the sheets. She responded by moving a long, shapely leg past his damp and quiescent genitalia and brought it to rest across his hips.

'Tried to convert you, has he?'

'No fear. For one thing Mummy and Daddy wouldn't stand for it.'

'Stationed near here?'

'Oh, God no. North Africa.'

'What a waste. Of you, I mean, Popsy.'

'I do wish you wouldn't call me that.'

'Why not? It's my own little private pet-name.'

'It's also the little private pet-name bestowed by all ranks upon their little wartime bit on the side.'

'Darling, I don't like you when you're coarse.'

She nuzzled his neck. 'Love me again, then.'

'I can't . . . daren't . . . I'm due at GHQ in less than an hour.' He nuzzled her back, his crisp moustache rasping pleasurably over her bare shoulder.

'Just a little quick one.'

'I honestly mustn't – fucking always makes me so sleepy afterwards. No, take your hand away, Popsy . . . darling Popsydoodlums. . . .'

Outside the hotel room a chambermaid was singing *Yours 'til the stars lose their glory, yours 'til the birds fail to sing* . . . to the accompanying purr of a vacuum cleaner. Watching the Brigadier clamber into his uniform Rose wondered whether being married to a Jew imposed some sort of taint, undetectable to oneself but apparent to others. She was glad that she had been chosen for an OCTU course and was now an Assistant Section Officer. Sammy of course was a Squadron Leader, but only because he was aircrew.

The train to Pitchipoi had been travelling for three days and two nights.

SS guards had taken over from the French gendarmerie at the German border but the doors of the cattle trucks had not been opened, and the cries of those in distress had gone unheeded. Children exhausted by boredom, heat, hunger and crying had fallen asleep like small animals resignedly on their way to market, and close to where Nat lay slumped with her elbow on her suitcase, a very old Jew had died quietly and almost apologetically. Although he was very thin and very shabby, there was a quality in his face that reminded her of her father; the powerful nose, the richly carved lips, the expression of mingled humour and pain at life's idiocies. She had often seen that expression on her father's face and now here it was on the face of a dead man. She felt no repugnance for his presence, but when her thoughts began to wander in the direction of Rodney Street she quickly switched them away. Contemplation of a corpse was easier.

The water bucket had long since been drained dry and the sanitary bucket had been upset by the jolting, its contents seeping into the straw. The smell of it, the smell of unwashed bodies and bad breath had long ago made breathing through the nose unendurable. Once again the gaunt woman on the other side of Nat tried to soothe her child back to sleep; in the briefly flickering light coming through the apertures in the woodwork Nat saw that its face was flushed and puffy, its temper obdurate. It looked about four years old.

She held her arms open, and with a tired grimace of a smile its mother surrendered it.

'Listen,' Nat said, holding it lightly against her, 'can you hear that little engine going bom, bom, bom? Good. Now, if you count with me you will hear that it's going at the same tempo as the train . . . listen hard . . . *un – deux – trois*. . . .'

It listened obediently, and resting her chin on top of its head Nat smelt dirt and the warm smell of lice, and sensed the trustful surrender of child to adult as it occupied itself with counting the beats of her heart.

'That's how music begins,' she said. 'With counting.'

'Can you sing, Madame?' The child raised its head. Its accent was hard to place.

'Not very well. I've got a voice like a crow.'

The child giggled briefly, then said, 'I can sing.'

'Can you? Go on then, let's hear you.'

Settling its head back beneath her chin it cleared its throat and then proceeded to make a long and indeterminate buzzing sound. When finally it had finished Nat said, 'What music was that?'

'Worship music.'

'Oh. I see.'

'It's good, isn't it?'

'Yes, very.'

'Would you like to hear some more?'

'What about another sort, for a change?'

'There isn't any other sort,' the child said with finality. 'All music is worship music.'

They jogged in silence, half-asleep. Then Nat said, 'What's your name?'

'Emil Rokhele, and I'm a Jew.'

'Yes,' Nat said. 'I thought perhaps you were.'

'Are you a Jew, Madame?'

'I don't know. I'm not sure.'

The child slept, his knees drawn up bonily into Nat's stomach. Peering sideways she could see that his mother was also asleep, her head back and little frowns and grimaces chasing each other across her forehead like clouds across a young summer sky.

It was night when they arrived. Two other people had died in their wagon and the water bucket had been empty for thirty-six hours. Cramped and dry-mouthed they waited for what was to come, the sharp smell of fear once again rising from their unwashed bodies.

The sides of the trucks were let down with a sudden crash and there was a concerted stampede by the able-bodied to snatch the first breath of fresh air. They gulped it in noisily, greedily, then became aware of the blinding lights and the barking of dogs.

'*Raus! – raus!* . . . *Schneller!*'

After two and a half days in the semi-dark, they couldn't see. Nat heard Emil Rokhele's mother calling him. 'Hold my hand – quick, my darling, give me your hand!'

Bags, bundles and suitcases were thrown out, their owners slithering, toppling, falling out after them, and all the time the hoarse German voices were urging them to hurry . . . hurry. . . .

The arc lights made everything bright as day and lurid as a nightmare. In its pitiless glare Nat saw German soldiers wearing leather coats glistening with rain and holding Alsatians on leashes; among them flitted strange ghostlike creatures without any hair and wearing striped pyjamas. They climbed up into the wagons and hauled the old and the sick out of the stinking straw, and the corpses they slung out like sacks of rubbish.

The steam from the engine was dying down and it stood hissing in the lightly falling rain. Dazedly gripping her suitcase Nat became aware that the SS were moving along among the crowds, pushing some in one direction, some in another, while the dogs snapped and snarled. She saw the first act of violence: an old woman in a headscarf clubbed to the ground to lie motionless beneath the milling feet. Perhaps she was dead.

Children and women began screaming as they were wrenched apart; she saw a baby thrown into the back of an open truck. The fleeing figure of a man was caught in the stare of an arc light and the crack of rifle fire brought him down. The pandemonium increased, and when she saw Emil Rokhele torn from his mother and sent spinning into the opposite crowd of deportees – the children and the old people – she lost all sense of prudence and dropping her suitcase fought her way towards him. She grabbed him and held him tight, his tears wetting her hands like the rain, and now she was no longer carefully inanimate. Now she was a human being screaming with rage and defiance, and just for a moment it seemed as if no one or no conceivable thing would ever be able to part them. It was as if they were welded indissolubly together by the power of a sudden terrible and desperate love.

'He's a living *person!*' she heard herself shrieking into the face of the Wehrmacht soldier who chopped them apart with his rifle. Stunned with pain and horror she staggered back and found that a man in a baggy cloth cap was trying to comfort Emil's mother.

'Weep not,' he kept saying in a strange and wilting French, 'he is gone to the children's place, that is all. . . .'

Cowed into submission the crowds were quieter now, and Nat managed to regain her suitcase before joining the queue that was being herded into the long line of open trucks. They stood tightly packed together, some of the women crying quietly, and Nat raised her head and concentrated on breathing in the cold fresh air. There were no old people among them now; neither were there any children.

Soon there were more arc lights on watchtowers, more barbed wire, and a strange, sickly-sweet smell of burning. Peering ahead she saw an occasional orange flame licking the top of a tall chimney and illuminating what looked like a heavy pall of smoke. The trucks passed through the main gates, which closed behind them, and listening to the whispered words around her she learned that this was not Pitchipoi; or if it was, then Pitchipoi was the other name for Auschwitz.

Miranda's restless irritability increased. Emrys had left her tolerably well off, she still loved Trellis House – preferably without Florence – but seemed unable to settle to anything of enduring interest. Most other young women of her age seemed to have disappeared from the locality, probably into the forces or into civilian jobs of national importance, while their mothers encouraged Victory in voluntary organisations which specialised in growing vegetables, bottling fruit, make-do-and-mend classes and cosy groups knitting for Russian orphans in wool dyed a bright and cheerful red. Everyone loved Uncle Joe, who was not to be confused with the American uncle of the same name, and we were all on the same side working like blazes to defeat Hitler and his gang.

Saturday night hops were held in the village hall and amazing tales told of invading Yanks' sexual prowess behind the WCs, and beneath the washed-out summer skirts of village maidens the first signs of little Anglo-Americans became visible. Older generations wondered if a German invasion would have been any worse, then shrugged over their watery beer in the Fox and Garter and came to the conclusion that a bit of new blood in the area mightn't be a bad thing.

But none of it seemed to have anything to do with Miranda, or with the war that was raging Out There. She too maintained a vegetable garden, and she worked one day a week in the library attached to the village papershop (twopence per week per book), and tried to sidetrack the few remaining evacuees from Ethel M. Dell and towards the Brontës

– 'I'm pretty sure you'll enjoy Charlotte. . . .' She also saw a good deal of the Ellenbergs, not only for pleasure but also because of a niggling sense of responsibility for their transfer to deepest Suffolk, although Esme was now putting together the material for a book on British birds. Despite all this activity the sense of purposelessness continued to dog her footsteps. Until the day she cycled to the local Red Cross depot with a bundle of books too good for salvage but too tatty for the village library.

'How jolly kind,' said the lady who received them. 'Honestly, our POWs are bitterly short of reading matter.'

She had a nice face, craggy with middle-age and lit by a gleam of humour. Miranda lingered, and recalled her unsuccessful visit to the branch in Liverpool. Since then she had pursued the whereabouts of Nat no further.

'I don't suppose,' she said diffidently, 'you could help us get in touch with an English girl who was in Paris when the Germans occupied it?'

'Our International Committee has a postal message scheme. Letters of no more than twenty-five words which can be sent to friends and relatives, and it's surprising how often they seem to get through.'

'Her parents have written to her address but there's no reply. We've all written, and we've also tried the music academy where she was a student.'

'I believe the Red Cross is setting up a special scheme to help trace missing people but we've received no details so far. Some sort of central tracing agency, but other than that I'm afraid I can't help much. So many thousands of people have been uprooted in Europe.'

'Yes,' said Miranda bleakly, 'I know.'

'Is she a relative of yours?'

'A friend. Just a very good friend.'

'Friends are very often closer than family.'

'I wish I could help in all this,' Miranda said, looking round at the bright recruiting posters on the wall. 'Do something useful, I mean.'

'Nothing to stop you. In the words of the song, Come and Join Us.'

'It wouldn't really be worth it. For one thing I'm not much good at blood and guts and stuff, and for another I'm due to be called up in six months' time.'

'Join us full time. As for blood and guts, that's only for the nursing side. We also want welfare workers. Once you're trained, though, you'd have to be prepared to go anywhere at any time.'

'Sounds fun.'

The older woman shook her head. 'It won't be fun. Not when this lot's over and we start cleaning up the mess. Anyhow,' she went over to the cupboard and sorted through some loose papers, 'take these forms home and fill them in if you're seriously interested. And once again, thanks for the books.'

With the forms stuffed in her handbag Miranda cycled back to Trellis House and met Florence looking conspiratorial in the front garden. She was wearing her ARP uniform.

'Come and see what I've just caught!' She beckoned towards the path that ran round the side of the house.

'Not a paratrooper?' Miranda propped her bicycle against a tree and followed.

'Better than that.' Walking on tiptoe Florence led the way to an unused potting shed between the wash house and what had once been a stable. Miranda followed.

'Ssshhh,' cautioned Florence. Finger to her lips she gently unlatched the door. 'Come in very quickly and shut it behind you.'

They stood in the wan light of early spring, a loop of old montana clematis tapping irritably against the window. A few flowerpots were still stacked on the slatted bench and over in the corner stood an unidentifiable chunk of garden machinery gingered with rust.

'What is it?' Miranda glanced round apprehensively.

'Oh blast, it's got out.' Florence peered beneath the bench and then behind the machinery. Then she pointed with a crow of triumph to the opposite corner. 'There – look!'

It was a wild rabbit. Very small, very frightened, and crouching with its ears down flat against its shoulders.

'I caught it myself, chickabid – honestly! I was just going to the bog and when I opened the door there it was – it must have got in underneath. Anyhow it was the easiest thing in the world just to catch it in my hands – its fur's so soft, you really ought to feel it – and just think what this means, chickabid. Rabbit pie! We could do it with carrots and onions – perhaps our marge ration will stretch to making a bit of pastry, otherwise rabbit casserole. . . .'

'Yes,' Miranda agreed. 'Lovely.'

'So we'll leave it there for now and kill it first thing tomorrow.'

'Yes. Or what about getting Bert to do it?'

'I don't know. He'd want some of it, wouldn't he?'

'OK, leave it,' Miranda said. 'Come on, we're frightening it.'

They went back to the house and ate half a tin of Spam and some boiled potatoes for supper. 'Never mind, chickabid, rabbit tomorrow.'

'Do you know how to kill rabbits?' Miranda asked later.

177

'Oh yes, I learned when I was a girl. You swing them up by the back legs and administer a sharp chop with the side of your hand against their necks. They're supposed to die instantly.'

'In the meanwhile, we've shut it up without anything to eat.'

'Yes, I know,' Florence said. 'I feel rather bad about it.'

They went to bed early, depressed by the war news and the cold east wind, and bored with one another's company. Miranda slept heavily for an hour, then awoke, wondering about the rabbit. They should have fed it. Even criminals condemned to die on the scaffold were given a last hearty breakfast, according to popular supposition. The rabbit was very small, and small things needed to eat with great frequency.

But we also need to eat, she thought. Elevenpenn'orth of meat a week is hopelessly inadequate. Before long we'll get deficiency diseases. And just think. Rabbit pie. Rabbit casserole. Rabbit pie . . . rabbit sandwiches. . . . All proper country people catch rabbits, wring hens' necks, shoot pigeons. . . . She slept, then woke again at five. It was still dark but the wind had dropped when she crept out of the kitchen door and down the garden. Shadows twitched and birds mumbled as she tiptoed towards the potting shed and then recoiled. A human shadow had joined her own, yawning its length on the closed door.

'Oh Christ, chickabid, what are you – ?'

'Probably the same as you.' Miranda's heart steadied slowly.

She pulled at the potting-shed door and held it wide open. Blackness filled the interior and the clematis had stopped tapping. Birds who had been disturbed settled to sleep again.

'Did you come out here to give it something to eat?'

'No.'

'No. Neither did I.'

They waited, growing cold in dressing gowns and thin slippers. Ten minutes later they heard a faint scuffle and then, peering, saw a small shape creep over the threshold, crouch motionless as if not daring to trust its luck, and then bound suddenly and rapturously away.

They closed the door and went back to the house arm-in-arm.

'I do love you, chickabid,' Florence said at the foot of the stairs. 'You're just like me.'

'I love you too,' Miranda replied.

Three weeks later she opened her morning post and discovered that the British Red Cross Society was inviting her to attend a nine-week course on First Aid.

I can't, she thought. The sight of blood makes me faint.

The reception hut of the women's block at Birkenau, which was the extermination camp of Auschwitz prison, had a long table running down the centre on to which all suitcases, bags and bundles had to be emptied. Uniformed SS women turned over the variety of objects which tumbled out – clothing, jewellery, photographs, little china trinkets, carefully hoarded cigarettes . . . . Fur coats were the first items to be confiscated, amid suppressed cries of grief; then jewellery, which included wedding rings wrenched from fingers which dared not protest. An SS woman wearing a hairslide pawed idly through the contents of Nat's suitcase and flicked through the books of music which lay at the bottom.

'What's this?' she asked in German.

'Music,' Nat replied in English.

'Yours?' The woman tried a guttural French.

'Yes.'

'Do you play it?'

'That's why I brought it.'

The woman grunted and chucked the books on the floor. No one else had brought music with them, so a separate pile had to be started; few people realised how much the smooth running of the Final Solution depended on an orderly approach to small details.

The next two hours of the procedure were unbelievable. Blunt scissors hacked at Nat's thicket of hair, then a blunt razor removed what remained. Cuts on her scalp trickled blood which she could only wipe away with her fingers. Dazedly she submitted to having a serial number tattooed on her forearm; no longer Natalie Ellenberg, she was now 69487.

The next stop was the shower, and icy-cold water drenching naked heads, naked bodies. A woman lost consciousness and was left to lie on the slimy concrete. Back in the reception hut they looked at one another timidly, shamefacedly; those who had been in Drancy for several months were already thin while others were still reasonably plump and rounded. One woman with large breasts drooping to her waist tried awkwardly to cover them behind her folded arms.

Then at last, clothes. These were thrown at them by the *blockawas*, the *fridolines* of Auschwitz, and were ludicrous both in style and fit. Although winter came early to that part of Europe, the majority of the garments were creased and skimpy summer dresses – there was no underwear – and Nat's allocation was a green cotton affair that might have been worn by an old-fashioned domestic servant, except that it had a yellow triangle sewn on the front. The yellow triangle, she discovered, signified Jew. The only other apparel she was given was a pair of men's shoes; size nine and without laces. Then at last, after three days and three nights, they were given food: a tub of soup baled out into tin bowls by more *blockawas*, who made it plain by their manner that they were dispensing a favour at personal sacrifice. There were no spoons, and despite her aching hunger Nat tried to avoid the odd lumps of unidentifiable substance as she raised her bowl between both hands.

No one spoke. No one dared to. Each woman strove in silence to come to terms with reality while maintaining a precarious hold upon sanity. Only Emil Rokhele's mother, weeping silently, laid aside her untouched bowl, which was snatched up by the woman sitting next to her. The woman with the big breasts.

They were shown into a large and evil-smelling shed, and in the faint light were just able to make out that it was filled with three-tiered bunks and that most of them were occupied. The place was restless with the sound of deep, lung-tearing coughing, with groaning, and with the fragmented mutterings of women tormented even in their sleep.

Fearfully, Nat climbed on to a middle bunk and lay down, trying not to touch the stinking straw with her face. She felt cold, bitterly cold, and clasping her stinging bald head in her hands tried not to cry out at the memory of the children of Drancy who had chattered so optimistically about Pitchipoi. She remembered her own contributions to the fantasy of sea and sand, food and toys, and bitterly reproached herself for what they must now see as a grown-up's cynical delight in misleading them. The only comfort lay in the hope that she might see them again, and be able to explain that her ignorance had been as great as theirs. If they were still interested, that was.

She learned next day that the chief language of Auschwitz was Polish, and that it was understood to a greater or lesser degree by the many deportees who had made the escape south-west to the Netherlands and France, only to find themselves transported back again as the German advance caught up with them. There was no one she met who spoke English, and those who spoke French tended to do so with an accent difficult to penetrate.

She also learned some of the other facts concerning Auschwitz, including the reason for the dividing of prisoners upon arrival at the railway siding; babies, children, the old and sick went straight to the gas chamber while the others would be put to work.

'*Et la grande cheminée, c'est pour . . . ?*'

'*Exactement. Et maintenant vous comprenez tout . . . .*'

Yes, I understand everything now.

On the morning of her third day the *blockawa* with the hairslide singled her out, and with a jerk of the head signified that Nat was to follow her. She did so, trudging with difficulty in her men's unlaced shoes across the frozen mud that stretched between Block A and Block B. From the outside it was just another barracks hut, but the inside was strikingly different. It was warm, and even contained a modicum of furniture, and the women within – there must have been twenty or so – were comparatively well dressed, their hair in varying stages of regrowth. Compared with the poor creatures in Block A they were aristocrats.

Nat seemed to absorb all this without really looking, because her eyes were fixed on one thing only. There, on a platform surrounded by music stands grouped like respectful attendants, stood a concert grand piano. Its appearance was so incongruous, grotesque even, in a place like this that she remained motionless, without breathing, while she tried to assimilate this latest proof that the world had indeed gone mad.

A grand piano. In a place where they gassed people by the thousand and then shovelled them into a furnace.

A woman detached herself from the silent group and came towards her. She was thin but had a full head of hair, and she wore an armband which obviously gave her some kind of official status.

'You are a musician?' She had the usual guttural accent.

'Yes.'

'What do you play?'

'Piano.'

The woman considered her in silence for a moment, then indicated the platform. 'Do so.'

It was an effort to start moving, to break out of the trance. Bald and dirty, clad in a ridiculous frock and men's shoes, she shuffled towards the piano, sat down on the stool and stared at the keys with her hands in her lap.

'She can't really play,' someone whispered in Polish. 'She's just trying to save her skin. . . .'

Her Jewish profile remained stony, obdurate, and only those nearest to her noticed the rapid blinking of her eyes. Then she raised her hands and crashed out a chord. The Bechstein responded. She crashed out another and another, and the huge magisterial sound swept through the room and was joined by a great sweeping cascade from the top of the keyboard down to the lowest bass note. She paused, still blinking, hands once more in her lap. Then she raised them very slowly and began to play.

She didn't know what she was playing. Her mind was blank. Only her fingers, hands and arms were responding to the great black-and-white smile of the Bechstein, and fragments of Bach and Beethoven, Schumann and Brahms joined together seamlessly and harmoniously as if they were all gallantly agreeable to being united in this one extraordinary moment in this one most terrible place.

She stopped playing when the woman with the armband touched her shoulder and said, 'That will do. I will have you in the orchestra.'

'Orchestra . . . ?' Her hands fell away from the keys.

'This is the Music Block, and we are the official Birkenau Women's Orchestra. We play cheerful marches for the prisoners going to their work each morning and coming back each night. That takes place out of doors. Indoors, we give our serious classical concerts.'

'Who for?' Nat's voice was a disbelieving croak.

'For the Gestapo. Who else?'

And so began for Nat perhaps the most bizarre interlude so far: her time as accompanist to the Women's Orchestra in the most renowned concentration camp in history.

There had been an all-male orchestra in Auschwitz since the first mass round-up of Jews in Germany, Austria, Czechoslovakia and Poland; all were professional musicians, composers or teachers who had been swept into the maelstrom, and all played regularly before the SS and their high-ranking visitors. Even Heinrich Himmler had attended a performance arranged for his delectation, but had left before the first interval. Fearful in case the performance had been declared substandard, they waited for reprisals, but none came. Perhaps Himmler just didn't care for music.

The Women's Orchestra had been formed later, and was regarded as an unusual and rather whimsical innovation on the part of Höss, then commandant of Auschwitz. They were given better food and clothes, and were also given to understand that each of them could be sent back to Block A and the gas chamber should they fail to please.

Fear spurred them to musical heights of which they would not have thought themselves capable, but even so the results were idiosyncratic and occasionally freakish. The balance of sound depended upon which musical instruments were available, and upon who was able to play them. Cellists were nonplussed at suddenly having to play violins, and a girl flautist who had played in the Czech Philharmonic flatly refused to consider switching to the oboe.

'But it's a *reed* instrument – don't you see that it works on an entirely different principle?'

Her mind was changed at the mention of a return to Block A, and so she applied all her concentration to mastering the oboe that had recently appeared. It was not unusual for instruments to appear and disappear without explanation, and Nat consoled herself with the knowledge that a grand piano could hardly be whisked away while no one was looking. Several other women also played the piano, but not as well, and Nat sensed that she had won the approval, if not the friendship, of the woman with the armband who conducted them. She was Block *kapo*, which Nat understood to be the rank assigned to head prisoner, and everyone regarded her with due circumspection. Obviously it paid to keep in with her.

The woman occupying the bed next to Nat's was Magda Wozniak, who was tall and spare with large intense eyes set in a prematurely lined face. Born into a musical family, she had been a violin teacher in a minor academy in Hungary, and had escaped the gas chamber by virtue of a desperately spirited performance with the men's orchestra in a work by Lalo, after the rightful soloist had been declared medically unfit to play. This had taken place during the initial planning of the women's orchestra, so her place as first violin was assured.

'It was the performance of my life,' she told Nat. 'I know I would never be able to do it again.'

'You can do anything at any time, if you're pushed hard enough,' Nat replied in the stumbling German she was slowly acquiring.

But she discovered that Magda's assessment of her own capabilities was probably accurate; she loved music, but for the formal nuts and bolts of it rather than for its emotional appeal. Unusual perhaps for a Hungarian.

She also discovered that the role of official pianist had one serious limitation, for as the *kapo* had already explained, the orchestra's main function was to play outside as the work groups were marched off each day and returned at night; and as it was obviously impossible to move the piano in and out each time, what other instrument did she play?

'I don't. My second subject was composition.'

'Then you had better learn one,' the *kapo* said tersely. 'And fast.' She shoved a mandolin into Nat's hands.

'I can't play this.'

'Why not? It's a stringed instrument.'

'But for God's sake – '

'Do you want to live?'

Nat drew her fingers across the bridge of the mandolin and brought forth a melancholy and discordant twang.

'That's better. Now we'll see about getting you some warmer clothes and some proper shoes. . . .'

The baptism of fire, as Nat thought of it, came only three days later. Clad now in a white blouse and dark skirt and a pair of women's shoes, and wearing a little white triangular scarf over her naked skull, she stood at the foot of her bed in line with the others while the two German *blockawas* bawled *'Achtung! Achtung! – Appell!'*

A crop-haired blonde, her SS tunic straining to cover a powerful bust, marched in. She spotted Nat instantly, and demanded to know who she was.

The *kapo* stepped forward and said that the prisoner in question was Natalie Ellenberg, English and a pianist.

'English . . .' The woman stepped closer to Nat; her eyes were very small and her breath smelt of onions. *'Und eine Juden?'*

'Yes. I am a Jew,' Nat said in English, and despite the tenseness of the situation was instantly carried back to the old childhood days of saying, *We're Jews, but not Orthodox*. She remembered saying it to Miranda when they first met at Queen Mary's. Perhaps she had been rather in love with the word 'Orthodox'. . . .

The SS woman spoke a few abrupt and rasping words to the *blockawas* who mumbled agreement while standing to attention, then the inspection was concluded and the Women's Orchestra was given leave to take up its instruments and march outside.

At the junction of Blocks A and B was an open space, in the centre of which stood a bandstand, complete with chairs. Its jaunty appearance was rendered even more incongruous by the hundreds of silent wraiths waiting outside their squalid huts for the order to quick-march. *Blockawas* and SS officers with whips shoved them this way and that, ostensibly pushing them into line, and when one woman collapsed on the ground her companions seemed too sunk in apathy to notice. A *blockawa* pushed her to one side with her boot.

Sickened, Nat gripped her mandolin in both hands and stumbled up the steps of the bandstand with the rest of the orchestra. They waited while the *kapo* took up her conductor's stance in front of them. The morning was misty, and her eyes seemed to switch on like two powerful and menacing headlamps.

There were no music stands and no music. The orchestra was supposed to have mastered the repertoire by heart. Most of them had, and they obediently raised violins and oboes while the two percussionists

– Rosa on the kettledrum and Jenni with the cymbals – poised themselves in readiness. The remainder of the ill-assorted group did likewise; four mandolins, a guitar, a piano accordion and, of all things, a mouth organ. Thus equipped, they plunged into the 'Rakoczy March' when the conductor gave the downbeat.

It was brave and it was ludicrous; stirring music thumped and piped out by an insane variety of instruments held together by the thin sounds of violins. Nat strummed, desperate as the rest, and tried not to watch as the columns of slave labour shambled forward in pitiful imitation of a brisk march. All had shaven heads and half were barefoot; some moved forward as if deep in a lost world of their own, while others turned their heads to stare at the comparatively well-fed and well-dressed orchestra and to spit hatred upon its privileged stature. Only one or two acknowledged the music-makers with a little flicker of understanding: a lift of the eyebrows, a wink or a half-smile that testified to the universal plight of those incarcerated in Auschwitz, the model extermination camp that was Himmler's pride and joy.

Head bent, Nat plunked an inaudible accompaniment to the two Suppé marches which followed, and tried to concentrate on listening to the voice of Magda's violin at her side, and when the last ghostly figures had finally passed into the mist the conductor laid aside her baton and gave the order to return to their quarters. They marched briskly and in step.

Back in the comparative warmth of their hut Nat lay face down on her bed and thought, twice a day, morning and evening, for weeks, months, perhaps years. How will I keep going? And if I do, what sort of a mindless creature will I be at the end of it?

'Don't worry, everyone feels the same to begin with. The first time's always the worst,' Magda said grimly.

At last the war seemed to be accelerating in the Allies' favour.

After a dank winter followed by a cold spring of irritable tension the great Normandy landing took place on June the 6th. Transferred from North Africa Sammy Ellenberg became part of the British/American Airborne Division and broke a leg as he pancaked down close to the Pegasus Bridge at Benouville. Two women from the café close by dragged him in under cover of darkness and kept him hidden in an attic until the enemy had been driven back from the area. His leg remained without medical attention for six days, but he was one of the lucky ones.

The Germans were retreating but not before contesting every step of the way, and on the day Miranda broke the news that she was being sent to France with a team of Red Cross relief workers, Florence gave a squawk of horror.

'You can't possibly go over there – it's far too dangerous! Jesus, chickabid, you'll get blown up!'

'Not if I'm careful.'

'But it's no place for a woman! Men start wars, they should bloody well finish them.'

'Exactly. But now I think it's time for a spot of the famous womanly touch. Why don't you come with me? You'd be awfully good at it.'

'I've half a mind to. . . .' For a moment Florence looked wistful.

'Oh no you don't,' Miranda said hastily. 'The Red Cross is full up.'

'Are you sure?' She seemed to dwindle a little, then added, 'Well, I don't suppose they'd have me. I mean, I'm not educated like some people I could mention, and the Red Cross has always struck me as a bit . . . well. . . .'

'Élitist?'

'What's that?'

'But it isn't. Anyone can join. But what's wrong with your ARP?'

'It's all become a bit of a bore, really. We still go through all the drill, but the last bomb we had was back in April last year, and even then it only fell in a field and killed a sheep.'

'Sheep have a place in this world too, you know,' Miranda said sternly. 'But don't forget that I'll be relying on you for all sorts of things like keeping the garden going – can you remember to sow some more lettuce seed if we get a shower next week? – and then Bruno and Esme rely on you to make them laugh.'

'I'll try.' Florence sounded dubious. 'But I wish you weren't going to France, chickabid. I mean, what are you supposed to do when you get there?'

'Provide medical care and general comfort, mainly. I'm also going to find old Nat as soon as Paris is liberated and tell her it's high time she came home.'

'She might be dead by now.'

'Of course she's not dead! For God's sake think positive.'

'Not always easy at my age, particularly when you've witnessed the tragedies I have.'

'Like a poor old sheep being bombed.'

'I didn't actually see it, I'm thankful to say. By the time we arrived with stirrup pumps and stretchers and things it was just a little red smear and a few tufts of wool. But oh, chickabid. . . .'

'That's probably all the Red Cross team'll have to cope with.' Miranda submitted gracefully to her mother's embrace. 'Just the odd little smear and the odd little tuft. You really mustn't worry.'

Florence and the two Ellenbergs waved her off in the village taxi the following day while Bert the handyman stood a little apart. The sky was of a peerless blue and the Common basked in shimmering gold.

'She looks very smart in her uniform,' Esme said to Florence as the taxi trundled out of sight. 'Come over and have a bowl of soup for lunch.'

Florence thanked her, but declined. She had grown fond of the Ellenbergs, fond enough to forget that they were Jews, and different, but the sense that they knew more because they were better educated – he must have been specially well educated to be a specialist – still gave her an awkward feeling. At any minute she might put her foot in it, and that would let Miranda down.

So she went back to the empty house where shafts of sunlight played over all poor Emrys' pretty bits and pieces and the placid country silence tore at her nerves. The cat was dozing on a chair in the dining room but woke at her approach and rather pointedly left the room, swinging its hips. They had never cared for one another.

She looked in the drinks cupboard, but there wasn't much in there; anyway, she didn't think that a drink would help. Neither would a cigarette, even if she had one. She sat down, nibbling her fingers and fighting an increasing panic of loneliness and despair. The place was awful and impossible without chickabid; it would swallow her in a great green tide and leave no trace.

An hour later she was upstairs packing a bag. She closed the windows, put out the cat, bolted the doors, left a note stuck in the letterbox to say that she had gone away for a few days, then set off across the Common. It was a long hot walk to the village, but the London train meandering down from Ipswich arrived ten minutes later.

A thunderous crash followed by the tinkling of glass greeted her arrival at Liverpool Street Station. She had heard on the news about the new peril of flying bombs, and she scuttled rapidly in search of a taxi. London looked drably dull, the taxi driver was uncommunicative, and looked sourly upon the threepenny tip she gave him.

'I'm only a poor widow,' she said ingratiatingly.

'I'm the father of six kids under eight.'

'If I was her I'd chop it off.'

She had a long wait for the train at Euston and listened apprehensively to further crashes, some distant and some near, as the flying bombs stuttered and then fell. She was relieved when they finally steamed out of London, and studied her travelling companions in the hope that they might yield a little interesting if ephemeral conversation, but they looked as drab and dull as London itself. The woman in the opposite corner had brought a thermos flask and a packet of sandwiches wrapped fussily in a white napkin, and the beguiling smell of hot tea and egg mayonnaise woke up the others. They stared at her resentfully, wondering where she got the egg from. There were few servicemen on the train, which was a pity, and Florence concluded that they must all be in France where poor silly old chickabid had gone. Gloom descended.

But Liverpool revived her. Directly the train arrived at Lime Street she felt invigorated; full of the old bright-eyed, spring-in-the-step youthful jauntiness that had wrenched her at the age of fifteen from a poor and unpromising background into the precarious world of ever-tantalising promise that she adored.

And in spite of the war and the bombing, Liverpool welcomed her back with a screech of the old familiar trams and the old familiar chatter delivered in nasal singsong. Rejoicing, she booked herself a room in a dingy little hotel just off Mount Pleasant, unpacked her bag, washed her hands and face and applied fresh make-up, then sallied forth.

The blackout made a difference of course, but she stood entranced watching the thousands of starlings swooping in to roost under the portico of St George's Hall as the summer sky darkened. Like a woman in a dream she retraced her steps up Mount Pleasant to Catherine Street, to Upper Parliament Street and the area where she had lived in so many different flats; each one rosy with new hope springing from a new relationship and none of them working out quite as she had imagined. There had been Harry in the basement in Bedford Street, Eddie in the top flat in Faulkner Square, then darling chickabid in Huskisson Street where that woman had falsely accused her of messing up the bathroom. . . . Then Morton Street with chickabid and Rob. But her busy, happy mind sheered away from Rob the marvellous lover and the filthy Fascist. He would still be sewing mailbags or whatever, and serve him damn well right.

She left Morton Street and wandered back past the bombed buildings surrounding the new Anglican cathedral, and rather like an act of purification found her way to the house in Rodney Street. It was still empty, its windows grimy and the door showing the patch where Bruno's brass plate had been removed. She wondered about the poor daughter who had been at school with chickabid; Jewish of course, but a very nice type in spite of the hole in her sleeve. 'I don't believe she's still alive,' Florence said aloud, before turning away. 'Such a shame because she played the piano quite nicely.'

The hotel in which she was staying offered only bed-and-breakfast, and after the long hot day she felt not only tired but also extremely hungry. Tucking her handbag firmly under her arm she left Rodney Street for the liveliness of Church Street and the hope of a nice pub meal.

It was different without the lights, of course, yet the war seemed not to have dimmed the old sense of expectancy, of warm friendliness and lack of inhibition. She pushed open the outer door of what had always been known as Marty's pub, and once inside saw the old cut-glass lamps gleaming over the long curve of mahogany bar just as they had always done. But Marty wasn't behind the bar, and when she asked about him the barmaid said, 'Ooh well, he's in the Mairchant Navy, isn'ee?'

They had some sherry in stock and she ordered a plate of potato hash with red cabbage before carrying it over to a secluded corner. The place was crowded, Liverpool voices and Liverpool laughter rising above the jukebox music, and she paused at a small table where a man sat with his back to her.

'Pardon me,' Florence said in upper-class London tones, 'may I join you?'

Without replying the man indicated the empty seat with a wave of his hand.

'I'm just up from London for a few days,' Florence said, sipping. 'I used to live here, many years ago.'

'Oh, yes?' He sat staring into his glass of beer.

'It's nice not having the flying bombs any more – that *awful* moment when the engine cuts out and you wait for it to fall.'

'Nasty things, flying bombs.' He took a mouthful of beer, appraising her while doing so.

'Sometimes after they cut out they drift.'

'I've heard that,' he said. Then added, 'How's Miranda?'

Florence drew a sharp breath, peered at him closely and then said in tones of disbelief: 'Stanley!'

'It's me,' he said, and gave her a painful little smile. 'How are things?'

'Stanley . . .' she repeated incredulously, and put out her hand almost as if to ward him off. Mistaking the gesture he seized it and shook it warmly. 'Nice to see you again, Flo.'

They continued to shake hands slowly and ritualistically while they stared into one another's faces. He's gone *bald*, Florence thought. And he used to have lovely thick hair like Miranda.

'You don't look any older, Flo.'

'Don't I?' She touched her cheek with her free hand, remembering how pretty she had been then, in a little cloche hat and with two kiss curls stuck to either cheek with Vaseline. 'I feel it, sometimes.'

They had met when colliding in the swing doors of the post office; Florence had conveniently dropped her handbag and Stanley had picked it up with one hand while raising his hat with the other. They had both apologised, and when she indicated that he had also trodden on her toe he was led to the tentative suggestion that they might share a pot of tea in the nearby ABC.

Being hard up, lonely and at an emotional loose end, she had fallen in love with him before demolishing her second toasted teacake; he was good-looking in a neat and unspectacular way, and he spoke like a gentleman. He was in insurance he said, and lived in the house that had been left to him by an aunt.

'I'm an orphan,' she said eagerly and untruthfully. 'I've absolutely no one in the world.'

'In that case, perhaps I can offer a little sympathy.' He spoke the words gravely, and his very obvious lack of philandering intent increased his attraction even more. She also liked the sound of his aunt's house.

The courtship had proceeded in a steady if unspectacular fashion, but the first doubts had set in even before the wedding. His parents (elderly, censorious and comfortably off) had not succumbed to Florence's flapper charm, and his aunt's house was only semi-detached. Love flew out of the window even before they had settled in, and Stanley, kind, unimaginative and immersed in the world of insurance, had taken it for granted that she was happy, especially when the baby was born. But Florence had wanted a boy called Marcus – if she had wanted anything at all – and the trials of motherhood added to the boredom of chaste suburbia proved too much. She decamped, leaving Miranda in the care of a friend, and returned thankfully to the old precarious life of existing by her wits while staying within the law. The divorce was painless and dignified like everything else about Stanley and his world, and within a short space of time Florence had few detailed recollections of their relationship, which left her free to invent whatever facts seemed to suit the occasion. But now, this unexpected meeting had temporarily deprived her of all her powers of invention.

She dropped her hand from her cheek, but not before he had noticed that she was still wearing the wedding ring he had placed on her finger, all those years ago. At least it looked like the same one, but it was hard to tell with wedding rings.

'Did you get married again?' He had to ask the question.

'No, just one or two near misses. Did you?'

'Yes, I married a girl from St Helens, but she died giving birth to Roger.'

'Roger. . . .'

'He's six.'

Florence began to cry quietly. He released her hand, patted it and said, 'Drink your sherry before it gets cold.'

It was the sort of weak little joke he used to make in the old days. Then, such jokes had invariably irritated her, but now she was grateful. Yet jokes were something you shared with people, and meeting Stanley again was making her freshly aware of her new loneliness.

She sipped, choked slightly, and fumbled again for her handkerchief. Then a waitress in a tight pink dress appeared with a small tray, shouted, 'Prater 'ash fer one!' and dumped the plate and a knife and fork in front of her.

'I don't think I want it now,' Florence faltered.

'Go on, I'll keep you company.' With a brief nod, Stanley ordered the same for himself.

'Now,' he said, returning from the bar with another sherry and another beer, 'tell me what Miranda's doing. I don't suppose you've got a snap of her, have you?'

She had; one taken last summer at Trellis House, sitting in a deck-chair with her knees showing and her toes turned in. She was laughing and tousled and very nearly beautiful. He studied it intently, a muscle twitching in his jaw.

'She's lovely and wonderful and clever and kind and I saw her off to France this morning with the Red Cross.' Tears came again but she forced them back. 'She's also a widow. He was older than her and he died of cancer.'

He returned the snap reluctantly, then showed her one of a little boy with curly hair sitting on a piano stool with his ankles crossed. He was clutching a toy dog.

'Is this Roger?'

'That's him.' There was quiet pride in his voice, and while they ate he went on to tell her that Betty's mother, Roger's grandma, looked after him during the week while he was working.

'Are you still in the same job?'

191

'Oh no, I'm in the Inland Revenue now. Have been since thirty-eight.'

'That's nice,' Florence said and meant it. Being something to do with the government was much nicer than being in insurance.

'Am I by any chance a grandfather yet?'

'There was no time. Miranda married this terribly nice chap called Emrys – comfortably off and very well connected – and she had a job with him to start with; he was a very big noise in the antiques business. As I say, he was older than she was. They moved down to the country when the bombing started and insisted that I went with them, but poor old Emrys got iller and iller and although we both did every mortal thing we could, he died last year.'

'Poor Miranda.' He looked weary and oppressed.

'I hope to God she'll be all right in France.'

'So do I.'

They ate in silence for a while. 'So you live in the country,' he said at length. 'I thought you said you were in London.'

'Yes, I used to be, and I still pop up from time to time to see old friends or go to a show.'

'You were always good at making friends,' he said wistfully.

'But I didn't have the knack of making them last, somehow,' she surprised herself by saying.

'Would you like to meet Roger?'

'No – I don't know. Well, not straight away.'

'No, of course not. There's plenty of time.'

Is there? she asked herself. We might still get killed in the war, and anyway, we're beginning to get old.

The noise in the pub was increasing. Someone was playing the piano and people were singing, and cigarette smoke was stinging her eyes. Funny how some people could always get hold of cigarettes.

'I think I'll go now, if you don't mind,' she said, and gathered up her handbag.

'I'll see you home.'

She wanted to argue, but couldn't be bothered. It had been a long and emotional day and she was very tired.

There were no taxis, and because of the blackout she held his arm. She remembered how punctilious he had been about walking nearest the kerb when they were out together, but then he, like Miranda, had had the benefit of a good education. Pity he hadn't done more with it, really. She thought of his life as she now knew it; from insurance to the Inland Revenue; divorce from one woman, then marriage to another one who had died leaving him with a small child. But had her own been any better? At least she hadn't had a child by Rob Allardyce, any more than they had actually gone through the formality of getting married, thank God. . . .

'I still love Liverpool,' she said, suddenly nostalgic. 'And I'm glad the old Liver Building's escaped the bombs.'

'Not a bad place, but I'm not sure I want Roger to grow up here. It's going to be tough after the war.'

'Come and live in the country, then.' She spoke lightly, flirtatiously, but sensed rather than saw him shake his head. She was glad that she couldn't see his face, only feel the warmth of his arm as it held hers.

He seemed surprised to discover that she was staying in a shabby little hotel. They stood beneath the dull blue glow coming through the fanlight.

'How long are you staying for, Flo?'

'Only a couple of days. I just came up on impulse after I'd seen Miranda off.'

'Shall we meet up again before you go?'

'I don't know. I mightn't have time. . . .' Sudden confusion made her sound evasive. 'Can you give me a phone number?'

He did so, then after a momentary hesitation they exchanged addresses, scribbling hastily on the backs of envelopes while a police constable pacing slowly past eyed them with mild interest.

They parted quietly and almost abruptly. He made no further suggestion about another meeting, but touched her cheek with the tips of his fingers and said, 'So long then, Flo.'

'So long, Stanley.'

She hurried into the hotel, collected her key at the seedy little reception desk and bolted upstairs as if she were afraid that he might be following her. Flinging her hat on a chair she sat down on the creaking bed with her head in her hands, too tired to think coherently. She wished tearfully that chickabid was with her, even though she would probably only say something nasty.

Very little news from the outside world was able to penetrate the secluded world of Auschwitz; any which did so was invariably inaccurate.

Of course there were always rumours – the war is over, we are going to be liberated – but even for those with sufficient life left in them to be interested, there was the certain knowledge that the Germans would refuse to leave anyone alive to tell the tale. Whatever the outcome of the war it was too late now. They were already doomed.

Sometimes it was possible to detect a heightened tension, a nervousness, among the Germans who ran the camp; invariably it displayed itself in scenes of increased and random brutality, and working prisoners had developed an almost uncanny ability to sniff the wind. To read behind the choking black clouds coming from the crematorium a sense of worried uncertainty among those in charge of them. But they never knew anything for certain; to be in Auschwitz was to be in limbo.

It was during one of these periods of restless foreboding that Natalie Ellenberg was invited to play the piano before the Camp Commandant.

'Word's got round that you play well,' the woman who conducted the orchestra said, 'so you'd better do your best. Not only is he Camp Commandant, he also knows about music, which is more than you can say for some of them.'

'I haven't been practising much lately.'

'Then you'd better start. If you impress him it could lead to all kinds of things.'

'For example?'

'Another pair of stockings. Even a box of chocolates, perhaps.'

'I'll think about it.'

'Let us be frank,' the *kapo* said, 'you haven't much choice.'

Because she was unable to play piano on her twice-daily appearances on the bandstand she had been neglecting the big Bechstein. Fellow members of the orchestra had to practise too, and the full-blooded sound of the concert grand drowned instruments of a less assertive nature. She was also aware of a covert watchfulness, the prelude to jealousy, on the part of the other pianists, and she had no desire to fan it into flame. She had no desires at all, except to survive, and preferred the company of Magda Wozniak the violinist because she too preferred to remain silent about the past.

The lust for music had died after leaving Saint-Denis for Drancy and had never returned. Perhaps it never would. Perhaps it had only been a child's passion anyway; something which was unable to withstand privation and fear. She wondered how long Liszt would have lasted in Auschwitz.

It was only when the *kapo* chucked a couple of music scores down on her bed that the old excitement began to stir. Miraculously they were the scores she had brought with her, and as she flicked through them, notation turning into the voice of the piano as she read, she was glad in a way that she had no option but to play. Although the old lustful joy was still absent, and she was determined that it should remain so, the sense of pleasure in sharing music was not. With whom she shared it couldn't be helped in the circumstances.

She chose Mozart's Sonata in C (K.545) which she had loved as a child, and the Beethoven Sonata No. 11 in B flat, which she had once played for an exam. Both were included in the two scores that had been returned to her, and after approving her choice the *kapo* left her alone to get on with it.

The other members of the orchestra also left her alone, and in their tacit withdrawal she read a kind of grudging respect which touched her. Of mixed race and background, she had never found them particularly easy to get on with; the Hungarians (with the exception of Magda) had the most inflammable tempers and the Polaks the best line in dumb insolence, Jews and the handful of Catholics mixed warily, the French considered themselves superior and the Czechs preferred their own company. The novelty of a lone Englishwoman had worn off long ago, although in times of stress she might still be called upon to answer for the sins of her country.

'Your King Tudor persecute Catholics.'

'Your Chamberlain he persecute Jews.'

'So why you burn Joan of Arc?'

'Because,' Nat said exasperatedly, 'we were cold. Now shut up.'

But they endured with stoicism her long hours of practice, and only one of them (the Polish girl who sucked and blew twice daily on the mouth organ) expressed aloud the foreboding that oppressed them all from time to time: 'You play bad, we all die.'

The recital was to be given in the Sauna, a large and forbidding structure in brick and concrete, and the piano was carried over there by male prisoners from the main camp. The *kapo* obtained permission from the *blockawa* on duty for Nat to have a bath, a luxury practically unheard of.

Her hair had now grown to an inch in length – heads were supposed to be shaved every three months but the orchestra was treated more leniently – and it covered her scalp in tight black curls. She wore her white blouse and dark skirt, and polished her shoes on her blanket because, although cleaning materials were unobtainable, the SS attached great importance to impeccably shining footwear.

A great deal had been heard about Herr Kommandant Josef Kramer, who now ruled the Women's Camp at Birkenau. Some said he was not too bad, while others whispered that he was a beast incarnate. Most had never set eyes on him, and Nat, waiting with forced politeness for the guest of honour to appear, wondered what he looked like. The remainder of the audience was already in place; SS men and women in uniform, removing their caps and placing them tidily at their feet, a sprinkling of civilians from various admin. offices, and a handsome, pleasantly smiling man whom the *kapo* had earlier pointed out as the doctor in charge of the Experimental Laboratory. Standing at the side of the piano she had watched them all come in, for in the world of Auschwitz the artiste awaited the audience, not the other way around.

And when Kramer entered, everyone stood. He came in swiftly, flanked by two SS men, and strode to his seat in the centre front. He had the build of an all-in wrestler; a large head set low on a powerful barrel-chested body, and long arms that gave the impression of waiting to grab his opponent and crush him to death.

Striving to concentrate on the fact that he was supposed to be musical, Nat continued to stand by the piano. Her throat felt dry and her hands were worryingly damp; discreetly she wiped them down the sides of her skirt. At length, when everyone was seated, Kramer nodded to her that the recital might begin.

She sat down at the keyboard and closed her eyes, summoning the music. Then she opened them and began to play.

The acoustics were bad and seemed to spoil the opening of the Beethoven sonata, but as the music settled down to a more thoughtful mood she sensed that the audience was listening attentively. *One wrong note and I'm for the gas chamber* . . . yet the sense that she was at least being taken seriously helped her in the early moments, and by the time she had reached the second movement she was no longer aware of them. She was only aware of the presence of Beethoven, lending her all the strength and concentration she needed. But with the opening of the Minuet she was suddenly back in the old days of love and warmth in Rodney Street. It hadn't happened once during all the hours of practice and she faltered for a second, blurring a couple of notes before wrenching her mind back to the present. Since the early days in Saint-Denis she had rigorously excluded all thoughts of the past; the past was dead – as dead as she would be if she allowed herself to slip into the treacherous false comfort of nostalgia.

She was playing better now, with muscles loosened and hands no longer damp, and when she reached the end of the sonata she was astonished to hear the audience applaud. Not wildly and unrestrainedly, but in a strange, grudging fashion; at least it was better than total silence. She stood up and bowed, hesitantly and rather jerkily, then sat down again to play the Mozart. She had been playing it since the age of ten, and its bubbling gaiety made a marvellous if temporary nonsense of the gloomy Sauna, of the wraithlike women of Birkenau and of the ever-present fear of the gas chamber.

This time the applause was less strained, and she saw Kramer smiling as he leaned towards one of his companions. She suddenly noticed what enormous ears he had. Then he turned towards the platform again, and indicated with a nod that she should play an encore. Confused and unprepared she launched into another old favourite, Mendelssohn's 'Rondo Capriccioso', but she was less than halfway through when a loud voice interrupted. She faltered, and her hands fell to her lap.

'That is Jews' music,' Kramer said.

She stood up very slowly, heart thumping with the sickened knowledge that it had all gone wrong after all; that it wasn't another scholarship at stake, it was her life. And the lives of others too, in all probability.

'And it's being played by a Jew.' The words seem to come of their own accord.

No one was prepared for what happened during the ensuing seconds. Two SS men entered the Sauna, glanced quickly about them and then made for where Kramer was sitting. They strode across to him, whispered rapidly, and the rest of the audience watched motionless as the Herr Kommandant snatched up his cap and hurried out after them, followed by his two companions.

It was difficult to break the frozen silence that followed, and in the end it was the pianist who did so. Left marooned by the side of the piano she braced her shoulders and marched from the scene.

'What a fool to play Mendelssohn!' the *kapo* stormed at her. 'Haven't you got any brains at all? Thank God for the diversion. . . .'

The other women in the music block greeted their return with eager questions. How did it go? Was he pleased? Did he smile at you? Living so precariously at the whim of others they knew the terrible difference between a smile and a frown. The *kapo* made no mention to them of the encore débâcle, which was nice of her, and gaunt, hollow-eyed Magda drew her to one side and whispered, 'I have saved your supper for you and there's an extra slice of bread.'

In less than an hour the whole camp was on special alert. All prisoners were ordered into their huts and even the *blockawas* looked frightened. Catholics prayed and Jews resigned themselves to the inevitable. Someone had escaped. There had been a mass escape, rumour said. Those of an optimistic nature even dared to wonder if the war was at an end.

The truth was that someone had attempted to assassinate Hitler. The attempt had failed; Hitler had emerged unscathed, and the perpetrators of the crime were immediately hunted down and dealt with in Nazi fashion. Hanging by rope was too merciful; they were hanged by piano wire.

Dear Mother,

Well, we've arrived at last. Can't say too much in detail because all mail's heavily censored, but we're somewhere in Normandy and living in quite luxurious quarters. I share a room with a nice girl called Dora. Not much activity at the moment but we're all unpacked and ready! There's an old lady here who's some kind of caretaker for the family who lived here and I practise my schoolgirl French on her. Dora's lucky, she can speak German as well, but then she's an interpreter while I'm only a humble relief worker. Will write again shortly. Take care, give my love to everyone and don't forget to water the beans and nip the tops out of the tomatoes.

Yours lovingly,
Miranda.

Sometimes it had seemed as if she would never get overseas. Grimly she had endured the nine-week training in First Aid, had quite enjoyed the Selection Board at the Joint War Organisation HQ, had passed the medical with ease, and had then sat back and waited.

Three weeks went by before the letter arrived requesting her to present herself at Rounham Camp in preparation for posting overseas. In the meantime the week which followed was filled with a dizzying rush to complete the necessary formalities; the form-filling seemed prodigious. Application for a passport, exit permit and contract form, and much hurried scurrying from one office to another. Then the issuing of clothing coupons and a £40 kit allowance. She bought her uniform (khaki) at Garroulds in the Edgware Road, filled in more forms, this time dealing with insurance and compensation, submitted to five different inoculations (the TAB giving her a high temperature and suicidal tendencies for twenty-four hours), and then came the panic-stricken realisation that she had forgotten to collect her camp equipment; camp bed, camp bath, canvas bucket, sleeping bag, mattress and pillow . . . . The list went on and on and she had to rush back to Garroulds to buy a special valise in which to carry it all. She already had a suitcase and a cabin trunk which, hastily packed, had been sent on to Southampton.

A three-ton lorry collected her at the port (no sign of luggage) and took her to Rounham which consisted of rows of tents threaded together by duckboards. It poured with rain from the moment she arrived. She ate off a tin plate and drank from a tin mug and caught a heavy cold, but the men and women who were now her companions exuded a resolute cheerfulness that rather appealed to her. It was impossible to feel homesick in their company and they boarded the Red Cross ship in a burst of dazzling sunshine that seemed a good omen for the future.

She had never been to France before, and as they travelled further inland the savagery of recent destruction appalled her; they passed small towns all but obliterated, many of them still smoking. Dora wanted to know why they couldn't stop and work here, but the Section Leader tersely informed her that she would soon have more work than she could cope with. So Dora shut up, but retained a mutinous expression.

The sandstone château at which they arrived was full of wounded British troops who were being tended by French nuns. Medical supplies were low and treatment rudimentary, and when the Red Cross medical team unpacked their own drugs and equipment the Mother Superior, with a large white apron over a billowing black habit, blessed them with calm ritualistic motions of a ghost-white hand.

Two weeks later all but the few servicemen too badly wounded to be moved were sent back to England; the Team packed up, said goodbye to the nuns and pushed closer to the fighting.

They were under canvas again and the tents throbbed to the roar of bulldozers driving impromptu roads down through woods and meadows to where assault engineers were hastily building pontoons and then a Bailey bridge over the River Orne. British and Canadian troops were working together in grim concentration and under constant enemy fire, for crossing the Orne was the final obstacle to linking up with the Americans.

Miranda found the new life extraordinary, and apart from the odd patches of terror, unexpectedly enjoyable. She discovered that the brief training had somehow prepared her both for obeying orders instantly and unquestioningly, and, on occasions when there were no orders, for being able to think clearly and act calmly. She had endured the First Aid course unwillingly and squeamishly, but after a preliminary gulp at the sight of blood was able to cope as the wounded were brought in, even to the extent of being present at an amputation and only feeling slightly swimmy at the sight of the poor hairy white leg lying on a towel beneath the operating table.

And they were all so kind to her. Dr Bennett, a sandily freckled man

199

in his early fifties, and Dr Paston who rigged up a badminton net and thwacked balls of cotton wool with a cardboard bat until remonstrated with by Beatrice the senior SRN who said that it was naughty to waste materials in wartime. There was Jenny who was in love with a chap in the Merchant Navy, Dodo who was half-French and who introduced them to the delights of strong French coffee laced with Calvados, then Dora and Michael, Phyllis and Bernard and Nancy and Pam and Steve, and as time wore on and they faced more physical dangers and more sudden emergencies in which there was little time even to think coherently, they became bound wordlessly together. It was impossible to imagine that peace could ever sever the ties.

But on an evening of incomparable beauty when there was a lull in the fighting – they were now near Le Tourneur – Miranda sat on a canvas chair with her evening ration of tinned Meat & Veg. on her lap and told Dr Paston about Nat.

'We were at school in Liverpool and I used to go and stay with her sometimes. I adored Nat and I adored the whole family because they taught me so much in a funny, casual sort of way. Nat was always going to be a concert pianist – I went to her début in London and honestly she was *cracking* good – then she went off to Paris to study some more with a woman called Boulanger who's apparently very famous, and that was the last we heard. She *must* have known when war was declared and we all expected her to come home pronto, but she didn't. And now God knows what's happened to her, because she's Jewish, for one thing. I suppose,' she laid aside her knife and fork and gazed at him earnestly, 'there's no hope of me taking my long weekend, which incidentally is long overdue, and going to Paris to find her?'

'Not the slightest,' Dr Paston said cheerfully.

'Why not? It's been liberated.'

'Only just. Hang on a bit longer until things get properly organised.'

'I'm fed up with hanging on.'

'We're doing all we can, dear,' he said in a voice that suddenly reminded her of Emrys. 'None of us can perform miracles, you know.'

'Sorry.'

'Don't be.' He descended from jocose falsetto and said sadly, 'I'm in love with a girl last heard of in Sumatra.'

'Being in love's much worse,' Miranda said with contrition. 'At least I'm a widow.'

'Nothing to stop you falling for someone else in the fullness of time.' Fondly he rumpled her hair, then said, 'Come on, finish your supper and then we'll have a little game of patball while Beatrice isn't looking.'

They put up the net and played with balls of screwed-up paper until it was too dark to see and the bark of gunfire shattered the country peace. She wondered whether she was falling a little bit in love with John Paston, then remembered about the girl in Sumatra and told herself that to do so would be a waste of time and emotion better spent elsewhere.

A few days later the Relief Team moved on again and followed the Allied armies into Holland where it was about to be embroiled in the bloodshed of the Battle of Arnhem.

'So that's that,' Sammy Ellenberg tried to say lightly.

'I'm sorry.' His wife Rose was standing at the window fiddling with the edge of the curtain.

After a certain amount of evasion on her part he had persuaded her to apply for a forty-eight-hour pass to coincide with his own sick leave, and they were staying at a small hotel in London. The leaves in Portman Square hung tired and dispirited, and they had just returned from a monosyllabic shopping spree in Selfridges. His broken leg, newly released from its plaster cast, was aching with fatigue and he hated walking with the aid of a stick.

'If anyone else says "There's a war on, madam" I shall scream,' Rose had said, emerging yet again from the curtained cubicle.

'You look very nice in that shade of blue.'

'It's turquoise, actually.'

'Well, whatever it is.'

'Does it make me look fat?'

'No. Sleek as a whippet.'

So she bought the turquoise dress, two blouses and a skirt, and a nightdress in white satin and then said, 'Oh damn, I've run out of coupons.'

'I've still got plenty.' Fumbling in his tunic pocket he extracted his own clothing coupon allowance. He gave her all he had and then paid for the purchases, and when they returned to the hotel and she told him that she wanted a divorce he felt initially stunned.

'But why? Is there someone else?'

'Afraid so.'

'And I've just provided your wedding trousseau.'

She turned on him sharply. 'What a beastly thing to say! Trust someone like you to think of something like that!'

'What exactly do you mean – someone like me?'

'Well. . . .'

'I take it you mean a Jew?'

She closed her eyes for a moment, then drew a deep breath. 'Well, that's what you are, isn't it?'

'Yes. But as my sister used to say when she was a kid, not Orthodox.'

'Does it make any difference?'

'You tell me.' He stretched out his leg to ease the pain.

'I'm sorry.' She began scooping the new clothes off the bed and hanging them rapidly on hotel hangers. 'But it's never really worked, has it? I suppose it's the war and everything.'

'The war's got nothing to do with it.'

'That's where you're wrong – the war's got everything to do with it.' The new blouses shivered on their hangers. 'The war's all about Jews, isn't it? If the Chosen Race hadn't tried to hog all the money and all the influence – '

'For God's sake, whose side are you on?'

'Ours, of course. I'm British to the core. But you have to admit that Hitler had a point.'

'Hitler's point,' he said, 'is the annihilation of every race, colour and creed, every shape of nose, every religious belief, every idea and every way of life that doesn't happen to correspond in every detail to his own warped vision of the human race. He has no interest in alien culture, in the richness of nonconformity. He has no desire to consider any creed or philosophy that doesn't happen to go along with his own curious ideal of a planet peopled exclusively by blond, blue-eyed giants versed in the martial arts and woefully incurious about everything else. His is a theory without grace, a world without beauty, variety, or wonderment at the unusual. Most of all it's a world based on the theory of intolerance, and let's face it, Rose, intolerance is the offspring of ineradicable stupidity.'

'Please spare me the lecture,' she said tiredly. 'I'm merely asking for a divorce.'

'I take it the lucky man is of pure Aryan stock?'

'As it happens, yes.'

'And he plays jolly good golf and has big feet and calls you Old Girl if he's under the age of forty – and probably something deeply embarrassing like Popsy if he's over – '

'As a matter of fact he's a Brigadier.'

'Aha, so it *is* Popsy!' Sammy cried, almost joyously. 'Red tabs and a nailbrush moustache. Little choleric blue eyes and a tendency to fart in the heat of battle – '

'Shut up!' she screamed at him. 'Shut up, shut up! You're venomous because you're a filthy blasted Jew! Venomous and spiteful and always hitting below the belt because you're not one of us!' She steadied herself before continuing. 'You want to be, but you can't be. Oh yes, you try hard enough, you all do, trying to join our various clubs and institutions and things and pretending you're British to the core, but when you realise that you can't – and you're *not* – then you try to run our financial world and struggle to gain power through the back door but you never will – not properly – because you're not one of us. You're a foreigner – you're all blasted foreigners – and you're all simply rotten with bitterness and jealousy – '

'Save the rest of it for Himmler,' he said, and taking up his cap and walking stick, hobbled out.

Without bothering to acquaint the reception clerk of his departure, and making no effort to pay the previous night's bill, he stumped down into the square and made for Baker Street Underground. Passengers smiled at him and a schoolboy gave up his seat because of the walking stick and the pilot's wings above his breast pocket.

He caught the train from Liverpool Street and when he reached the Overseer's House they asked with gentle offhandedness how Rose was.

'Fine,' he told them. 'Absolutely and utterly wizard.'

'Splendid. . . .' They smiled and nodded, and refrained from commenting on the fact that he had returned twenty-four hours too soon and without the small canvas holdall with which he had set out.

Aware that his father was keeping a carefully unobtrusive eye on his injured leg, he was at pains to alternate periods of rest with bouts of suitable exercise without being told to do so. He loved his parents for their careful avoidance of fussing and sympathised with their obvious puzzlement about Rose and the absence of news concerning her, but during the late summer of 1944 he found it impossible to speak of how things were – either with his marriage or his part in the war.

So clad in old grey flannels and an open-necked shirt he limped around Clatterfoot Common and tried to absorb a sense of healing peace from the wild scabious, rusting ferns and ripening blackberries that thronged his path. Without telling his mother he began to note birdlife activity; swallows (or were they swifts or house martins?) began to assemble in twittering groups ready for the flight south. They had a freedom unknown to the man in uniform who flew the skies on artificial wings, but they faced much the same hazards. Men shot down birds with the same impartiality with which they shot down one another.

Then his thoughts returned to Rose and her attitude towards the Jews. He had always known that she would have preferred him to be like her and her family – decent and unobtrusive C of E – and he had been well aware of her parents' scarcely concealed hostility towards him during their early meetings. He had been amused by it, fortified by Rose's frequent and passionate declarations of undying love which had overcome the old fundamental sensitivity. If he and Rose belonged together, then he belonged to all the world. My God, it had been so pathetically simple in the early days.

So he had met the local vicar, and had allowed himself to be married charmingly and painlessly in a Christian church lined with brass plaques devoted to the memory of (and extolling the virtues of) an impressive number of Rose's ancestors. Not that it had mattered, quite honestly – all a bit of a joke really; as an unorthodox Jew with no burning desire to embrace any kind of faith, the Church of England ceremony was as good as any other so long as the ultimate reward was Rose. Rose Pomfret into Rose Ellenberg, and his parents had welcomed their new daughter-in-law with gentle dignity.

The first slight jarring had come with Rose's suggestion, while nestled lovingly under his chin, that he might consider changing their name from Ellenberg to Ellendale.

'Why?'

'It sounds nicer.'

'But Ellenberg's my rightful name. My father's name.'

'He wouldn't mind.'

'I think it's a crazy idea.'

'Don't forget it's my name too.'

And that, he saw now, had been the beginning of the inevitable slide towards disenchantment and doom once the gloss, the excitement and yes, OK, the sex had begun to fade a little. Nothing serious, nothing dramatic; just a series of light pinpricks and small put-downs, all of them aided and abetted by the war. She had been called up less than a year after their marriage and their ways had naturally diverged; different RAF stations, difficulty of synchronising their leaves, the frustrations of wartime travel. . . . He had kept on hoping until there was no hope left.

His thoughts turned from Rose and wandered towards his sister Nat. He had always tried to visualise her safely ensconced in a nice little Paris flat somewhere, but Paris had been liberated for almost a month now and there was still no word from her. They only mentioned her name once during his leave at home, and that was in order to assure each other with a brightness as false as their conviction that they would be hearing from her any day now.

'She's probably married and the mother of four,' he said gaily, 'in which case it's bound to take a bit of time to get passports and things organised.'

They smiled, and agreed that it was silly to be impatient, and he loved them with a great surge of emotion that made it difficult not to put his arms round them and rock with them to and fro in an effort to soothe the long slow agony of longing for the absent child of their flesh. For Nat was a part of him too; bound to him by the indissoluble ties of family that made his relationship with Rose, he now saw, a poor, hollow thing by comparison. The fact of it comforted even while it brought fresh anguish. He had so loved, and been so proud of Rose's classically cool English beauty.

He was wandering over the Common and reliving yet again the last scene in the hotel bedroom when a smallish and rather skinny woman with dyed red hair and brightly enquiring eyes approached him. She was carrying a shopping basket in one hand and a string bag filled with a newspaper parcel in the other.

'You must be Sammy!' she said, and put down her shopping basket. 'I'm Florence, Miranda's mother.'

'Yes, of course.' They shook hands. 'I've been meaning to call and see you. How are you, and how's Miranda?'

'I'm fine, and she's living in a tent,' Florence said. 'I do wish she wouldn't.'

'Wouldn't what?' He picked up her shopping basket and retraced his steps. They walked together towards Trellis House.

'Get mixed up in all this battle stuff. It's all right to see it in the newsreels but not in real life.'

'I expect she's coping,' he said. 'The same as my sister.'

'Still no word from her?'

'Not yet.'

'I don't understand girls any more,' Florence sighed. 'In my day they were so peaceful and chic.'

'Depends on the times you're living in. Anyway, I hear you're a doyenne of civil defence.'

'That's different. I don't have to live in a tent for one thing.'

They had reached Trellis House when Florence turned to him suddenly. 'You're limping on that bad leg of yours.'

'No, it's fine. Honestly.'

'You should be walking with a stick.'

'I'm trying to do without it.'

'Does your father know?'

205

'My father's got nothing to do with it. I come under the medical section of an RAF station.'

'My God, you sound just like Miranda!' Florence began to laugh, then beckoned him through the gate. 'Come on in and have a sit-down. I've got a drop of Sandeman port that'll do us both good.'

He limped after her into the kitchen and sat at the table while she poured two small glasses and then pushed one towards him.

'Ah well, here's to victory!'

'Victory. . . .'

'And to the return of our darling girls.' Florence busied herself unpacking her shopping. 'Got my rations today. Two tins of soup, one of sardines, a packet of gravy browning and a scraggy-looking lamb chop. How's your wife, by the way? I've never met her but Esme showed me some photos – she looks very classy.'

'She is,' Sammy agreed. 'And she's fine.'

His gaze fell on a photograph on the window ledge of Miranda. Her hair was swept back from her forehead and she seemed to be gazing at him with an intensity that suddenly made his heart contract. He supposed it was because he had known her for a long while and because she was a friend of Nat's. Even so . . . .

'Oh, won't it be smashing when it's all over? – the war, I mean. I don't suppose you managed to bump into Miranda when you were in Normandy, did you?'

He had to admit that he hadn't, but added that the Red Cross was doing a marvellous job.

'Funny isn't it, your sister and my daughter being chums at school. I remember little Natalie coming to tea with us all those years ago when we lived in Morton Street. What a lively kiddy she was.' Slowly Florence unwrapped the newspaper parcel and disclosed a large cod's head. 'Just look at that! I got it in Sudbury market for twopence.'

'Magnificent,' Sammy said politely, and averted his eyes from its agonised stare.

'If the war's taught us anything at all, it's how not to waste anything.' Cautiously Florence manoeuvred the fish head into a saucepan without touching it. She added water and a shake of salt, and clapped the lid on. Then she poured two more glasses of port.

'What a lovely house this is.' Sammy glanced round at the beautiful china on the dresser, some of it a little chipped now. Two slender Sheraton chairs were drawn up at the kitchen table and a faded yet still brilliant Turkish rug reminded him fleetingly of the flat in Rodney Street. It pleased him to think that this was Miranda's home.

'Most of the things belonged to my poor chickabid's husband.' Florence reseated herself. 'A sweet boy who died soon after we all moved down here. Chickabid was marvellous of course, she nursed him day and night and when she flaked out I took over. I don't mean that I did anything out of the ordinary – just what any other loving mother would have done.'

Sammy murmured sympathetically, and remembered having tea with Miranda in London all that time ago. How happy she had seemed – until she suddenly remembered another appointment and darted away. It was strange to think of her as a widow now braving the horrors of Normandy with a Red Cross team.

'Aren't you bored down here, after Liverpool?' he asked.

'Oh no, not a bit,' Florence said. Then added another trickle to their glasses and said, 'Well, perhaps just a wee bit. I mean, I adore your parents, then of course I have other friends around. Country people are very anxious to be pals, you know. Also I've recently met up with an old friend from Liverpool who might be coming down to stay. His name's Stanley.'

'That'll be nice.' He eased his aching leg, and Florence seized his ankle and propped his foot on a stool.

'That better?' She sat down again and gazed at him lovingly.

'Great. Thanks a lot.' He took another sip of Sandeman's.

'Never mind, Sammy dear – the war will be over soon and then our darling girls will be home – ' The expression on her face changed abruptly as an urgent hissing came from the stove. The stench of boiling fish filled the kitchen.

'*Bugger!*' She leapt up, dragging the saucepan off the stove, and after peering through the steam staggered back with a shriek of horror. 'Oh my God, its eyes have fallen out!'

'Here, give it to me.' Sammy limped over to the stove.

'They're rolling around as if they can still see!'

'Never mind, I'll get them out. . . .' Arming himself with a slotted spoon he dexterously hooked out the offending articles and deposited them in the crumpled newspaper.

'They were staring at me.' Florence shuddered violently and collapsed at the kitchen table with her head in her hands. 'Oh sweet Jesus Maria, I'll never get used to the country – it's all spiders and beetles and rats in the woodshed and wild rabbits in the bog. . . .'

'What are you going to use the rest of it for?' Sammy scooped the cod's head on to a clean dish. Its mouth had come open to reveal a row of little fine white teeth.

'I don't know, it just seemed a good bargain,' Florence whimpered. She got up and opened the door to let the smell out. 'Some sort of stew, I suppose.'

'You could make marvellous glue with it.'

'I've got nothing I want to glue. Although chickabid might have something when she gets home.' She began to cheer up.

'Do you want me to throw it away?'

'Yes . . . no . . . Oh come on, let's get out of the smell.'

She led him out into the garden, past Emrys' tree and the wash house to where runner beans hung in thick clusters and tomatoes blazed in the warm sun. There were other things too: leeks and cabbages and the beginnings of brussels sprouts, and he admired everything gallantly.

They parted, Florence seeing him to the gate and watching him limp along the little footpath that led to the Overseer's House before she went back into the kitchen in preparation for dealing with the fish head. But there was no need; the cat had got there first and had already eaten most of it.

The Allied race through Normandy cost some 83,000 casualties over a period of three months. Five years to the day since Britain declared war on Germany Brussels was liberated, and it seemed as if the end was in sight. Then came the desperate battle for Arnhem followed by the German breakthrough in the Ardennes. Once again the balance shifted as the Americans were forced to yield ground to the Panzer divisions. Christmas came and passed unnoticed during the savage fighting, and Miranda held the hand of a young Canadian dying on a blood-soaked stretcher as the year 1945 was born.

She was used to death now. She had seen the light fade from pain-clouded eyes, had seen puzzlement, anger and fear, and had leaned close to catch last whispered requests. Write to Mum, give my love to Joan . . . . It was part of her job to do these things when the eyes had been closed, the sheet gently pulled over the face. And lying aching with tiredness on her camp bed she wondered when it was all going to end.

She spent a weekend's leave from the casualty clearing station at the Hotel St-Continaire in Brussels where she washed her hair and had a bath before creeping exhaustedly into bed. It was the first time she had lain in a proper bed for four months and she slept for seventeen hours.

The hotel was filled with Allied service personnel, and an ATS serving with a mixed anti-aircraft battery asked on the following morning if she would like to see the battlefield of Waterloo. It wasn't far away. Miranda thanked her and declined; she ate an enormous meal which included (she suspected) a horsemeat steak, and went back to bed again. She felt drunk with the luxury of it all, and on returning to the CCS where there was a lull in customers, Dr Paston asked her to marry him.

'What about the girl in Sumatra?'

'I've come to the shameful conclusion that it was only lust.'

'I had a stab of lust for you, at one time.' Strange how one could talk openly about such things these days. She wasn't sure whether it was the war or the medical background, but it was a pleasant relief to jettison the stupid, vapid, feminine pretences of her mother's generation.

'Has it faded?'

'I think so. I suppose it's all the blood and guts.'

'Take these pills and see me in ten days' time,' he said lightly, and blew her a kiss. She almost loved him for it; she would have been able to if it hadn't been for the carnage and the sense of madness that governed their days.

The new Allied offensive began in early February with a desperate drive towards the Rhine. Operation Veritable lumbered forward through mud and floods and choked roads, and the German losses were severe. Back home someone had written a song, *Berlin or bust, we didn't want to do it but we must* . . . and plodding about the duckboards in gumboots and mud-stained dungarees Miranda thought, How much longer? How much strength and resolution have we got left in us?

They were wondering the same thing in Auschwitz extermination camp.

The Women's Orchestra of Birkenhau had had their calorific intake reduced yet again, but at least they were not expected to do manual labouring. Thin, irritable and cynical they sank petty differences because they dared not do otherwise. The only alternative to performing music was the gas chamber, and months of living in close proximity to it had still not extinguished the dogged hope of life, of liberation. Sometimes the hope was no more than a glimmer, a weary little matchlight flickering in an infinity of darkness, but it was still there.

Some while ago a new railway line had been constructed between the old sidings and the gas chambers in order to save time and trouble, and it ran close to the Music Block where Nat was incarcerated. They could see the passengers only too clearly as they arrived, dirty, hungry, ragged and confused; weeping children without parents, old people falling and too weak to rise, and corpses being slung out like bags of rubbish. They too had arrived at Pitchipoi.

Some of the women in the Music Block turned away weeping hysterically, while others watched as if mesmerised. *Blocksperres*, or roll-calls, became more frequent, while whistle-blowing and the stamp of boots heralded confinement to quarters as another Selection was made. Mostly these selections for the gas chamber were made from the newly arrived trainloads, but as numbers in the camp had to be kept to a consistent level, additional victims were rounded up from the prisoners' huts. Anyone might be chosen, at random or because of illness or some trifling misdemeanour, and Nat would lie watching the searchlights playing on the wooden ceiling and listen to the shouts and yelping of dogs while she pictured the moment when her turn would come.

Rumours became wilder. The most common one was that France had been liberated and that the Allied armies were penetrating Germany. But no one knew anything for certain and no one believed the rumours. They didn't dare. So the ragged, half-starved Women's Orchestra continued to play its poor ragged music to the hollow-eyed spectres who staggered off each morning to work in the fields. And the number that returned was always less than the number that had set out.

Among the survivors soaring hope now clashed with a new and savage pessimism; there can be no end to this except death; once Hitler knows that he's lost he'll kill us all so there'll be no one left to tell the story. Defeated, what has he got to lose? Illness racked them; typhoid, dysentery, tuberculosis. Limbs broken by casual blows from the SS and the *blockawas* hung loose, and hands that had once been warm and kind were now like birds' claws; frail bundles of twigs scratching in the frozen mud for an extra morsel to eat.

In the Music Block they had taken the grand piano away some weeks ago. Like other musical instruments it disappeared without explanation; maybe to the Men's Orchestra, or perhaps it had been chopped up to help fuel the furnace of the crematorium, which was now belching out its thick black smoke day and night. But Nat still had the mandolin, the cheap and nasty version of the lute which she twanged twice daily on the bandstand outside. She had never been tempted seriously to explore its potential, partly through youthful musical snobbery and partly because it was a part of Auschwitz.

She developed bronchitis pretending to play Sousa marches dressed in a thin cotton skirt and blouse as the stinging snow of early winter swept in gusts through the bandstand. Her cough deepened and it hurt to breathe, and Magda Wozniak managed to filch some lung syrup from the stores and give it to her with the unnecessary injunction that she was not to tell anyone. The stores, known for some strange reason as Canada, contained almost every form of medical necessity and feminine luxury, the goods having been obtained either from the prisoners as they arrived, or from parcels sent to them and never handed out. The SS women, *blockawas* and *kapos* helped themselves freely.

It was late October when they heard the planes. Wave after wave of them, followed by the distant crump of bombs.

'It's them!' someone whispered.

'It's *us*!' Nat thought.

They were exultant, and at the same time filled with a new and searing terror. To die now, with liberation on the horizon, was a prospect no one could face. Two days later they heard the wail of the camp air-raid sirens, followed by the rapid thud of boots as the SS scurried for shelter. Prisoners were left in the huts to take their chance, and the strange mixture of fear and exultation made some of them cling together, sobbing. They bombed the gas chambers and the crematorium, but not sufficiently, it was later discovered, to put them out of action completely.

But when they heard that the camp was to be evacuated Magda turned a gaunt ashen face towards Nat and said, 'I'm not going. I'm staying here.'

'Don't think you've much say in the matter,' Nat croaked.

'I'm staying. I came here with all my family, all nine of us, and I'm the only one left.'

'So be the only one to survive.'

'Why? What for?'

It was a difficult question to answer, and they stared in silence through the window to where the chimney belched out its sickly-sweet cloud beyond the railway line.

'Come on, I'll help you.'

'Where are we supposed to be going?'

'God alone knows, but it can't be worse than this.'

They had no packing to do apart from the few pathetic treasures they had managed to keep hidden during the routine searches: a crumpled snapshot, a hunk of bread, and in Nat's case the remains of the lung syrup which she held carefully between her two books of piano music. They were herded into a cellar with at least a hundred other women, Nat and Magda remaining close together as the old SS game of dividing them up – some to the left, some to the right – was played yet again.

211

Trying to suppress a fit of lung-tearing coughing Nat stood unsmilingly erect as the uniformed figure approached. He had a riding whip under his arm and he rocked to and fro on his heels as he appraised her.

'Name?'

'Natalie Ellenberg.'

'Ah. You play the piano.'

She nodded.

Removing the whip from beneath his arm he flicked the tip of it across the books of music. He flicked harder, the whip stung her cheek and although she remained motionless the bottle of syrup slid from between the covers and smashed on the floor.

'What was that?'

'Cough mixture.'

'How did you come by it?'

Sensing Magda about to speak, Nat said, 'I stole it.'

'You won't need it where you're going,' he said, then brought the whip down hard on the arm that was holding the music. She suppressed a cry of pain and the books slid to the floor. One lay in the puddle of syrup.

'You won't be needing those either,' he said, and with a jerk of the head indicated that she was to join the group on the left. The fit of coughing refused to be denied any longer and she bent double beneath the agony of it. When it was over she saw that she was in the group containing the old and the sick and the children too young to be of use. The group that wasn't worth the bother of evacuating.

Magda was in the other group, and she managed a smile and a little wave of the hand as they were marched away.

Nat's group stayed in the cellar all night. Old and young huddled together on the stone floor. Some prayed, some wept, while others like Nat maintained an obdurate silence. They had been given no water, no means of sanitation and the air became putrid. Yet the children remained quiescent, as if they had learned from other small defenceless creatures the importance of remaining unnoticed.

So this is the night before my death, Nat thought. This time tomorrow I'll be a nothing. I doubt if they keep a record of our names any more. We're all nothings; the last visible sign of us will be a new cloud of black smoke coming out of a chimney. My smoke mingled with theirs. Perhaps one last little greasy smut of me might drift as far as England if the wind blows in the right direction. . . .

I wonder what it'll be like. How long it'll take. They say the more they shove in the quicker it works because a lot of people get trampled to death. The worst thing will be if somebody panics; if one person does, we all will. Dad always said that hysteria was as catching as measles, but I don't think he ever envisaged anything like his dear daughter's going through now. If the truth ever gets out I bet they won't believe it. . . . Her thoughts turned to the flat in Rodney Street and she wrenched them quickly away. She had always known that she would have a fair chance of facing up to the final ordeal provided she kept her mind firmly on the here and now. On the world in which she found herself.

Lying huddled on her side she noticed a small child, little more than a baby, crawling on hands and knees towards her. No one in the vicinity seemed to be concerned with it. She put out her hand as she would to a stray cat, and it crept closer.

'Come, little baby. *Viens, mon petit* . . . . ' It hesitated, a small pale blob on the icy floor, then reached out and touched her fingers. It was like being touched by something already dead. She put out both arms and gathered it to her and it tried to fold itself against her. Its head felt very heavy in comparison with the rest of it, and it breathed with a rasping sound that matched her own.

'You comfort me and I'll comfort you,' she whispered to it. 'Cheer up, it won't be all that bad.'

She understood now what Magda had meant when she said, Why survive? What for? She wondered what the gaunt violinist was feeling now, wherever she was; whether she envied Nat for being in the group for whom there would be no tomorrow, or whether surviving this last and final *blocksperre* had changed her mind.

In the meanwhile, thought Nat, I've developed something of her sense of acceptance; the inevitability of it all has brought an odd kind of peace. I've no desire to question why me and not her. . . . It's a relief to let go of life; to contemplate dissolving in a whiff of smoke that will curl and fragment and then vanish in the cold pure air above the snow clouds. It'll only take a little while. Being gassed will only be like having an anaesthetic, except that it'll be permanent.

Although the baby weighed so little it was making her arms ache. It had hooked its little dead cold fingers into the front of her blouse and its head was resting beneath her chin. A meagre warmth was coming from its body and she hoped that she was giving out a little heat of her own in return. She imagined she must be doing so because she had a temperature.

As dawn filtered a mud-coloured light into the cellar she saw that several people around her were already dead; one of them a huddled young woman in a headscarf, who might have been the baby's mother. It's not only rats who leave a sinking ship.

'How sensible of you,' she whispered. 'We might as well stay together for the last few hours.'

The cellar doors were flung upon to the familiar roars of *'Aufsteben! Raus, raus!'* and torches were shone in their faces. Whistles blew and the yelping of dogs echoed round the stone walls. Groaning and weeping, those who could staggered to their feet. Coughing weakly, Nat held the baby close to her and then glanced round the vicinity in a flash of torchlight. Another woman was lying nearby; almost fleshless, she was lying on her back with the palms of her hands upturned as if in a gesture of surrender. She also could have been the baby's mother, but it no longer mattered.

'We're all surrendering,' she croaked to it. 'But it'll soon be over and then we'll be free. Free as air, you might say.'

Those too ill to move were kicked to their feet and told to stand in line. Outside in the stinging cold the baby began to cry quietly and tearlessly and Nat shuffled forward with the rest and kept her hand over its great bare skull in an effort to shelter it a little more.

'Be nice and warm where we're going,' she told it with a trace of the old sardonic smile.

They came to a ragged halt some fifty yards from the gas chamber. The chimney of the crematorium was still belching smoke and the sweet-rotten smell of it was almost worse than the stench in the cellar. They waited. The old man standing beside Nat began to sob, his twig fingers over his eyes. She wanted to touch him, to impart a little of her own calm acceptance, but couldn't because of the baby. So she nudged him with her elbow and whispered, *'Courage, mon père.'*

He didn't seem to hear. Perhaps he was deaf, or maybe he was beyond comfort.

They waited. And it was extraordinary that everyone should be so calm, so patient. We might be queuing for a bus, Nat thought. What's happened to us all? Are we already dead? Have all these months of terror killed the living spark in us and left us just a lot of mindless automatons? I made myself forget the old life, I forced it out of my mind and I've achieved what I set out to do. I can mention names but they mean very little to me now. . . . I realise now that people in our situation don't die just at the moment they're killed; they start dying from the time they first realise that death's inevitable. And that's what I've been doing; I thought that by blotting out the past I was enabling myself to survive, but in fact I was turning myself into a dying person. . . .

Then somewhere ahead of them a woman began to scream. She was silenced with the butt of a rifle. As if infected by her sudden loss of control a man broke away from the line and ran for it. A watchtower machine gun brought him down and he lay huddled like a heap of rags. The iron cold ate into them and there was no more hysteria, no more wild-eyed attempts to escape. Blank-faced they waited, and nowhere in the world was there any compassion. The baby had stopped crying and seemed to be sleeping.

The end came a little before midday. With kicks and curses they were told to about-turn and march back the way they had come. Dimly, shamblingly, they did so, but not before Nat had caught a glimpse of the reason why. Corpses were piled to a height of six feet outside the doors of the crematorium and the gas chamber was already hard at work producing more. The famed efficiency of Auschwitz was limping to a halt beneath the weight of numbers.

She felt no sense of gratitude or relief, merely bitter disappointment accompanied by peevishness. The thought of being reincarcerated in the dark stench of the cellar was destroying her mood of peaceful surrender to death and nothingness, and merely bringing back the old miseries of hunger and illness and fear. And now there was an additional problem: she had saddled herself with someone else's baby.

It was still asleep – or unconscious or dead – but its small white fingers were still hooked in the front of her blouse as they trudged, hobbled, crept like beaten animals, past Block A and Block B, past the Sauna and the cellar, to the single-track railway where an ancient steam engine was hissing before a long line of cattle trucks.

A heavy blow from a truncheon caught her across the shoulders and one of the dogs snatched savagely at her skirt as she hauled herself up with the baby in her arms. The old man who had been crying reached down and tried to help. She wouldn't surrender her burden, but allowed him to take her by the elbow and add his frail strength to her own. She stood coughing and wheezing helplessly, then wiped her eyes on the back of the hand that was still trying to protect the baby's head from the cold.

'*Shalom*,' the old man said with a courtesy that made her gasp.

The train started, jerked to a halt, then started again. This time they were in open trucks, standing packed together so tightly that if anyone fainted or died they would go on standing up because there was no space in which to fall down. There was no food, no water. They had received nothing to eat or drink for more than two days and nights, and they had no idea where they were going.

She looked at the old man and thought that perhaps he was a rabbi. She looked at the other people standing so close to her that the sharpness of their bones seemed to grind against her own. Then she lifted her head and inhaled the smoke from the engine, and it wasn't the greasy black cloud billowing from the crematorium chimney. It was clean.

And crazily, the urge to go on, to survive at all costs, poured back. It was painful, like the jerky spasms of a new life being born, but it brought back with it the old incomparable sense of joy.

During the hours which followed people urinated and defecated where they stood. Some died, many more passed into the trancelike state which precedes death, but all remained upright; a grim army standing to attention with unseeing eyes and snow piling against them as they travelled further east. The old Jew next to her seemed to telescope down within himself, shrinking from the cold, but now and then she saw his blue lips move as if he were praying.

The snow softened, and with a slight shift in temperature the flakes fell large and soft. They fell like clean caresses, like lingering kisses that melted on the naked skulls, and she raised her face to receive them – so that they might wash away the dirt and the fever. She was going to live.

Fumblingly she put her head under the baby's chin and gently raised its face. As babies go, it was pretty nondescript; white-faced and filthy, with a runny nose and sores round its mouth, but it opened its eyes and gave her an odd little grimace that could have passed for a smile. It hadn't cried for a long while, and she concluded that like the rest of them it had moved beyond hunger and thirst.

She had no idea of its name or its nationality, she didn't even know what sex it was, but it didn't matter. It was still alive; it was destined to go on living the same as she was, and her fingers began drumming a light, half-frozen scale on top of its head as they chugged slowly across the whitened landscape on the way to Bergen-Belsen.

Life had come back, and so had music.

'Chickabid,' Florence said, smiling tremulously, 'you'll never guess who this is.'

Hot and dusty from travelling and not yet adjusted to the deep calm of rural England, Miranda dumped her suitcase on the hall floor of Trellis House, and said, no, she couldn't.

'This is my Stanley. Your father.'

'Really?' She touched his fingers politely. 'I was given to believe you were dead.'

'There was a mistake,' explained Florence. 'And I rather leapt to conclusions.'

'Hullo, Miranda.' He spoke quietly, his watchful eyes never leaving her face. 'Nice to see you again.'

'I've been around for quite a while.' More affected than she cared to admit, she turned away from him. Picking up her valise she paused at the foot of the staircase and said, 'I think I'll go and lie down for a while. I didn't sleep much on the boat.'

'That's my chickabid,' Florence said when she had gone. 'Heart of gold beneath a gruff exterior.'

Closing her bedroom door Miranda wandered round looking at things, touching things; moving a silver candlestick a fraction this way, a bowl of potpourri an inch or so that way. Florence had seen that everything was kept swept and polished and ready for when she returned. Summer frocks and winter skirts hung in the big cupboard where she had left them, and a jar of freshly picked daffodils stood on the bedside table. She began to unpack, then left it. She went over to the window to see the fresh spring buds breaking, and then looked across at the Overseer's House. She wanted to visit Esme and Bruno, but not until tomorrow. She didn't want to see anyone until she had been able to subdue, if only a little, the memories of the last months. The blood and pain and remorselessness of it all. The young German from the 5th Panzer Division peering dimly from a charred face and mistaking her for his mother; the American who had told funny jokes about dying and had then done so, composing himself like a pleasantly tired man settling down for a nap.

Nationalities no longer mattered; enemy and ally were treated impartially, and the Relief Teams had followed close behind the fighting, moving step by step deeper into Germany and the link-up with the advancing Americans. The link-up had been achieved on the 3rd of March, and as the Germans withdrew Dr Paston had liberated a bottle of Schnapps from a village inn close to the Rhine. She still liked John Paston very much, but wasn't sure that she loved him.

A general sense of comradeship was all she seemed to require, but on the day that Dora, their interpreter, drove over a landmine and was killed instantly, she couldn't stop crying. The tears poured out of her eyes in a steady blinding stream, and the more she tried to regain control of herself the worse it became. She had always been fond of

Dora; they had done their initial training together and had shared a tent off and on for about eight months. She had grown used to the sound of her snores, to the way she cleaned her teeth, screwed her hair up in fuzzy brown pipecleaners each night, and the way she always said, 'Oh, jam-and-plaster!' as a ladylike substitute for damn-and-blast. She had been brought up partly in France and partly in Germany yet had remained incorrigibly English, with nut-brown hair and eyes, and a sentimental love of animals, horses in particular. She had won lots of red rosettes in gymkhanas.

And now she was gone. Blotted out in a single brutal explosion, and weeping copiously Miranda tried to sort through her kit and pack it up in readiness for its return to England.

'Come on, old love.' Paston took her by the shoulders and eased her gently on to her camp bed. The hypodermic slid under the skin of her forearm, and when she awoke sixteen hours later she discovered that she had been granted a week's leave.

She was grumpy and suspicious until they assured her that it was not sick leave. It was part of her ordinary entitlement which was in fact long overdue. So she went back to England, dry-eyed now but with feelings curiously muffled, to be greeted by the presence of a father who she had been told was either dead or divorced, according to Florence's whim of the moment.

She didn't mind either way. She had seen too much, been immersed for too long in the raw and brutal side of life to bother about a comparative triviality. Collapsing on to the soft double bed that she had once shared with Emrys she pulled the quilt over her head and slept dreamlessly. Downstairs her mother and father ate lunch without her.

But it became better. A healing skin began to form over the wounds in her mind, helped by the sound of birdsong in place of gunfire, the sight of faces untwisted by pain, and by the unchanging tempo of country days. She spent time with the Ellenbergs, slow gentle hours in which she could almost seem to hear the spring leaves unfolding, and for the first time no one mentioned Nat. They told her that Sammy had been home on sick leave and Esme even confided to her that his marriage was probably suffering from wartime strain, but his sister's name remained unspoken. She's dead, Miranda thought. They've been officially notified in some way and they can't bear to tell me yet. The idea was sad and depressing, but sank into the morass of other deaths she had seen and would mourn for the rest of her days.

She walked down to the village and did some shopping. Rationing was tighter than ever, but the lady who ran the library greeted her warmly and made her a cup of tea. She sat by the narrow river and watched the moorhens fussing round their new nest in a clump of reed-mace. She caught the bus into Sudbury and saw a film with Rita Hayworth in it, and a newsreel of our troops surging through Germany – 'The going may be tough but these are tough lads and they're spurred on by the knowledge that victory is just around the corner. . . .' A fulsome voice accompanying pictures of grinning soldiers riding on armoured cars, weeds draped over their tin hats and giving the thumbs-up sign. . . . All so simple and all so jolly, with not a man screaming in agony in sight.

She caught the bus home again, and walking over the Common saw someone coming towards her. When they drew level he turned and strolled along by her side. A thrush was singing piercingly from the top of an elm. *'Bridget – Bridget – Bree, bree, bree . . . !'*

'Are you really my father?'

'Afraid so.'

'What makes you afraid?'

'I haven't been a very attentive one, have I?'

She didn't reply immediately, then said, 'I suppose it wasn't easy.'

'Your mother,' he said, 'would make a first-rate romantic novelist.'

'I know.' She smiled down at her feet.

'It's going to take time.'

'Are you planning to settle down together?' Her voice sounded rough with suspicion.

'We've talked about it, yes. We'd rather like to retire to one of the weavers' cottages over there,' he waved his hand, 'but I've got to think of Roger, too. Your mother and I really were divorced, and I married again and have a son who is now almost seven.'

'A half-brother I've never met.'

'Betty died when he was born.'

'I'm sorry,' she said automatically, and it was strange how little the death of a civilian meant. I've been conditioned to death in khaki, she thought. If it hasn't been shredded by mortar fire it isn't real.

'Where is he now – your son?'

'Staying with Betty's mother. She's been a brick the way she's looked after him during the day. I've just had him at night and at weekends.'

'What a lonely sort of life.' She spoke musingly.

'No, not at all. I'm finding it exceptionally rewarding, as it happens.'

'Sorry. I didn't mean to sound disparaging.'

Yet she quite liked him for remonstrating with her. This quiet man with thoughtful eyes and a bald head is my father, she reminded herself.

219

The bits I remember about him – or *think* I remember – are all so entangled with Flo's fantasies and self-justifications that we'll have to start again. But not until the war's over . . . the war's over.

They reached the house and Florence handed Miranda a telegram. It was a request to return to Germany immediately.

'But you've still got three more days!' wailed Florence. 'How can they be so mingy?'

Stanley said little, but unobtrusively gave her his month's sweet ration to take back.

'What about Roger?'

'He's got his own.'

They both went with her to the railway station, and as the London train steamed in she said, 'When am I going to meet him?'

'Perhaps next time. In the meanwhile, good luck.' He didn't kiss her, which she appreciated, but stood looking after the train long after Florence had turned away.

The date was the 20th of April.

'We gather it's some kind of POW camp or something,' John Paston said when she got back. He kissed her publicly and resoundingly. 'The Jerries apparently surrendered it waving a white flag some time last week and I gather other Red Cross teams are steaming towards it with all speed. Sounds like a biggish job.'

'Whatever it is, the war's almost over now.'

'Except for the mopping up.'

They set off at first light on the following morning, the ambulances and the big surplus lorry jolting over the shell holes and making endless detours round villages where the streets were blocked with rubble. Miranda took her turn driving one of the trucks, and the desolation around them reminded her of a lunar landscape. The only signs of life came from the twists of smoke slowly rising from tumbled houses. God knows where the inhabitants were.

The first sign of their destination came in late afternoon. The stretch of broken country road was punctuated by signs hastily painted with the skull and crossbones, and driving up to the big closed gates heavily reinforced with barbed wire, a British soldier in a beret checked their credentials and then murmured to Miranda, 'Take a deep breath before you go in, chum.'

More barbed wire punctuated by dark and silent watchtowers; rough concrete paths running between long wooden huts with no windows, and no one about except a few soldiers. Complete silence reigned, and their tired wonderment increased when they saw that the soldiers were wearing gas masks.

'Looks as if we're too late,' John Paston said, alighting and stretching his cramped legs. 'They've already been evacuated.'

On a patch of greasy bare ground Miranda noticed a small heap of blue-and-white striped rag. She moved closer, and recoiled hastily when it moved. A long white bone with fingers on the end was extended, then the rag fell back a little to disclose a lard-white skull bordered by two huge ears. The eyes which turned towards her appeared almost equally huge; two round dark shapes burnt into the bleached cranium, and there was no expression in them at all. They moved in their sockets but they were unseeing.

'What in God's name is it?' she whispered.

The smell hanging over the place was indescribable; a mixture of excreta and burning boots and rags, Miranda thought fragmentarily, and turning aside saw her co-driver being quietly sick behind their truck.

Six Red Cross teams had been hastily mustered and one Friends' Relief Service, and they were given a rapid briefing by Brigadier Glyn Hughes, who had already assumed the role of Chief Medical Officer and Administrator. He told them that they were in an extermination camp, and although there had only been time to make a rough assessment of the situation it was estimated that the place contained some forty to fifty thousand prisoners within its square-mile area, a large proportion of them dead but unburied, and the remainder suffering from a variety of contagious diseases aggravated by acute malnutrition.

The immediate plan was to convert some of the barrack buildings which had been used by German personnel into a hospital, and to move the gravely ill prisoners into it as soon as possible. The Army was working round the clock setting up casualty clearing stations and had already mobilised five hundred beds and straw mattresses in one day. The Brigadier's face showed signs of fatigue as he warned them that their own living quarters would be somewhat inadequate, then after a brief word of welcome strode hurriedly away.

Horror froze into disbelief at what they saw, and an initial attempt was made to forbid non-medical personnel entering the barrack huts. But the decision was ignored, and Miranda followed in the wake of an Army medical orderly. Although it was broad daylight, the interior of the place was so dark that they could only see by torchlight, and its beam illuminated the racks of corpselike figures, some motionless and some still moving feebly. The smell was like a physical blow in the face, but repugnance was banished by pity as a tattered, hairless scarecrow raised a wavering claw to Miranda. She grasped it and held it in both hands, trying to warm it and instil into it a sense of hope. She couldn't tell whether it was man or woman.

'You're going to be all right . . . it's all over now,' she whispered, bending close to the desperate, gaping face.

They moved on. Other hands reached out, clawing the air with an animal desperation. Those too weak to move merely stared with huge eyes set in shrunken faces, and the dirt and the horror and the stench were as nothing compared with the need to help. There were children, babies even, some dead and some lying in their own excrement on the floor, too weak to move or cry, and the medical orderly flashed his torch round the walls, saying softly, 'Jesus Christ, where do we start?'

Working tirelessly, sleeplessly, the Army backed by the civilian medical teams organised a decontamination centre into which each sick prisoner was carried, gently stripped of its rags and bathed in warm water liberally laced with disinfectant, then transferred to the improvised hospital. Medical supplies were desperately short and the British Army units stationed nearby gave up their blankets.

Wearing dungarees, a Red Cross armband, and with a triangular bandage covering her hair, Miranda, like the rest of them, performed any task that was needed. She carried water, carried stretchers, fed watery soup or black coffee which was all the poor shrunken stomachs could tolerate, and helped to wrap corpses in blackout material ready for the Death Wagon that came round morning and evening. As a social worker it was her job to find out their names if possible, but her rate of success was low. Some were too ill to speak; some couldn't remember, and they were dying at the rate of five hundred a day.

But steadily the work went on. They were oblivious to the gunfire on the other side of the Elbe, and took no notice when the remnants of the Luftwaffe swept in low over the camp, and if Miranda had any pity to spare it was for John Paston, who was one of the doctors burdened with the task of deciding who among the inmates was worth saving as opposed to those for whom help had come too late. Suffering from dysentery, typhus, typhoid, and covered in suppurating sores, those still with breath in their lungs begged wordlessly for a chance to live, and Miranda saw a young medical student, one of the volunteers who had arrived from the London teaching hospitals, weeping helplessly over a young girl who refused to let go of his hand.

She had been working all morning with Bernard, a new orderly from her own team, when she was asked to help with the evacuation of one

222

of the last barrack huts. She hurried off to join the doctor and the other stretcher-bearer, and in the familiar stench and gloom began to deal with an emaciated corpse lying with closed eyes and open toothless mouth on a bunk furnished with a small quantity of urine-soaked straw. She made sure that she was dead – no heartbeat, skin already ice cold – and then became aware of the creature lying next to her. A fuzz of filthy black curls surmounting a parched skeletal face in which only the eyes seemed to be alive. They glowed up at her from the filth, from the shadow of the open-mouthed corpse, and Miranda shone her torch closer.

They continued to glow up at her without blinking; they were the usual deep, sunken eyes, but with an expression in them that suddenly made Miranda's heart contract.

'Nat . . . ?'

Rigid, she watched the swollen white tongue make a painful attempt to moisten lips coated with sores. The creature swallowed, drew a rasping breath, then managed the painful flicker of a smile. 'What kept you?'

The doctor was gentle, pitying, and like the rest of them rocking on his feet with exhaustion, and Miranda saw from his expression in the torchlight that Nat was one of the dying. It wasn't worth moving her. Agonised, Miranda saw the comprehension in Nat's eyes.

Gripping his sleeve she drew him to one side and hissed, 'She's English! I know her, for God's sake – she's a friend of mine!'

He shook his head.

'She'll be OK, I know she will – oh, what can I say to make you *believe* . . . ?' She began to cry, jerking at his sleeve as if she were pulling a bellrope.

He applied the stethoscope again, pushing away the filthy remnants of blue and white. Then he heaved a sigh. You're wasting your time, his expression said. You're merely depriving someone who's got a better chance.

They gathered her gaunt bones carefully in case they broke through the skin, and laid her on the stretcher. Her eyes sought Miranda's with urgency and once again she tried to gasp a few words.

Miranda bent close.

'Baby. Got a baby. . . .'

A baby? In here? Unreality seemed to be piling upon unreality as Miranda took her hand again and said, 'Don't worry, darling, we'll find it. Is it a boy or a girl?'

With what seemed like a tired shake of the head Nat closed her eyes, and the doctor came back down the hut carrying a squalid heap of rag which emitted a faint mewling cry.

'Is this it?'

He held it close. Nat opened her eyes for a moment, attempted a smile and then closed them again. The doctor took Miranda's end of the stretcher while she followed, carrying Nat's baby.

Faint sounds of entreaty followed them, stick arms held out in mute supplication, and huge eyes burning like candles in the gloom followed them as they left.

'We're coming back,' Miranda said from the door, and smiled with the exaggerated brightness used hopefully to take the place of half a dozen European languages. 'Don't worry, we'll be back in a minute.'

The news that an Englishwoman had been found in the camp by one of her friends spread among the rescue teams, and in spite of dizzying tiredness several immediately volunteered to take Miranda's place as temporary stretcher-bearer. The evil of Belsen had cut through all sense of rank and profession; doctors helped to carry stretchers and to organise transport, while orderlies and drivers helped nurse the sick and bury the dead, and Miranda went with Nat to the human laundry where she was divested of her rags, gently washed, then wrapped in a blanket and sent with others in the three-tonner transport to the hastily improvised hospital. She was suffering from typhus and her chances of recovery were nil.

'And imagine her having a baby,' Miranda said tiredly to John Paston as they crouched on upturned buckets drinking black coffee. 'She didn't seem the type, somehow.'

'What type was she, then?'

'Musical. I told you about her, didn't I?'

'Yes, I remember now.' He massaged his forehead. 'But so much has happened since then.'

Because everyone was so engrossed in their own particular task of the moment it was difficult to follow every aspect of the dismantling of Belsen. Miranda caught only one glimpse of the uniformed SS women standing in line during their formal arrest, and gained a mere fleeting impression of plump, well-fed bodies in shabby shirts and tunics. She missed seeing Irma Grese, the burly blonde with the thin mouth and deep-set eyes who had been personally responsible for the deaths of thousands of women and children, and she also missed the sight of male SS officers being made to dig the communal graves needed to bury the ten thousand corpses that had greeted the arrival of the British troops.

But almost everyone was present on May the 21st when Brigadier Glyn Hughes climbed on to a trestle table and announced with the aid of loudspeakers that all the barrack huts were to be burned down in order to prevent the spread of infection. The flame-throwers moved in, and they watched in silence as the huge picture of Hitler which someone had nailed to the wall of the first hut writhed and then disintegrated in the leaping conflagration.

One or two people raised a cheer but most remained silent, oppressed by the knowledge that for so many thousands liberation had come too late.

A shaft of sunlight lay like a yellow path across the bed. Tiredly she put out her hand to touch it, but the hand wasn't hers. Each bone was shining like a dark matchstick through the skin, and the fingernails were far too big and white and prominent because the flesh had fallen away from them. It was the hand of a dead person. She stared at it in slow surprise and then let it drop, too light and too withered even to make an indentation in the blanket. Blanket . . . a real blanket all to herself. A bed with no one else in it. No cold, spiny limbs lying against her own. Her mind clouded; voices, and the sound of footsteps receded, and she slept.

Woke again. Darkness, and a stream of horror. Back on the old sodden-straw shelf in the old stifling hut. Life dying out like the gleam of light behind a closing door. No hope, no hope. Human life at its lowest ebb. Last breaths rattling through hollow chests, a last splash of urine on to the inert bodies lying below. I tried to keep going. I tried, I tried, because I wanted to so much. One more week, one more day, one more hour, but there's a limit. Everything has a beginning and an end except time and space. The blackness and endless space I'm adrift in now, like a little boat. Oh well, it doesn't matter. At least I'm in a little boat on my own. Horror fades in the calm of resignation. I can't fight any more. Let me sleep now. Die now . . . .

'Nat.' The voice came to her from the edge of the world. 'Nat, open your eyes. It's Miranda.'

Can't. Don't want to. Sleep now.

'Nat, listen to me. You're very ill, but you're going to get better. You're going back to England. Everything's all right, Nat . . . it's all over.'

Flimsy blue eyelids covering eyes too weak to focus any more. A thin blade of nose prominent between gaunt cheekbones. This is what it really means to see someone naked, Miranda thought; it means seeing the shape of their bones beneath the polite clothing of flesh.

'Listen to me, Nat. You're getting better. They've just flown in another supply of a new drug called penicillin and you've been given some and you're responding to it. The doctor says you are. The doctor I work with, and he says that it all depends now on your will to live. So *try*, Nat. It must have been unspeakably dreadful, all the things you've gone through, but you're nearly there now. You're coming out the other side, Nat. So don't give up – think of home and love and music and all of us waiting for you. We all love you, Nat.'

No response.

'So OK, I'll just keep on and on at you until you open your eyes and stop being so blasted feeble. And what about your baby? She's come off glucose now and she's taking half-strength milk. She's trying hard to sit up, Nat, which is more than you're doing. Would you like to see her? I could bring her in from the babies' ward. . . . '

Silence. Miranda took Nat's hand and traced with her eyes the serial number burnt into her forearm. 69487. Like the branding of cattle. . . .

Perhaps I should let her die after all, Miranda thought. Perhaps all that she's been through will be too much for her to bear for the rest of her life. Even with all of us helping her and loving her, how will she be able to endure the memories? How will she ever be able to laugh at jokes again?

But she had to keep trying, and during the hours she could have spent in precious sleep she continued to sit on the edge of the Army-issue bed and pour out words to the motionless figure lying beneath the blanket.

'The doctor I work with – the one who says you're going to be all right – has asked me to marry him, Nat. I said no to begin with, but now I'm not so sure. I've always liked him, and the work here has brought us very close together. I mean, you can't be formal and status-conscious in an outfit like ours – I'm with the British Red Cross, by the way – did I tell you? I joined last year and volunteered for Europe because I always had this idea of coming to find you. Only I didn't think it'd be in a place like this. No – I was hoping to get to Paris, where I was going to enquire at your music college. . . . What was that woman's name you were having lessons with? Nadia something-or-other. . . . But I never got there, not even on a weekend pass. I went to Brussels once, and that was quite nice. Have you ever been to Brussels, Nat? Nat, open your eyes and tell me if you've ever been to Brussels. . . .'

I'm so tired I could sleep for a month. My back aches, my hair's gone like string and I've got the curse.... And I promised to relieve Bernard for a couple of hours this evening....

'All right then, don't answer me if that's how you feel. It's all the same to me. I'm so bloody exhausted I don't give a bugger what you do. I'm only trying to persuade you to pull yourself together because the senior MO's coming round tomorrow to see who's fit to travel home. If they've got a home, that is. You're one of the lucky ones, Nat. You've got a lovely home in the country you've never even seen yet, you'd go in a transport plane, and can't you just imagine your parents' reaction when they see that you're alive and getting better? So come on for God's sake – Caesar cup of hot Oxo, pull yourself together and start working on it. Just open your eyes, Nat. Or keep them shut if the light hurts and just say a couple of words. Any words'll do, just to show you're listening.'

'Stop bossing,' Nat said in a parched whisper.

The camp was emptying slowly but steadily. The dead had been buried, the captured SS removed to a place of safety in readiness for the coming war trials, and the poor lost and nameless souls found scratching in the soil for potato peelings had been duly cleansed and fed and issued with clothing donated by Americans and Britons sickened and aghast at the newsreel films of Hitler's extermination camps.

The problem of setting up Displaced Persons' Camps, of trying to trace and reunite parents and children, husbands and wives torn apart during the years of madness, was now top priority, and on the afternoon that the tall gaunt woman in ill-fitting jumble-sale clothes stood in front of Miranda and said that her name was Madga Wozniak and that she had played the violin in the Women's Orchestra at Birkenau, Miranda laid aside her pen.

'A women's orchestra? In Auschwitz?'

The woman nodded.

'You're quite sure?'

She nodded again. Sighing, Miranda made a note to the effect that Magda Wozniak should be referred to the unit for Psychiatric and Mental Rehabilitation.

Nat out of quarantine. Nat with sores healing, hair beginning to thicken, and skeletal legs able to support her provided she clung on to someone. And on the day of her departure from the hospital Miranda had taken ten minutes off to say goodbye.

'Can't you come too?' Nat was wearing a pink swagger coat that was

227

much too large, its bright jollity striking a bizarre contrast with the rest of her.

'I'd love to, but we're a bit busy at the moment. Look, do you mind getting yourself on to this? You needn't lie down.'

'Why have I got to go home on a stretcher?'

'Because we've no wheelchairs. And because they're easier to manipulate in and out of ambulances.'

'Efficient, aren't we?'

'Someone's got to be.' This was more like the old days, and Miranda's heart rejoiced. 'And speaking of efficiency, they've got the baby all ready for you. What's her name, by the way?'

Nat hesitated for a moment, then said, 'I've forgotten.'

'Gosh, I'm not surprised,' Miranda said feelingly. 'But I expect it'll come back to you. Loss of memory due to stress is generally only temporary.'

'Thanks,' Nat said laconically. Despite the heavy weight of lassitude she was touched by Miranda's tactful suppression of curiosity. (*Were you married? Who was he? What happened?*) She had never asked, and they remained silent now; then a young VAD came in with the baby in her arms. It was sitting up rather waveringly and its thin little streak of hair had been brushed up in a single curl on top of its head. The nurse gave it to Nat, wished her goodbye and all the best, and departed.

'She's lovely,' Miranda said heartily, 'and her name'll soon come back to you.'

'Yes, I'm sure.' Nat regarded the baby doubtfully. It didn't look much like the one she had befriended in the Auschwitz cellar, but what with one thing and another it was hard to be sure. Although she had held it in her arms for so long she hadn't made a point of studying it too closely, and appearances had played little part in the desperate intimacy that had been forced upon them. At the time, it had seemed as if the bond would never be broken, that they would recognise one another from halfway across the world by touch, by voice, by smell. Especially smell.

'What are you smiling at?' Miranda looked at her fondly.

'Oh, nothing really.'

'I think she looks a little bit like you,' Miranda said. The baby was sitting on Nat's chest, its huge extermination-camp eyes fixed hungrily on one of the buttons on the pink swagger coat. It looked as if it might be good to eat.

'Yes. . . .' Nat murmured. Then put her arms round the small creature and hugged it to her.

Although still hazy about the length of time she had spent in Belsen, and too weakly indifferent to calculate, she imagined that the baby, if it was the original one, would have been bigger by now – assuming that it was possible for anyone to grow bigger and not smaller in Belson. Still, one baby's much the same as any other, she thought, so I might as well take this one. It's somebody's poor little bit of flotsam.

Stroking its cheek with her index finger it occurred to her that perhaps she too had developed something of the concentration-camp philosophy; this one to live, that one to die, it's all the same to me. The choice is strictly impersonal.

'I've just remembered,' she said, as the field ambulance arrived. 'Her name's Rachel, after my little sister. Remember her?'

'So far as I'm concerned, it all began with her . . . all this.' Miranda indicated their surroundings.

'You always felt it was your fault, didn't you?'

'Wouldn't you have done if you'd been me?'

Nat grinned at her. 'Whatever the rights and wrongs, you've certainly expiated any possible guilt, working here.'

They were suddenly very close. As close as they had ever been, including the old days of rambling round Liverpool streets and squares on the way home from Queen Mary's.

'I'm not entirely sure about expiation,' Miranda said, 'but I sometimes get the feeling that it had to happen like this. The violence and cruelty as propounded by people like Rob Allardyce had to come to a climax and wear itself out before we could be rid of it, once and for all.'

'And you think we are rid of it, once and for all?'

'For God's sake! . . . Don't you?'

'I wouldn't bet on it.'

The ambulance doors were opened, and Miranda picked up the baby while Nat was carried out on the stretcher.

It was raining outside, warm, early-summer rain cleansing away the last of the filth and the degradation. Four weeks after its liberation Belsen was almost completely dismantled. Soon wild flowers and butterflies will gentle the mass graves, Miranda thought. But we will never forget, and we will never let it happen again.

She watched the ambulance jolt past the British sentries on its way to the airstrip, then she went back to work. Tomorrow she was being transferred to 119 Section of the Displaced Persons' Camp at Osnabruck. She would miss Nat, and she would miss John Paston.

The flight in the old Lancaster was not exactly comfortable, and the baby wept and was sick. Having wiped the worst of it from the pink swagger coat Nat peered through the cracked, mist-bound window and allowed the first cautious trickle of optimism to return. And with it, the first thoughts of the old life. Faces, and places. Having denied them for so long in the effort to keep going, there was a strange sense of the forbidden, which made her smile.

But the prisoners who had tried to live on memories had been the first to sicken and die; she had seen it. She had seen crumpled snapshots, pathetically and dangerously hidden, and had heard of engagement rings and other love tokens smuggled in bedding, even secreted in various orifices of the body in an attempt to defy authority and to remain in touch with the past. But it had never worked. Sooner or later they were discovered and defiled, their owners beaten and abused and sent with the next batch to the gas chamber.

In order to survive, one had had to strip oneself bare; to admit to no past and to no hope for the future, and the dimly remembered wild surge of hope experienced in the cattle truck from Auschwitz had been no more than truant instinct fostered by delirium. She had brushed it away like a stray lock of hair.

But now was the time to start easing herself back into life. It would be difficult at first, probably more painful than the massaging and stretching of the shrivelled muscles in her body, but she would work at it. And she would have help.

A sergeant in flying kit loomed through an aperture and gave her some coffee in the mug of a thermos flask. He looked very young and very English.

'Is the kiddy OK?'

'Yes thanks, she's fine.'

'Sorry it's a bit noisy. . . .'

'No, I like it.' How like the English to apologise for things outside their control.

He left her, the baby slept, and Nat resisted the temptation to wonder whether it was Polish or Czech, French or Russian or whatever. It didn't matter. It was a survivor, and that was sufficient.

'What we've got to do is get ourselves fit,' she told it, 'and the moment we are, we're off to Paris to look for a father for you. I've already got someone in mind.'

At last she could allow herself the luxury of thinking about him. Of speaking his name. It hurt, with the same kind of sweet healing ache that was in her hands when she tried to stretch the fingers wide. *Raoul* . . . . The word was lost in the roaring racket of the plane, but he was coming back to her. No sensuality as yet; merely the revitalising of a deep and loving need that had been carefully kept on ice during the past six years.

J'attendrai...
Le jour et la nuit
J'attendrai toujours,
Ton retour....

She dared herself to let the little tune come back too, and it began to interweave with the voices of Brahms and Haydn, Beethoven, Mozart and Mendelssohn, the friends and colleagues who had been waiting patiently during the long years of barbarism.

Half an hour later the plane landed. Her parents were waiting to greet her, and the sun was shining.

The day had unfolded out of early mist to display itself in tones of gold and blue, and at Trellis House Miranda and her husband breakfasted in the garden under what was still known as Emrys' tree. Birthday cards were propped up on the table and the new cashmere shawl was draped round her shoulders.

'It's *lovely*,' she said again, touching it with her cheek. 'But a bit naughty to spend so much money.'

'You're quite right. I'll ask them if they'll take it back.'

'I love being cuddled into things,' she said, ignoring him. 'It makes me feel precious and wanted.'

'You become more feminine as time goes on.'

'What an awful thought.'

'I'm not complaining.'

A wood pigeon purred in the branches above their heads. Sunlight glanced down through the leaves and illuminated a birthday card heavily adorned with roses and bluebirds.

'What was I like before, then? Masculine?'

He considered. 'No. Just a bit brisk.'

'I think we were all a bit brisk during the war. We had to be.'

'Maybe. I don't think Nat's ever said anything about you being a brisk schoolgirl.'

'Isn't it nice she'll be here for lunch – which reminds me, I should be up and doing – '

'Lots of time. It's barely half past nine.'

'But everything takes me longer these days. Don't forget I'm sixty.'

'Only as from today.'

'Oh my duck, how soothing you are.' She leaned across and kissed his cheek.

'Careful, the end of your expensive present's dangling in the marmalade.' Love shone in his eyes.

'So what are you going to do while I'm busy?'

'Me? I thought we'd arrange that I should cut the grass.'

'Be nice if you would, it stops the weeds showing. And if the weather holds we can eat al fresco. . . .'

Stacking the breakfast dishes on the tray she hurried towards the house, the shawl still resting on her shoulders, then paused by the kitchen door: 'Don't forget to change into your blue shirt and clean trousers, will you, Sammy?'

Lunch for midday. She had already poached the salmon and roasted the chicken. The fresh fruit salad was assembled in its cut-glass bowl in the fridge, and the trifle only wanted its final decorating. Cold consommé for starters presented no problems, and neither of course did the cheese and biscuits. As Sammy had said, there was plenty of time; but when you're getting on in years you get a bit nervous, and you hate leaving anything to chance, Miranda thought. Plus the fact that your standards tend to rise. So many smart restaurants open now, including the one in what used to be the old railway station; so many luscious cookery books and TV programmes that make us all struggle harder and harder to keep up. Florence turns her nose up at asparagus and hollandaise sauce these days, and when you think of what we had to put up with during the war . . . .

Beating up mayonnaise in the blender she wondered why today of all days she should be thinking about the war. Then she remembered the dream, the monstrous nightmare she hadn't had to endure for many years until last night. What had brought it back? What stray word or random thought had innocently sprung the trap? She didn't know – didn't want to know – and she concentrated instead on worrying about the mayonnaise, which looked such a bright yellow. Although it was only due to the freshness of the free-range eggs it had the appearance of being full of additives . . . .

Then she remembered the sound of human voices she had heard out on the Common during the early hours of the morning. Leaving the finished mayonnaise in its bowl she hurried through the hall and out into the front garden, and drew in a sharp breath of surprise. The place was dotted with transit vans and Range-Rover-drawn caravans, although when she looked more closely she saw that dotted was hardly the right word; they were drawn up in neat rows that gave them a businesslike appearance. Young people in holiday clothes were moving among them and a large brown dog was rolling on its back with its legs shooting ecstatically into the air. On a clear stretch of the Common, a little apart from the vehicles, someone had set up what appeared to be a tall, thin mast. A caravan club, she thought, and it looks as if we might be in for a disco or something. Strange that no one had heard about it.

She went back to the kitchen and found Florence there. Now in her mid eighties, Florence had dwindled in size and had developed a little nid-nod of the head which gave the impression of someone in perpetual agreement. Her hair had thinned, but what was left she had shampooed and set into careful little waves once a week. She was frail now, and subject to the variety of minor ailments common to the degenerating human body, all of which were more or less controlled by a daily intake of pills, but her eyes still shone bird-bright with enjoyment of the present and hope for the future.

'Many happy returns, chickabid!' she cried, and gave Miranda a package wrapped rather clumsily in red paper patterned with robins and snowmen. Vaguely, Miranda recognised it as the covering of her last year's Christmas present to her mother.

'Well now, whatever's this?' she asked playfully. Conscious of Florence's beady expectation she made an exaggerated performance of opening it, and although her smile remained wide her eyes glazed slightly at the sight of a red-and-black frou-frou petticoat embroidered with butterflies. 'It's lovely. . . .'

'It's *you*, chickabid,' Florence crowed, then added with a leer, 'and Sammy will adore it. . . .'

'Yes, I'm sure.' Miranda quelled a vision of protruding stomach and clumpy legs twirling seductively in a wild bedroom flamenco. At least it had an elasticated waist.

'You're still young – to me at any rate.' Florence checked a little tear, and adjusted her hearing aid while Miranda carefully rewrapped the petticoat and laid it gently on top of the fridge.

'Very sweet of you to say so.'

'Aren't you going to kiss me?'

Obediently Miranda stooped to kiss a cheek soft and finely creased as tissue paper, then said, 'Why don't you go and sit in the garden while I finish off the cooking?'

'I could help you.'

'There's not much to do, really.' Swiftly Miranda changed tack. 'Anyway, what's Stanley up to?'

'He's still in bed, the lazy old sod.'

'You mustn't call him that when he's eighty-five.'

'What about me? I'm eighty-three and a half!'

How proud we become of our age once we're over the hill, Miranda thought. As pleased as small children. It's only during the middle stages that we prefer reticence, I suppose for sexual reasons, but once we're over that . . . . And today I'm sixty, which puts me just over the brow of the hill, past which there is no return.

'Can I cut the bread and butter?' Florence hovered.

'We're not having bread and butter – '

'What are we having, then?'

'Cold consommé to kick off with – '

'We'll want bread and butter with that for a start.'

'No, we won't! We're having Melba toast – '

'What's that when it's at home?'

'It's a very thin slice of toast, and you don't have – '

'Well, I want bread and butter and so does Stanley. We can't eat toast because of our teeth.'

'Go and sit in the garden,' Miranda said, her own teeth becoming clenched. 'Or better still, go back to Stanley and cut him some nice bread and butter and make him a pot of tea and take it up to him in bed for a treat. Breakfast in bed . . . go on, now. . . .' She made a shooing motion in the direction of the door.

'That petticoat cost every penny I have.' Florence edged sideways, then added, 'By the way, there's a lot of funny-looking people camping out on our Common.'

'It's not our Common.' Miranda had also become argumentative. 'It's open to everyone.'

'It's ours because we live round it. And these people look very funny to me.'

'It's a caravan club. Just a group of ordinary people who feel like spending a weekend in the country away from it all.'

'They've got a flagpole – '

'Rubbish, it's a loudspeaker mast thing. They're going to have a disco. Now, if you'll just get out of the way I can get to the sink.'

'OK, I know when I'm not wanted.'

'That,' said Miranda with heavy sarcasm, 'is a state of affairs I never thought I'd live to see.' The door banged. 'Come back for drinks at twelve,' she shouted, 'and don't forget to bring Stanley.'

Stanley. She had grown very fond of him over the years but still found it difficult to think of him as her father. I sprang from his loins, she thought, covering the mayonnaise with clingfilm. Impossible. As impossible as the idea of calling him Daddy darling. Yet the fondness was deep and genuine and laced with sympathy that he should be sacrificing a tranquil old age to the ups and downs of living with Florence.

It was eleven o'clock and the lunch was prepared when there came a rap on the kitchen door. Shiny-faced and ruffle-haired, Miranda opened it and said, 'Oh, Bert. How nice.'

He too was in his eighties, with wisps of pale fluff clinging to a cranium speckled like a bird's egg.

'Best respects.' He proffered a crumpled bit of newspaper. 'I pulled these for you special.'

Radishes, rosy-red and round as marbles. Forty years of rural living had developed in Bert an ability to grow the best vegetables in the district and to make wine, cordials and various pick-me-ups from the most unpromising weeds in the hedgerows. Though he now read the *Daily Mirror* instead of the old *Daily Worker*, and had ceased to harangue acquaintances with a view to conversion, preferring these days to watch television, he remained in essence a product of the old tough part of Kilburn.

Miranda thanked him warmly, then reminded him that his presence was requested at twelve o'clock, followed by lunch at one.

'Better put on me Peckham Rye.'

'Come as you are, it's only family.' Miranda wondered fleetingly whether to prepare the radishes for the salad, then decided to change into her other dress first. Sammy came in.

'Bloody mower's packed up. I think it went over a stone.' He looked hot and cross.

'Never mind about it now. Put it away and get changed.'

'But I'm only half done – '

'In that case you wouldn't have time to finish it all, would you?'

'Why? What time are they coming?'

'I've told you lots of times – drinks at *midday*.' Miranda was also looking hot and cross. 'Have you got glasses and things organised? Hell, I've still got to put out the nibbly bits – '

'Bert can do that while you get ready.'

'I don't think I've got enough parsley – '

'I can pick some more.'

'No, you can't, you haven't got time. You've still got to change – and don't forget it's your *blue* shirt – '

'Dear God,' he rumpled his hair distractedly, 'anyone would think the whole of Suffolk was coming.'

Left alone in the kitchen Bert surveyed the assembly of plates, bowls and dishes that constituted Miranda's birthday lunch. Everything was covered in clingfilm which could be removed at the last moment, and he raised the edge of the piece protecting the plate of sliced cold chicken. Carefully he filched a little chunk of breast, shoved it into his mouth and then smoothed the clingfilm down flat again. Chewing rapidly he retreated towards the Common. The people from the caravans and transit vans were sitting in a circle and they all appeared to be studying sheaves of papers. A lot of them were wearing shorts and T-shirts and he could see very few women. Concluding that they were some sort of religious sect he skirted them fastidiously and hurried home to clean his shoes and put on a tie in readiness for Miranda's party.

'They're still there,' Miranda said.

'Who?' Clad now in his blue shirt, Sammy was climbing into his clean trousers. 'God, these are getting tight round the waist.'

'The people camping over on the Common. And it's not the trousers, it's you, my darling. You must stop eating biscuits.'

'I only eat them when I'm hungry – ' A tap came on the bedroom door. Miranda opened it.

'I thought you might like to wear my beads, chickabid.' Florence proffered the triple string of artificial pearls. 'They'll look lovely with your black dress.'

'I'm not wearing my black dress – '

'And is the petticoat all right? Does it fit?' She edged further into the bedroom and watched in the mirror as Sammy knotted a cravat in the neck of his shirt.

'Yes, it fits perfectly, and thank you again.' Miranda groped in the darker reaches of the cupboard for her high-heeled sandals.

'And do you really like it?' Florence's head nid-nodded with anxiety and the desire to please.

'Yes of course I do, lovey – but run along now, there's a good girl. I've still got things to do.'

'Your father's fussing about being home in time to watch Wimbledon – '

'Tell him he can go whenever he likes.'

Gently but firmly Miranda closed the door, and heard Florence say on the other side of it, 'I'll leave my beads on the hall table, chickabid, in case you change your mind. . . .'

'She's forever under my feet!' Miranda exploded, then drew a deep breath and blew the dust off her sandals. 'Wherever I go, there she is – I sometimes think she creeps in through the fanlight.'

'Calm down, there's a good girl – remember that it's your birthday and that we all love you.'

'Sixty,' Miranda said dolefully, 'and look, my hair's coming out.'

'You're not alone.'

'But it's socially acceptable for men's hair to come out. Some women

237

go potty over bald men – look at Yul whatsisname.' She buttoned her flowered silk dress and smoothed the collar. Then she sat down and began to apply her make-up; a few strokes of moisturiser followed by a light coat of liquid powder in a pale tan shade, then a flick or two of mascara and she was ready.

'You look marvellous,' Sammy said, embracing her fondly, 'and I adore you even more now you're an old-age pensioner.'

It was ten minutes to twelve and they went downstairs in readiness to greet the guests.

Lunch for sixteen, three of them children, and all signs of pre-party tension melted at the sight of the first arrival. He came in slowly, leaning heavily on the arm of his companion, and there was a red rosebud in his buttonhole which matched his bow tie.

'Dear daughter. . . .' With arms outstretched Bruno Ellenberg embraced Miranda.

Age had been kind to him, the familiar leonine head of hair surmounting a face in which the features had merely become a little more pronounced, his nose a little more commanding and his strong eyebrows emphasised by a new shagginess. Miranda kissed him fondly and his companion gravely extended a small square package tied with ribbon. She was a tall and somewhat angular woman in her seventies and although the day was warm she was wearing a black cardigan over her summer dress.

'Happy greetings, Miranda.' She spoke with an accent.

'*Thank* you, Magda.' Miranda kissed her. She had kissed her on many occasions during the past thirty-seven years, and never without a feeling that she was invading a carefully guarded sense of privacy. She had frequently come across the same reaction during the years spent working in Displaced Persons' Camps and recognised it as one more symptom of long-suffered brutality. Gas them and burn them, but first make sure that you destroy the psyche, the personality that dwells within the outer wrapping.

Ultimately, Magda had been lucky. Suffering from typhoid and the inevitable gross malnutrition, she had been found in the barrack hut next to the one in which Nat was incarcerated. Yet for her, the miracle of release brought with it no immediate blessing; all it brought was the renewed memory of her family.

All nine of them had arrived at Auschwitz in a tight-knit, defensive little group – grandparents, parents, two brothers, one sister and an aunt. Her grandparents and her mother had been sent to the gas

238

chamber upon arrival and her father and two brothers she had never seen again. She had spent ten days in the same fetid hut in Block A as her aunt and sister, and when it was discovered that she played the violin, and knew the solo part in the Lalo, she grabbed the chance to play it, in the hope that to do so would be of benefit to all three of them.

But it hadn't worked like that; instead, she had found herself in the Music Block scratching out Strauss and Suppé on the bandstand each morning while her aunt and sister marched off to forced labour in the fields. And each evening she played as they returned. They always looked for her, and gave her a cheery little wave as they passed. They knew that she had done it all for the best, and that she would try to exert in their favour whatever precarious influence she had obtained.

Autumn came, bringing cold mornings of weeping mist; influenza and bronchitis spread, and she saw her aunt bowed low beneath a lung-tearing cough. She no longer waved, and neither did Magda's sister. They still smiled however; brave, fixed smiles that grew to mean less and less as the wind settled in the east and the snows came. Magda approached the *kapo* of the Music Block on their behalf, but she had never been adept at wheedling favours. The *kapo* dismissed her with a snort of derision. 'Worry about your own skin,' she advised, 'and leave others to do the same.'

The smiles faded, and were ultimately replaced by hostile, hollow-eyed stares as they shambled unsteadily past. As the flesh melted from their bones so the love withered in their hearts. There was no hope now, and no understanding; merely a bitter accusation that seemed to come from the depths of their souls.

On the evening her aunt failed to return from the fields Magda asked the *blockawa* if she could be transferred from the Music Block back to Block A. Deeply suspicious the *blockawa* demanded to know why, and afraid to draw attention to the remnants of her family, Magda said that she was tired of playing the violin. She hated music. The request was refused and she was forced to continue as before. By the time Nat arrived in the Music Block she had ceased to look for her sister in the long ragged column of women who crept back and forth. Familial love could no longer withstand the remorseless pressure of evil, and they had become strangers. She never knew when or how her sister died.

And with the gradual return to health after the liberation came the silent agony of loss and guilt. She could tell no one, and remained stonily indifferent to Miranda's discovery that she was a friend of Nat's, and apparently ungrateful that with the aid of official manipulation she had been admitted to England and given a home with the Ellenbergs on Clatterfoot Common. She had been living there for thirty-six years.

Florence and Stanley arrived behind Bruno and Magda at the party, and Miranda thought, my God, I've just realised that I've got four octogenarians helping me to celebrate my entry into old age . . . .

'What time's Nat coming?' someone asked.

'The plane was due in at ten this morning, so they should be here in time for lunch. Oh, *thank* you, Jenny – ' Miranda knelt down to receive a lumpily wrapped present from Stanley's small granddaughter.

'It's from Nicholas too.'

'Thank you very much indeed, Nicholas.'

Nicholas surveyed her in silence, thumb in mouth.

'He's always stupid before lunch,' Jenny explained.

'Then we must find him something to eat straight away – Sammy!'

'Jenny, are you being authoritative again?' Roger, son of Stanley, swept his small daughter up in his arms and held her aloft. She shrieked with delight.

'Her knickers are showing,' Florence complained.

'I bet you've shown yours often enough in your time.' Miranda took the dish of cocktail crisps from Sammy and offered it to Nicholas. 'Not too many or you'll spoil your lunch.'

'I want some too – ' Jenny struggled to get down, then darted after Nicholas.

'I hope we're bringing them up the right way,' Roger said to Miranda. 'I sometimes think we ought to go on a course.'

'They seem OK so far.' She watched the retreating Nicholas with a smile. 'Funny to think I'm their half-aunt, isn't it?'

'I always think of you as an older sister.'

Roger had gone to live with Florence and Stanley soon after they set up home together in one of the weavers' cottages. Miranda had seen little of him until she left the Red Cross and married Sammy, but they had slowly built up an easy, bantering relationship, and he had seemed extravagantly pleased when she gave him a Victorian microscope in a fitted mahogany case that had once belonged to Emrys.

He was now senior partner in a firm of chartered surveyors in Sudbury; a pleasant, self-effacing man with something of his father's unobtrusive good looks. He had married a girl called Helen whom everyone liked, except Florence, who considered her common.

The party had now congregated in the garden at the back of Trellis House, Bruno sitting in a recliner chair close by a large shrub rose in full bloom. Sunlight formed a halo round his head and Magda hovered behind him, remaining impassive as Florence sank into the neighbouring chair.

'I can't believe my chickabid's sixty,' she said, then patted his brown-speckled hand affectionately. 'The next party will be your ninetieth, dear.'

'Ninety? Me?' His Jewish features, more pronounced in old age, assumed a fierce and hawklike expression.

'Yes, you. And I have to admit, Bruno, that you're wonderful for your age. So strong and so upright.' Aware that Magda was listening above their heads, Florence added diplomatically, 'And of course, a lot of it's due to Magda. If anyone ever asked me to describe her, I would say to them, quite frankly, Magda is a saint.'

'She has learned to make rice pudding.'

'How lovely!'

'But she won't stop. Every day it's rice pudding – ' He looked petulant for a moment, then glanced round him. 'Where's Nat? Isn't she supposed to be coming?'

'Yes, Miranda said her plane was due in at ten. She should be here any time now.'

'All this travelling is getting ridiculous.'

'Yes, Bruno dear, but we must remember that she is a great *artiste*. I always knew from the very first time I met her – a dear little girl with a hole in her jersey – that she was destined for great things.'

'Rice pudding,' Bruno said, 'nothing but rice pudding. . . .'

'Shall I get you another glass of wine, dear?'

'He must drink only water now.'

'*Water?*' Outraged, Florence turned in her chair to meet the dark and obdurate stare of Magda. 'But my dear girl, this is my daughter's birthday!'

'Water, please. Otherwise he swell.'

'Oh, rubbish!' Seizing Bruno's empty glass Florence struggled up from her chair and tottered away.

'Why are you such an old cow?' Bruno asked mildly, and failed to notice when Magda touched his hair with a fleeting movement that was probably the nearest she would ever come to a caress.

'Because you are stupid old man who knows nothing.'

A short distance from them an admiring group had gathered round the daffodil-yellow carry-cot that contained a very small baby lying asleep, little hammer fists folded on either side of its head.

'Three weeks old yesterday – '

'She's beautiful!'

'And she's like you, Rachel!'

'But I think she's got Johnny's chin, hasn't she?'

'What a lovely lot of hair – '

'I remember what a lot Miranda had.' Florence paused, two glasses of wine held carefully aloft.

'Won't Nat be thrilled to see her!'

'Where *is* Nat?'

'Someone said they'll be here about midday. Depends on the traffic from Heathrow.'

'It's almost one o'clock now – '

'Sammy,' Miranda said in an undertone, 'I think we'd better start eating. Nat won't mind.'

Roger's wife Helen offered to help Miranda, and seeing that Florence had absentmindedly given the glass of wine destined for Bruno to someone else, Magda left her place behind his chair and followed them to the kitchen. The old trestle table belonging to Bert had been set up in the shade of Emrys' tree and covered with a red-and-white check cloth. The three women carried out trays of food while Sammy and Roger assembled more bottles of wine.

The four octogenarians were supplied with cushions for their chairs, and Bert, seated next to Florence, wondered whether anyone would notice if he helped himself to salmon as well as chicken. Then Nicholas demanded the use of his potty and had to be hurried away with crossed legs and an agonised expression. The baby continued to sleep, undisturbed by the increasing animation, and flexing her feet under the table Miranda thought, I shall have to take these damned sandals off soon. . . .

But the pleasures of the day shone in their smiles and illuminated their laughter as the sun twinkled in the wineglasses and lit the faces of the roses nearby, and Sammy was about to propose a toast to his wife when Bruno gave a sudden great cry, like a cry of pain.

He was the first to see her as she came quietly round the corner of the house. Natalie Ellenberg, internationally acclaimed concert artist, ruffled black curls threaded with silver, and wearing a black-and-white dress with a bow under the chin. Now unashamedly plump, she bore little resemblance to the girl who had come home from Germany on a stretcher in 1945. She stood looking at them all for a moment as if imprinting the scene upon her memory, then with a little crow of delight hurried forward and seized Miranda in a powerful embrace.

'*Sixty!* My God, how can anyone *be* so old?'

'Hang on, you're only six weeks off target yourself!'

'How are you? Oh, you look great!'

'So do *you*!'

They embraced again, and Nat moved round the table smiling the old smile and gleaming with affection. She left Bruno until the last; he reached out to her blindly with his stiff, old man's arms, and she rocked with him to and fro.

'Oh my goodness . . . oh my goodness . . .' he kept repeating against her shoulder. Then she sat down at the empty place opposite him and grabbed a nearby glass of wine. A new air of excitement had entered with her, almost as if the concert was about to begin, Miranda thought fragmentarily, then looked round her and suddenly exclaimed, 'Where is he?'

'He is here.' He came round the corner as Nat had done and he was carrying a large airport carrier bag in either hand.

'*Raoul!*' Her eyes stung with tears because the family party was now complete. 'It's worth being sixty having you all here like this,' she said, but her words were lost to everyone except Sammy. He took her hand under the table.

Raoul and Nat had brought champagne, and as the corks flew Bert helped himself to a little more chicken, then to a nice little morsel of salmon which had obligingly detached itself from the main body. Glancing round he caught the large dark eyes of Magda, who was sitting opposite, and she smiled at him. He didn't think he had ever seen her smile before. He smiled back, cheeks bulging.

Raoul was now sitting between Florence and Roger's wife Helen. That man gets more and more handsome, Florence thought. Those dark blue eyes, those marvellous features . . . even his limp is dead sexy.

She asked him where they had arrived from and he told her New York. 'Natalee has given twelve concerts in ten days which is too merch. She must rest here now before the English tour and the Proms.'

'She is a wonderful darling girl.' Florence sipped dreamily. 'And you, if you don't mind my saying so, dear, are a wonderful boy. You are the rock on which she depends.'

'I drink to that,' he laughed, 'although it is not true.'

'And it's wonderful to have you in our family. . . .' Four glasses of white wine and one of champagne had dimmed Florence's recollection of who was actually related and who was not. Not that it mattered, because she loved everybody. Even poor little Helen, who was so common. She leaned across Raoul towards her, breathing in the scent

243

of aftershave as she did so, and said, 'I do love your long dangly earrings, darling. No one else could wear them but you.'

'Thank you, Auntie Flo,' Helen replied with equal sweetness.

'Florence, dear.'

'Oh, but Auntie Flo's so much more *homely*. . . .'

Bitch, thought Florence, then straightened her smile and adjusted her hearing aid as Stanley, on the other side of the table, rose to his feet.

'I would just like to say a few words,' he began, clearing his throat. Obediently everyone fell silent except Nicholas, who was singing a song.

'Ostensibly,' continued Stanley, 'it is with the idea of proposing a toast to Miranda, and congratulating her upon attaining the wonderful age of sixty. And I say wonderful not in the sense of wonderful *old* age of sixty but, having already been there, I have proved to my own satisfaction that sixty is an age full of new wonderment and joy.' He paused, and there was a subdued murmur of agreement from the elders.

'In our thirties and forties we are sometimes apt to lose our way, and I'm betraying no secrets when I say that Miranda's mother and I found our paths diverging for a while. We both discovered happiness elsewhere, and it was only in our sixties, after a somewhat circuitous route, that we found our way back together again. And the result,' he smiled rather shyly, 'has been well worth waiting for.'

'Hear, hear – ' His son Roger banged the table with his fist, and Florence's head nid-nodded in gratification. Nicholas continued to sing quietly.

'I'm not, however, suggesting that Miranda and Sammy should part purely for the joy of coming together again – ' (one of his dear little weak jokes, bless him, thought Miranda, smiling affectionately) ' – but when I look round at us it occurs to me that we have all, at one time or another, been swept apart from each other by the hand of either God or fate – the choice is a personal one. Some of us have endured unspeakable suffering which others among us have done everything within their power to heal, but the coming together again has enriched our two intertwined families of Ellenberg and Whittaker with new members who over the years have become increasingly dear to us. . . .'

Sitting close to Miranda, Sammy noticed Little Rachel bite her lip and look down at the tablecloth (why do we still call her Little Rachel now that's she in her mid-thirties), and his glance took in Magda, carefully hatchet-faced, brushing a crumb from Bruno's linen jacket.

'. . . It only remains for me to ask you to raise your glasses, not only to Miranda, but to all of us who live here in harmony and love now that the storm is over. May we continue to value the peace that surrounds us and our little ones, and may these same little ones grow up tall and honourable and unafraid.'

'To Miranda!'

'To all of us,' she responded.

Memories floated in the warm summer air, painful memories now softened a little by time. Nat, smoking a gold-tipped cigarette, smiled across at Magda and their eyes locked together.

Do you remember when we played in the Women's Orchestra, Magda?

Of course I do. Is it likely that I will ever forget?

You seemed such a private, untouchable person in those days.

And I still do, don't I? I had so much to lock away, to try to forget, and any form of change is difficult at my age.

Yes, I also have holes in my skin; places it hurts to touch.

But it has also enriched us, my dear. It gave us an extra dimension. We, more than other people, know the meaning of fortitude.

My God, Magda, do you remember when we ate raw cabbage stalks?

There was cannabilism, too. The starving pillaging the bodies of the dead for their kidneys and their liver.

And the sickness, the griping bellyache of dysentery . . . I lost sight of you on the train to Belsen, Magda.

I was there, in another cattle truck. I remember the snow and the wind, and the smoke from the engine wreathing past over our heads like a column of ghosts in the darkness . . . . Yes, we learned the meaning of fortitude.

We have also learned the meaning of joy. Of waking up in the morning and being able to contemplate the certainty of a full day's living. No one's going to suddenly snatch it away from us at a *Blocksperre* . . . remember the blowing of whistles, the barking of dogs, the shouts of *Achtung – achtung*? That was how life ended for millions of people.

I remember. But we were two of the lucky ones, weren't we?

Yes, my dear. We are two of the lucky ones.

Unobtrusively Nat raised her glass in a silent toast. Here's to us, Magda.

Here's to us, Nat.

There was no need for words.

The remains of the salads were cleared away, their places taken by a trifle of heroic proportions, a Jamaican rum *torte*, a Pithiviers cake and a bowl of fresh fruit salad. Bert eased his collar a little before taking up his spoon, and Johnny, Little Rachel's husband, wondered whether a brisk game of tennis would deal with the day's calorific excess. He had been prone to chubbiness since he was a small boy, and now his doctor was nagging him to lose weight. Accepting a portion of rum *torte* he caught his wife's eye and hurriedly switched to fruit salad.

Conversation was still animated, and Raoul watched Nat chatting to Miranda, while at the same time he listened with half an ear to Florence describing her daughter's education. 'She's a college girl, dear. Very well qualified, like her father. And I have to admit that I *do* believe in education, and that I was only too happy to shoulder the hardship of working for her fees ... thirty guineas a term *plus* extras ... children don't come cheap, dear – I even paid fifteen guineas on her teeth alone. Her front ones were crooked and a woman's smile is so important. . . .'

'Yes,' Raoul said, rousing himself. 'Corsican eggs.'

'Beg pardon, dear?'

'*Oeufs Corse* ... it is a stupid joke we have because of my accent.'

'Oh, I see,' said Florence, who didn't. Undeterred, she continued to prattle in a low monotone which blended with the warmth of the sun, the taste of good food and wine, the scent of flowers and the atmosphere of relaxed goodwill that enfolded them all.

Ten more days before the English tour – Liverpool, Manchester, Birmingham – that would culminate with the Prom concert at the Royal Albert Hall, thought Raoul. Ten days of relaxing at the Overseer's House with his father-in-law and old Magda, of roaming the quiet countryside with the bloke, and listening to her keeping her fingers in trim at the grand piano in the evenings . . . .

The one and only bloke. His mind went back to the days of the occupation of Paris. To their life in the attic, to the day when he found her gone, and to the day when he sewed the Star of David on the breast pocket of his jacket in the hope that he too would be rounded up in a *grande rafle* and taken to the same place of internment.

But love had destroyed his normal commonsense and filled the resulting space with romantic impracticality, and on the following day the café owner for whom he worked had said, 'Why are you wearing that stupid emblem? You are not a Jew and you never have been. Take it off.'

Fists clenched, he had been on the point of leaving without notice, of smashing the window as he went past, then the café owner had lowered his voice and added, 'In these times it is unwise to be precipitate, but one hears that foreigners are sent to an internment camp out at Saint-Denis.'

So in spite of all his precautions even his employer knew about the bloke.

He found the place at Saint-Denis and hung about outside until a couple of gendarmes began to take an interest in him, and when one of them showed signs of moving towards him he limped hurriedly away, sickened by his own ineffectuality. It was easy enough to be arrested in wartime Paris, but another matter to be sent to Saint-Denis.

So he went back to the café, where his employer showed no further sign of sympathy for his private affairs, and Raoul continued to work the long hours, hobbling rapidly between tables where Germans spent loudly and lavishly and where the old French clientele sat with their backs to the wall and made one cup of bitter acorn coffee last all evening. His wages paid the rent and bought his meagre food ration, but the main reason for remaining in the café lay in the hope of picking up more information, more odds and ends of tittle-tattle that could be used to his own advantage.

He heard about Drancy, and his misery of loss became augmented by a gross foreboding when it became clear that Drancy was the deportation centre for Jews. Paris was now openly anti-Semitic, with hook-nosed Shylockian figures remorselessly cartooned in the newspapers and *À bas les juifs* scrawled interminably on walls and placards. So he went out to Drancy one afternoon and saw, with conflicting emotions, that the prisoners were clearly visible from the other side of the wire fence. They were walking to and fro in the aimless fashion of animals in a zoo, and even more appalling was the presence of casual sightseers – he supposed that he must count himself as one of them – peering in from the outside.

There was no sign of her. Male prisoners seemed to predominate, or perhaps the women preferred to stay in their quarters rather than submit themselves to the casual stare of onlookers. He didn't know. So he went home again to the cold and empty attic, and averted his eyes from the Tante Honorine and stretched out on the small divan in which he always slept these days. He had a cigarette in his pocket which another waiter had given him, so he lit it, then leaned over the side of the bed and wound the gramophone. The needle hissed painfully, and the voice of Tino Rossi came to him like that of a poor little ghost. His life now was full of ghosts . . . .

And then he met the man in the café who changed it all. The man who asked if he liked travelling, and if he loved France. Indifferently, he said that he did, and his indifference melted when he realised

247

that he was in the initial stages of being vetted for the Resistance Movement . . . .

'Try a bit of Pithiviers cake.' Miranda's voice broke into his reverie. 'I made it with you in mind because it's French.'

Leaning close, she saw the shadows pass from his face and the glow of his smile break through. Although he was now in his early sixties the life of husband and concert manager to Nat had added a pleasantly international charm to his spectacular good looks. Dressed in clothes that might have come from Paris, Rome or New York, he was at ease in any milieu, and with the knife poised above the Pithiviers cake Miranda's mind flashed back to the thin white-faced boy, newly released from the horrors of Fresnes gaol, who had found his way to Liverpool, and from Liverpool down to Clatterfoot Common, in search of Nat.

'Ah, Meerandah!' He seized her hand and kissed it, laughingly adopting the role of archetypal Frenchman as imagined by the British. 'You are a darling leetle woman and I adore you!'

She sat down on the vacant chair next to him. 'I thought you were looking a bit bereft just now.'

'Bereft?' He examined the word carefully.

'Lost, defenceless.'

'My mind was in the past, but now it is returned.'

'I think today's brought back the past to several of us older ones,' Miranda said. 'I suppose it's inevitable when families get together.'

'And share a past of tumult.'

Miranda watched him draw a ribbon of cream over his Pithiviers cake, then said, 'You still haven't written your book, have you?'

'Book?' He pretended not to understand.

'About what happened . . . after Nat.'

'Ah, that. It is all over now.'

'No, it's not,' she said vehemently. 'Stories like yours should be kept alive for future generations – what about Jenny and Nicholas, and Little Rachel's baby? They've got to know in order that they can learn.'

'One day, perhaps.' He smiled at her. 'In the meanwhile I am too much occupied with my Natalee – the old bloke never stops giving concerts, giving recitals, giving pleasure.'

'She wouldn't be able to do it without you perpetually smoothing the path. But even so, I do think you ought to write your memoirs, Raoul.'

'I have written them already.' He tapped his forehead. 'They are written and stored away up here.'

'That's not good enough. They should be stored in libraries and on people's bookshelves.'

'One day. Perhaps one day.'

She left him to eat in peace, and walked barefoot back to the kitchen with the idea of making coffee. The lunch party was running down now, fragmenting into little groups. She could hear the voices of Jenny and Nicholas playing a game of their own invention, and in a patch of shade Little Rachel was breastfeeding her baby. Before going into the house she saw Magda slowly escorting Bruno back to the Overseer's House for a nap.

She found her father in the kitchen stacking dirty plates into the dishwasher.

'Oh my dear, you don't have to do that! There's lots of youngsters around to give a hand.'

'Did your mother really play championship tennis?' he asked.

'Not that I know of.' Miranda giggled briefly. 'Why?'

'She keeps saying she wants to be home in time to watch Wimbledon.'

'But she told me – ' Miranda paused. 'Anyone who wants to watch tennis is perfectly free to do so here, without traipsing back over the Common.'

She began to make the coffee while Stanley fiddled with plates and glasses. He was very stooped now, and tufts of white whiskers sprouted from each ear.

'How long are those people staying on the Common?' he asked.

'I don't know. But they're not being a nuisance, are they?'

'Oh no. It's just that one becomes a shade proprietorial.'

She finished grinding the coffee beans then heaped the grains into the percolator. 'I'm very proprietorial about this house, and about all of us.'

'Including me?' He smiled at her shyly.

'You're almost at the top of the list – Father.'

They set out the coffee cups on two trays, and the word *Father*, uttered at last, seemed to hang in the air like a moment of grace.

'It's funny,' Miranda said, 'but I had the old nightmare again last night. Haven't had it for years.'

'About the baby Ellenberg?' She had told him about it shortly after retiring from the Red Cross. 'Probably because you were tired after all the preparations for today. You've put on a wonderful show, Miranda.'

'Sammy's done a lot to help, and so of course has Florence.'

'Yes,' he said. 'Of course.'

They began to laugh, silently and guiltily with their arms about one another, and when Stanley insisted upon carrying one of the trays she hoped fervently that he wouldn't trip.

249

The elders slept. Florence in a recliner chair with her mouth wide open, Bruno beneath a brightly coloured shawl on the sofa in his own drawing room, and Bert, minus collar and tie, full length on the garden bench. Stanley, having helped to distribute the coffee, drifted in a light doze with his panama hat shading his eyes.

Wandering down the garden Nat found Little Rachel with the baby spread on her lap while she changed its nappy.

'Worth waiting for, wasn't she?'

'Thirty-seven's pretty old for having a first baby.'

'If the experts told you that, forget it. Experts, like critics, are a load of hooey.' Nat sat down beside her and when the baby's toilet had been completed took her in her arms. And the sensation of a small living thing cradled against her brought back memories of the last cattle-truck journey to Belsen.

She had been pretty certain from the time she regained consciousness that Rachel was not the baby she had held so fiercely and protectively as the snow had whirled down on them, and as the sudden violent urge to go on living had come roaring back. In some ways it was a pity because it had always seemed to her that on that last nightmare journey an unbreakable bond had been forged between two ill-assorted human beings who had been thrust together by chance and allowed, for a brief space of time, to share an interdependence that was almost sublime. She remembered the baby's individual presence rather than its physical appearance, but her memory of the journey ended before they reached their destination. Perhaps she had been one of the prisoners who had lost consciousness before they arrived, in which case the baby would have remained wedged in place in the same way as everyone else, because there was no room in which to fall. But when the sides of the trucks had been let down and those still alive scrambled in terror to avoid the whips, the fists and the jackboots, the baby was in all probability trampled underfoot. She didn't know. She had no real recollection. But she must have said something about a baby when the camp was liberated, because they had presented her with the girl sitting quietly beside her.

Pot luck, Nat thought, that's all it amounts to. But in all that insane and prolonged upheaval of millions, what else do you expect? And although Little Rachel had been brought up to know the truth about her origins, Nat had never told her (indeed, had never told anyone) about the little spectre still drifting in her memory. Funny that Miranda and I are both haunted by babies and that we should both be childless, she thought.

She looked down at the baby in her arms, and watched its eyes growing blank with sleep.

'How did you come to choose me?' It seemed as if Little Rachel had been following her thoughts. It was a question she had never broached before, and for a moment Nat was disconcerted.

'I can't really remember,' she said slowly. 'But probably because you stank less than the others.'

'That's as good a reason as any.'

'I've never had cause to regret it.'

'Needless to say I haven't either.'

Let's leave it at that, shall we? Answer any questions that are necessary with a lightness of touch that will leave the sediment of pain undisturbed. They smiled at one another.

'Will you be playing for us later, Nat?'

'If anyone asks me.'

'I mean, you're not too tired? Jetlagged, and all that?'

'I grew out of such self-indulgence years ago, dear child.'

'You've certainly done some travelling in your time.'

'In all sorts of conditions, too,' Nat said laconically, and thought, why does the past keep coming back, today of all days? I've been remembering things I haven't thought about for years .... A sign of growing old, no doubt.

Without Miranda being aware, it had been arranged with Magda that Nat should play for them over at Bruno's house, and that tea and birthday cake would be provided.

With studied casualness it was suggested that guests might like to wander across to the Overseer's House as Bruno was too tired to walk back to Trellis again. So they straggled across the patch of Common in twos and threes, Little Rachel and Johnny pushing the baby in its folding pram, Jenny and Nicholas indulging in a short sharp quarrel, and Bert sidling along with a blade of grass between his teeth.

'More of them have arrived!' Florence said exasperatedly to Stanley. 'Just look at all those cars.'

'I expect they're going to have a barbecue.' He glanced across to the new and orderly line of vehicles. 'Yes, look, they're making a fire.'

'There's going to be loud pop music and a horrible smoky smell and people getting drunk and girls getting raped – '

'What an imagination,' Stanley murmured.

'You may not know about these things, but I *do*,' Florence retorted. She felt tired and oddly petulant; perhaps it was because Miranda had insisted with exaggerated fulsomeness that she should be shut up all alone in the drawing room with the curtain drawn and the TV on while white-clad silly buggers smacked tennis balls to and fro. She had slept, and had woken with a headache and a sense of having been deliberately excluded from better things.

'Miranda's very bossy now she's sixty,' she said, 'although she's always had a tendency that way. I could see it, even if no one else could.'

'Don't criticise her on her birthday.'

'I'm not criticising, I'm merely speaking the truth.'

Truth, thought Stanley, what cruel and inaccurate pronouncements are uttered in thy name.

Bruno, refreshed by an hour's dreamless sleep, greeted them at the door. He remembered everyone's name, and when Miranda, who had walked over with Raoul, asked where Nat was, he closed one wrinkled basilisk eye and said, 'Most probably attending to the requirements of nature, my dear.'

The drawing room was cool after the heat of the day, and the scent of roses and peonies greeted them. So did the careful arrangement of chairs, and the grand piano, whose lid was raised like a great sail.

Nat strolled in unconcernedly, seated herself at the keyboard and said, 'Every silver lining has a cloud and every celebration has a short period of boredom. This is it.'

They laughed and clapped, and Nat smiled the old sardonic smile and said, 'Happy birthday, Miranda.'

She began to play, her spine a little hunched now after years spent at the keyboard, her Jewish profile a little more obdurate beneath its elderly plumpness. But the magic was still there, and the sound of it rippled and danced from beneath her fingers and old Bruno nodded his head and clasped the hand of Magda, who was sitting next to him.

Miranda and Raoul were also holding hands, and in the warm grasp each was conscious of a love born from past history; from pain and fear, from hope and ultimate triumph. When you are old you are free to love people simply and unrestrainedly, Raoul thought, in French. I can tell this woman that I love her because she is good and strong and kind and because she found my bloke when she was dying and made her well, and because her family made me welcome here. A family is a good thing . . . .

And Little Rachel's husband Johnny, who came from a nonconformist background, thought, how strange and interesting Jews are. *And He will assemble the dispersed of Israel and gather together the scattered of Judah from the four corners of the earth*, as Isaiah said. But I suppose the only thing that matters is for Jews and Gentiles, believers and non-believers, to try getting on together for a change. Rachel thinks she's probably a Jew by birth and has no idea of her nationality, but she's no need to. She's just Rachel, and that's enough.

Helen, wife of Roger, squeezed the hand of Miranda's husband Sammy and thought, I love music. I always have. Listening to it relaxes me, makes me calm, makes me feel better. Like a drink or a warm bath. But it's different for the casual listener like me – imagine what it's like to be Nat. A professional, a soloist. OK, it's glamorous, and I'm not above boasting that she's a sort of relation when I see her photo in the papers and her name in the lists of forthcoming concerts, but I don't think I'd like to be her. She hasn't any children. Well, she's got Rachel of course – why do they call her *Little?* – but she didn't actually give birth to her, did she, so it's not the same thing at all . . . .

She cast a glance at Jenny who was sitting on the other side of her, and at Nicholas who was on her lap and drowsily sucking his thumb.

No, it isn't the same thing at all . . . although she does play beautifully.

She was playing only short pieces: a Chopin prelude, a Beethoven bagatelle, and then Debussy's *Children's Corner* suite, and each one when she came to it sounded perfect and yet unpremeditated; lovely little trifles flicked effortlessly from the keyboard and sent floating into the subdued glow of late afternoon.

All I hope is she doesn't develop arthritis, thought Florence, sitting between Stanley and Bert. I've got it . . . that's what these little lumps are. If her fingers go like mine she's had it. Goodnight all. She'll have to stop all this jaunting round the world dragging that poor husband of hers and settle down like the rest of us. Chickabid's settled down . . . . Florence dozed, jerked awake and began to nid-nod when everyone clapped, and then Jenny went up the the piano and said, 'I can play like that.'

'Come on then, let's hear you.' Nat indicated that Jenny should climb on to her lap, and to each splodge of sound the child made she added a graceful little curlicue that transformed it into a lilting tune.

'No – you don't know how to play properly – '

'Auf . . .' Ruefully Nat stuck her fingertips in her mouth while Jenny continued her solo splodgings, then Magda, who had quietly left the room, reappeared in the doorway and announced tea.

Bruno entered the dining room supported on either side by his son and daughter, and when he was seated Nat went across to Magda.

253

'Did you do it all yourself?' She indicated the large and elaborately iced birthday cake.

'I like to cook. Yes.'

'It's wonderful, Magda.'

'So is your playing, Nat.'

They stood side by side watching Little Rachel pouring out the tea and once again memories were reawakened.

When Magda first arrived at the Overseer's House she had been in a state of emotional aridity, and had passed through the days as if she barely noticed them. She ate frugally, slept fitfully, and watched with large suspicious eyes every movement on the part of her hosts. The bang of a door would make her start convulsively and they learned to laugh quietly and to move slowly as if they had a wild bird at large in the drawing room.

Nat was released from hospital two weeks later, and while her appearance did a certain amount to reassure Magda, it also brought back the past with a new and searing horror. She stayed in her bedroom, refused to dress, wash or eat. She sat on the floor in a corner away from the window, rocking to and fro with her thin white arms clasped round her knees and the tattooed serial number showing up stark and shocking below the sleeve of her nightdress.

Still weak and gaunt after the ravages of typhus Nat had tried to talk to her, to explain that the past was all over; but her presence now caused the older woman such distress that it seemed pointless to continue. They took the baby to see her, but Magda merely turned her head away, and it was several years before they discovered that Magda had never greatly cared for babies anyway.

She had been equally unresponsive to Bruno, seeming to sense through the pores of her skin that here was yet one more authoritative presence which could only be bent upon inflicting fresh torment, and so he had withdrawn, nonplussed and appalled by the damage that had been done to her.

'But she seemed the strongest of us all,' Nat had said, lying rug-draped on the drawing-room sofa. 'She seemed so hard and practical. She was the one who never wept.'

'And now she's paying for it.'

The one person she seemed to respond to was Esme, who appeared and reappeared without speaking. Sometimes she would bring in two cups of tea and sit on the bed drinking one of them while Magda sat in the corner rocking to and fro, empty-eyed. Then Esme would go away again, and the soft rustle of her skirt made a soothing sound.

'One day she will break down and cry,' Bruno prophesied. 'It will be like the bursting of a great dam, and we must be prepared to receive the full force of it.'

But it didn't happen like that. She unfroze gradually, at times almost imperceptibly, and they entered into the stage when she was unable to bear Esme out of her sight. In Esme's silent presence she would get dressed, brush her mop of short grey hair and even accompany her downstairs, taking one step at a time like a child learning to walk. They became adept at pretending she wasn't there, in case a word or a glance or a sudden unguarded movement would send her scurrying for the stairs. Only Esme could speak to her; slowly and very quietly, sometimes in English, sometimes in schoolgirl German and sometimes using the odd Russian words that the old aunts and uncles had used; and more and more it seemed to Esme that she was dealing with a wild bird, lost and injured, that had come into their care.

She had been restored to health for several years when Esme died; long enough to withstand the loss without breaking, but incapable of making any kind of separate life for herself. The Overseer's House on Clatterfoot Common had become her world and there was no question of leaving it.

The new pattern only emerged gradually; confused and shattered by the loss of his wife, Bruno's zestfulness faltered; he became like a man who had lost his sense of direction and his elderly plight had the effect of rousing Magda's frozen sensibilities. Although still incapable of demonstrating any outward sign of affection she began to assume responsibility for his welfare. She learned without too much difficulty to cook and, with a mind that had always been essentially methodical and practical, began to run the house with calm efficiency. When Nat came back to stay she could even listen to her music without anguish. The old wounds were healing, but there would never be much sensation where they had once been.

She gave little outward sign of caring for anyone in a personal sense but exhibited a fierce protectiveness towards the little group of family and friends living around the Common, and to Bruno in particular, now that he was in his ninetieth year. He clung to her, and he appeared to feel safe in her hands.

'It's been a long road, Magda,' Nat said as they stood together by Miranda's birthday cake. Sammy and Roger had lit the sixty candles and they gleamed like smiling little eyes.

'A long road, Nat.'

'And we've come through, haven't we?'

255

'Yes, my dear. We have come through.'

Impelled by some shy and private motivation they lightly touched their bare forearms together and the serial numbers burnt into the flesh met fleetingly.

'You never had yours removed, Magda?'

'I am too proud. And you?'

'I suppose I couldn't be bothered. Perhaps one day I will. . . .'

They remained standing close together, aware that they both belonged to one of the most exclusive clubs in the world.

The long summer day died slowly, the sun slashing the western sky blood-red and outlining the trees in black. Thrushes and blackbirds carolled a last song before retiring, and the four younger guests were departing with their offspring. Magda had begun helping Bruno on his way to bed.

'They *are* going to have a barbecue,' Sammy stood, looking out over the Common from the front garden of Trellis House, his arm round Miranda. 'Are people allowed to light bonfires without permission?'

'No idea, but they'd better be careful because everything's so dry.'

Miranda began counting the transits and cars parked in their neat lines, but the gathering dusk made it difficult; tents had also been erected during the course of the day yet the campers still appeared curiously reluctant to take advantage of their rural surroundings. One or two had sunbathed and a man had walked about throwing sticks for his dog. Earlier on they had been observed holding some kind of seminar, but that had appeared to be the only joint activity. The idea came that it was a religious gathering, too devout to engage in the more frivolous summer pastimes; no girls in bikinis, no shrieks from happy children.

'They're saving it all up for the barbecue.' Nat had now come over to join them. 'Any minute now they'll light the bonfire and let fly with an ear-shattering blast of pop.'

'Beethoven can be equally ear-shattering,' Sammy murmured.

'Who's arguing?'

'And who's coming in for a drink?'

'All of us old-age pensioners,' Miranda said. 'My arms are getting chilly.'

The party had ended. The jollity had died, and all that now remained was the sweet quiescence of elderly friends who could admit to being pleasantly exhausted. Florence arrived, and said that only a small gin and tonic could stop her legs aching; Stanley, appearing behind her, asked for no more than a small dash of something because his water-works played up at night.

'In other words, he has to dash,' piped Florence, reviving.

Raoul had a glass of wine, and Bert, appearing stealthily through the French windows, accepted a half of bitter. He was wearing his cap and his carpet slippers.

'They're up to something funny.'

'Who are, Bert?'

'Them on the Common.'

'Ah, live and let live. . . .'

Bert subsided, muttering.

'Is Magda coming over?'

'I doubt it. She's too intent on playing watchdog to Father.'

'Gosh,' Miranda hugged the cashmere shawl round her, 'it's so nice to think Nat and Raoul are going to be here for ten whole days.'

'Even after that we'll only be in the provinces, and then London.'

'We've already sent for our tickets for the Prom – Oh, *Caesar cup of hot Oxo!*' Miranda cried.

'Beg pardon, chickabid?'

'Just an old expression from Queen Mary's.'

'Yes, of course,' said Florence, nid-nodding. 'Funny how I always insisted that you should have the best education money could buy.'

'I'd still manage to love her if she was totally illiterate,' Sammy remarked.

'I daresay, dear. But she'd never have got into the Red Cross, let alone ending up a Commandant – '

'For God's sake stop exaggerating, Flo.'

'Don't call me Flo.'

'Well, Maria then. Or was it Tania?'

They bickered lazily, contentedly, then Bert set down his empty glass and said he'd best push off now, so ta-ta.

Stanley said that they must be going too, yet no one else moved. No one even bothered to switch on a lamp to dispel the soft silver-grey twilight that filled the room.

'You'd best come and take a look,' Bert said, abruptly reappearing from the garden. 'Gawd knows what they're up to but I don't like it.'

They all rose to their feet simultaneously and stood looking at one another, and out of the ensuing silence came the faint sound of music.

'It's a military band, isn't it?' someone said wonderingly.

They followed Bert through the French windows and round to the front garden, Sammy grabbing at Florence as she stumbled in the deep gloom. Assembled by the front gate they saw with a shock of surprise that the camp site was now brilliantly illuminated by car headlights aided by the leaping flames of the bonfire, and as if an ants' nest had been disturbed a multitude of black-clad figures was hurrying to and fro. The music was very loud.

Had they been there all day? Miranda wondered uneasily. Keeping quiet in the seclusion of the caravans and tents until darkness began to fall? If so, why?

'I don't like it,' she said, unconsciously echoing Bert.

The figures began to draw together in a homogenous mass, then they separated a little and with quick shuffling steps formed themselves into four long columns. And then remained motionless. As motionless as the six elderly people watching spellbound from behind the gate of Trellis House.

The brisk music crackled and died, and as a bareheaded man in boots and riding breeches stepped out in front of them Sammy pointed to the top of the metal mast that had been erected earlier in the day. Only Florence had seen it as a flagpole and not a radio mast, and in the violent light from the bonfire they saw that a swastika banner had been unfurled from it.

'Dear God in heaven,' Sammy whispered. 'I read about this in the paper. Councils and private landowners had refused permission and it was suspected that they might try to pick on some out-of-the-way place and hope to get away with it unnoticed.'

The public address system had been adjusted so that the speaker's words were audible to his followers but not to the world in general. Miranda's ears, though, were still sharp enough to catch many of the old sickening phrases she had heard many years before.

'Sooner or later we have to come to terms with reality, and to realise that it is only by re-establishing a Britain for the British that we can hope to restore our beloved country to its former power. Socialism has failed, dismally, lamentably, and now at last we are on the brink of a mass movement towards sanity. . . .'

Instinctively she glanced at Florence, who was standing huddled close to Stanley, but there was no sign in her crumbling profile that she had ever been familiar with the old dogma. If I recited a Hail Mary in her ear she wouldn't recognise that either, Miranda thought.

The posturing figure in the knife-edged breeches and glittering boots was now pounding the ball of his fist in the open palm of his other hand. 'There is no room left in this country for undesirables! There is no room left for Asians and blacks and those of alien culture who do not think and feel as we do! We are frank in our condemnation of all those who do not actively strive for a return to the glory of Empire!'

It's starting again, Miranda thought incredulously. It really is. We got rid of it once, but it's creeping back like a dirty disease . . . .

The six spectators by the gate had instinctively drawn close together and Miranda saw Nat staring sombrely at the swastika illuminated by the bonfire flames. Since June 1945 bonfires had come to mean jollity and peace; barbecues, fireworks and the gentle days of piled autumn leaves, but suddenly they were back to the Reichstag fire, to the burning of books, to the bombing of open cities and to the flames leaping from crematorium chimneys. Very quietly Miranda unlatched the gate.

The man in breeches and boots finished speaking and stiffly raised one arm in salute, and the fervour which had been carefully kept in check burst like a thunderstorm. They cheered with raised arms, and the combined flare from bonfire and car headlights caught the shining sweaty faces and cropped haircuts.

'*Ein volk, ein reich, ein fuhrer!*'

Unseen on the shadowy perimeter Magda joined them, a shawl covering her head and shoulders. 'What happens? What are they *saying?*' Her voice was hoarse with disbelief.

'The same old slogan,' Nat said.

'They're only playing.' Sammy strove to sound reassuring. 'It's one of the eccentricities of our age to dress up and pretend to be someone else, preferably from the past. Re-enacting our fantasies, the psychologists call it.'

'They are not acting,' Raoul murmured with his arm round Nat. 'They believe.'

The shouts died as the loudspeaker crackled and the flood of music covered them. It also covered the sound of car engines and the slam of doors. Headlights died before they had been noticed.

'It's starting again,' Miranda said dully. 'After all we went through. After all we suffered.' Glancing past Sammy she saw that Raoul had put his other arm round Magda and drawn both women close to him.

The men on the Common had begun to march, singing as they went. There was no sign of caution now, and their voices rose exultantly as they pounded in step across the short springy turf. For a moment or two it looked as if they were making straight for Trellis House, then the man in breeches yapped an order and they right-wheeled smartly.

Of course they're playing, Miranda thought. They must be. They practise in their local drill hall once a week. . . . All the same, the idea of a lot of men playing soldiers like little boys is a bit unnerving . . . .

259

But when they turned back again she knew that Raoul was right. They *believed*. It glistened in their sweating faces and proclaimed itself in the deep baying of their voices. This was no charade; this was a large group of well-drilled and hate-ridden men shouting their rejection of humanity. It was all beginning again. Sick with despair her mind went back to the grey day in Liverpool when a runaway pram collided with a police horse and a baby died a violent and unnecessary death. She had taken the blame upon herself, and during the latter war years and after had worked, sometimes with manic desperation, to eradicate the misery of guilt. The living presence of Nat and Raoul, of Little Rachel and Magda on this lovely day had seemed like an absolution, a bestowal of grace by some unseen, unknown hand. But the pardon had been withdrawn, and once again those whom she loved were under threat. Perhaps once again the whole world was under threat.

Drawing a deep breath she quietly pushed the gate open and began to walk through it, then found herself abruptly shoved to one side as the small figure of Florence suddenly darted past. Sammy made a grab at her but she evaded him and ran with rapid, little-old-lady steps towards the column of marchers.

'Stop it at *once*! Go home, before I ring for the police! You're *mad*, all of you!'

Her high shriek was lost in the braying music, but, as if her action had been the signal for concerted protest, a sudden barrage of bricks and bottles flew from the hands of shadowy figures now emerging from behind bushes and trees.

'Come back!' Miranda bawled, rushing after her mother. The marchers broke step in temporary confusion before proudly continuing in a hail of thudding missiles. Then some broke away in pursuit of the counterdemonstrators, and what sounded like shots rang out.

Florence lay on the grass face upwards, her arms flung wide, and in the eerie light the blood on her forehead looked like black mud.

'For God's sake why did you have to – ? Oh, my poor little darling. . . .' Panting, Miranda dropped to her knees and attempted to wipe her mother's face with the hem of her skirt. The music was still blaring but the tumult of shouting had moved further away. Distractedly she caught the first sound of a police siren.

'Gorgeous end, chickabid.' Florence smiled up at her through the streaks of blood. 'You called me darling.'

They all knelt round her, and it was Sammy who very gently lifted her and carried her back to the house. Miranda was sobbing with shock and carrying Florence's powder-blue high-heeled sandals – so bravely

260

unsuitable for an octogenarian – and Stanley drew her close against his thin old man's body and led her away.

Twenty minutes later the police called in search of witnesses, and told them what they already knew. Florence was dead.

The Common was silent. The ambulance and the police cars had departed, the transits and caravans had gone; the bonfire had subsided in a last shower of sparks, and hatred had died with the heat of the day.

The moon came up mistily, then rose cool and serene above the trees where the old houses grouped companionably together gleamed silver-grey in its light.

At the Overseer's House old Bruno had come downstairs in his pyjamas saying that he had heard shouting and strange noises.

'Only holiday peoples on the Common,' Magda assured him. 'They are gone home to bed now.'

'Time we all went to bed,' Nat said. 'Come on, give me your arm.' She led him back to his room, and as she plumped his pillows and then tucked the blanket round him he said, 'I keep having dreams. . . .'

'I know.' She bent to kiss him. 'We all do. It's what keeps us going.'

Over at the weaver's cottage next to the one in which Florence had lived with Stanley, Bert removed his cap in order to scratch his head, and then replaced it. He felt snackish. Drama always had that effect on him. Always had done, even during the war.

Funny to think of her gone. So bright and lively one minute, and the next gone; snuffed out like a light. Best way really, he thought, and hoped that he would manage his own exit as speedily when the time came.

The cause of her death he viewed with stoicism; people would always fight, it was human nature. There would always be quarrels and squabbles and disagreements over politics – he had felt strongly about politics himself, once – and there would always be wars. Very often people didn't mean anything by it; nothing personal. It was just human instinct and you couldn't do anything about it. At least it helped to keep the population down.

He went through to his kitchen and opened the fridge. A nice piece of English cheddar greeted him. He cut some bread, plastering it thickly with butter, then got out the jar of ploughman's pickle. Still wearing his cap he sat down to eat, cutting the cheese into neat squares and carrying each one to his mouth on the point of his knife.

Yes, a pity about tonight's little to-do, and it was a shame her getting

261

in the way like that. Mind you, she wasn't getting any younger – none of them were – and he was glad that old Stan was staying over at Trellis House. It wouldn't do for him to be on his tod, not on the first night.

Give him a day or two and he'll be over the worst, Bert thought, munching. He got up to make a cup of tea.

Sammy and Miranda sat at the trestle table beneath Emrys' tree. The red-and-white cloth still covered it although all the plates and glasses had long since been removed. Twinkling silver moonlight filtered through the leaves and touched chairs that had been pushed back by their occupants, one or two of them still holding a crumpled table napkin. Noticing a small gleaming object near her feet Miranda bent down and picked it up. It was the little plastic aeroplane, probably out of a cornflakes packet, with which Nicholas had been playing.

'I do wish they didn't all seem so remote now.'

'Who?' Sammy's thoughts had been with Florence.

'Everyone who was here. It seems extraordinary that there's nothing left of the happy part except empty bottles and half a trifle.'

'Don't you remember the voices? The laughter?'

'I suppose so, in a dim kind of way.' She fiddled with the little aeroplane.

'It was a marvellous day,' Sammy said firmly. 'Everyone enjoyed it tremendously, including you and me. As for Florence, she was in her element from start to finish.'

'Trust her to kick the bucket on my birthday. She was always hellbent on upstaging me.'

'That's my girl.' He leaned close and took her hand.

'Did you ever fly planes like that?' Through her tears she indicated the little toy resting on the tablecloth.

'No. I was never a child of the jet age.'

'Come to think of it, neither of us were.'

They sat in silence listening to the cry of the owl. An elderly couple too tired and too sad to go to bed.

'It's all going to start again, isn't it?'

'Not if we don't let it.'

'How can we stop it?'

'Think of Florence.'

'She did her best, and died for it.'

'Come on,' he said, gently helping her up from the table. 'It's been a helluva day and everything will seem different in the morning.'

Bibliography

Aftermath, M. F. Beardwell (Arthur H. Stockwell)
La Force de l'Age, Simone de Beauvoir
The Musicians of Auschwitz, Fania Fenelon (Sphere)
And We Shall Shock Them, David Fraser (Hodder & Stoughton)
The Holocaust, Martin Gilbert (Collins)
Little Resistance, Antonia Hunt (Secker & Warburg)
Swastika Over Paris, Jeremy Josephs (Bloomsbury Press)
Curfew in Paris, Ninetta Jucker (Hogarth Press)
La Grande Rafle du Vel d'Hiv, Claude Levy (Robert Laffont)
Vichy France and the Jews, Michael R. Marrus & Robert O. Paxton (Basic Books Inc. New York)
This Europe, Girija Mookerjee (Saraswaty Library, Calcutta)
Paris in the Third Reich, David Pryce-Jones (Collins)
The Work of the Prisoners of War Department during the Second World War, compiled by Sir Harold Satow KCMG OBE & Mrs M. J. See (Foreign Office)
Jackals of the Third Reich, Ronald Seth (New English Library)
Women Who Went to War 1938–46, Eric Taylor (Robert Hale)
The Meaning of Treason, Rebecca West (Macmillan)
Holocaust and Rebirth, Bergen-Belsen (Memorial Press, New York)
Belsen, Irgun Sheerit (Hapleita Me'Haezor Harbriti, Israel)
The Red Cross & St John War History 1939–47, compiled by P. G. Cambray and G. G. Briggs.